PRAISE FOR DAVID DOWNING

'Stands with Alan Furst for authentic detail and atmosphere'
Donald James, author of *Monstrum*

'Think Robert Harris and *Fatherland* mixed with a dash of
Le Carré'
Sue Baker, *Publishing News*

'A wonderfully drawn spy novel . . . A very auspicious début,
with more to come'
The Bookseller on *Zoo Station*

'Excellent and evocative . . . Downing's strength is his
fleshing out of the tense and often dangerous nature of
everyday life in a totalitarian state'
The Times on *Silesian Station*

'Exciting and frightening all at once . . . It's got everything
going for it'
Julie Walters

'One of the brightest lights in the shadowy world of
historical spy fiction'
Birmingham Post

David Downing is the author of several works of fiction and non-fiction. His first novel in the 'John Russell and Effi Koenen' series, *Zoo Station*, was published by Old Street in 2007, followed by *Silesian Station* in 2008 and *Stettin Station* in 2009. *Potsdam Station* is the fourth in the series. He lives in Surrey with his wife and two cats.

POTSDAM STATION

DAVID DOWNING

First published in 2010 by Old Street Publishing Ltd
40 Bowling Green Lane, London EC1R 0NE
www.oldstreetpublishing.co.uk

ISBN 978-1-905847-94-5

10 9 8 7 6 5 4 3 2 1

A CIP catalogue record for this title is available from the British Library.

Printed and bound in the UK by
CPI Mackays, Chatham ME5 8TD

For David Reynolds and Charlie Viney,
who made this series both possible and better

POTSDAM STATION

Franco's furniture

April 6 –7

As they walked south towards Diedersdorf and the battalion command post, Paul Gehrts realised that he and his companion Gerhart Reheusser were grinning like idiots. The cloudless blue sky, warm sunshine and dust-free easterly breeze were responsible, banishing, if only for a few minutes, the grim anxiety that filled their waking hours. For the moment the occasional rattle of a distant machine-gun, the odd boom of a tank cannon or gun, could be ignored.

About five kilometres behind them, the Seelow Heights fell sharply away to the Oderbruch, the meadowlands which lay between the escarpment and the Oder River. Soon – in a few days, most likely – the men and tanks of the Red Army would storm across those meadows and throw themselves at the German defences. The Russians would die in their thousands, but thousands more would follow. It would only be a matter of time.

But a sunny day was a sunny day, with a power all its own.

The two men were approaching the first houses of the small town when they came upon a large group of soldiers spread out along the side of the road. Few looked older than fifteen, and one boy was actually passing round his army-issue bag of sweets, as if he were at a friend's birthday party. Most had their panzerfausts lying beside them on the grass, and all looked exhausted – the disposable rocket-launchers were a crippling weight for all but the strongest children. Their troop leader, who was probably almost out of his teens, was examining a weeping blister on one of his charges' feet. As Paul and Gerhard walked past he looked up, and offered them a brief rueful smile.

Almost all of Diedersdorf's usual residents had left or been evacuated, and were now presumably clogging the roads leading westward, but the town was not being neglected – in the small central square an over-zealous staff-sergeant was supervising another band of young recruits in sweeping the cobbles.

'The madness of the military mind,' Gerhard muttered, not for the first time.

As if prove his point, a half-track drove across the square, sending eddies of dust in every direction. The sergeant endured a violent fit of coughing, then ordered his boys back to work.

The division mechanics had set up shop in the goods yard of the town station, close to where a large dug-out had been excavated in the railway embankment for the battalion command post. The corporal at the im-provised desk in the goods shed groaned when he saw Paul's machine-gun. 'Don't tell me – it jams.'

'It does.'

'How often?'

'Too often for comfort.'

The corporal sighed. 'I'll get someone to have a look,' he said. 'Come back in an hour.'

Two bench seats from the nearby railway station had been left outside the battalion command post entrance, offering a place to wait and watch the war go by. The two of them had only been sitting there a few minutes when a captured Red Army jeep pulled up. A Wehrmacht major and two NCOs leapt out, shoved their manacled Russian prisoner onto the other seat, and disappeared into the dugout. He looked like an ordinary rifle-man, with dark dishevelled hair and vaguely Mongoloid features. He was wearing a blood-stained kaftan above badly frayed trousers and worse-worn boots. He sat there with his mouth slightly open, his eyes gazing blankly into space.

But he wasn't stupid. Catching Paul's look he returned it, and his eyes, once focused, seemed full of intelligence. 'Cigarette?' he asked.

That, at least, was one thing the Reich wasn't short of. Gerhart got up and gave him one, placing it between the Russian's lips and offering a lighted match.

'*Spasibo*.'

'You're welcome, Ivan.'

'No, he fucking isn't,' another voice exploded behind them. It was one of the NCOs who had brought him in. He knocked the cigarette from the Russian's mouth, throwing sparks all over his face, and swung round on Gerhart. 'What the fuck do you think you're doing?'

'What I hope...'

'Shut the fuck up. And get out of my sight.' He turned away, grabbed the Russian under one arm and hustled him through the curtained door of the dug-out.

'Wonderful,' was all Gerhart said. He looked at the still-swaying curtain, as if contemplating pursuit.

'Let's try and find some hot water,' Paul suggested.

'I'm not going anywhere,' Gerhart told him. 'I'm not going to let a shit like that order me around.'

Paul shrugged and sat down again. There was no use arguing with Gerhart at times like this.

They'd been sitting in silence for about a quarter of an hour when shouting started inside. This went on for several more minutes, and culminated in a gunshot. A few moments later, there was another.

Gerhart leapt to his feet.

'Let's go and find that hot water,' Paul said quietly.

Gerhart spun round, anger in his eyes, but something in his friend's expression did the trick. He closed his eyes, breathed out heavily, and offered Paul a rueful smile. 'Okay' he said. 'If we both take a bath, the war might stink a little less. Let's go and find one.'

But they were out of luck. The only hot water in town came complete with a queue, and was already brown. A drink proved easier to come by, but the quality was equally dire, and after scorching their throats with a single glass neither felt hungry for more. They went back to the workshop, but the mechanic still hadn't got round to checking the machine-gun. Rather than return to their seat outside the command post, they pulled a couple of armchairs out of the empty house next door, and settled down to wait. Paul thought about checking the location of the nearest basement, but found he couldn't be bothered. The sun was still shining, and it looked like the Red Air Force was having an afternoon off. If worse came to worst, they could simply throw themselves into the dugout across the yard.

Gerhart was devouring a cigarette, angrily sucking in smoke and flicking off ash while he wrestled with his inner demons. He was still pissed off about the Russian prisoner, Paul realised. Which might be admirable, but was unlikely to serve any useful purpose.

Paul had known him a long time. They'd been best friends at their first school, but Gerhart's father had moved his family to Hamburg when both were nine, and they'd only met up again two years ago, when both were drafted into the same *flakhelfer* unit at the Zoo Bunker Gun Tower. Gerhart had persuaded Paul that pre-enlistment in the Wehrmacht made sense, partly because he wanted out of the *flakhelfer*, partly to avoid SS recruitment. Paul had resisted for one reason – the girl he had just fallen in love with was one of those directing the neighbouring tower's searchlights. But after Madeleine's mounting took a direct hit he could hardly wait to get away. He and Gerhart had started their compulsory labour service together, and then been called up as seventeen-year-olds when the age limit was lowered early in 1944. They were still gunners, but now they were soldiers of the 20th Panzergrenadier Division.

They had been with their Pak-43 88mm gun for almost a year, somehow surviving the collapse of Army Group Centre the previous summer and the winter battles in Poland. When they had left Berlin for their first *Ostfront* posting, Gerhart's mother had taken Paul aside and asked him to look after her son, but if anything he had looked after Paul. Gerhart's relentless negativity when it came to the war, the army and the Führer was sometimes irritating, but he never let it lessen his sense of duty toward his comrades. In fact, the one probably reinforced the other.

These days, Gerhart was the closest thing Paul had to family. His father John Russell had deserted him in 1941; his mother Ilse and stepfather Matthias Gehrts had died in a car crash the previous year. His stepsisters were alive as far as he knew, but Paul hadn't seen them since their evacuation two years ago, and the relationship had never been really close. He hadn't spoken to his mother's brother Thomas since their argument about his father almost three years ago.

'Here he comes,' Gerhart interjected. A mechanic was walking towards them, the machine-gun over his shoulder.

'Is it fixed?' Paul asked.

The mechanic shrugged. 'Seems to be. I just a filed off a few micrometres. Give it a proper test in the woods – random gunfire this far behind the front makes people nervous.'

Paul hoisted the gun over his own shoulder. 'Thanks.'

'No problem.'

They walked back through Diedersdorf's empty streets. The young recruits on broom duty had vanished, but a Waffen-SS staff car was sitting in the otherwise empty square, and the gruppenführer sitting in the back seat turned a surprisingly anxious pair of eyes in their direction.

'He's seen the future, and it's not looking black,' Gerhart joked.

The sweet-sucking youths had also moved on, and the road running north was empty. After about a kilometre they turned off into the trees, and followed the winding track to their position on the eastern edge of the wood. The unit's two cruciform-mounted 88mm anti-tank guns were dug in twenty metres apart, covering the distant Seelow-Diedersdorf road, which curved toward and across their line of vision. The first few Soviet tanks to bypass Seelow would certainly pay for their temerity, but those coming up behind them... well, their fate would depend on whether or not Paul's unit received another shipment of shells. They currently had nineteen, and two of those would be needed to destroy their own guns.

They'd been here for over two months, and the dug-out accommodation was as spacious as any Paul had known in his short military career, three steps leading down to a short tunnel, with a tiny command post on one side and a small room full of bunks on the other. The ceilings weren't exactly thick, but they were well-buttressed, and even a direct hit should prove survivable. The half-tracks they needed to move the guns were parked a hundred metres away in the forest, and heavily camouflaged against a sighting from the air. They had fuel enough for sixty miles between them, which seemed unlikely to be enough. Then again, if no more shells were delivered, the guns would become effectively useless, and they could all ride back to Berlin in a single vehicle.

It had been a quiet day, Sergeant Utermann told them. The artillery barrage had been shorter than usual, and even less accurate – nothing had fallen within a hundred metres of their small clearing. There'd been no Soviet air raid, and three Messerschmitt 109s had appeared overhead, the first they'd seen for a week. Maybe things were looking up at last.

'And maybe Marlene Dietrich came home,' Gerhart added sarcastically, once they were out of earshot. Utermann was a decent man, but a bit of an idiot.

Out in the clearing Hannes and Neumaier were kicking the unit's football to and fro. Hannes had found it in a Diedersdorf garden the previous week, and had hardly stopped playing with it since.

'Shall we challenge them?' Gerhart asked.

'Okay,' Paul agreed without much enthusiasm.

Greatcoats were found for posts, and two men from the other gun team cajoled into making it three-a-side. Paul had played a great deal as a child, and had loved watching his team Hertha. But the *Hitlerjugend* had turned the game into one more form of 'struggle', and he had always gone to the Plumpe stadium with his dad. A wave of anger accompanied that thought, and before he knew it he was almost breaking Neumaier's ankle with a reckless tackle.

'Sorry, sorry,' he said, offering the other boy his hand.

Neumaier gave him a look. 'What happens to you on a football pitch?'

'Sorry,' Paul said again.

Neumaier shook his head and smiled.

The light was starting to fade, but they played on, engrossed in moving the football across the broken forest floor – until the Soviet planes swept over the trees. They were Tupolevs, although right until the last moment

Paul was somehow expecting Sergeant Utermann's Messerschmitt 109s. Like everyone else he dived for the ground, instinctively clawing at the earthen floor as fire and wood exploded above him. He felt a sharp pain in his left leg, but nothing more.

A single bomb, he thought. Turning his head he could see a wood splinter about ten centimetres long protruding from the back of his calf. Without really thinking, he reached back and yanked it out. His luck was in – there was no sudden gush of arterial blood.

Two large trees were in flames on the western edge of the clearing, where Gerhart had gone to collect the ball. Paul counted the figures getting to their feet, and knew that one was missing. He scrambled to his own and rushed across to where his friend should be.

He found Gerhart lying on his back, a shard of wood driven deep into his throat, a bib of blood spread across his chest. Sinking to his knees, Paul thought he caught a flicker in the other's eyes, but they never moved again.

It seemed at first as if the DC-3 had landed in a forest clearing, but as the plane swung round John Russell caught sight of a long grey terminal building. The legend 'Moscow Airport (Vnukovo)' was emblazoned across the facade in enormous Cyrillic letters, beneath an even larger hammer and sickle.

He had expected the Khodynka airfield, which he had last seen in August 1939, decked out with swastikas for the welcoming of Ribbentrop and the signing of the Nazi-Soviet Pact. He had never heard of Vnukovo, and hoped it was closer to the city centre than it looked.

A wooden stairway on wheels was rolled out to meet the plane. It looked like something left over from the siege of Troy, and creaked alarmingly as the passengers stepped gingerly down to the tarmac. The sun was still above the tree line, and much warmer than Russell had anticipated. He joined the straggling procession towards the terminal building, a concrete edifice with all the architectural interest of a British pillbox. The constructivists would be turning in their graves, he thought, and they wouldn't be alone. As Russell had discovered in 1939, trips to Stalin's Soviet Union were guaranteed to disappoint those like himself who had welcomed the original revolution.

He joined the end of the queue, thinking that on this occasion a sense of ideological let-down was the least of his worries. First and foremost was the question of whether the Soviets had forgiven him for refusing their offer of hospitality at the end of 1941. After his escape from Germany – an escape which German comrades under Soviet orders had died to make possible – Stalin's representatives in Stockholm had done their best to persuade him that Moscow was an ideal place to sit out the war. They had even plucked his old contact Yevgeny Shchepkin out of the international ether in a vain attempt to talk him round.

He had explained to Shchepkin that he wasn't ungrateful, but that America had to be his first port of call. His mother and employer were there, and when it came to raising a hue and cry on behalf of Europe's Jews, the *New York Times* seemed a much better bet than *Pravda*.

What he hadn't told Shchepkin was how little he trusted the Soviets. He couldn't even work out why they were so keen to have him on board. Did they still see him and his rather unusual range of connections as a potential asset, to be kept in reserve for a relevant moment? Or did he know more about their networks and ways of operating that he was supposed to? If so, did they care? Would he receive the Order of Lenin or a one-way trip to the frozen north? It was impossible to tell. Dealing with Stalin's regime was like the English game of Battleships which he and his son Paul had used to play – the only way you found out you were on the wrong square was by moving onto it, and having it blow up in your face.

The queue was moving at a snail's pace, the sun now winking through the pines. Almost all the arrivals were foreigners, most of them Balkan communists, come to lay gifts at Stalin's feet. There had been a couple of Argentineans sitting across from Russell, and their only topic of conversation had been the excellent shooting in Siberia. Diplomats presumably, but who the hell knew in the violently shuffled world of April 1945? As far as Russell could tell, he was the only Western journalist seeking entry to Stalin's realm.

For all his apprehensiveness, he was pleased to have got this far. It was seven days since his hurried departure from Rheims in north-east France, the location of the Western Allies' military HQ. He had left on the morning of March 29th, after receiving off-the-record confirmation that Eisenhower had written to Stalin on the previous day, promising the Red Army the sole rights to Berlin. If Russell was going to ride into his old home town on a tank, it would have to be on a Russian one.

A swift exchange of cables with his editor in San Francisco had given him sanction to switch his journalistic sphere of operations, and, more importantly, some sort of semi-official fig leaf to cover up an essentially personal odyssey. Accompanying the Red Army into Hitler's capital would prove a wonderful scoop for any Western journalist, but that was not why Russell wanted to do it.

Just getting to Moscow had been complicated enough, involving, as it did, a great swing round the territories occupied by the Wehrmacht, an area which still stretched from northern Norway to northern Italy. Three trains had brought him to Marseilles, and a series of flights had carried him eastwards via a succession of cities – Rome, Belgrade and Bucharest – all with the unfortunate distinction of having been bombed by both sides. He had expected difficulties everywhere, but bribery had worked in Marseilles and Rome, and broad hints that he would put Tito on the cover of *Time* magazine had eased his entry into Belgrade and, by default, the wider area of Soviet control. The rest had been easy. Once you were in, you were in, and the authorities in Bucharest, Odessa and Kiev had waved him on with barely a glance at his passport or papers. No doubt the various immigration bureaucracies would recover their essential nastiness in due course, but for the moment everyone seemed too exhausted by the war to care.

Moscow, though, was likely to be different, and Russell was half expecting orders to leave on the next return flight. Or worse. But when his turn finally came he was let through with only the most cursory check of his documents. It was almost as if they were expecting him.

'Meester Russell,' a voice said, confirming as much. A youngish man with prematurely grey hair, piercing blue eyes and thin lips had appeared in front of him. One arm of his shiny civilian suit was hanging empty.

Russell wondered how many arms and legs had been detached from their bodies in the last five years. They weren't the sort of statistics that governments publicised, always assuming they bothered to collect them. 'Yes?' he replied politely.

'I am from Press Liaison,' the man said. 'You will come with me, please.'

Russell followed, half expecting a room somewhere in the bowels of the terminal building. Instead, he was led outside, to where an American single-decker bus was pumping thick clouds of black exhaust into the rapidly darkening sky. Those who had scurried for pole position in the terminal queue had been rewarded with a better-than-average shot at carbon monoxide poisoning.

The double seats all had one or more occupants, but the man from Press Liaison swiftly cleared the one at the front with a wave of his identity card. He ushered Russell into the window seat, and sat down beside him. 'My name Semyon Zakabluk,' he volunteered in English, as the driver clanked the bus into gear. 'You first time Moscow?'

'No,' Russell told him in reasonably fluent Russian. 'I was here in 1924, for the Party's Fifth Congress. And again in 1939, when the Pact was signed.'

'Ah,' Zakabluk said, probably for want of anything better. In 1924 Trotsky had been one of the country's leaders, and six years on from Ribbentrop's visit the Nazi-Soviet Pact was probably almost as unmentionable. 'And you speak Russian?' he asked with more than a hint of truculence.

'I try,' Russell said. He had devoted a considerable chunk of the last few years to learning the language, partly with such a visit in mind, but more because its sphere of use seemed certain to increase.

'Why have you come to Moscow?'

'To report on the victory of the Soviet people.'

'Ah.'

'You served in the Red Army?' Russell asked.

'Yes, of course. Until this –' Zakabluk shrugged what little remained of his left arm. 'A tank shell, in the Kursk battle. One minute I had two arms, then only one.' For a moment he looked sorry for himself, but only for a moment. 'Many friends were not so lucky,' he added.

Russell just nodded.

'You were too old for your army?'

'I was in the First War,' Russell said. 'A long time ago,' he added without thinking. Lately, with all the horrors he had seen in Normandy and the Ardennes, the memories of his own time in the trenches had become depressingly vivid.

The bus wheezed to a halt alongside a railway station platform. This was good news – Russell already felt as if several joints had been jolted from their sockets. The passengers trooped off the bus and into the Victorian-style carriages which were waiting to carry them to Moscow. Much to everyone's surprise, the train set off almost at once. The small locomotive signalled their departure with a triumphant blast of its whistle, and was soon hurrying through the silver birch forests that surrounded the Soviet capital. Night had fallen by the time they reached Moscow's Kiev Station, and Russell had a fleeting glimpse of the red stars adorning the distant Kremlin as his companion hustled him towards the Metro.

Their train, which came almost immediately, was full of tired-looking faces and bodies in shabby oversize clothes. Like people all over Europe, Russell thought. If ever there was a time when people might understand what others were feeling, then surely it should be now, at the end of a terrible war against a wholly discredited foe. But even if they did, he didn't suppose it would make any difference. Their governments might still be talking like allies, but already they acted like future enemies.

Back in the open air, the familiar shape of the Metropol Hotel was silhouetted against the night sky. They walked across Sverdlov Square and in through the main entrance.

'You must report to the Press Liaison office in the morning,' Zakabluk told Russell, after checking that his room was ready. 'At ten o'clock, yes?'

'Yes,' Russell agreed. 'Thank you.'

Zakabluk bowed slightly and turned on his heels. As he walked towards the door, he gave a slight nod to a man in one of the lobby chairs.

Russell smiled to himself, and took the lift up to the second floor. His room looked remarkably similar to the one he'd had in 1939. The Soviet security police, the NKVD, had supplied a naked woman with that one, but, for reasons both virtuous and pragmatic, he had declined to take up the offer.

Since his parting from Effi there been other opportunities, equally appealing on a physical level and much more free of political risk, but he had refused them all. Staying faithful seemed the least he could do, after saving himself – albeit with her encouragement – at her expense. He wondered if she had been faithful to him, and how he would react if she hadn't. At this moment in time, he just needed to know she was alive.

He stared out of the window at the empty square. It was only seven-thirty in the evening, but the city already seemed asleep. He had meant to check in at the American Embassy the moment he arrived, but tomorrow morning would do – he didn't think the NKVD would have gone through all the rigmarole of settling him into a hotel if they planned an early hours arrest.

Dinner, he decided, and made his way down to the cavernous, ornate restaurant room. A few Russians were dining at two of the tables, but otherwise it was empty. There was only one meal on the menu, and by the time it eventually arrived, he was drunk enough not to notice the taste.

The tram that limped to a halt at the stop on Schloss Strasse had at least one seriously damaged wheel, but Effi and her fellow would-be travellers were hardly spoilt for choice. The wide avenue stretched emptily away to both east and west, offering the sort of pre-industrial calm that earlier generations of Berliners had deemed lost for ever. Getting it back had, of course, proved rather costly – most of the grand terraced houses were now detached or semi-detached, and the fires ignited by the latest raid were still smudging most of the sky with their smoke. It was almost four in the afternoon, and the city was making the most of the several hours' breathing space which the RAF and USAF usually allowed between one's departure and the other's arrival.

The tram started off, bumping noisily along the rails as it headed north towards the Schloss Brücke. Four out of five passengers were women, which Effi assumed was a fair reflection of the city's population in April 1945. Most of the children had been sent to the country, and most of the men had been sent into battle. Only those over forty-five remained in the battered city, and there were rumours that all under sixty would soon be marched to the various fronts. The Russians had been on the eastern bank of the Oder River – little more than sixty kilometres from Berlin – for almost three months now, and a resumption of their westerly progress was daily anticipated. The Americans, approaching the Elbe River, were not that much further away, but only wishful thinkers and supreme optimists expected them to reach Berlin ahead of the dreaded Red Army. Another month, Effi thought, maybe two. And then, one way or another, everything would change.

The tram was grinding its way around the bend into Alt Moabit, and she had a distant glimpse of the synagogue on Levetzow Strasse from which so many Jews had been sent to the east. Few of Effi's gentile acquaintances mentioned Berlin's Jews anymore – it was almost as if they had never existed. Goebbels had even stopped blaming them for all the Reich's misfortunes.

The star-shaped Moabit Prison loomed on the left, and the tram swung left onto Invaliden Strasse. Up ahead, smoke seemed to be rising through the shattered roof of Lehrter Station, but it proved an illusion – as the road arched over the station throat she could see, across the Humboldt Harbour, several fires raging among the buildings of the Charité Hospital. The red-on-white crosses adorning the tiled roofs might just as well have been targets.

Five minutes later the tram reached Stettin Station. Effi hurried in through the archway, half expecting the worst. If there were no trains to the suburbs before the usual evening air raid, and she couldn't get out to the rendezvous point, then her fugitives would be left in limbo, and those who had risked life and limb bringing them out of Berlin would have to take them back. She offered a silent prayer to whatever gods were looking after the Reichsbahn and stared up at the still-functioning departure boards.

There were no announcements of delays or cancellations, and the next train for Frohnau was allegedly leaving in five minutes.

It left in fifteen, which was good enough. Given the almost non-stop bombing, it seemed amazing that so many things continued to work. According to Ali the public library on Bismarck Strasse was still lending books, and when the wind was in the right direction they could smell the hops fermenting in Moabit's breweries. And the police showed no signs of loosening their grip. If anything, there seemed to be more of them, all scouring the streets for any male with four limbs who hadn't had his turn in the Wehrmacht's mincing machine.

As they pulled out past the freight yards Effi found herself re-living that night in December 1941, waiting for hours in the freezing boxcar, then rattling out of Berlin with bombs falling all around them. It seemed so long ago.

He seemed so long ago.

But assuming he was still alive, assuming he still loved her, assuming she could survive for however long the Russians were going to take... then maybe...

She looked round at her fellow-passengers. Again they were mostly women, all with that look of mental exhaustion that even the best-fed Berliners habitually wore on their faces. More than three years of shortages and almost two of regular bombings had worn the city out. Everyone wanted it over, everyone but him and his desperate disciples. Gröfaz, as people sarcastically called him, an abbreviation of Grössler Feldherr aller Zeiten, the 'greatest general of all time'.

The train was passing under the Ringbahn, and a decrepit-looking steam engine was towing a rail-mounted flak gun along the elevated line, pumping more smoke into an already sated sky. Several *flakhelfer* were perched on the gun's mounting, and none of them looked older than fifteen. Two years ago Effi had seen John's son Paul in a *flakhelfer* uniform, but he would be eighteen by now, and probably in the regular forces. If he was still alive.

She shook her head to dismiss the thought, and turned her attention to the here and now. Most of the other passengers were clasping newspapers, but no one was reading – the chronic shortage of toilet paper had obviously reached the suburbs. One woman caught Effi looking at her, and stared back, but Effi resisted the impulse to smile – her smile, as John had once told her, was her most recognisable feature. Not that she expected to be recognised, not anymore. These days she always wore glasses, and the grey streaks in her frumpily cut black hair were depressingly authentic. Sitting and walking like a person fifteen years older than her actual age had become so ingrained over the last three years that she sometimes wondered if the process was reversible.

The train had stopped, and the view through the window of unbroken houses and trees was a reminder of the past. It was not representative, of course – the moment the train restarted more bombed-out buildings and charred trees swam into view, and a group of people could be seen gathered, heads bowed, around an improvised grave in someone's back garden. The damage was less widespread away from the city centre, but still considerable. If the Western allies were targeting anything more precise than Berlin, then their aim was poor.

The light was fading by the time the train reached Frohnau. She resisted the impulse to hurry out of the terminus, and took her time walking across the mostly intact town square. The local Rathaus had lost an end wall to a bomb, but lights were burning in the rest of the building, and people were sitting, wrapped in their winter coats, outside the café restaurant next door. Most of their ersatz coffees looked untouched – maintaining the ritual was clearly more important than the actual drink. The familiar smell of kohlrabi soup drifted out of the open doorway.

There were no uniforms in sight. Effi headed up the street opposite the station, as she and Ali had done on the previous Saturday. They had been carrying a picnic basket on that occasion, but today she was only toting a small bag of extra rations. If she was stopped, these were for an imaginary friend, the one who owned the abandoned lakeside cottage that they had stumbled across at the weekend. As explanations went it was rather thin, but much better than nothing.

There was no traffic, and little sign of life in the neat suburban houses that lined the road. Effi's watch told her it wasn't yet seven. She held it against her ear, and listened to a few reassuring ticks. The watch had only cost a few pfennigs in a rummage sale – it had probably been found in the rubble of somebody's home by a professional scavenger – and had seemed more appropriate to her current identity than the elegant Cartier which a lustful studio boss had given her several years earlier.

Back in the days when she was acting for a living, rather than for her life.

She smiled to herself and wondered, not for the first time, if she would ever act again. Would she want to? She really didn't know. It was hard to imagine what life would be like after the Nazis, after the war. So much seemed lost, and irretrievable.

The last houses were behind her now, trees leaning out to enclose the road. Effi had brought along a flashlight – a priceless treasure in 1945 Berlin – but hoped she wouldn't need to use it. The batteries were fading, and replacing them would probably take more time and effort than it was worth.

The hiker's trail left the road about half a kilometre into the wood, and she had covered around half that distance when she heard the approaching vehicle. The sound preceded the thin gleam of the slit-sealed headlamps, and Effi barely had time to get off the road before the dark shape of a truck rumbled by. She could see nothing of the driver, and no movement in the open rear, but it was worrying nevertheless – unofficial motor transport was rare these days. It might just be a farmer with access to petrol – someone had to be delivering the blue slop which passed for milk in Berlin – but it didn't seem very likely.

She made her way back to the road as the sound of the lorry faded. Had it been full of Gestapo, there was nothing she could have done. By this time all her co-conspirators would be in motion, beyond warning.

No other traffic disturbed her walk to the turn-off. She turned onto the hiker's trail, the last flashes of the setting sun splintering through the trees ahead. By the time she reached the lakeside the orange orb had vanished, and the sky was a kaleidoscope of reds. As Berliners were fond of remarking, in their usual bittersweet way, blasted bricks made for wonderful sunsets.

The cottage sat a few metres back from the shore, and Effi used what light remained to check that nothing had changed since the weekend. The door was still half off its hinges, the windows mostly broken, and there was no indication that anyone had been making use of the mouldy chairs or bedding. A weekend retreat rather than a permanent home, the cottage had clearly been abandoned early in the war, its middle-class owners too busy or dead to make use of it.

She went back outside and sat on the rickety jetty. The lake stretched away like a sea of blood, darkening as the minutes went by. The sound of sirens carried faintly across the water, so faintly that she thought she might be imagining them, but then searchlight beams sprang into life, columns of cloudy white crossing over the distant city like giant pairs of scissors. A few minutes more, and they were joined by thinner beams of red and green, desperately swinging to and fro.

It was a quarter-past eight. She went back into the cottage, sat herself down on one of the upright chairs, crossed her arms on the table and rested her head upon them.

Somewhere out there a engine driver was waiting for the all-clear to sound. And when it did his train would jerk into motion, trundling its way around the north-eastern edge of the city, heading for the cutting which lay three kilometres north of where she was sitting. It was a freight train, and one of the covered vans was loaded with crates containing Spanish Embassy furniture. All the friendly embassies had been moved out of Berlin and away from the bombing in 1944, but their new location, some fifty kilometres east of the capital, was in imminent danger of Russian occupation, and the Spanish had requested permission to ship their valuable furniture home through neutral Sweden. The criminal idiots at Ribbentrop's Foreign Office had decided that the threat to Franco's sideboards was more important than their own forces' chronic shortages of supplies, and had ordered the Reichsbahn to divert the necessary rolling stock from military duties.

Franco knew nothing of this, and nor, Effi suspected, did his ambassador. The shipment had been suggested by Erik Aslund, and organised by an attaché whose hatred of the Nazis stemmed from his devout Catholicism. It wasn't the first time Aslund had used a furniture shipment for his own ends, which centred around getting prospective victims of the Nazi regime to safety. Two years earlier, when the bombing first became serious, the Swedish Embassy had supposedly crated and shipped its own furniture home to Stockholm. Tables and chairs had been carried aboard at one end, Jews helped off at the other. The switch had been made in these woods, the furniture broken up and buried once the fugitives were on their way.

It was soon after that that Effi began working with Aslund. She had never found out what position he held at the Swedish Embassy, but assumed he had one. When she had eventually asked him, as a personal favour to her, to check whether an Anglo-American journalist named John Russell had arrived in Sweden around the end of 1941, it had taken him only a few days to come up with a positive answer.

She knew he had ties with at least two of the Swedish churches in Berlin, but he had never given her any other reason to think him religious. He was obviously a brave man, but she never got the feeling that he enjoyed taking risks – there was something irreducibly sensible about him which reminded her of Russell. He was younger than John, around thirty-five, and conventionally good-looking in the classic Nordic way. She had seen no evidence of a sense of humour, but given the sort of world they shared that was hardly surprising.

As far as she knew, Aslund had no idea of her own true identity. He knew her as Frau von Freiwald, a gentile widow who was willing to shelter fugitive Jews for a few precious days and nights in her spacious Bismarck Strasse apartment. He also, as far as she knew, had no suspicion that Ali, far from being her aryan niece, was one of several thousand Jewish fugitives – or 'U-boats' – living illegally in Berlin. He had never offered any explanation of his involvement in dangerous anti-state activities, but perhaps he assumed that common decency needed none. He was a Swede, after all.

Outside, the natural light had vanished, but the night battle over Berlin was throwing moving shadows on the wall behind her, and she could just about hear the familiar medley of droning planes, anti-aircraft fire and exploding bombs. She felt her fists tightening with the usual anger – what possible purpose could so much death and destruction serve? The war was won and lost, and punishing the women of Berlin for the crimes their fathers, sons and brothers had committed elsewhere – many and terrible as these undoubtedly were – seemed like something her own despicable government would have done. For reasons that now escaped her, she had expected better of the British and Americans.

She laid her head back down and closed her eyes. She wondered how John felt about his country's bombing campaign, and the fact that most of the people he loved were among the millions on the receiving end. She remembered his outrage when the Luftwaffe had bombed the Spanish town of Guernica for Franco, and an argument not long after with his diplomat friend Doug Conway. 'The bombing of civilians is always, always, a war crime,' Russell had insisted at the dinner party in question. No one had agreed with him. He was being naive, Conway had said. They had the planes, they had the bombs, and they weren't going to let an inability to hit precision targets stand in the way of their use. 'No doubt about that,' John had agreed. 'But that won't make it less of a crime.'

She hoped he still felt that way, that the war hadn't changed him too much. That he would still recognise her.

She remembered a trip to the Zoo with him and Paul. It had been one of those spring days when everything seemed right with the world, even with the Nazis in power. Paul had only been about seven, so it must have been early in their love affair. The three of them had clambered aboard the same elephant, and clung to each other as it lumbered along the wide path between the iron cages...

She woke suddenly, thinking she'd heard a noise outside. There were no lights, no banging – it must have been an animal, perhaps a fox who frequented the cottage and had suddenly scented its human occupant. She hurriedly used her flashlight to check her watch. It was almost two o'clock. Another half-hour and she would have been late for the rendezvous. How could she have been so careless?

There were no moving shadows on the wall, no distant thunder – the air raid had ended. Outside the fires raised by the bombing were reflected in the clouds, casting the world in an orange glow. She selfishly hoped that her own building had been spared – finding new accommodation with her current identity papers shouldn't prove too difficult, but any contact with the authorities involved some sort of risk.

It was cold, and she could feel the damp of the cottage in her bones. She thought about using the outside toilet, but a memory of dense cobwebs persuaded her to squat down in the garden. She was almost forty years old, but spiders still frightened her more than the Gestapo.

She decided to get going. There were only two kilometres to walk, along an easy-to-follow path, but it would be prudent to reach her destination early, and give herself the chance of sizing up the situation from a distance.

Walking as quietly as she could, she followed the path around the northern shore of the lake and up into the woods. The rendezvous point was a designated picnic area close to, but above, the road from Frohnau to Bergfelde. As she and Ali had discovered at the weekend, it had several wooden benches and tables, along with a board bearing faded pictures of animal life and stern warnings against dropping litter. Engraved arrows on a plinth directed viewers towards prominent landmarks of the distant capital, and one recent visitor had brought the display up to date by scratching 'ruins of' in front of several names.

Effi approached the area with extreme caution. No lights were visible, which was as it should be. She thought she heard murmurs of conversation, but was far from sure.

She worked her way off the path and through the trees, grateful for the masking effect of a noisy breeze as she got closer to the edge of the clearing. Stopping, she thought she could make out several figures, some standing, some sitting at one of the picnic tables. Another few metres and she was sure. There were six of them.

They looked innocent enough, but that was the mistake tigers made about staked-out goats.

She told herself that the person or persons who had brought them would still be watching from hiding, if only to confirm her own arrival. She would not see them, and they would only see her from a distance – Aslund had a keen appreciation of cell structures and the security they provided. Which was why he wanted her to take the group from here to the train, to provide a cut-out between his organisation in the city and the railwaymen.

It was always possible that the initial escorts had been arrested en route, their places taken by Gestapo agents. If so, the latter would be close by, watching and waiting for Effi to reveal and condemn herself.

She forced herself to wait a little longer. As she strained ears and eyes for sign of any other watchers, one of the figures at the table suddenly got to his feet and stretched. 'I imagine many ways in which it would all end,' he said to his companions, 'but I never considered a midnight picnic.'

The other men laughed, removing Effi's suspicions. These men had not been brought by the Gestapo.

She took a deep breath and strode out of the trees. The six men, hardly surprisingly, all jumped at her sudden appearance.

'I am your guide,' she said softly. 'We have about two kilometres to walk, and I want you to follow me in single file. Move as quietly as you can. And please, no talking.'

They did as they were told.

She led them back down the path she had taken, turning off onto another after two hundred metres. This new path led north, climbing into the trees and around the side of a low hill. Effi doubted whether the paths in this wood saw much traffic anymore, but *Hitlerjugend* playing soldiers had infested all woods within easy reach of the capital until the end of 1942, and nature had not yet succeeded in erasing all proof of their perambulations. This path was still easy to follow.

An occasional noise, probably an animal evading their passage, broke through the constant swish of the wind in the trees, and Effi could feel the nervousness of those behind her. She had no idea how far they had already travelled, or how much they knew of where they were going. She remembered her own aborted flight from Germany three years earlier, and the sense of utter powerlessness she had felt in the hands of those trying to help her. All that waiting, all that tension.

It was easier in motion. She could hear the heavy breathing of the men behind her, could imagine the hope at war with the fear. A few more days and their fate would be decided – sanctuary in Sweden or some impromptu execution yard.

They walked steadily on through the rustling forest. A barely risen moon was soon ghosting the tops of the trees, and by the time they emerged above the cutting it was high enough to reflect off the receding rails. These stretched straight as arrows in both directions: south-east towards Berlin, north-west towards the Baltic coast.

She turned to the six fugitives, and saw them properly for the first time. Three were in their forties or older, all wearing the sort of suits and shirts with high collars which the old upper class favoured. Army politicals, Effi thought, potential victims of the never-ending hunt for anyone even remotely involved in the previous summer's plot to kill the Führer. The Reich might be on its last legs, but Hitler was determined that all his German enemies should die before he did.

The other three were younger, wearing cheaper, less formal clothes. Jews, Effi guessed, from the look of two of them. She realised with a shock that she recognised one man. A year or more ago, he had spent a night at the apartment.

His eyes told her the recognition was mutual, which boded anything but good. But there was nothing she could do about it now.

'I'm leaving you here,' she said, raising a hand to still the sudden alarm in six pairs of eyes. 'See the railwaymen's hut down there?' she added. 'Wait behind it. The train will stop, someone will come and get you, show you where to get on.'

'When is it due?' one man asked.

'Soon,' Effi told him. 'In the next half-hour.'

'When does it get light?' another voice asked.

'Not for another three hours,' one of his companions told him.

'Okay, good luck,' Effi said, turning away.

'Thank you,' several voices murmured after her.

It felt wrong leaving them to fend for themselves, but Aslund had insisted that she retrace their steps as quickly as possible, and make sure they were not being followed. If they were, she was supposed to lead the pursuit off in a safe direction. Safe, that is, for everyone but herself.

With the pale light of the half-moon suffusing the trees, without her charges to worry about, she was able to walk much faster, and as her fears of meeting the enemy began to fade, so her progress through the forest began to feel almost exhilarating. She felt like bursting into song, but managed to restrain herself. There'd be plenty of time for singing when the war was over.

And then, somewhere up ahead, she heard the dog bark.

At this point the path was curving down from the crest of a low ridge. She scanned the darkness below, searching for lights or movement in the tangle of trees.

A second round of barking sounded different. Was there more than one dog, or was that just her imagination?

A light – maybe lights – flickered in the distance. They were several hundred metres away, she thought, though it was difficult to judge distance. Far enough in any case that she heard no voices or footfalls.

What should she do? If it was the Gestapo, then the dog or dogs would be following their scent. There was no way she could erase it, but she could add another trail by moving away from the path. In fact that was all she could do – she certainly couldn't go forward or back. Without further thought, she left the path and hurried into the trees, moving fast as she could across the broken slope. The ground beneath the trees was spongy enough to absorb the sound of her passage, and no more barks broke through the background swish of the breeze. When she stopped after several minutes and took a long look back, there was no sign of lights.

Had they simply gone on down the path? And if so, would they reach the cutting ahead of the train? She hadn't heard the latter, but it should have arrived by now.

It was out of her hands. 'Save yourself, Effi,' she murmured, and pressed on. A few minutes later she stumbled into a narrow ditch. There was water at the bottom – not much of it to be sure, but it was trickling down, and presumably in the direction of the lake. She followed it down the slope for what seemed an eternity, casting the occasional anxious glance back over her shoulder, but there was no sign of a pursuit. She began to hope she had imagined it. Could the lights and the barking have come from something as innocent as a woodsman and his dog? Did such people still exist in the Third Reich? It was possible. It often felt as if all normal life had been consumed by the war, but things kept popping up to prove the opposite.

She suddenly found herself on the path which ran around the lake, no more than a couple of hundred metres from the borrowed cottage. Paul would have been proud of her, she thought, remembering the boy's own joy at winning a *Hitlerjugend* orientation exercise on a pre-war weekend. She felt pretty proud of herself.

There were no indications that the cottage had received any visitors. She ate one of the rolls she'd brought with her, drank some of the water, and tried to decide on a course of action. It wasn't five o'clock yet, which meant another two hours of darkness. Should she stay or go? She had counted on returning to Berlin around 8 am, and hadn't bothered to note the time of the first train – if she walked back to Frohnau station now she might find herself alone – and conspicuous – on an empty platform. Staying put for another couple of hours seemed, on balance, slightly less fraught with danger. She settled down to wait for dawn, wishing she knew whether or not the six men had caught their train. If they had, she should be safe for the night. If they hadn't, someone would soon be talking.

Once again, she found herself waking from an unexpected sleep. This time it was probably the sunlight that woke her – it was almost eight o'clock. She went outside to have a pee, only to hear the sound of male voices in the distance. And a barking dog. They were coming from the direction of Frohnau.

Should she run? If they were looking for her, then the station would be covered in any case. And the dogs would surely track her down if she went back into the woods. Her only hope was to bluff it out.

She needed to be sure of her facts. Hurrying back inside, she went straight to the drawer where she and Ali had found the letters. Two were addressed to Harald and Maria Widmann and bore Heidelberg postmarks. Inside both were a few dutiful lines from 'your loving son, Hartmut'. He was allegedly 'working hard', presumably at his studies. The third was a bill for boat repairs, addressed only to Herr Widmann.

She repeated the names out loud, then closed the drawer and took a quick look along the shelf of mouldering books. There were a couple by Karl May, and several books on birds and fishing.

The voices were outside the cottage now. She stood still, not wishing to gave away her presence, hoping they would walk on by.

No such luck. 'Check inside,' someone said.

She walked to the doorway and cried out 'good morning', as if overjoyed to meet a posse of passing strangers. The man coming towards her, and two of those remaining on the lakeside path, were wearing light blue-grey *Bahnschutzpolizei* uniforms; the man in charge was wearing the long leather coat beloved of the Gestapo. He walked slowly towards her, enjoying each step.

'Is something wrong?' Effi asked innocently.

'Who are you, Madame? Where are your papers?'

Effi took them from her bag and passed them over.

'Erna von Freiwald,' he read aloud, with a slight, but unmistakable hint of disdain for the 'von.'

'Yes,' she agreed cheerfully.

'And what are you doing here, Frau von Freiwald?'

'Ah,' Effi said. 'This is slightly embarrassing.'

'Yes?'

'This cottage is owned by old friends of mine. My late husband and I used to visit them before the war. Rainer was a keen fisherman, like Harald. They used to spend whole nights out on the lake, and Maria and I would talk...'

'Your social life before the war does not interest me. What are you doing here now?'

'I came to see if I could stay here, away from the bombing. It's getting so bad in the city, and, well, I came up here last night. The train took forever, and I had trouble finding the cottage after all these years, and by the time I did it was too late to go back. So I stayed the night. I was just getting ready to leave when you arrived.'

'And where are the owners?'

'I don't know. Harald was always a bit secretive about what he did, so I imagine he's doing war work somewhere. I haven't seen them since 1940.'

'But you decided to take over their house?'

'I'm sure they wouldn't mind if they knew. I was only hoping to stay a few weeks. Until the miracle weapons are ready,' she added, hoping that she wasn't overdoing it, 'and the enemy has to stop bombing us.'

He looked at her, then started through her papers again. He doesn't believe me, she thought, but he doesn't know why, and he can't really bring himself to believe that a middle-aged woman is what he's looking for .

'Is there trouble in the area?' she asked. 'Has a foreign prisoner escaped from one of the camps?'

'That is not your concern,' he said sharply, and thrust out a hand with her papers. 'If you wish to live here, you must get the written consent of the owners, and a residence permit from the local Party office. Understood?'

'Yes. Thank you.' She resisted the temptation to curtsy.

He took one more look at her and turned abruptly on his heels. The dog whined happily at the prospect of resuming its walk.

As the sound of their progress faded, Effi let her body sag against the door jamb, closed her eyes, and let her breath escape in an explosive sigh of relief.

Führer, we thank you!

April 7 – 9

Russell woke early, which was just as well, as he'd forgotten to request a wake-up bang on his door. Assuming the American Embassy hadn't moved in the last five years, he had time for breakfast and a quick visit before his appointment with the Soviet authorities. He washed and shaved in unexpectedly hot water, got dressed, and hurried down to the restaurant.

It was better patronised than the evening before, and those idly playing with the suspicious-looking slices of cold meat included one British and two American foreign correspondents. One of the latter, Bill Manson, was an old acquaintance from pre-war Berlin. He'd represented various East Coast papers in half a dozen European capitals since the 1920s, and his eternal crew-cut was suitably grey. He had to be well over sixty.

'I thought you were with Ike,' Manson said as Russell sat down.

'I was. I needed a change.'

'Well, if you needed a rest, you've come to the right place. Nothing's happened here for months, and nothing will until the victory parade. Lenin's birthday or May Day, depending on how quickly Zhukov and Co. can wrap things up. If you like watching tanks roll by for hours on end you'll be in seventh heaven.'

'Sounds riveting. I'm John Russell,' he told the other two. '*San Francisco Chronicle*.'

'Martin Innes, *Daily Sketch*,' the thinner of the two Englishmen said. He had slicked-back brown hair and rather obvious ears book-ending a pleasant, well-meaning face.

'Quentin Bradley, *News Chronicle*,' the other chipped in. He had wavy blonde hair, a chubby face, and the sort of public school accent which made Russell's teeth stand on edge.

'Is this the usual breakfast?' he asked.

'Never changes,' Manson confirmed. 'One day I took the meat away with me, just to make sure they weren't bringing the same pieces back each morning.'

Russell reached for the bread and jam. The former was dark and stale, the latter surprisingly good. Cherries from the Caucasus, most likely.

'How did you get here?' Innes asked.

Russell went through his itinerary, raising a few eyebrows in the process.

'You must have been really keen,' Manson commented when he'd finished. 'Any particular reason?'

Russell told them he was hoping for a ringside seat when the Red Army entered Berlin.

Not a chance, was the unanimous response.

'Why not?' Russell asked. 'Don't they want witnesses to their triumph? Are they treating German civilians that badly?' He hadn't wanted to believe the reports coming out of East Prussia – of German women raped and nailed to barn doors.

'They probably are,' Manson said, 'but that's not the whole story. I think the main reason they won't allow any foreign reporters near the Red Army is what it might tell them about the Soviet Union. They don't want the world knowing how utterly reckless they are with their own soldiers' lives, or how backward most of their army is. The front-line units are good, no doubt about it, but the rest – no uniforms, not enough weapons, just a huge rabble following on behind, stealing wristwatches by the dozen and wondering what flush toilets are for. It's hardly an advert for thirty years of communism.'

Russell shrugged. 'I have to try.'

'Good luck,' Manson said with a sympathetic smile.

He was probably right, Russell thought, as he made his way across

Sverdlov Square and down Okhotnyy Ryad in the direction of the American Embassy, trying to ignore the man in the suit walking some twenty metres behind him. It was his first glimpse of the city by day, and Moscow seemed a much sorrier place than it had in 1939. There was a lot of visible bomb damage, given that years had elapsed since the last real German attacks. The shop windows were empty, and people were queuing in considerable numbers for whatever was hidden inside.

He supposed things were slowly getting back to normal. Trams trundled along the wide boulevards, and hordes of plainly dressed pedestrians hurried along the pavements. In what had once been shady parks, a few surviving trees were budding into spring. It was certainly hard to believe that only three years had passed since the Wehrmacht came hammering at the city's door.

As Russell approached the embassy building he noticed two of the new Gaz-11s parked on the other side of the road. There were at least two men in each, and they were presumably waiting for someone to follow. The regime's paranoia was scaling new heights.

Once inside, Russell was asked to sign the usual book, and told to wait.

'I have another appointment in twenty minutes,' he objected.

'This won't take long,' the duty officer told him

Half a minute later, a dark-haired, bespectacled man in his early thirties came down the stairs. Russell hadn't seen Joseph Kenyon since late 1941, when the diplomat was stationed in Berlin. He'd first met him in Prague two years earlier, during his own brief stint working for American intelligence.

After they'd shaken hands, Kenyon ushered him through the building and out into a large and barely tended courtyard garden. 'The rooms are all bugged,' the diplomat told him, as he reached for an American cigarette. 'Or at least some of them are. We find them and destroy them, but they're surprisingly efficient at installing new ones.'

'It's good to see you,' Russell said, 'but I only came to register my presence. I've got a meeting at Press Liaison in fifteen minutes.'

'Just tell me who you're here for,' Kenyon said. 'We've received no word.'

The penny dropped. 'I'm here for the *Chronicle*, no one else. I gave up working for governments in 1941.'

'Oh,' Kenyon said, clearly surprised. 'Right. So why Moscow? Nothing's happening here.'

Russell gave him a quick précis.

'Not a chance,' Kenyon told him, echoing the journalists at the Metropol.

After scheduling a drink for that evening, Russell hurried back up Okhotnyy Ryad, his NKVD shadow keeping pace. The sky, like his mood, was darkening, and large drops of rain were beginning to fall as he reached the Press Liaison office on Tverskaya Street. A minute late, he was kept waiting for a further twenty, quite possibly as a punishment. There was a picture album of Soviet achievements on the anteroom table, all dams, steelworks and happy *kolkhoz* workers driving their brand new tractors into the sunset. He laughed out loud at one photograph of Stalin surrounded by nervously smiling women in overalls, and received a withering glare from the young receptionist.

Someone arrived to collect him, a thin, balding man in his thirties with a worried look who introduced himself as Sergey Platonov. Upstairs, Russell discovered the reason for Platonov's anxious expression – another man of roughly the same age with bushier hair, harder eyes and an NKVD major's uniform. His name was Leselidze.

Russell was reminded of another interview he had endured, in Berlin several years earlier. Then too, the monkey had asked the questions while the organ grinder just sat there, making everyone nervous.

The room was like a small lecture hall, with several short rows of seats facing a slightly raised dais. They all sat down, Platonov and Leselidze behind the lecturer's desk, Russell in the audience front row. It felt like more like a tribunal than an interview.

Platonov asked, in almost faultless English, whether Russell was aware of the wartime restrictions on movement applicable to all non-Soviet citizens.

'Yes,' Russell replied in the same language. A moving crane caught his eye in the window, proof that some rebuilding was underway.

'And the general rules governing conversations between foreigners and Soviet citizens?'

'Yes.'

Did he understand the specific rules governing foreign reporters in the Soviet Union, particularly those regarding the transmission of any information deemed detrimental to the Soviet state?

'I do,' Russell affirmed. He had no knowledge of the current details, but the gist was unlikely to have changed – foreign journalists would be allowed to prop up the main hotel bars, sit quietly at official press conferences, and have spontaneous conversations with specially selected model workers at tractor assembly plants. Anything else would be forbidden.

'Do you have anything you would like to see?' Platonov asked. 'A collective farm, perhaps.' He sounded every inch the caring host, but his companion's face told a different story.

'I would like to see Berlin with the Red Army,' Russell said, tiring of the game and switching to Russian. 'The rest of the world should know who really defeated the Germans.'

Flattery made no impression. 'There is no possibility of that,' Platonov replied calmly in English. 'We have strict rules – only Soviet journalists are allowed with Soviet forces. We cannot be responsible for the safety of foreign journalists in a war zone. That is quite impossible.'

'I...' Russell began.

'What makes you so certain that the Red Army will reach Berlin ahead of the Americans?' Leselidze asked him in Russian. Platonov slumped back in his chair, as if relieved that his part was over.

Russell answered in the same language. 'About ten days ago General Eisenhower wrote a personal letter to Comrade Stalin. He told the Generalissimo that the Allied armies would not be advancing on Berlin, that their next moves would be towards Hamburg in the north, Leipzig in the centre and Munich in the south.'

Leselidze smiled. 'I was unaware that the details of this letter had been made public in the West. But that is not important. What matters is whether General Eisenhower was speaking the truth. We know that

Churchill wants Berlin, and that all the generals do too, both British and American. Why should Eisenhower be any different? He's a general; he must want the glory which goes with the biggest prize. So why does he tell us he doesn't?' The Russian leaned forward in his seat, as if eager to hear Russell's answer.

'You're mistaken,' Russell told him. 'You don't understand how things work in the West. The war is effectively won, but a lot more soldiers are going to die before it ends, and the US government would rather they were Russians than Americans. The occupation zones have already been agreed, so they don't see any point in sacrificing lives for territory that they'll have to hand back. And on top of all that, they've got this ridiculous bee in their bonnets about diehard Nazis heading south to the Alps, where they've supposedly built a fortress to end all fortresses.'

Leselidze shook his head. 'You are clever enough to see through this, but your leaders are not?'

'I know the Nazis better than they do. If Hitler and his disciples knew how to plan ahead they might have won the damn war. And one last thing. Eisenhower loathes Montgomery, who would have to be given a leading role in any advance on Berlin. Believe me, Ike would rather let Zhukov take the prize than give Monty that sort of glory.'

Leselidze sat back in his seat, still looking less than convinced. 'Very interesting. Thank you, Mr Russell. But, as Comrade Platonov has explained to you, the policy forbidding journalists from travelling with Soviet forces is an extremely strict one. So...'

'I'm sure it's a very good policy. But it would be in your interests to make an exception in my case.'

Leselidze looked blank. 'I don't understand.'

'Comrade Leselidze, I have personal reasons for wanting to enter Berlin with the Red Army. My wife and child are probably in the city. My wife, who helped me escape from Germany in 1941, has been a fugitive from the Gestapo for more than three years. And now the Red Army is coming. The soldiers have all read Comrade Simonov's articles calling for punishment of the German people...'

'Yes, yes. But Comrade Stalin has now issued an order calling for the troops to only punish Nazis...'

'I know. And a very wise order it is. But after what the Germans did to your country and your people, an army of saints would be out for revenge. And while I can appreciate that, I still want to protect my family. Can you understand that?'

Leselidze shrugged. 'We all wish to protect our families,' he said blandly. 'But I fail to see how helping you protect yours will benefit the Soviet Union.'

'Because I have something to offer in exchange,' Russell told him.

'What?'

'My knowledge of Berlin. Whatever your generals need to know, I can tell them. Where everything is, the best roads, the vantage points. I can save Russian lives in exchange for my family's.'

Even to Russell himself, it sounded dreadfully thin.

'I would be very surprised if we did not already possess this information,' Leselidze told him. 'I will of course pass your offer to the relevant authorities, but I am certain that the answer will be no.'

Alighting from the tram at her Bismarck Strasse stop, Effi checked that her building was still standing. Reassured, she scanned the rest of the wide street for fresh bomb damage. None was apparent. The smoke still rising away to the north-west suggested that the latest British attacks had fallen on that area of the city, where many of the larger war industries were situated. Which made for a pleasant change.

She walked up to their second-floor apartment, feeling the tiredness in her legs. She also felt emotionally numb. Had she grown accustomed to living with fear, or more adept at suppressing her feelings? Was there a difference? She was too tired to care.

Ali wasn't home, but a note on the kitchen table promised she'd be back by four. There was no mention of where she was, which caused Effi a pang of probably unnecessary anxiety. For all her youth, Ali was never careless of her own safety, and only the previous day had lectured Effi on the importance of not growing over-confident. It would be so terrible to fall at the very last hurdle, after all they'd been through.

Ali had left her some soup in a saucepan, but there was no gas, and Effi didn't feel hungry enough to eat it cold. She nibbled on a piece of bread instead, and walked through to her bedroom, thinking she'd lie down for however long it took the Americans to arrive overhead. It would probably make more sense to go straight downstairs, but the idea of spending any unnecessary time in the basement shelter was less than appealing.

She lay down on the bed, closed her eyes, and wondered what Ali would do after the war. Marrying Fritz would be a good start, and no less than she deserved. The girl had lost so much – her parents deported and presumably killed, her first boyfriend the same – but she'd grown into such a resourceful young woman. She had certainly saved Effi's own life. When the two fugitives had run into each other in the Uhlandeck Café in June 1942, it had been Ali who had put Effi in touch with the forger Schönhaus, and he who had documented the fake identity that had served her ever since.

Where was he, she wondered. In 1943, he'd been recognised and al-most caught by one of the Jewish *greifer* – 'catchers' – that the Gestapo employed, and had taken off for Switzerland. No one had ever heard from him again, which was probably good news – if the Gestapo had caught him, they would have gloated. His story would make a good film, she thought. A final pan-out filling the screen with Alps...

She was woken by the air-raid sirens. Was she imagining it, or were they sounding increasingly the worse for wear? How many air raids did the average siren last?

She walked quickly downstairs, out across the rear courtyard and down the narrow stairway to the large basement shelter which served her own building and four others. There had sometimes been as many as a hun-dred and fifty people camped out down there, but lately there seemed about half that. The Volkssturm call-up and evacuation programme had taken most of the remaining men and children, and several women had fallen prey to the bombing. Many of the latter had recently lost a husband or son, and had, in their grief, stopped taking any precautions for their own safety.

Strangely, but somehow predictably, the occupants of the different houses stuck together in their shared shelter, arranging their camp beds and chairs in a laager-like circle, regardless of how little contact they had with each other above ground. And each group, Effi guessed, would have the same cross-section of stereotypes. There was the cynic who disbelieved everything the authorities said, and the old Nazi who still clung to his faith in ultimate victory. There was the woman who talked of nothing but her missing son, and the old man who had fought in the First War, when things were done so much more efficiently. There was the couple who held each other's hands and always seemed to be praying. Sometimes Effi sat there casting the movie, assigning actors and actresses of past acquaintance to the various parts.

Frau Pflipsen was the one she would like to play, in the hopefully distant future. The woman claimed to be ninety, and quite possibly was, having lost two grandsons at Verdun in 1916. A diminutive physical presence, all of 1.45 metres tall and weighing in at not much more than 40 kilos, she was more than happy to share her feelings about the authorities in general, and the Nazi leaders in particular. She had a reluctant soft spot for Goebbels – 'you have to admit it, the little shit is clever' – but thought the rest should be lined up against a wall and shot. A few months earlier, Effi and Ali had amused themselves by scripting a meeting between Frau Pflipsen and the Führer. The latter had hardly got a word in.

That morning, Frau Pflipsen was reading aloud from the single sheet that passed for a daily paper. The Red Army's assault on 'Fortress Königsberg' was in full swing, and Promi – the Propaganda Ministry – was obviously determined that other German cities should be fully aware of their possible fate. Why, Effi wondered, as Frau Pflipsen cantered through lurid accounts of Soviet atrocities, and the faces around her grew more alarmed. What good did scaring people do? If Goebbels really believed that German defeats were down to a lack of backbone, then he wasn't such a clever little shit after all.

Once Frau Pflipsen had finished her recitation, Frau Esser raised an arm in hopeful pursuit of silence. Her husband had been block-warden until mid-March, when an unheralded raid had killed him and his infant cabbages on a nearby allotment, and she had inherited the post by default – no one else wanted the job, and no one else could read his handwritten lists of the local residents. Frau Esser was less than keen herself, a fact that aroused occasional feelings of guilt in her own breast, but bothered no one else. During these final weeks, less than keen seemed a highly appropriate response.

'I have a short announcement,' she said. 'Any woman who wishes can register for a half day's firearms training at the barracks down by the Lietzensee. The instructors will be from the SS. If you're interested come and see me.'

A couple of women did, and Effi thought about joining them. Were they handing out guns with the training? If so, it might be worth risking a few hours in the company of the SS. She smiled inwardly at the memory of the last such occasion, when she and Ali had accepted a poster invitation to an SS Christmas party on Potsdamer Platz. The food and drink had been wonderful, and their only problem had been shaking off Ali's newly acquired SS suitor. He had insisted on escorting her back to the apartment, and only relented when Ali explained that her husband – a Wehrmacht major – was expected home on leave that day, and would be outraged if his wife returned with another man.

Those were different days, Effi thought. In 1943 neither had really expected to survive the war, and the feeling of nothing to lose had encouraged the taking of risks. Now that survival seemed almost in reach, the instinctual urge was to do nothing that might attract attention. She would forget about the firearms training, Effi decided, but she might still try to get hold of a gun. Men behaved badly in wars, particularly in their final days, when neither winners nor losers had much to gain by behaving well.

She lay back on her camp bed, hoping to get some more sleep, just as the sound of exploding bombs penetrated the shelter. They were falling at least a mile away, Effi guessed – like most Berliners, she had grown quite proficient at estimating such things.

The next stick was closer, but not close enough to shake dust from the ceiling. A quarter-mile at least. She looked up, wondering for the umpteenth time whether the floor above would hold if the building above collapsed. They had done their best to shore it up, but no one really knew. If it did come down, she hoped it came down on her head. The thought of being buried alive filled her with dread.

More explosions, and this time little specks of dust floated down from above. Like everyone else, Effi braced herself for the sudden crack of thunder, but as the moments lengthened it became apparent that none were coming. There were muffled explosions in the distance, then more still further away.

The all-clear sounded earlier than usual. Provided there was no British daytime raid, the streets should be safe until dark, and Effi knew she should use the opportunity to do some shopping. With the Russians on the Oder, who knew when the city's ration supplies would suddenly dry up?

It was still grey outside, and most of the eastern sky was full of smoke. The government district, she guessed. Serve them right. She didn't suppose Hitler had been standing by a window when it blew in, but one could always hope.

The queue at the local grocery was long, but there was still no sign of food running out. Effi used her and Ali's ration cards to buy rice, lentils, dried peas, a small amount of fat and an even smaller piece of bacon. There was, unusually, no ersatz coffee to be had, but few seemed disposed to lament the fact. And in general, the mood seemed one of almost cheerful resignation. For months the favourite joke among Berliners had been 'enjoy the war – peace will be dreadful', but lately things had got so bad that even a Russian occupation might be some sort of improvement.

It was almost three when Effi left the shop, and the sun was struggling to break through the clouds. She thought about walking to one of her favourite cafés on Savigny Platz or the Ku'damm, not for the barely drinkable coffee and barely edible cakes, but because taking a seat on the sidewalk and watching the world go by was a way of stepping back in time, to when such pleasures could be taken for granted. It was too risky, of course – the Gestapo *greifer* hovered around those cafés like vultures. They, above all people, understood the fugitive's desperate desire to relive a few moments of his or her former life.

She walked home. Discovering to her surprise that gas was available, she put water on for a pot of tea. The flame was pathetically low, but half an hour later, just as Ali was letting herself in through the apartment door, steam began to rise.

'How did it go?' Ali asked as she took off her coat.

She was looking good, Effi thought. Too thin, of course, and their diet was doing nothing for her skin complexion, but she would be a lovely young woman again when all this was over. A real catch for any man who could cope with an independent spirit, and she believed that Fritz could. 'I don't really know,' she admitted in answer to the question. She gave Ali a run-through of the night's events, ending with the Gestapo officer. 'I don't know whether he believed me or not,' she concluded. 'If he didn't, then we may have visitors. But we've had them before,' she added, seeing Ali anxiously purse her lips, 'and we sent them packing. Remember the ice?'

Ali laughed. About eighteen months earlier, the Gestapo had suspected 'Frau von Freiwald' of harbouring a Jewish U-boat. She and her 'niece' had been living in a ground floor apartment then, and watchers had been stationed front and rear. One evening Effi had poured boiling water across the path at the back, and the freezing temperature had done its work. A few hours later they were treated to the sound of a heavy fall and subsequent volley of curses. Soon thereafter the watchers were withdrawn, and a month or so later Effi was able to resume her provision of temporary sanctuary for those in desperate need.

'And Erik will warn us if things have gone wrong,' she added.

'If he's not the first one they arrest,' Ali protested, but without too much conviction.

Years earlier, Effi had listened to a conversation between John and his ex-wife's brother Thomas about their times in the trenches. There were some men, they agreed, whom everyone knew would remain unscathed. The Swede, she realised, had that sort of aura.

Of course, Russell had added at the time, the intuition was sometimes mistaken, and when one of the certain survivors was killed everyone else became twice as depressed.

'So how was internment?' Russell asked Joseph Kenyon that evening. Like all the American diplomats and journalists marooned in Berlin when the Japanese carrier fleet hit Pearl Harbor, Kenyon had endured five long months of 'protective custody' at Bad Nauheim's Grand Hotel. Russell had been on the run by then, or he would shared the same fate.

'It was probably a decent hotel before the war,' Kenyon said. 'But by the time we arrived the staff were all gone, and the heating and electricity had both packed up. Things got better, I suppose. After we kicked up a fuss, we probably ate better than the local Germans, but that wasn't saying much.'

'I can't say I'm sorry to have missed that,' Russell admitted. He reached for his drink and took in their surroundings. The bar of the National Hotel bar was large and almost deserted; there were a couple of Swedish journalists sharing a bottle of wine on the far side of the room, and an obvious NKVD snoop at a table close to the door. He kept checking his watch as if expecting relief.

'And how did you get out of Germany?' Kenyon asked.

Russell gave the diplomat the expurgated version, which had him passed, like a parcel in the children's game, from one group of selfless anti-Nazis to another, until Sweden loomed on the horizon.

Kenyon wasn't fooled for a second. 'The communists got you out.'

'I suppose most of them were Party members,' Russell admitted ingenuously.

'And once you got to Stockholm?'

'I got passage on one of the neutral sailings the Swedes had arranged with the Germans. Got dropped off in Havana, took a flight to Miami, arrived just in time for my mother's funeral, which was really sad – I hadn't seen her since 1939. I spent the next six months trying to tell America what was happening to the Jews, but no one wanted to hear it. Would you believe the *New York Times* has only had two lead editorials on the Jewish question since the war started? Lots of short pieces on page 11 or page 19 – 19,000 Jews killed in Kharkov, how Treblinka operated, etc etc – but no one would spell it all out in capital letters. It became a minor running story.'

Kenyon lit a cigarette. 'Did you work out why they wouldn't?'

'Not really. Several of the editors were Jews, so you couldn't put it all down to anti-Semitism. I think some of them convinced themselves that a war for the Jews would be harder to sell than a war against tyranny. Some journalists told me the stories were exaggerated, but their only reason for thinking so was that most of the atrocity stories from the First War had turned out to be fakes.' Russell grimaced. 'When it came down to it, they couldn't bring themselves to believe that the Nazis were murdering every Jew they could get their hands on. Apart from being inconvenient, it was just too much to take in.' He took a swig from his glass. 'Anyway, I tried. You can only go on flogging an unwilling horse for so long. After that, well, I was feeling a long way away from the people I loved.'

'They're still in Berlin?'

'As far as I know. My wife – she's my girlfriend really, but people take a wife much more seriously – anyway, she was on the run with me, but things went wrong, and she had to stay behind. If the Gestapo caught her, they never let on, and I'm praying that she's been in hiding all this time. My son was only fourteen when I left, and he's more German than English. There was no way I would have put him at risk, even if his mother – my first wife – would have let me.'

'And you haven't heard from either of them since '41?'

'No. The Swedes got their Berlin embassy to let Paul know I was safe. He thanked them for letting him know, but he had no message for me. He must have been furious with me, and I can't say as I blame him. When

I got to London at the end of '42 I tried to persuade the BBC to broadcast a message that only Effi would understand, but the bastards refused.'

'Three years is a long time,' Kenyon mused.

'I'd noticed,' Russell said wryly.

'So you left the States,' Kenyon prompted.

'I was lucky. The *San Francisco Chronicle*'s London correspondent wanted to come home – family reasons of some sort – and my old editor asked if I was interested. I jumped at it.' He smiled at Kenyon. 'I'm afraid having an American passport hasn't made me feel any less English.'

'It'll come.'

'I doubt it. There's a lot I love about America, and a lot I loathe about England and Germany, but Europe still feels like home.'

'Try Moscow for a few years. But how was London?'

'Okay. In any other circumstances I'd have probably loved it, but all I did was sit around and wait. I began to think that the Second Front was never going to happen. When it did, I managed to convince my editor that a year in the trenches qualified me as a war correspondent, and I've been trailing after the troops since Normandy. Until now, that is.'

'They're making a huge mistake,' Kenyon said.

'Who is?'

'Well, Ike, to start with. But the president as well, for not overruling him.'

'Word is, Roosevelt's not long for this world.'

'I know, but there must be someone at the wheel. Ike's telling everyone that his business is winning the war as quickly and cheaply as he can, and that winning the peace is down to the politicians. If he doesn't get the connection, then someone should be getting it for him.'

'Career soldiers rarely do. But if the occupation zones are already decided, what's the point?

'The point,' Kenyon insisted, tapping the ash from the end of his cigarette, 'is to show some resolve, give the Russians something to think about. If the Red Army takes Berlin, the Soviets will come away with the impression that they've won the war on their own.'

'They damn near have.'

'With a hell of a lot of help. Who built the trucks their soldiers are riding on? Who supplied the cans they're eating from? Who just surrounded three hundred thousand of the bastards in the Ruhr Pocket?'

'Yes, but...'

'Take it from me, the Russians will go from friend to foe in the time to takes to say "Hitler's dead". They've already got their hands on half of Europe, and they'll be eyeing the rest. They might not be as nasty as the Nazis, but they'll be a damn sight harder to shift.'

He was probably right, Russell thought. But if the Americans had been through what the Russians had, they'd also be looking for payback.

'What are you going to do when they say no?' Kenyon asked, changing the subject.

'I've no idea,' Russell admitted.

He was still pondering that question as he walked back up Okhotnyy Ryad to Sverdlov Square and the Metropol. He seemed stuck in what bomber pilots called a holding pattern; he couldn't 'land' until he knew what had happened to Effi and Paul. One or both could be dead, which would change everything. But even if both were alive... Paul was eighteen now, and more than ready to strike out on his own. Effi might have fallen in love with someone else. Three years, as Kenyon had said, was an awfully long time.

And if she still loved him, well, where would they live?

In the ruins of Berlin? She might be longing to leave the city behind. She might feel more tied to the place than ever.

He had no idea where he wanted to be. Living in hotel rooms and lodgings for three years had left him with an abiding sense of rootlessness. This war had set millions in motion, and some would have trouble stopping.

'I can't see what I'm doing,' Effi said, putting the half-sewn dress to one side. Outside the light was fading, and there'd been no electricity since that morning's bombing.

'Have my seat,' Ali suggested. 'The light's better.'

'No, it's all right. It's not as if there's any hurry. I don't think the Skoumal sisters will be going out gallivanting any time soon.' When Effi and Ali had set up the business in late 1942, Frau Skoumal had been one of their first clients, and fashioning dresses for her and her daughters had yielded them a steady supply of food and ration stamps. They had lived above the shop in Halensee in those days, because residents of commercial premises were not obliged to register with the local authorities.

Effi stood up and stretched her arms above her head. 'I can't believe how...'

She was interrupted by an urgent series of knocks on their front door. The two women looked at each other, and saw their fears mirrored.

'Did you hear a car?' Effi whispered, as she headed for the door.

'No, but...'

There were more knocks.

'Who is it?' Effi asked, remembering to put a few years on her voice.

'It's Erik,' a voice almost hissed.

She let him in, wondering what new disaster had occurred. It was only the second time he had been to the apartment, and he looked shabbier than usual – his coat was missing a button, his trousers badly frayed at the ankles. He was also unshaven, she realised – the first time she had seen him so.

'I'm sorry for coming here,' he said at once, 'but there was no time to contact you in the usual way.'

'Were those men caught?' Effi asked.

'No. At least, not as far as I know. We still haven't heard from Lübeck, and no news is usually good news. But that's not why I'm here.'

'One of them knew me,' Effi told him. 'And he stayed here.'

Aslund looked mortified. 'Oh, that's bad. I'm sorry. It's just... there's no excuse, but the arrangements... there was no time. I am sorry,' he repeated.

'Have a seat,' Effi offered. Her anger was already turning to guilt. Aslund had saved so many innocent lives.

'No, I can't stay. The reason I came – I have someone in need of a refuge.'

'Of course,' Effi said instinctively, and tried to ignore the sense of resentment that suddenly welled up inside her. They had not had a 'guest' for several months, and she had grown accustomed to living without that particular hostage to Gestapo fortune.

'I know,' Aslund said, as if he could feel her reluctance. 'But...'

'For how long?' Effi asked.

'Until it's over,' the Swede admitted. 'This one's different,' he continued, seeing the look on Effi's face. 'She's only eight years old. Her mother was killed by a bomb about a month ago, and the woman who's looking after her – who sheltered them both for more than two years – she's seriously ill. She can't look after the girl anymore.'

'She's Jewish?' Ali asked.

'Yes. The name on her new papers is Rosa. Rosa Borinski. She's a lovely little girl.'

Effi hesitated. She wanted to say no, but she didn't know why. One risk too many, perhaps.

'There's no one else,' Aslund said softly.

'Of course we'll take her,' Effi said, looking at Ali. How could they refuse?

Ali looked concerned. 'There's something I've been meaning to tell you,' she said. 'I told Fritz that I'd move in with him until it's all over. There'll be more room, but I won't be around much to help.'

'That's all right,' Effi told her. She felt upset that Ali was going, but hardly surprised. 'I can manage the girl on my own,' she told Aslund.

'That's wonderful,' Aslund said, as if a huge weight had just been lifted from his shoulders. 'Someone will bring her here tomorrow. After the day raid, if there is one.'

'They haven't missed a day for weeks.'

'True. But it can't last much longer. Once the Russians are in the city, the Western allies will have to stop their bombing.'

'And how long before the Russians are here?' Effi asked him.

Aslund shrugged. 'A few weeks. No more than that. And maybe less.'

Russell was woken by the early morning sunlight, and found it impossible to go back to sleep. With two hours to wait until the restaurant opened, he enjoyed a long soak in the oversize bath and then sat by the window with his Russian dictionary, checking through words he might need to use. When the Cyrillic letters began to blur he put the book down, and stared out at the square. A group of four women cleaners were gathered beside the statue of Marx, leaning on their brooms like a coven of witches. Marx hadn't noticed them, of course – he was staring straight ahead, absorbed in saving humanity.

He ate breakfast alone surrounded by yawning waiters, and then went for a walk, cutting round the back of the Lenin Museum and into Red Square. On the far side, a couple of people were crossing in front of St Basil's, but otherwise the vast expanse was free of movement. There were no guards outside Lenin's tomb, a sure sign that the mummified corpse had not yet returned from its wartime vacation in distant Kuybyshev.

Russell ambled across the cobbles, wondering what to do. Would the Soviets actually communicate a refusal, or just leave him dangling for days? Probably the latter, he thought. He needed to push for an answer – it wouldn't hurt and it might even help. The Soviet Union was one of those strange places – like Oxford or the Church – where money didn't talk very loudly, and where making yourself heard called for a certain directness. Like shouting, or banging one's fist on a table.

If the British introduced a National Health Service he could almost guarantee that those who shouted loudest would get the best treatment. Which would still be better than rationing according to income.

His mind was rambling. What if the shouting failed to shift them? What should he do then – travel back to the West? Once the Red Army took Berlin, the Americans, British and French would insist on their own people going in to administer the agreed zones, and he, as a Western journalist, should have no trouble going with them. But who knew how long it would be before the Red Army declared the city safe, and allowed their Allies in? Weeks probably, maybe even months.

Was there nothing more he could offer the Soviets? He couldn't think of anything. He needed a friend, a sponsor.

Shchepkin, he thought, without much hope. But there was no one else.

Yevgeny Shchepkin was the closest thing he had to a friend in Moscow. When Russell had refused the Russians' invitation to the Soviet Union at the end of 1941, he had gained the impression that Shchepkin had actually been pleased, as if he knew that his bosses meant Russell no good, and was pleased that their plans had come to nought. That might have been wishful thinking – it was hard to know. When they had first met in 1924, both had been enthusiastic communists. At their meetings in 1939, Shchepkin had still seemed committed, but on a much more pragmatic level, and by 1941 Russell had gained the distinct impression that his old comrade was just going through the motions.

Shchepkin might speak in his favour, he thought. Always assuming he could – the average life expectancy of Stalin's international reps had taken something of a dip in recent years.

But how could he find him? There were no private numbers in the Moscow telephone directory.

He could just go straight to the NKVD. Put them at their ease by sticking his head between their jaws. Say Shchepkin was an old friend whom he wanted to look up while he was in Moscow. Witter on about internationalism and other mad ideas from Lenin's day. What did he have to lose? They could only say no.

The young woman who brought the child seemed cold and brusque to Effi, as if she was passing on a parcel rather than another living soul. 'This is Rosa,' was all she said, handing over the false papers and a small and very battered suitcase. She was clearly disinclined to linger, and Effi did nothing to detain her. The child could answer any questions about herself.

Rosa seemed small for her age, with large hazel eyes, a small straight nose and soft lips. In better times, she would have been pretty, Effi thought, but hunger and grief had taken a toll. The curly fair hair was short and roughly shorn, adding to the waif-like impression. More to the point perhaps, there was nothing in the girl's features or colouring to suggest her Jewish heritage.

'I'm Erna,' Effi said. 'Erna von Freiwald. And this is Mathilde,' she added, introducing Ali. 'She's moving out in couple of days, but she'll still come to see us.'

Rosa solemnly shook hands with both of them. 'Rosa is not my real name,' she said. 'But I can't tell you my real name until the war is over.'

'That's good,' Effi said. 'Erma and Mathilde aren't our real names either. When the war's over we can all tell each other.'

The girl nodded. 'Are you my mother now?' she asked Effi, with a discernible hint of challenge.

'We're both going to be your friends,' Effi offered, uncertain of what to say. 'And we'll try and look after you the way your mother would have wanted.'

'For ever?' the girl asked.

'I don't know. Until the war is over, at least. I'm sorry, but no one has told us about your family – what happened to your father?'

'I don't know. Mother told me he might be alive, and we must hope, but I don't think she believed it.'

'When did you last see him?'

'I don't remember. I was very small. He just went away one day.'

'Do you have any brothers or sisters?'

'I don't think so. Is there any food, please? I'm very hungry.'

'Of course. I'm sorry, I forgot. I made some soup this morning for when you arrived.'

There was no gas to heat it, but Rosa gulped it down. After she'd finished, Effi showed her round the apartment. 'You'll sleep with me,' she said. 'I hope that's all right.'

'I think so,' Rosa agreed. 'I go to bed at eight o'clock.'

'Where you were before,' Effi asked, 'did you go down to the shelter for the air raids?'

'Not when my mother was alive. We had to stay in the shed where we lived. We used to get under the bed, but mother went out to get something.' Her eyes brimmed with tears, which she angrily wiped away. 'Frau Borchers took me down after that. She said I was her niece from Dresden, and that my mother and father had been killed.'

'That's a good story,' Effi agreed. 'We shall say the same here.'

Later that evening, as the British thundered overhead, she told the same story to Frau Esser. The block warden wrote down the fictional details, which someone somewhere would doubtless try to verify. Most such stories, as many U-boats had found to their cost, could eventually be checked, but surely the time was now too short. With any luck at all, the Gestapo would be much too busy looking for last-ditch ways of saving their own skins.

Watching Rosa interact with the other children in the shelter, Effi was reassured by the child's obvious reticence. She wouldn't be giving herself away – her mother had taught her well.

Later, lying awake upstairs with the sleeping girl's arm possessively draped around her, Effi found herself wondering how many millions of children would enter the coming peace as orphans.

Russell's Monday morning visit to the NKVD headquarters on Dzerzhinsky Street was long and fruitless. His arrival caused consternation, his request for Shchepkin's address a look of such incredulity that it almost made him laugh out loud. The young officer stood there mute for several seconds, torn between a transparent desire to send him packing, and an equally obvious fear that doing so would render him personally liable for any other outrageous acts that Russell might commit in the temple of socialism. After ordering him to take a seat, he disappeared in search of help.

He returned five minutes later with a senior officer, a much older man with a prominent scar on one side of his neck, who coldly asked what Russell wanted.

He repeated his story. He had attended the Fifth Conference of the Party in 1924 as a fraternal delegate, and made friends with a young Russian, Yevgeny Shchepkin. Since his job as a journalist had brought him back to Moscow, he was hoping to renew their acquaintance. But, unfortunately, he had lost his old friend's address.

'And why have you come here?' the officer asked.

'I met Yevgeny again in Stockholm in early 1942, and he told me he worked for State Security. These are the State Security offices, are they not?'

The NKVD officer gave Russell a long look, as if trying to determine what he was dealing with – an idiot or something more threatening. He then spent five minutes examining the passport and papers which Russell had voluntarily submitted to his first questioner. 'I hope this is not some journalist's scheme to make trouble,' he said eventually. 'I find it hard to believe that you expected us to tell you the address of a security officer.'

'I did not expect it. I just hoped. And I have no wish to make trouble.'

'Perhaps. In any case, there is no one of that name working for this organisation. I think you have been misinformed.'

'Then I'm sorry to have troubled you,' Russell said, extending a hand for his passport.

After a moment's hesitation, the officer handed it back. 'Where are you staying?' he asked.

'The Metropol.'

'It is a good hotel, yes?'

'Very good.'

'Enjoy your stay, Mr Russell.'

He nodded, and walked back out onto a sunlit Dzerzhinsky Street. A mistake, he thought. Entering the monster's lair was always a bad idea, especially when the monster was as paranoid as this one. As far as he could tell, he hadn't been followed since his first visit to the American Embassy, but he was willing to bet that a fresh human shadow would be soon be waiting at the Metropol.

So why go back? He altered course, turning left down the side of the Bolshoi Theatre and eventually finding a street which led him through to Red Square. As on his last visit, the vast expanse was almost empty. A few lone Russians were hurrying across, and a party of middle-aged men were conversing in Polish as they gawped up at Stalin's windows. The next government in Warsaw, Russell guessed.

He walked on past St Basil's and down to the river. Leaning on the parapet above the sluggish-looking water, he wondered how else he could search for Shchepkin. What had made him think that the NKVD man lived in Moscow? Had he just assumed it? No, he hadn't. He remembered Shchepkin telling him so, if not in so many words. In Stockholm, the Russian had taken him out in the embassy car – a minion had done the actual driving – and walked him round the city's Northern Cemetery. Standing in front of Alfred Nobel's grave, Shchepkin's had said how much he enjoyed cemeteries. 'They make you think about life,' he had said. 'And its absurdities. Nobel probably thought his prizes would stop people associating him with dynamite, but of course the juxtaposition was too perfect – people who remember one always remember the other.'

And then Shchepkin had half joked that some graves were a constant reproof, and that he lived near Moscow's Novodevichy Cemetery, where Vladimir Mayakovsky, the Revolution's most famous poet, was buried.

Where was the Novodevichy Cemetery? The first three passers-by that Russell asked gave him looks of alarm and hurried on, but the fourth – an oldish man with a thumb-sucking child in tow – told him what he wanted to know: the cemetery was next to the monastery of the same name, an hour or so's walk along the river. Or if he was in a hurry, he could walk straight down Kropotkin Street.

Russell set off, walking west between the Kremlin and the river, and eventually found the head of Kropotkin Street. As he strode down the broad avenue, he remembered more of what Shchepkin had said. To reach Mayakovsky's grave, it was necessary to pass Kropotkin's. And Shchepkin often talked to them both. 'I try to answer their criticisms of where the Revolution has taken us.'

'And are they convinced?' Russell had asked him with a grin.

'Who knows?' Shchepkin had admitted with an answering smile. Chekhov's grave was another that gave him pause for thought. The playwright had died in 1904, the year before the first Russian Revolution, and had therefore missed the most tumultuous years of his country's history. But Chekov's own times had been just as compelling, just as challenging to him, as these times were for those who lived through them.

'It might be a lifetime to us,' Shchepkin said, 'but no one experiences more than a brief span of history.'

'So only history can judge itself,' Russell had suggested, half ironically.

'No, we have to make our own judgements. But we do so on insufficient evidence, and we should always bear that in mind.' And having said that, Shchepkin had tried to persuade Russell that the Soviet Union should be his temporary home. Russell had told him he could never get used to the weather.

No one could complain about it today – the sun was still shining in a mostly blue sky, and out of the slight breeze it actually felt warm. When he finally reached the unguarded gates of the Novodevichy Cemetery, the lure of a bench under shady trees proved irresistible. He sat for a while enjoying the sense of peace and beauty, the grey stones amidst the greenery, the golden onion domes of the adjacent monastery gleaming in the bright blue heavens. He thought about looking for Kropotkin, but the stones were myriad, and there was no one to ask.

Outside again, he began the search for Shchepkin's home. He remembered the Russian mentioning an apartment, but it soon became apparent that all the houses in the cemetery's vicinity had been converted into flats. Most of the buildings looked at least a century old, and were quite beautiful – Russell found it easy to picture Tolstoy's Natasha gazing rapturously out of one of the large bay windows, or dancing down a flight of steps to a waiting *droshky*.

He began knocking on doors, expecting a long and probably fruitless afternoon. Several nervous rejections confirmed his pessimism, but then, at only the sixth or seventh attempt, he struck unexpected gold. A young man leaving by the front door simply held it open for him. 'Number four,' he said.

It was on the first floor, at the back of the building. Russell's knock was answered by a smartly dressed young woman. She was slim, with blonde hair and blue eyes, and looked about nineteen. She had her father's mouth.

'Yes?' she asked, almost angrily. There was fear there, too.

'My name is John Russell,' he said. 'I am looking for Yevgeny Shchepkin.'

'He's not here,' she said abruptly, and started to close the door.

'Who is it?' another woman's voice asked anxiously from further inside the apartment. The young woman's answering burst of rapid-fire Russian contained the word 'father'.

'I am a friend of your father,' Russell told her.

The second woman appeared in the doorway. She was probably in her forties, with grey hair tied back in a bun, and clothes that had been worn too long. She had been a beauty once, but now looked worn-out. There was a large spoon in her hand, and Russell realised he could smell borscht.

'My name is John Russell,' he said again.

'You are German?' she asked, worrying him somewhat. Was he speaking Russian with a German accent?

'I'm English. Are you Comrade Shchepkina?

'Yes,' she admitted.

'I met your husband in Poland in 1939, and again in Sweden in 1942. And as I was here in Moscow, I thought I would visit him.'

'He's not here,' she said dully. 'He is away.'

'Will he be back soon?'

'No, I do not think so. I'm sorry. We cannot help you. Please.'

The young woman said something to her mother about Russell being a friend of father's, but she was still opening her mouth to reply when they all heard the creak of a door opening further down the landing.

No one appeared.

'I will show Grigori Sergeyevich back to the Metro,' the daughter said in a loud voice. Her mother looked like she wanted to argue, but forbore from doing so. 'Come,' the daughter said, almost pushing Russell towards the head of the stairs. The door down the landing clicked shut.

Outside on the street, she turned towards the river. 'The spiteful old cow won't be able to see you if we go this way,' she told him coolly.

Like father, like daughter, Russell thought to himself. 'I know my way back,' he told her.

She ignored him. 'Tell me about my father,' she said with more than a hint of hostility.

'What?'

'I've hardly seen him since I was a child.'

'Surely your mother...'

'She knows him the way a wife knows her husband. The world out-side – she doesn't like to even think about it. When he leaves, it's as if he was never there. Until he suddenly appears again, and then it's as if he had never left. It drives me crazy.' She put an arm through Russell's. 'So tell me.'

'I don't really know him. We met more than twenty years ago, here in Moscow. We were both in the First War...' He paused to order his thoughts. 'I think we both became communists because of what that war showed us about the way the world was run. But we didn't get to know each other, not really. We were both involved in the same discussions and arguments about the Revolution, and where it should be headed. Your father was always full of passion,' he added, remembering as he did so that Shchepkin had said the same of him in that Danzig hotel room six years earlier.

'Passion?' she murmured, as if trying the word on for size. They had reached the river, and the half-repaired roof of the Kiev Station was vis-ible to the north. A line of empty barges was chugging downstream.

'That's how all this started,' Russell said, as much to himself as to her. 'Hard to believe now, perhaps. But twenty years is a long time. Once it becomes clear that your passion will also cause innocents to suffer, it begins to wear you down. First there's good and evil, and then the good gets tarnished, and soon it's only a lesser evil. Some quit at that point; they walk away, either physically or mentally. Those that don't, it just gets harder. Your father kept going – that's the one and only thing I really know about him.'

'You make him sound like a hero,' she said, with more than a trace of anger.

'Do I? I don't mean to. People like your father, they lock themselves in. Like a sailor who ties himself to a mast in a storm. It makes sense, but once you're tied up there's not much you can do for anyone else.'

'Why did you really come looking for him?'

'I need help, and he's the only person I could think of.'

'I don't think he can help himself anymore,' she said.

'You think he's been arrested?'

'We don't know, but we haven't seen him for over year. I went down to Dzerzhinsky Street just before Christmas, and they said his whereabouts were unknown. I asked why they had stopped sending my mother his pay, and the man promised he would look into it. But we've heard nothing.'

'If he was dead, they would have informed you,' Russell said, with more conviction than he felt.

'I hope so,' she said. 'You can take a tram from that stop over there,' she said, pointing across the street. 'It goes up Arbat and along Mokhavaya.'

'Thank you,' he said.

As she turned to walk away, he asked what her name was.

'Natasha,' she said.

Emerging from the soldiers' mess on Koppen Strasse, Paul Gehrts could see flames still leaping from the buildings further up the street. They had been hit a couple of hours earlier, courtesy of an idle or incompetent Allied bombardier. The rest of the bombs had fallen, to rather more relevant effect, in the marshalling yards beyond Silesian Station.

There was only one fire engine visible, and no sign of hoses in use. A couple of uniformed men were leaning against the engine, puffing on cigarettes, watching the dancing flames.

Paul walked the other way, towards Stralauer Platz, in hope of finding a tram to take him across the city. Four days had passed since Gerhart's death. The loss had numbed him, but not for long – the shock had worn off all too quickly, and left him seething with an anger he could hardly contain. His sergeant, sensing that he might do something stupid, had persuaded battalion to let Paul take some of the leave he was owed.

Reaching the capital had taken all night, and his first sight of the city in over six months had been a sobering experience. The streets were like obstacle courses, and in places it seemed as if almost half the buildings had been damaged beyond repair. After Russia and Poland, he was used to ruins, but this was Berlin, his home and one of the world's great cities. Germany's heart, as his stepfather had used to say.

There were no trams in Stralauer Platz, but he managed to hitch a lift on an ammunition lorry heading for the Tiergarten. The city centre had taken several hits that morning, and blankets of smoke hung above the streets. Pedestrians crossed his line of vision, striding purposefully this way and that, as if they hadn't noticed that their city was on fire.

As the lorry crossed the Schloss Brücke he saw two bodies floating in the Spree, both head-down with arms stretched forward, like frozen swimmers. As the driver wove his way down Unter Den Linden, he noticed that the Bristol Hotel had been almost razed to the ground – only the revolving doors remained, opening onto rubble. On the other side of the boulevard a line of identical posters bore the message: 'Führer, We Thank You!'

The Brandenburg Gate loomed ahead, and he remembered his feeling of pride when German soldiers had paraded through the Arc de Triomphe in Paris. Five years ago. Five long years.

The Adlon Hotel loomed to the left, still intact, and now enclosed by a grim protective wall that reared up to the first floor balconies. He had a sudden memory of an afternoon there – he must have been about ten – sitting at the bar drinking Coca-Cola through a striped straw as his father interviewed someone on the other side of the room. It must have been the first time he drank the America soda – it had tasted so different, so good. He had wanted it to last forever.

He felt the familiar pang of resentment, the feeling of betrayal that he couldn't really justify, but which rankled deep inside. His head told him – had always told him – that his father had done the right thing, but his heart could not believe it.

This, after all, was the father who had told him that being right was often the consolation prize.

The lorry was skirting the eastern end of the Tiergarten, which looked more like a desert than a park, an area of churned nothingness punctuated by bomb craters and the angular stumps of murdered trees. The Zoo Bunker gun and control towers loomed in the distance, like the gravestones of brother giants.

His lift was going no further, so Paul walked down Budapester Strasse towards the end of the Ku'damm. As a child, he had assumed that his father was just being loyal to the country of his birth, but later he had come to realise that his was not the case – his father felt no attachment to England either; his beliefs transcended nationality. Paul had a rough notion of what those beliefs were – a commitment to fairness, a hatred of prejudice? – but nothing more. It was never easy to work out what other people really believed in. Take Gerhart – he had hated the Nazis, but had he actually believed in anything? He was German through and through, so he must have believed in a different Germany. But different in what way?

What did he believe in himself, come to that? Nothing really. War took away the option of belief, left you too busy fighting for survival, your own and that of your comrades. Particularly a losing war.

But maybe that was the answer. It was how you fought that mattered – you had to fight and lose with honour, or defeat would leave you with nothing.

People like Gerhart would die. Thousands of them, millions of them. He couldn't blame the Russian pilot who had dropped the bomb. He was just doing what he had to do; on another day he might have come down in flames.

But that Russian prisoner in Diedersdorf – he hadn't deserved to die. His death had been a matter of convenience, nothing more. Killing him hadn't been right.

He suddenly remembered something else his father had said. Paul had used to pester him about the First War, and every now and then his father had responded, usually in a vain attempt to undermine all the *Hitlerjugend* stuff which had swirled so happily around his young brain. 'You can't afford to turn off,' Russell had said. 'Both your mind and your emotions – you have to keep them turned on. You own what you do. You live with it. If you can, you use it to make yourself kinder or wiser or both. You make sense of it.'

His father had always believed in making sense of things. Paul could remember an exasperated Effi telling his father that some things would never make sense. Russell had laughed, and said she was living proof of her own argument.

Paul wondered where he was now. Where she was. He remembered the weeks after their disappearance, how he'd scanned all the newspapers he could get hold of, dreading news of their arrest or execution.

And that day in the spring when he'd finally discovered that his father was safe. The relief. The rage.

He skirted round what was left of the Memorial Church, and started up the Ku'damm. A gang of Russian women prisoners were hard at work clearing rubble, one sharing a joke with the German overseers, and the sidewalks were surprisingly crowded, mostly with tired-looking women. Several elderly couples were sitting outside one of the surviving cafés, and most seemed to be nursing their cups between both hands, as if the warmth mattered more than the drink.

The trams were still running in the West End, and one took him down Uhland to Berliner, where he caught another heading east to the Hohen-zollerndamm S-Bahn station. Crossing the railway bridge, he forked right down Charlottenbrunner Strasse. Grunewald's suburban avenues had lost many trees to fuel hunger, and several of the detached houses and villas had been damaged or destroyed by bombs, but an air of serene gentility lingered on. In one large garden an elderly man in a wing collar was digging a grave for a grey-haired corpse in a wheelbarrow. The legs dangling over the end were still stockinged, the feet encased in purple slippers. In another garden, two old women were absorbed in a game of croquet, the sharp crack of mallet on ball echoing down the empty avenue.

Paul finally reached Herbert Strasse, the northern section of which seemed almost intact. Reluctant to reach his destination, he slowed his pace, and even found himself hoping that the house would be gone, and Gerhart's mother with it – with the father and brother already dead there would be no one left to inherit the grief.

But the neat little villa was still standing in its large tree-shaded garden, just as he remembered it from their school days. He opened the wooden gate, walked slowly up the path, and let the knocker fall.

She smiled when she saw it was him, but only for the briefest of moments. Realisation dawned, and her face seemed to collapse in front of him. 'No,' was all she said, without even a trace of conviction.

'I'm sorry,' he said.

Her hand grasped at the door-jamb for support. She looked entreatingly at him, tears coursing down her cheeks. 'Why?'

There was no answer to that, so he told her how: the Russian plane, the bomb, one moment there, the next moment gone. No time to think, no pain. The grave in the woods outside Diedersdorf. He would take her there after the war.

'But why?' she said again, this time with anger. 'Why are you still fighting? Everyone knows the war is lost. Why don't you just say no?'

There was no answer to that either, or none that would help. Why were they still fighting? For each other. And because someone would shoot them if they refused. 'I'm sorry,' was all he found to say. 'I loved him too,' he added simply.

She shut her eyes, reached for the door like a blind woman, and closed it in his face.

He stared at it for a few seconds, then turned away. Back on the street he took out the family photograph which Gerhart had always carried. He had meant it to give it her, but it would have been like slapping her in the face with all she had lost. He would bring it round later. If there was a later.

His own house, the one he and his step-sisters had inherited, was less than a kilometre away. He hadn't intended to go there, but he found himself walking that way, drawn by the need for solitude to the only private space that was available to him.

The key felt strange in his hand as he opened the front door. He half expected to find the place full of refugees, but privilege was obviously still able to exercise its malign protective spell – those members of the Grunewald rich now hiding in the countryside would be expecting to find their homes the way they left them when peace made it safe for them to return.

The house had been empty for almost a year, since his parents' death in the car crash. By then permission to drive a private car had been granted to very few, and his stepfather would have appreciated the irony of it – death by privilege. His mother would not have been so amused. Why, he wondered, had she married two men whose sense of humour so exasperated her?

The rooms smelt stale, and looked, for some reason, like one of those film sets he had seen when Effi gave him a tour of Babelsberg. Uncle Thomas had written to say he would look after the place, but had probably been called up to the Volkssturm not long after that. He might be dead by now.

On impulse, Paul unhooked the telephone, and much to his surprise, it still worked. He looked up Uncle Thomas's number in the book on the side table, and dialled it. He could picture it ringing in the hall of the house in Dahlem, but no one answered.

He went upstairs to his old room. It was as he'd left it, a shrine to his childhood, lined with maps and pictures of his boyhood heroes: Ernst Udet performing aerial acrobatics at the Berlin Olympics, Rudolf Caracciola beside his Silver Arrow at Monaco, Max Schmeling after defeating Joe Louis.

More usefully, he found a drawer-full of socks and underwear that might still fit him.

The bed was only slightly damp, and almost obscenely comfortable. He lay on his back, staring up at the pictures on the walls, and wondered what had happened to the boy who put them there. Several hours later he was woken by the sirens, and chose to ignore them. There were worse things in life than a bomb through the ceiling.

The ghost of a star

April 10 – 13

They came in the night, as they always did. A half-heard key in the door, a rough hand on the shoulder, a succession of barked orders – 'get up, get dressed, get a move on.' Then the back staircase, the Black Maria parked beside the rubbish bins, the short drive up an empty Mokhavaya Street, the archway and gates swallowing him up.

He was bundled in through a side door, walked down a blue-lit corridor and into a yellow-lit reception room, planted on a stool in front of a desk. His personal details were copied from his passport and other papers onto a new form, and he was asked, somewhat bizarrely, whether or not he smoked. When he asked the official across the desk the reason for his arrest he was given nothing more than an if-you-don't-know-I'm-not-going-to-tell-you smirk.

Registration complete, he was hustled along barely lit corridors and up barely lit stairs to his new quarters. His escort shoved him in, pulled the door shut, and flicked up the metal flap to make sure he was still there. It was a six-by-four-foot cell. The bed took up half the available space, a battered tin bucket sat in the far corner. He was not going to get much exercise.

Nor much sleep if the light bulb hanging from the ceiling was always on, which it doubtless was. He could see other yellow lights through the window, which suggested his cell overlooked the inner courtyard, but what the hell did that matter? The quality of the view was hardly a priority.

He lay down on the bed, wondering if the solo cell boded well or ill.

Privacy was nice, but so was someone to talk to. And he would have liked someone other than the authorities to know he was there.

He should be terrified, he thought, but all he could feel was a damning sense of failure.

He had let Effi and Paul down, behaved like an idiot. Making a pain in the arse of himself hadn't worked in the US or Britain, where the only sanction was refusing his calls. So why in God's name had he expected it to work here, where swatting away human pests was almost a national sport?

Stupid, stupid.

But this was no time for self-flagellation. If there was any flagellating to do the Soviet authorities would be only too happy to oblige. He needed to calm down, keep his wits about him. 'Sobriety breeds success', as one puffed-up schoolmaster had written on one of his essays, the day before Archduke Franz Ferdinand bit the dust.

He wondered whether someone had overheard him at the Shchepkins' door, and reported him for breaching the 'general rules governing conversations between foreigners and Soviet citizens?' He hoped not – Shchepkin's wife and daughter would also be under arrest if that was the case – but it seemed the logical explanation. Of course, if Shchepkin himself had been carted away on some ludicrous pretext of consorting with foreign agents, then a foreigner trying to contact him would be a dream come true to those who'd done the carting. It would provide them with 'evidence' that Shchepkin was in touch with 'foreign powers'. The irony was, the only real spying Russell had ever done had been *for* the Soviet Union. His work for the Americans had involved him in nothing more dangerous than lining up potential contacts.

His request to join the Red Army's triumphal progress could hardly have given them reason to arrest him. They only had to say no, as indeed they had. And if they wanted to punish him for chutzpah, then a swift deportation would surely have been more than sufficient.

So why was he here? He supposed they would tell him eventually, always assuming there was a reason.

* * *

In Berlin, Effi woke soon after eight with the sun in her eyes – it was reflecting off an unbroken window on the other side of Bismarck Strasse. She examined the sleeping face of the child beside her for traces of the nightmare which had woken them both a few hours earlier, but there were none. The face was almost serene.

In the thirty-six hours which had passed since her arrival, Rosa had given no additional cause for concern. True, she didn't talk very much, but she replied when spoken to, and did all that was asked of her. She had objected only once, albeit with an almost desperate intensity, when Effi suggested they get rid of a particular blouse. It wasn't that the blouse was badly faded and frayed, though that in itself would have been reason enough. The problem was the incompleteness of the fading, and the star-shaped patch which had held its colour beneath the yellow badge.

'My mother made this blouse,' Rosa had pleaded. 'It's the only thing I have. Please.'

Effi had relented. 'But we must hide it well. And you must never wear it. Not until the war is over.'

Rosa had accepted the conditions, folded the blouse with the sort of care one reserved for religious relics, and placed it at the bottom of a drawer.

Other items in her suitcase included a chess set and a pack of cards, both homemade. Her mother had taught her many games during their years of hiding, and Rosa had become particularly good at chess, as Effi soon discovered. She could also sew, though not with the same proficiency.

Her real talent was for drawing. Effi had assumed that the beautifully crafted cards and chess 'pieces' were the work of Rosa's mother, but it soon became apparent that they were the child's. Given a pencil and paper that second afternoon, she produced a drawing of the street outside that astonished the two adults. It wasn't the rendering of the bomb-gapped buildings opposite which caught their attention, accurate though that was. It was the figure in the foreground: a man walking by with a suitcase, looking back over his shoulder, as if in fear of pursuit. Real or imagined, he was utterly convincing.

In the Lyubyanka, the sun had risen and fallen before they came for Russell again. Breakfast had been a bowl of thin soup with a hunk of stale bread, dinner the same. Yet he didn't feel hungry. It had been like that in the trenches on the eve of a German attack – the mind was too busy fighting off fear to take note of what the body was saying.

They passed along many corridors, ascended and descended several staircases, as if his escort had orders to disorient him. Eventually they came to their destination – a large, windowless room that smelt of mould. There were seats on either side of a table, one upholstered leather, the other bare metal. Ordered onto the latter, Russell tried to bolster his spirits by compiling a probable list of the books in the prison library. Kafka, of course. The Marquis de Sade and Machiavelli. The Okhrana Book for Boys. What else? Had Savonarola written his memoirs?

The door opened behind him, and he resisted the temptation to turn his head. A tall faired-hair man in an NKVD uniform walked briskly past him, placed a depressingly thick file of papers on the desk, and took the leather chair behind it. He was about thirty-five, with wide nose, full-lipped mouth and blue eyes just a little too close together.

He placed his cap on the side of the desk, positioned the desk-lamp to shine in Russell's face, and turned it on.

'Is that necessary?' Russell asked.

'I am Colonel Pyotr Ramanichev,' the man said, ignoring the question and opening the file. He looked at the top page. 'You are John David Russell, born in London, England, in 1899. You lived in Germany from 1924 to 1941, and became an American citizen in 1939. You lived in the United States for most of 1942, and then returned to England. You describe yourself as a journalist.'

'I am a journalist.'

'Perhaps,' Ramanichev admitted, as if he didn't much care either way. 'In 1939 you did other work for us – courier work – in exchange for our

- 64 -

help with some fugitives from the Nazi Gestapo. Jews, I believe. You were paid by us, and presumably by the Jews as well.'

'I was not paid by the Jews, and I was forced to use all the money I received from you – money I received for writing articles – to bribe my way out of a trap that one of your people set .'

'The traitor Borskaya.'

'If you say so.' The glare of the lamp was annoying, but only debilitating if he allowed it to be so.

'And was the traitor Shchepkin your only other contact?'

'Why traitor?' Russell felt compelled to ask. He had long feared for Shchepkin – the man was too honest with himself.

'He has admitted serving the interests of a foreign power.'

'When did this happen? Is he dead?'

'These matters do not concern you. I repeat: was Shchepkin your only other contact?'

'Yes.'

'Later that year you suggested that a German railway official named Möhlmann might be willing to provide the Soviet Union with information on military movements.'

'Yes.'

'You suggested this to Shchepkin.'

'Yes.'

'And in 1942, after escaping from Germany, you met Shchepkin in Stockholm. Following that meeting, at which Shchepkin was supposed to invite you to the Soviet Union, you chose to visit the United States instead.'

'Shchepkin did invite me to the Soviet Union,' Russell retorted. He wasn't sure whether his own supposed guilt was supposed to rub off on Shchepkin, or the other way round, but it was beginning to look as if their fates were intertwined. 'And he was very upset when I refused.'

Ramanichev smiled for the first time, albeit fleetingly. 'So you say. But I'm sure you can see how this looks. In all your dealings with us, over many years, your only contacts have been with proven traitors. Why would such people have dealt with you if your sympathies were really with the Soviet Union?'

Russell resisted the temptation to ask Ramanichev if he had ever read *Alice in Wonderland*. 'That's absurd,' he said.

The Russian lifted an eyebrow. 'Absurd? And yet the moment you arrive in Moscow, you are knocking at Shchepkin's door. You know where he lives, you have an animated conversation with his daughter.'

'I only knew that he lived near the Novodevichy Cemetery. I knocked on a lot of doors, as I'm sure you know. And I had no idea he had been arrested,' Russell explained patiently. 'I was hoping he could help me.'

'With further plots against the Soviet state?'

'Of course not. I have already explained my reasons for coming to Moscow. On Saturday, to your colleague Leselidze.'

'Explain them to me.'

Russell went through it all again: his wish to reach Berlin as soon as possible, in case his wife or son needed help; his realisation that the Red Army would reach the city first, and his request to accompany the leading units as a war correspondent.

Ramanichev was having none of it. 'You could have arrived with the Americans once the city was secure. But knowing that members of the capitalist press have never been permitted to accompany the Red Army, you spend a full week travelling to Moscow, just on the off chance that we are willing to abandon our policy. And all in the cause of reaching Berlin just a few days earlier.'

'What other reason could I have?'

'As far as I can see this elaborate ploy can only have one purpose. You were sent here to convince us that the Americans and the British have no interest in taking Berlin.'

All right, Russell told himself, they're not just crazy, they do have reasons for distrusting the West. But even so. 'I believe General Eisenhower sent Comrade Stalin a letter saying exactly that,' he said.

'Yes, he did. And knowing that we might find the general's message hard to believe, the Americans also sent you, with the same message wrapped up in what I believe they call a "human interest story" – the man who can't wait to see his wife and son again, who has been told that the Soviets are certain to be first in Berlin. Reinforcing an important lie with a second, less consequential-looking falsehood – it's a classic tactic.'

'That's ridiculous...'

'Ridiculous?' Ramanichev exclaimed, raising his voice for the first time. 'Ridiculous that you should work for American intelligence? Wasn't that who you were working for in Prague in 1939?'

'Yes, but..'

'And did you not act as a contact between German military intelligence and the American Embassy in 1940 and 1941?'

'Yes...'

'But you expect me to believe that the moment you escaped from Germany – and chose to go to America – you also stopped working for American intelligence?'

'That's what happened. It's the truth. Just like Ike's letter is the truth, and the reasons I gave you for coming here. The Americans have no plans for taking Berlin.'

Ramanichev shook his head. 'On the contrary. Over the last two weeks three Allied airborne divisions have been making the necessary preparations.'

'I don't believe it,' was all Russell could say.

'According to our information, the British 1st, US 101st and US 82nd airborne divisions have orders to seize Oranienburg, Gatow and Tempelhof airfields.'

'That'll be a contingency plan,' Russell argued. 'They'll have dropped it by now.'

'Our information is up-to-date, Mr Russell.'

'Yes, but from whom? I doubt if anyone's bothered to tell the airborne troops that they're not going.'

Ramanichev sighed. 'Your lies get less and less convincing. I should inform you that under Soviet law any foreigner caught disseminating false information is deemed guilty of espionage. Those convicted are usually executed.'

He carefully closed the file, and looked at his watch. 'Before we meet again, I would recommend that you consider your position very carefully. In view of your past services to the Soviet Union – no matter how marginal these might have been – that sentence might be commuted. But a full confession will be necessary. We shall want to know exactly what your orders were, who you received them from, and who your contacts are here in Moscow.'

He reached forward and restored the light to its original position, got to his feet, and strode from the room. Russell was escorted back to his cell by the same pair of guards, along the same labyrinthine route. Slumping onto his bed, the clang of the closing door still echoing around the walls, he was ready to admit it. He felt frightened.

It had been dark for more than an hour, and Effi was mentally preparing for the sirens and their evening trip down to the shelter, when the now-familiar knock sounded on the apartment door. Ali had gone to Fritz's that morning, and Rosa was playing one of the patience games her mother had taught her by the light of a precious candle.

The moment Effi saw Erik Aslund's face, she knew it was bad news.

'We've heard from Lübeck,' he said without ado. 'The men you took to the train – they've all been caught. They were already on the ship, believing they'd escaped. And then the Gestapo swarmed aboard.'

'But that doesn't make sense,' Effi protested. 'If they knew the men were on the train, then why wait until they were on the boat?'

'We don't know. Maybe they wanted to put pressure on the Swedish government. Or perhaps they had a tip-off from someone in Lübeck. One of the sailors even – not all my countrymen are against the Nazis. It doesn't matter now. The point is, they're in custody, and you told me that one of the Jews had stayed here. Our contact in Lübeck says that they're being brought to Berlin for questioning, so this place should be safe over-night. But no longer than that. You must leave in the morning. I'll try and find somewhere, but...'

'Don't bother,' Effi interrupted. She had spent a good many sleepless nights anticipating this turn of events, and knew exactly what she intended to do. 'We'll get a train east, to Fürstenwalde or Müncheberg, somewhere like that, and then return as refugees. There are thousands arriving in Berlin, and half of them have lost their papers. I'll just make up a sob story, and we'll have new identities. I used to be an actress,' she added in response to Aslund's doubtful look. 'Quite a good one.'

'I'm not surprised,' he said, smiling for the first time.

'How will I get in touch again?' she asked.

'You won't,' he said after a moment's hesitation. 'It can't be long now, and I think we must all keep our heads down and hope for the best. And meet again in better times.'

She gave him a hug, and let him out the door. As she pushed it shut behind him Effi remembered that she was meeting her sister Zarah on Friday. With any luck they would be back by then.

'You won't leave me?' a small voice asked from across the room.

'No, of course not,' Effi said, walking across to embrace her. 'We'll go together.'

'On a train?'

'Yes.'

'I used to hear them from our shed, but I've never been on one.'

Russell woke to the sound of a scream, but it was not repeated, leaving him unsure whether or not he had dreamed it. He felt as if he had only slept for a couple of hours, and fitfully at that. Each time he had tried to still his mind with thoughts of something pleasant, Vera Lynn's 'We'll Meet Again' had started up inside his head, until he cried out loud in frustration.

Breakfast arrived through the lower flap in the door, a meal as enticing as the one before it, and the one before that. But this time he actually felt hungry, and the soup tasted slightly better than it looked. What was in it was hard to tell, but whatever it was, his stomach was unimpressed, and he was soon getting used to the stench of his own waste.

Several hours went by, and his only visitor was another prisoner, who transferred the contents of his bucket into a larger receptacle. Russell thanked the man, and received a disbelieving look in return. The smell showed no sign of fading.

He had half expected another session with Colonel Ramanichev, and felt absurdly aggrieved at being ignored. Get a grip, he told himself. This could go on for months, or even years. They had no reason for haste – on the contrary, the longer they left him the weaker he would be. He could lie there for ever, turning soup into shit and letting the same stupid song drive him slowly nuts.

Staring at the wall, he resisted the temptation to start scratching off days. Some clichés should be avoided.

He wondered if his sudden disappearance had been noticed. His fellow journalists at the Metropol might be wondering where he had got to, if they hadn't already been fed some story. Kenyon would eventually realise he was missing, and would certainly question the Soviet authorities. But would the American diplomat be able to push matters any further than that? The politicians in Washington were not going to put their relationship with the Soviets at risk for one difficult journalist, not at this juncture.

He went through what Ramanichev had said on the previous day. He had to admit it – if you examined his story from the Soviet perspective, it did seem a trifle suspicious. Write to Stalin forgoing Berlin, and then send him a journalist who was desperate to reach Hitler's capital – as neat a way of confirming the original message as could be imagined. Over the previous seven years Russell had met so-called intelligence people from most of the warring countries – British, American, Soviet, German – and they had all delighted in tricks like that. The fact that he was telling the truth was completely beside the point – Ramanichev couldn't afford to believe him.

So what would happen? Would they put him on trial? Only if he confessed – there was no way they would give him a public platform to protest his innocence. But what could he confess to? Foolish but innocent contacts with Soviet traitors? Shchepkin was probably dead, and Russell realised, rather to his own surprise, that even betraying the Russian's memory was hard to contemplate.

But the alternatives were worse. If he refused to confess, then the best he could hope for was a long prison sentence, probably in some God-forsaken labour camp within spitting distance of the North Pole. They might do their best to persuade him, which would be seriously unpleasant. Or they might just take him down to the basement and shoot him. His body would turn up in some Moscow alley, another foreign victim of those anti-social elements that Comrade Stalin was always talking about.

When the all-clear sounded Effi and Rosa returned to the flat. Afraid that Ali might walk into a Gestapo trap, Effi hung the end of a light-coloured scarf across the windowsill – their long-agreed signal for such an eventuality. After one last look around, she and Rosa picked up their already-packed suitcases and set off down Bismarck Strasse. There was still no sign of dawn in the eastern sky, but the street was already quite crowded with people eager to reach work ahead of the next raid. They joined the crush working its way down the steps at Knie U-Bahn station, and shared in the collective sigh of relief when it transpired that the trains were running.

The one that arrived a few minutes later was almost full, despite having only come two stops. Effi resigned herself to standing, but a young army major with an arm in a cast gallantly gave up his seat. Rosa clung to a handrail, small suitcase wedged between her legs, eyes scanning her fellow-travellers with enormous interest. They were not much to look at, Effi thought; if hope was being kindled by the seemingly imminent end of the war, it had yet to reach these faces. On the contrary, her fellow-Berliners were hollow-eyed, anxious and depressed-looking, as if fully convinced that the worst was yet to come.

More people got on at Zoo, filling every available space in the carriage. She and Rosa could have taken a main-line train from there, but Effi had reasoned that the longer they stayed underground the better, and the same service could be joined at Alexanderplatz, ten stops further on. The U-Bahn train was smelly and slow – these days every journey seemed to take three times as long – but it felt much safer.

At the Alexanderplatz booking office she purchased two singles to Fürstenwalde. She had thought long and hard about their destination, and this town an hour or so east of Berlin seemed far enough away to give them credence as refugees, yet close enough to spare them several checks en route. Of course, she might have got it completely wrong, and picked a journey that was short on conviction and long on inspections. She knew her papers would stand up to a cursory look, and was fairly confident that Rosa's would too, but neither would survive a proper investigation. They were, after all, only tissues of credible lies.

The first check came sooner than she expected. At the top of the stairs to the elevated platform one officer in plain clothes – Gestapo most likely, though he wasn't wearing the trademark leather coat – was sharing a checkpoint with two military policemen. As one of the latter examined their papers, Effi stole an anxious glance at Rosa, and was amazed to see her beaming happily at the probable Gestapo officer. Even more surprisingly, he was smiling back at her. Fifteen years as an actress, Effi thought, and she finally had a protégé.

It was fully light now, or as fully light as Berlin ever got these days. Several fires were burning in the Old Town, and smoke from those already extinguished still hung in the air. A Fürstenwalde train was scheduled to arrive in a few minutes, but after half an hour an announcement on the station loudspeakers admitted that it was only just leaving Zoo. Like many of her fellow would-be travellers Effi kept one eye on the sky, silently praying that their train arrived before the US Air Force.

It finally appeared in the distance, chugging slowly around the long curve from Börse. Like their U-Bahn train, it was already full, but they fought their way aboard and laid claim to a window spot in one of the vestibules. As they cleared the station the sirens began to wail, and the train seemed to falter in its stride, as if uncertain whether to continue. But instead it gathered speed, rumbling through Silesian Station without making its scheduled stop, leaving several shaking fists in its wake.

Once the city had been left behind the train slowed markedly, as if the driver was allowing his locomotive a rest after the rigours of its pell-mell escape. It was now wending its way through the lakes and forests of the Spreewald, but hardly steaming towards safety. They had, as everyone on board knew only too well, merely exchanged the threat of high-level American bombing for the closer attention of prowling Soviet fighters.

The latter had already been active that morning, as one official announced during a long stop at Friedrichshagen, and only a few minutes after resuming its journey the train clanked to a halt once more. Everybody was ordered out, and in the resultant panic several people managed to injure themselves making overeager exits. Effi and Rosa helped one old woman down the steps and into the shelter of the woods which lined each side of the tracks. She was visiting her daughter in Fürstenwalde, and had already decided that this would be 'the last time.'

They waited for the best part of an hour, but no plane swept down to attack the stationary train, and eventually the driver sounded his whistle to announce the resumption of their journey. Everyone climbed back on board, and the train set off again. A stop at Erkner was mercifully brief, but long enough to allow an inspection team aboard. These men were meticulous, Effi noticed, as they slowly advanced down the corridor, and for a few seconds she entertained the wholly ridiculous idea of jumping from the train. Instead, she gave Rosa a comforting pat on the shoulder and reminded herself that idiots like these had been checking Frau von Freiwald's papers for years without noticing anything amiss.

They were finally in front of her, two plump, fortyish men in plain clothes with bile for brains. The taller of the two took the papers from Effi, and began to examine them. 'And why are you going to Fürstenwalde?' he asked without looking up. He made it sound the most unlikely of destinations.

'To see my sister. I'm hoping that I can persuade her to return to Berlin with me. This is her daughter, my niece.'

'What is your mother's address?' the shorter man asked Rosa.

'Nordstrasse 53,' the girl said promptly. With no time to visit the library, Effi had picked the name out of the ether the previous night. 'Do you think the Führer is still in Berlin?' Rosa asked her questioner, improvising rather too freely for Effi's peace of mind.

The man opened his mouth and then shut it again, apparently reconsidering his answer. 'The Führer's whereabouts are not a matter for public discussion,' he eventually decided.

'Oh, I'm sorry, I didn't know,' Rosa said with a look of surpassing innocence.

'Well now you do,' the man said weakly. His colleague was going through their papers for a second time, as if determined to find something amiss. Failing, he almost flung them back at Effi.

'She's very young,' Effi told the shorter man in part-apology. 'But she means well.'

'I'm sure she does,' he said coldly. He gave them a quick nod, and turned away. His partner scowled at them both before moving on into the next carriage.

'He stank of onions,' Rosa whispered.

And so much else, Effi thought to herself.

When they finally reached Fürstenwalde late in the afternoon, Effi was still hopeful of their getting back to Berlin that day. But the news was all bad. A bridge had been bombed a few miles to the east, a locomotive had broken down a similar distance to the west, and nothing much was moving.

The station platforms were already crowded with families in flight from the east, and looking at them convinced Effi that a quick change of clothes was in order for herself and Rosa. Reasoning that an outward show of respectability should help them through checkpoints, they had ventured east in fairly smart outfits, but Effi had also thought to pack some shabbier clothes in their suitcases for this eventuality. Rosa had even remembered something one of her mother's friends had once said – that tying a piece of string around a suitcase made the owner look more desperate.

Once darkness had fallen, they changed clothes in the still-immaculate station toilets. They flushed as well as they looked, and Effi took the opportunity to dispose of her papers. She had grown rather fond of Erna von Freiwald, and felt slightly bereft at losing her.

Looking suitably distressed, they availed themselves of the free food on offer from the NSV – the National Socialist Welfare Agency – in the forecourt outside. Feeling unusually replete, they returned to a different end of the crowded platform, found a space for themselves, and settled down to wait. Rosa soon fell asleep, but Effi lay there, her head resting uncomfortably on the edge of her suitcase, listening to the conversations going on around her. There were two main themes – the horror of what had gone before, and the fear of what was to come. Rape and murder had apparently been commonplace in those parts of Germany now overrun by the Russians, and if the voices in the dark could be believed, the popular stories of crucifixions and other atrocities were not just the product of Goebbels' imagination. When it came to the future, it was Berlin and its people that seemed to worry the refugees most. Everyone knew that all Berliners were liars and thieves, and the thought of living in this modern day Gomorrah seemed almost as frightening as what they'd already been through.

Many of the stories were hard to listen to, and Effi was glad that Rosa was sleeping. But she kept her own ears open. These were the experiences that her new fictional identity would remember, and she needed every conviction-enhancing detail she could get.

It was a few minutes after six, and the light of the unrisen sun was leaking into the eastern sky, when Paul let himself out of the Grunewald house, locked the front door and set off without a backward look for the Westkreuz S-Bahn station. He had spent most of the last forty-eight hours indoors, going out only once to eat at a restaurant in nearby Halensee. He had listened to the BBC for a couple of hours each evening, and heard nothing that really surprised him. He had used the daylight hours to tidy and clean, working on the house like a doctor feverishly intent on saving a patient. It had felt absurd – he was not really expecting to see the place again – but also deeply satisfying. One small part of his world was in order.

He was heading for Westkreuz because a clerk at the Halensee station had told him that Stadtbahn trains were still running out to the eastern suburb of Erkner, and that from there he could take a suburban train on to Fürstenwalde. He was leaving at first light in hope of getting across Berlin before the morning air raid, and because he suspected that his sixty-kilometre journey would take most of the day. Whatever fate and the Russians had in store for him, he had no intention of being shot for desertion.

Half an hour later he was part of the crowd waiting on the Westkreuz eastbound platform. He didn't have long to wait. A train ran in, already full to bursting, and he joined those forcing themselves aboard. The closing doors almost took his head off, leaving him squeezed inside with his arms pinioned to his sides. Once turned around, face up against the glass, he found himself with a panoramic view of what the Western allies had done to Berlin. Street upon gap-toothed street, the demolished Zoo and the scoured Tiergarten, the hollowed-out dome of the Winter Garden. The train sat for a while beneath the skeletal roof of Friedrichstrasse Station, then ventured onwards, almost tiptoeing around the long elevated curve above Dircksen Strasse. Many got off at Alexanderplatz and Silesian Station, but even more seemed to get on. Where were they all going?

In the yards beyond Silesian Station two railway cranes were clearing away debris, and a crowd of prisoners was at work replacing damaged sections of track. Soon they were running under the Ringbahn tracks and into Köpenick, passing several allotments full of old men tending vegetables. Like the farmers a few miles further on, they knew that the war was about to roll over them, but no one was expecting the Russians to feed Berlin. Every potato and carrot would count.

The train terminated at Erkner. Alighting, Paul was almost bowled over by the smell of the soldiers crowding the platform. There was no train east for several hours, so he went in search of food. There was none at the station, and getting into town involved passing through a military police checkpoint. As an officer checked through his papers, Paul surveyed the wall behind him, which was plastered from floor to ceiling with identical posters threatening death for desertion.

Paul walked on into the town, which had clearly been bombed more than once. He eventually found a restaurant with something to offer, though it was only thin soup and stale bread. He ate it with a soldier's gusto, and made his way back to the station, where the crowd seemed somewhat thinner. His train, when it came, was absurdly full, but once the MPs had cleared the front five carriages of civilians the soldiers were able to get on board, and they were soon steaming out across the orbital autobahn and into open country. There were watchers fore and aft looking out for Russian planes, but none put in an appearance, and in mid-afternoon they reached Fürstenwalde.

The service was continuing east, and those wanting the Seelow line had to change. As Paul jostled his way through the crowd his train pulled noisily away, revealing an equally packed westbound platform. A woman in a long black dress caught his eye, though he couldn't have said why. She was talking to a small girl, and perhaps it was the way she inclined her head that made him think of Effi. At that moment, as if aware of his stare, she suddenly looked across at him, and almost broke into a smile.

And then a train slid between them, hiding her from view.

He told himself it couldn't have been her. He had always assumed that she had left with his father, that the two of them had spent the last three years enjoying life in New York or Hollywood. But even if she'd never left Germany, what would she be doing in Fürstenwalde? And with a girl who was at least seven, and couldn't be her daughter. And the woman had been too old – Effi couldn't have aged that much in three and a half years. No, it had to be someone who looked like her. Had to be.

He searched the windows of the stationary train, but the face did not reappear. And when the train pulled out, she was not among the passengers who had failed to get aboard. He shook his head and made his way to the Oderbruch Railway platforms, which stood ominously empty. The line ran much too close to the current Russian positions for comfort, and its northern section had been closed several weeks before. A shuttle service to Seelow had survived, but this, as a harassed railway employee told him, was now only running under cover of darkness. He had six hours to wait.

Paul wandered out of the station, passing the spot where he and Gerhart had sat the week before. He would have found it difficult then to imagine his friend dead; now he found it hard to imagine him alive. Life seem punctuated by implacable, irreversible events, like a series of doors clanging shut behind him in an endless straight corridor.

He walked on into town, hoping to pick up a lift, but nothing seemed to be going his way. He did find a relatively well-stocked shop, and exchanged his remaining ration coupons for a pound of sugar. Neumaier, who liked four spoonfuls in any hot drink, would be deep in his debt.

As he walked back outside, a water lorry drew up beside him and the driver, a Volkssturm man in his forties or fifties, leant out and asked directions for Seelow. 'I'll show you,' Paul told him as he climbed aboard.

They drove out of Fürstenwalde and up onto the plateau, Paul scanning the sky for hostile aircraft while his taciturn companion watched the road. As they drew nearer to the front the sounds of sporadic gunfire grew louder, and it became apparent that the driver was unused to such proximity. 'Do you think the offensive has started?' he asked.

'No,' Paul told him. He had been through offensive-opening barrages, and conversation had not been possible. 'When they do attack it'll be just before dawn,' he added reassuringly.

The driver let him off in the woods between Diedersdorf and Seelow, and Paul, watching the lone lorry motor off down the sun-dappled avenue of trees, had a sudden inexplicable urge to cry. He resisted it, feeling angry with himself. What did he have to be upset about? He was alive.

Ten minutes later he was back at the clearing. Neumaier and Hannes were still kicking their ball to and fro, which momentarily angered him. But football hadn't killed his friend.

Sergeant Utermann was at his usual post, sitting on the fallen tree trunk outside their dugout. The soldier perched beside him looked young from a distance and younger close up – his uniform was way too big for him, and when he stood to salute the trousers bunched up around his ankles. More depressing still, he had the look of someone pleased to be there.

'This is Haaf,' Utermann told Paul.

Half a soldier, Paul thought, remembering his English. Well it wasn't the boy's fault. He offered a hand.

'Haaf heard some good news at battalion,' Utermann went on, as Neumaier and Hannes came over to join them. 'The British and Americans are about to make peace. With any luck they'll soon be fighting the Russians alongside us.'

'And there are 500 new tanks on the way,' the boy added with barely suppressed excitement. 'And special divisions with new weapons.'

'Is that all?' Hannes asked drily, causing the boy to blush.

'It's what I heard,' he insisted.

'It could be true,' Utermann said, backing him up. 'Someone at battalion told me that everything's being held back for the Führer's birthday.'

'Which is next Friday,' Haaf added. 'He'll be fifty-six.'

'I wouldn't put any bets on him reaching fifty-seven,' Paul heard himself say. It was, he realised, exactly the sort of thing his father would have said.

In Russell's Lyubyanka cell two more meals implied the passing of another day. He had been expecting his anxiety levels to rise, but actually felt calmer. A sudden realisation that the war might end without his knowing induced only a mild panic, which soon dissipated. He felt distanced from his own plight, almost philosophical.

It seemed somehow appropriate that he should end up in a Soviet prison. The final stop of a long and almost predictable journey. From the Flanders trenches to the Lyubyanka; from one murderous balls-up to another. A true twentieth-century Odyssey. Or should that be Iliad – he could never remember which was which.

How would he explain it all to Paul, assuming he ever got the chance? Where would he start?

He remembered that evening in Langemarke, the Belgian village behind the lines where he first heard news of the Bolshevik Revolution. He had carried the excitement back to his unit, and seen haggard faces break into smiles. Few of his fellow-soldiers were socialists, let alone Bolsheviks, but the war had given anyone with half a brain a pretty fair idea of how things really worked, and most needed little convincing that their world was ripe for radical change. The Bolshevik Revolution seemed like the first decisive breach in the wall, a great strike against privilege and exploitation, a wonderful harbinger of equality and brotherhood.

The desire for some sort of revolution had been intense, and support for the only one on offer was bound to reflect that fact. Despite the many indications, over succeeding years, that life was considerably less than perfect in the new socialist paradise, many found it hard to give up on the Soviet Union, and even those that did seemed burdened with a lingering affection. Russell had left the Party in the twenties, but had still given Stalin the benefit of the doubt for many more years than he should have. And now he had run the full gamut, from fraternal foreign comrade to enemy of the state. How many thousands – millions, even – had traversed the same path? For him, the straw that broke the camel's back had been Stalin's return of exiled German communists to the Nazis. But there'd been plenty of others to choose from.

And yet. There were still thousands of communists out there – millions even – who thought they were fighting for a better world. They had taken the fight to the Nazis and fascists before anyone else, and they still led most of the resistance armies, from France through Yugoslavia and all the way to China. Communists like Gerhard Ströhm in Berlin, and the Ottings in Stettin – they had fought the good fight. They had saved Russell's life in the process, and probably paid with their own.

He supposed the same could be said of Christians and Christianity. Russell had been an atheist as long as he could remember, and generally despised all religion, but there was no denying the integrity and bravery of those individual Christians who had stood up to the Nazis, and who were now either dead or languishing in concentration camps. Perhaps both Christianity and communism only worked in opposition, as inspirational ideologies for the have-nots of any particular time and place. Once the proponents of those ideologies became established in power, moral corrosion always set in.

It was not an original thought, but he was very tired. He could think up a new universal theory tomorrow, or perhaps the day after. There seemed no shortage of time.

It was him, Effi thought; she was certain it was. She tried to force her way through to the windows on the other side, but made little headway. The train was packed with real refugees, bearing all the belongings that they'd managed to rescue from the ruins of their former lives, and they weren't about to surrender another square foot.

'What are you doing?' Rosa shouted after her, the obvious anxiety stopping Effi in her tracks.

'I thought I saw someone I knew,' Effi told her, once they were together in the corridor.

'Who?' Rosa asked excitedly. 'No, don't tell me,' she quickly added, having obviously realised than the 'someone' might well be out of place in their new fictional existences.

'He was the son of an old friend,' Effi told her. 'I haven't seen him for two years,' she added. And then only for a few seconds in the Tiergarten. He'd been a *flakhelfer* then, but now he was wearing an army uniform. He looked about a foot taller. And he was heading east, into the disaster which everyone knew awaited the army.

Both before and during the war – right up until his illicit exit in December 1941 – John had often talked about taking Paul and her away from Germany, but they had always known that the boy would refuse to go. His father might be English, but his mother, stepfather, stepsisters, friends – his life – were German.

And this was where his generation of German boys had ended up.

She felt like weeping, but that was nothing new.

At least she and Rosa were on a train, with a chance of reaching Berlin before the Russians. And after almost twenty-four hours in Fürstenwalde that was something to be thankful for.

After around an hour the train jerked back into motion, and was soon moving at a surprisingly respectable speed. This remained so until they reached Köpenick, where it slowed to a crawl before eventually stopping completely. There was a fine view of the sunset through the window, but no explanation given for the delay. By the time they got going again darkness had fallen, and the refugees were spared an early sighting of their capital in ruins.

It could hardly have made them more anxious. There was near-silence among the refugees as the train rattled in towards Silesian Station, even the children hushed by their parents' obvious concern. There was no rush for the doors when the train came to a halt, which suited Effi very well. She knew where the NSV desk was, and hoped to be first in the queue. In the event, she settled for fourth, and while those in first place began filling in forms, she took a look around the familiar concourse. Before the war, this was where their old enemy Drehsen had met his victims, and she had dangled herself in front of him as a means of discovering where he had taken the others. It seemed a long time ago. She remembered sitting in the car with Russell on Dragoner Strasse, eager to confront the bastard in his lair. He had made her wait, and she had admitted that patience was not one of her virtues. Well, that had at least changed. If the Nazis had taught her anything, it was patience.

They had reached second place in the queue when all the lights went out. There were gasps and shrieks from the waiting refugees, which a subsequent announcement through the loudspeakers only partly allayed. When the sirens began, somewhat belatedly, to wail out their warning, several people burst into hysterical laughter.

Red Cross workers bearing flashlights soon brought some order to the proceedings, leading everyone down to the shelter under the station. The lighting was dim, the smell dreadful, but the ceiling seemed, to Effi's practised eye, reassuringly substantial. She and Rosa laid claim to an empty corner and watched their fellow refugees get used to city life. One family had lost a suitcase, and the father was soon telling anyone who'd listen that they'd been right about Berliners – they really were all thieves.

Yes, and all East Prussians have the brains of sheep, Effi thought to herself. It had been a long day.

The settling-in process was just about complete when the all-clear sounded, and this time the queue was almost halfway across the concourse by the time they reached it. A helpful Red Cross worker pointed them in the direction of a canteen, and while they were eating their bowls of dubious stew a couple of well-mannered *Hitlerjugend* came over to ask if they needed help.

Effi seized the opportunity. 'My handbag's been stolen,' she said, clearly close to tears. 'I don't care about the handbag, but my papers were in it.'

'Don't worry,' the elder of the two youths told her, placing a tentative hand on her shoulder. 'You just need to report the loss. Once you've finished your dinner I can show you where.'

He was as good as his word, escorting them both to the relevant station office. A form was provided, which Effi filled out and signed with her new name – Dagmar Fahrian. The official presented her with a carbon copy, which he said she would need for obtaining replacements. The people at the NSV desk would explain it all.

But not today. The sirens began wailing again, and everyone hurried back underground. By the time the all-clear sounded two hours later, the NSV desk had closed and all public transport had ceased for the night. There was nothing for it but to sleep in the shelter.

Russell reckoned it was around ten in the morning when they next came for him, a surprisingly civilised hour by NKVD standards. And their route to the interrogation room seemed more direct, which also might bode well.

He reminded himself that hope was dangerous.

This time there were two of them, Colonel Ramanichev in his usual place, another uniformed officer sitting slightly to one side. He was probably in his early forties, stockier than his companion, with swept-back black hair, sallow skin and a Stalin moustache. He looked Georgian or Armenian, and was wearing a variant of the NKVD uniform which Russell didn't recognise.

Russell sat down. There was a bad smell in the room, and he had no difficulty in identifying the source. It was himself.

Ramanichev, who had obviously noticed it too, got up to open a window. As he sat back down a distant peal of laughter was audible. The world was still out there.

'Has the war ended yet?' Russell asked pleasantly.

Ramanichev gave him a look. 'No,' he said after a moment, 'it has not.'

'Pity.'

Ramanichev glanced briefly at his fellow-officer, as if seeking permission to proceed. 'When I questioned you three days ago,' he began, 'you stated with absolute certainty that the American Army had abandoned its plans to advance on Berlin.'

'Correct,' Russell agreed, with a lot more confidence than he felt. What had bloody Eisenhower done now?

'The American 9th Army reached the Elbe River the day before yesterday, and yesterday they crossed it. At Schönebeck, near Magdeburg. You know where that is?'

'Of course.'

'They are only a hundred kilometres from Berlin.'

'Are they still advancing?'

'No,' Ramanichev conceded reluctantly, 'not as yet.'

Russell shrugged. 'You know how it works. Front-line generals like to put pressure on their bosses. Whoever's in charge of the 9th Army – his orders were probably to stop at the river, but he'll have found some good reason to send a few men across, and if there's any resistance they'll have to be reinforced. If there isn't, he'll have shown the top brass that the road to Berlin is open. He'll want to push on, but they won't let him.'

'Why not?'

'Because that's what was decided. Those airborne divisions you claimed were making preparations – are they still?'

'That is unclear.'

'So they're not. I'm telling you the truth. Eisenhower is going to let the Red Army take Berlin. And the casualties that go with it.'

'You'd stake your life on that.'

'I think I probably have.'

Ramanichev smiled his agreement. 'My colleague has some questions for you.'

'What do you know about the German programme to create an atomic explosive?' the other man asked without preamble. He had a slightly rasping voice, and several gold teeth which glinted when he opened his mouth.

The sudden change of subject caught Russell out. 'Only that it didn't amount to much,' he said without thinking. 'Nothing' would have been a much better answer.

'Explain,' the man said peremptorily.

'I have no inside knowledge of the subject...'

'That is hard to believe. This must be a matter of great importance to American intelligence.'

Russell sighed. 'As I've told the comrade here, I no longer have any connection to American intelligence. As a journalist, I did hear certain stories.'

'Such as?'

Russell paused, wondering what to say. He had tried to keep abreast of atomic developments over the last few years – had even tried to understand the scientific and engineering problems involved – but there seemed no point in admitting as much in a Lyubyanka interrogation room. 'I know one of the journalists who covered the Strasbourg story last December,' he said. 'When the French stumbled across that laboratory. He wasn't given any access to the scientific details, but it was no secret that the American scientists who went over the place were all profoundly relieved. Whatever it was they found, it convinced them that the Germans were a million miles away from building an atomic bomb. But that's all I know.'

'You said stories, in the plural.'

'I was exaggerating. I don't know anything else about the German programme. Any fool could tell you that the Americans will be trying for an atomic bomb, but only the scientists will know how far they've got. And maybe the president, if they've bothered to tell him.'

Ramanichev smiled at that, but his companion just seemed disappointed. Five minutes later Russell was back in his cell, wondering what had just transpired.

Effi and Rosa were first in line when the Welfare Agency staff arrived at their Silesian Station desk that morning. Rosa had been working on a sketch of the concourse for about half an hour, and the two welfare workers spent so long admiring it that Effi's patience was sorely tested. Wherever they were going, they needed to get there before the morning raid.

Once fully engaged, however, their young woman helper proved both kind and efficient. She took down every false detail she was given, and asked where Effi wanted to go.

'We plan to stay here in Berlin,' Effi said, realising as she did so that she'd never considered doing anything else.

'Are you sure?' the woman asked. 'The bombing is very bad, and most refugees choose not to stay here. They go further west, to a small town, or into the countryside.'

Effi wavered, but only for a second. It would be safer for Rosa, and probably for herself, but no. She couldn't leave without letting Zarah know she was all right, or God only knew what risks her sister would take to find her. Even leaving the house was a risk these days. And then there was Ali, who would also be worried. And she knew Berlin. Anywhere else she would feel like a fish out of water. 'I must stay here,' she replied. 'We have relatives here, distant cousins of my late husband's. I'm afraid I don't have their address any longer – it was in my bag. But they live in Friedrichshain. Their name is Schmidt.'

'There are a lot of Schmidts in Friedrichshain...'

'I know, it's a common name. But if you could find us a room in that area, then maybe I can find them. We visited them before the war, and I think I would recognise their street if I saw it.'

'That may not be as easy as you think,' the woman told her. 'The bombing has been quite fierce, you know.' She opened a large ledger, and sought out the relevant page. 'Of course you may be lucky,' she added, as she ran her finger down a margin. 'And Friedrichshain is one of our best areas for empty properties.'

Which is why I chose it, Effi thought. A lot of Jews had lived in Friedrichshain.

'We have a room on Olivaer Strasse,' the woman said. 'It belonged to an old woman who died. There may be relations with a claim to it, but for the moment... well, it is a long way out, but in present circumstances that's almost a bonus – you'll have less chance of being bombed. She took a map from a drawer and spread it in front of Effi. 'Olivaer Strasse is somewhere in here,' she said, circling the area between Friedrichshain Park and the stockyards.

Rosa found it almost immediately.

'That looks perfect,' Effi said.

The woman added the address to the papers she'd already made out, checked through each one, and stamped them both. 'You must take these to the local NSV office, and they will issue a residence permit,' she said as she handed them over. 'And you must keep drawing,' she told Rosa.

As they walked away Effi breathed a huge sigh of relief. With any luck at all, they would sit out the last few days in the suburbs.

But first they had to reach this haven, and that, as soon became obvious, was easier imagined than done. There was no U-Bahn out to Friedrichshain, so their trip would be on the surface, and an air raid was almost guaranteed for later that morning. Travelling by tram would require at least one change, and with the service in its current state of repair might take most of the day. It would be safer to walk the four or five kilometres, but it wasn't a part of Berlin that Effi knew at all well. She nipped back to the NSV desk, and tried to memorise the names of the streets they needed to take.

Rosa had stayed with their luggage in the middle of the concourse, and was now talking to their *Hitlerjugend* friends from the previous night, who had doubtless noticed her standing alone, and sallied forth to offer their protection. By the time Effi reached the threesome, Rosa had explained their circumstances, and the taller of the two had offered to escort them to their new home. She felt like refusing, but knew she was being foolish. The young man seemed nice enough, and he was no more to blame for the uniform than Paul had been. There had been a time, she remembered, when Paul had loved his shirt and shorts and ceremonial dagger. 'That would be very kind of you,' she said. 'Are you sure you're allowed to leave the station?'

He returned five minutes later with the necessary permission, and soon they were out in the open air. A blanket of grey cloud hung low above the city, threatening rain. They started walking up Frucht Strasse towards Küstriner Platz, the young man carrying Effi's suitcase, she carrying Rosa's. The buildings of the Eastern Goods Station were missing most of their roofs and some of their walls, but trains were still being loaded by squads of foreign prisoners. Küstriner Platz had suffered serious damage, with several buildings reduced to rubble, the square itself combed with craters.

On the far side, Frucht Strasse continued north towards Frankfurter Allee. As they walked the young man told them his name was Franz, and that his father had died at Stalingrad. They wouldn't let him fight just yet, but when the Russians reached Berlin he planned to have his revenge. When Effi asked after his mother the boy shook his head. 'She has a boyfriend now,' he told them. 'She doesn't need me anymore.'

Approaching the elementary school on the corner of Frankfurter Allee they saw people lined up on the pavement, and a few moments later the roar of approaching vehicles provided a reason why. It was a military column heading out of the city, presumably bound for the not-so-distant Oder. It was mostly composed of trucks, all of which gave the impression of having been to Moscow and back. Two, Effi noticed, had French registration plates, so perhaps they'd gone with Napoleon.

There were also several horse-drawn guns and three well-worn tanks. Black-uniformed officers stood ramrod straight in each turret hatch, reminding Effi of Roman chariot riders. The tanks looked almost as ancient, but had probably come from the Spandau repair shops.

Turning her head to follow the procession, Effi suddenly caught sight of two men in leather coats. One chose that moment to glance in her direction, but seemed sufficiently reassured by her *Hitlerjugend* escort to resume his perusal of the passing column.

The noise was quite deafening, and the first sign of trouble was the sudden disappearance – like a Jack-in-a-box in reverse, she later remembered thinking – of one of the tank commanders. The hatch slammed shut and the tank accelerated, its treads whipping up a storm of brick dust. She was still wondering why when the first bomb exploded on the far side of the school, throwing earth and brick across Frankfurter Allee and up into the sky, and she was still looking round for Rosa when the second lanced down through the school roof and blew her off her feet.

If she passed out, it was only for a split second – the rest of the stick was exploding behind her, the school roof still crashing back to earth. There was pain and blood above her left ear, but otherwise she seemed uninjured. Raising her head, she could see people struggling to their feet.

But not Rosa. The girl was lying flat on her back a few metres away. Her eyes seemed to be closed.

'Please no,' Effi heard herself beg as she half crawled, half scrambled her way across the glass-strewn pavement. The girl's suitcase had been blown open, her meagre possessions scattered across the stone.

She could see no blood. 'Rosa! Rosa!' she entreated

The eyes opened, took Effi in. The mouth tried hard to smile. 'Am I all right?' she asked.

'I think you are,' Effi told her, putting an arm around the girl's neck and gently pulling her into a sitting position. Over Rosa's shoulder she saw that Franz was collecting the clothes, and carefully folding each item before putting it into the suitcase. And that now he was reaching for the tell-tale blouse.

'Franz,' she said, but he had already seen the faded star. Ignoring Effi, he simply stared at it for several seconds, and then went on with his folding.

But by then it was too late. One of the leather coats had seen it – or perhaps only Franz's reaction. He pushed the boy aside, knelt down beside the suitcase, and unfolded the blouse once more. 'Ha!' he said, and held it up for his partner to see.

The partner's eyes swivelled to take in Effi and Rosa. 'Jews!' he said, with the triumphant surprise of someone who had just happened upon a pair of living dinosaurs. 'You're under arrest,' he added superfluously.

Effi looked at the two of them. There was no kindness in their faces, and not much in the way of intelligence: nothing, in short, to which she might appeal as one human being to another. She helped Rosa to her feet, swaying slightly as she did so. Her head wound was beginning to throb.

'Don't leave me,' Rosa said numbly.

'I won't.'

Franz had closed the girl's suitcase. He gave it to her, and then looked up at Effi, offering a silent apology with his eyes.

'Thank you for your help,' she told him, picking up her own suitcase.

'This way,' one of her captors insisted, and gave her a gratuitous shove. She stumbled down onto her knees, and her head started whirling around. A hand grabbed her upper arm, and she could hear Rosa screaming: 'Leave her alone! Leave her alone!'

'I'm all right,' she managed to say. 'Help me up,' she told the man, and much to her surprise, he did. A crowd of women was watching them, and Effi found herself wondering how many of them had seen her in the movies.

They were ushered across the wide street, and up the opposite sidewalk, the two leather coats striding along behind them. They seemed in ridiculously high spirits, and Effi could almost feel them preening themselves when a ready-made audience of women erupted from the Memeler U-Bahn station. Effi had not heard the all-clear, but the air raid was obviously over. Come to think of it, she hadn't heard a warning either. Even the sirens were admitting defeat.

The nearest police station was a hundred metres further up the road. The front desk was untended, but voices could be heard below – the local *Orpo* officers were either still waiting for the all-clear or wholly engrossed in a game of cards. One Gestapo man headed for the stairs while the other stood watch over their prize. Lowering herself onto a bench, Effi still felt a little woozy, but after a minute or so something seemed to shift. Her wound continued to throb, but she no longer felt like passing out.

The other Gestapo man reappeared with a suitably chastened sergeant, and soon the former was describing their capture on the telephone. His voice grew less jaunty as the call progressed, and Effi deduced that their future was no longer in his hands. He confirmed as much when he came out. 'Dobberke's people will collect them later,' he told his partner. Catching Effi's eye, he hesitated for a moment, as if there was something he wanted to say, then continued out through the doorway. His partner followed without so much as a glance in their direction.

'Are they going to kill us?' Rosa asked in a whisper.

'I shouldn't think so,' Effi said, although she really had no idea. 'The war's almost over,' she added, as if that was bound to make a difference. The girl looked less frightened than she should, and Effi had the strange feeling that their arrest had almost come as a relief.

'I'm sorry about my blouse,' Rosa said after a few moments. 'I should have let you burn it.'

'No,' Effi said. 'I'm glad you kept it. This isn't your fault. It's just bad luck. But don't worry, I think we'll be all right.'

'We deserve to be,' Rosa said. 'That's what my mother used to say – we deserve to be safe.'

'We certainly do,' Effi agreed, laughing in spite of herself.

The sergeant's face appeared in the hatch, with a look that suggested she'd lost her mind.

It was two hours before 'Dobberke's people' arrived, two hours in which every policeman on the premises found time to give them the once-over. Only one man looked actually pleased to see them there, whereas several sighed with either sympathy or exasperation. Most gave them mystified stares, as if they found it hard to believe that Jews were still walking their streets. The uniformed Gestapo who came to collect them were obviously more used to dealing with fugitive aliens, and shoved them through the doors of the Black Maria with hardly a second glance.

There was a small barred window in the back, but Effi already knew where they were going. She had heard of Dobberke: one of the Jews she had sheltered at the Bismarck Strasse flat in 1943 had escaped from the collection camp on Grosse Hamburger Strasse, which Dobberke then ran. All Jews captured in Berlin had been taken and held there, until their numbers were sufficient to justify a transport. A year later another fugitive had told her that the Grosse Hamburger Strasse camp had been closed, and its functions transferred to the old Jewish Hospital out in Wedding. And that Dobberke was now in charge out there. The *greifer* – those Jews who scoured Berlin's streets and cafés for U-boats on the Gestapo's behalf – were also based at the hospital.

In most situations, Russell had once told her, there were some things beyond an individual's control and some things that weren't, and what mattered was realising which was which. He'd been talking about some politician – she couldn't even remember which one – but the principle held true for all sorts of things, from acting in movies to surviving the Nazis. Or, in this particular case, a Jewish collection camp. So which things in this situation were still in her control?

Her identity, above all. Who was she claiming to be? They had assumed she was a Jew, and she hadn't denied it, mostly for fear that she and Rosa would be sent to different fates. But now...

What did she want? To live, of course, but not at the cost of abandoning the girl.

Were they still killing Berlin's Jews? They couldn't send them east anymore, so were they killing them here? Was there a gas chamber out at the Jewish Hospital? It was hard to imagine such a thing in the heart of Berlin. Even the Nazis had shrunk from that – it was why they had bothered to move the Jews east before killing them. But maybe now they had nothing to lose.

If she wasn't a Jew, then who was she? Not the film actress Effi Koenen, who was still wanted for treason – a definite death sentence there. And not Erna von Freiwald, who was probably now being hunted in connection with the Lübeck-bound fugitives. Helping the Jews might not see her executed, but helping those involved in the plot to kill Hitler probably would. So Dagmar Fahrian, the woman whose papers she now carried? Dagmar had to be a better bet, particularly if Fürstenwalde soon fell to the Russians. Perhaps Dagmar's sister had married a Jew before the Nuremberg Laws came into force, and then given birth to a *mischling* daughter after that became illegal. Perhaps the sister had died, and the Jewish husband had sent the child to Dagmar for safe keeping, before disappearing himself.

As a story, it had a lot to commend it. She and Rosa would be kept together, and both would have a better chance of survival – Effi as a misguided aryan, Rosa as a *mischling*. As the van zigzagged its way up the rubble-strewn Müller Strasse she gave Rosa a whispered account of their new mutual history.

The girl listened intently, only frowning slightly at the end. 'But we will get our real history back one day?' she half asked, half insisted.

'We certainly will,' Effi promised her. She wondered what Rosa would make of the fact that her new protector had once been a film star. Through the rear window she could see the S-Bahn bridge by Wedding Station. They were almost there.

A few minutes later the van pulled to a halt. The back door was flung open, and one of the uniforms gestured them out. Stepping down onto the street, Effi saw that they had stopped beside a tall iron archway. A plaque announced the address as Schulstrasse 78, and the building behind it as a Pathology Department.

Beyond the arch there was a two-storey gatekeeper's lodge, and this, they soon discovered, was used for administration. A woman took their papers, timed their arrival, and told the bloodstained Effi that she would be taken to the hospital for medical treatment. When Effi asked that Rosa be allowed to accompany her, the woman sighed in exasperation, but made no objection. A young orderly escorted them down a long underground corridor and up several flights of stairs to the medical facility, where a nurse with a Jewish star found Effi a trolley to lie on, and then disappeared in search of a doctor. The man who turned up ten minutes later looked like a *Der Stürmer* stereotype of a Jew, but lacked the star to prove it. He examined Effi's head wound with none-too-gentle fingers, pronounced it superficial, and marched off, shouting over his shoulder that the nurse should apply a bandage.

She stuck her tongue out at his retreating figure.

'Are all the staff here Jewish?' Effi asked.

'Staff, patients and detainees,' the nurse told her, rolling the bandage around Effi's head. 'In varying degrees, of course. Most of the people on the second floor are half-Jews or quarter-Jews who were married to aryans. Or just had influential friends. The Jews scheduled for transport are in the old Pathology building.'

'But the transports have stopped, haven't they?'

'Weeks ago.'

'So what's going to happen now?'

'That's what we all want to know,' the nurse admitted with a shrug. She examined her handiwork. 'There, that'll do.'

The orderly took them back down the long tunnel, up the stairs and across the courtyard to the Pathology building. There was a guardroom just inside the entrance, and steps leading down to a large, semi-basement room. It was the first of four such spaces, and each seemed home to between twenty and thirty detainees. Most were women over thirty, but there was a smattering of younger women with children, and several men past middle age. As Effi and Rosa wandered through the rooms a few eyes looked up in curiosity, and a couple of the older women even managed a wan smile of greeting, but most of the faces held only fear and mistrust.

The first room seemed the emptiest. Having picked out a space for themselves, they examined the outside world through one of the high barred windows, Rosa perched precariously on her upturned suitcase. A barbed wire fence ran across their line of sight, bisecting the area of cratered lawns and broken trees that lay between them and the ivy-covered buildings of the main hospital. An almost idyllic setting, Effi thought. Once upon a time.

She was helping Rosa down when the sirens began to wail, and soon feet started tramping down the steps. The room began to fill up – these basements, Effi realised, were air-raid shelters for prisoners and guards alike. There were several men in Gestapo uniform, and one small bow-legged man in a black civilian suit who seemed to be in charge. Dobberke, she thought, as his black German shepherd cocked a leg against a metal table leg.

'We're all in the same boat now,' a satisfied voice said behind Effi, confirming her previous thought. One of the sleeping women had woken up, and was now grinning at the coterie of Gestapo in the far corner. 'I'm Johanna,' she said, as the first bombs exploded in the distance. She looked about fifty, but could have been younger – her face was gaunt, her body painfully thin.

'Dagmar and Rosa.'

'Have you just been caught?'

'This morning. And you?'

'A few weeks ago. I flushed the toilet without thinking, and one of the neighbours heard.' She smiled ruefully. 'Three years of effort down the toilet. Literally.'

'Are there no young people here?' Effi asked.

'They're in the cells. Through there,' she gestured with a hand. 'Mostly men, but a few young women too – anyone they think might make a run for it.'

'And the *greifer*, aren't they here too?'

Johanna's face darkened. 'They're not usually here during the day, and there are several I haven't seen for a while. Either Dobberke has given them a head start, or they've just taken one for themselves. Whatever happens to us, they have no future.'

'And what will happen to us?' Effi wondered out loud.

Johanna shook her head. 'Only God knows.'

Plunging into darkness

April 14 – 18

Russell had only just finished his breakfast when the usual escorts arrived. Three men were waiting in the interrogation room. The golden-toothed questioner from last time occupied Ramanichev's place; an NKVD officer with a shiny bald head and sharp-eyed Tatar face sat to his left. The third man was Yevgeny Shchepkin, Russell's old partner in espionage.

'I am Colonel Nikoladze,' Gold Teeth admitted, with the air of someone revealing a state secret, 'and this is Major Kazankin. Comrade Shchepkin I believe you know.'

Shchepkin's hair had turned white since Russell last saw him, and his body seemed strangely stiff in the chair, but the eyes were alert as ever.

'We have sad news for you,' Nikoladze began briskly, conjuring instant images of dead Effis and Pauls. 'Your president died yesterday.'

The relief was intense. 'I'm sorry to hear that,' Russell heard himself say. He supposed he was. He had never much liked Roosevelt, but he had admired him, particularly in the early years.

'To business, then,' Nikoladze said, laying both palms on the table. 'We have a proposition for you,' he told Russell. 'As I understand it, you have family in Berlin, and concerns that they might come to harm when our forces reach the city.'

'That is correct,' Russell told him. Surely they couldn't have changed their minds?

'I believe you offered assistance. "Whatever your generals need to know",' Nikoladze read from the paper in front of him. '"Where everything is, the best roads, the best vantage points".'

'That's what I said.' He could hardly believe it.

'So how would you like to arrive in Berlin several days ahead of the Red Army?' Nikoladze asked, with a singularly unconvincing smile.

Russell looked up. 'Ahead of?'

'We are sending a small team into Berlin. Major Kazankin will be in command. A second soldier, a scientist and, we hope, yourself. You will all be dropped at night in the surrounding countryside, and will work your way into the city. You, Mr Russell, will act as the guide. And you will handle any accidental contacts with the local population – Kazankin here speaks a little German, but not enough to pass himself off as a native.'

'Where exactly are we going?' Russell asked, suspecting he already knew the answer. 'Scientist' was a bit of a clue.

'You've heard of the Kaiser Wilhelm Institute?' Nikoladze asked, confirming his guess.

'Any one in particular? There are several of them.'

'The Institute for Physics,' Nikoladze said, with some irritation.

This was not a man, Russell thought, who took life as it came. 'It's in Dahlem,' he said. 'Or was. It may have been bombed.'

'As of last week, it was still intact. You know exactly where it is?'

'Yes.'

'And the Technische Hochschule in Charlottenburg?'

'Yes.'

'According to our information, these are the most important atomic research establishments in Berlin. We want to secure all the available documentation from these facilities, and get an accurate assessment of what materials and equipment they contain.'

'Why not go in with the Red Army?' Russell asked. 'Are a few days going to make any difference?' He knew he was arguing against his own interests, but the more he understood of the Soviets' reasoning the safer he would probably be.

'They might,' Shchepkin answered him, speaking for the first time. Even his voice seemed weaker than it had. 'The Germans may well decide to destroy everything, and if they do not, the Americans probably

will. Three weeks ago they tried their best to destroy the uranium pro-
duction facility at Oranienburg from the air, and they may well decide to
send in a ground team.'

'I doubt there's anything they need,' Russell protested.

'There isn't,' Shchepkin agreed. 'But they don't want us to get it.'

That sounded right to Russell. Hitler might still be breathing fire, but
his two principal enemies were already getting ready for the next war.

'You will guide the team from the drop zone to the Institute, and then
on to Charlottenburg,' Nikoladze continued. 'You know the city. And you
speak Russian – so you can help our scientist translate from the German.'

Russell idly wondered what the cost of refusal would be. Siberia, in all
likelihood. Which was neither here nor there, because he didn't intend to
refuse. He could see several drawbacks to acceptance – in fact, the more
he thought about it the more occurred to him. Berlin was probably going
to be the most dangerous place on earth over the next few weeks, and the
Americans would be seriously displeased with anyone who helped the Soviets to an atomic bomb. To top it all, the idea of jumping from a plane
with only a sheet of silk to combat gravity was truly petrifying.

But what did all that matter if it gave him the chance to find Effi and
Paul? 'I assume we won't be wearing uniforms,' he said.

'You will wear the uniforms the Nazis give their foreign labourers.
Many were captured in East Prussia.'

That made sense. 'And once I've guided the team to these two loca-
tions... where do we go then?'

'The team will go to ground and wait for the Red Army.'

'Where exactly?'

'We are investigating several possibilities.'

'Okay. But once the team is safely in hiding I assume I'll be free to
look for my family?'

'Yes, but only then. I understand your concern for your family, but
you can only leave the team when Major Kazankin agrees to your release.
This is a military operation, and the usual rules apply. I'm sure I don't
need to remind you of the penalty for desertion.'

'You don't,' Russell agreed. Nor did he doubt their ability to enforce it. The NKVD had a global reach, and peace or no peace, they would eventually hunt him down. And he could see how important this must be to them. If, as some experts claimed, the Soviets had sacrificed an eighth of their population to win this war, they hardly wanted to end it at the mercy of an American atomic monopoly. The stakes could hardly be higher.

'So you accept,' Nikoladze said, looking slightly more relaxed.

'I do,' Russell replied, glancing at Shchepkin. He seemed almost grateful.

'Have you ever jumped from a plane?' Kazankin asked. He had a deep voice, which somehow suited him down to the ground.

'No,' Russell admitted.

'Your training will begin this afternoon,' Nikoladze said.

'But first a bath,' Russell insisted.

Half an hour later, he was standing under a near-scalding downpour in the warders' shower-room when a further drawback suggested itself. Regardless of success or failure, by the end of the operation he would know far too much about Soviet atomic progress – or the lack thereof – for them to ever consider letting him loose. The most likely culmination to his involvement was a quick bullet in the head from Kazankin. One more body on the streets of Berlin was unlikely to attract attention.

For the moment they needed him – Nikoladze had been visibly relieved when he'd agreed to join the team. Even knowing he wanted to reach Berlin, they had feared a refusal. Why? Because they still believed he was working for American intelligence, and a real American agent would hardly agree to help the Soviets gather atomic secrets. And on the off-chance that he was telling the truth, and no longer working for the Americans, they had brought along the only man whom he might conceivably trust. Yevgeny Shchepkin. Resurrected, dusted off, and asked to help them bring Russell on board.

They must want the German secrets very badly.

Dried and dressed in clothes collected from his hotel, he found the major waiting for him. 'The car's outside,' the Russian said.

A thin young man with dark wavy hair and spectacles was waiting in the back. 'Ilya Varennikov,' he introduced himself.

'The scientist,' Kazankin growled.

For Effi and Rosa, Saturday was a day spent learning the ropes. The morning meal of *wassersuppe* and a few potato peelings served notice that yesterday's dinner had not been a fluke, but, as Johanna wryly remarked, starvation seemed unlikely in the short time remaining. They were allowed exactly forty-five minutes of exercise, circling a small courtyard under a square of smoke-streaked sky, and were then left with nothing to do but wait another twelve hours for another bowl of *wassersuppe*.

Once one of the guards had been cajoled into sharpening Rosa's only pencil, the girl seemed happy to draw, and Effi embarked on the task of learning as much as she could about their place of imprisonment. Johanna knew quite a lot, but residents of longer standing were more aware of how different the place had been only a few months earlier, and how it had changed in the meantime.

There were, it seemed, about a thousand Jews still resident in the hospital complex. As the nurse had told Effi, those living in the hospital proper – the half-Jews and quarter-Jews, the dreaded *greifer* – were the privileged ones. The atmosphere on that side of the barbed wire was said to be increasingly febrile, with much drinking, dancing and promiscuous coupling. The non-Jewish authorities, far from forbidding such activities, were avidly joining in. Everyone was fiddling while Berlin burned.

Still expecting a summons to interrogation, Effi sought information about her likely interrogator. SS Hauptscharführer Dobberke, as everyone seemed to agree, was a thug of the first order, but many of the same people seemed, almost despite themselves, to have a sneaking respect for the man. Yes, he did punish any serious rule-breaking with twenty-five lashes of his favourite whip, and yes, he would stick anyone lacking funds on a transport east with hardly a second thought, but he never exceeded the twenty-five, and once he had taken a bribe he always delivered his side of the bargain.

And not all the bribes were monetary. Dobberke loved the ladies, and was more than ready to stretch the rules in a woman prisoner's favour if he received a favourable response to his overtures. Effi forced herself to consider the possibility – would she let the bastard fuck her if it improved her and Rosa's chances of survival? She probably would, but doubted she'd be given the chance. Dobberke was said to like his flesh tender, and though she had become many things over the last four years, young wasn't one of them.

The church bells were ringing as Paul, Neumaier, Hannes and Haaf walked into Diedersdorf that evening. A gesture of defiance, Paul guessed, in that no one was left to attend any services. The only show in town was at the village hall – a screening of the movie *Kolberg*, which rumour claimed had cost as much as a thousand new tanks. According to battalion some idiot from Personnel had delivered the tickets in his staff car, engine still running, eyes nervously scanning the eastern horizon and sky.

Reaching the village hall the foursome discovered that their tickets, far from being free, simply entitled them to come up with a four Reichsmark entrance fee. After some grumbling – Hannes was all for telling the doorman to stuff his wretched movie – they came up with the cash and filtered inside. The hall lacked sufficient chairs for the likely audience, and those available, arranged in rows at the back, were already occupied. But the large area of floor space at the front was still only sparsely populated, and they managed to secure a stretch of wall on the far side to sit against. Looking round, Paul could see that most of the men were from artillery units like their own. The few tank men present had managed, with characteristic arrogance, to seize the front row of chairs.

The hall gradually filled, the babble of conversation growing steadily louder, until the ceiling lights abruptly went out, and the film began flickering on the large white sheet which covered half of the end wall. The first scenes drew deep sighs of appreciation, less for their content than for the fact that the film was in colour.

Paul, like almost everyone else in the hall, already knew the story – the

Pomeranian town's defiance of the French in 1807 had been a staple of school history lessons and *Hitlerjugend* meetings for as long as he could remember. It had, however, ended in failure when the overall war was lost, and Paul was intrigued to discover how Goebbels and his film producers – Effi's 'nightmare machine' – had finessed this unfortunate fact. He soon found out. *Kolberg* opened in 1913, after the eventual defeat of the French, with one of the characters reflecting on the importance of civilian militia, and the crucial role the men of the town had played in pointing the way towards victory.

Most of the rest was flashback. The indomitable mayor first overcame the doubters in his own camp – some seduced by foreign liberalism, others weakened by cowardice or too much self-importance – and then held the French at bay with the usual heady mixture of ingenuity, courage and extraordinary will-power.

It was impressively done, and almost insultingly lavish. He remembered Effi explaining how salt was always used for snow, and that hundreds of railway wagons would be used to transport it to a set. And then there were the soldiers – thousands of them. Where had they come from? They looked too much like Germans to be prisoners. They could only be real soldiers, taken out of the front line at some point in the last eighteen months. It beggared belief. Paul felt anger rising inside him. How many men had died for lack of support while Goebbels was making epics?

Let it go, he told himself. This might well be the last movie he would ever see. He should enjoy the spectacle, enjoy imagining a night in Kristina Söderbaum's arms. Forget everything else.

And, for most of the film, he did. It had to end though, and when the lights came on it felt like a slap in the face from reality. Most of the faces around him reflected similar feelings – the sense of angry hopelessness as the hall emptied out was impossible to ignore. Haaf had enjoyed it of course, but even he seemed aware that overt enthusiasm was inappropriate, and the four of them walked back to their woods in almost complete silence. If the film-makers' intention had been to stiffen resolve, and to foster the belief that eventual victory was still possible, they had made it several years too late, and shown it to the wrong audience.

Of course, Paul thought later, as he clambered up into his bunk, it didn't help that the real Kolberg had surrendered to the Soviets more than a month ago.

The level of noise suggested to Russell that the transport plane was slowly shaking itself to pieces, but Varennikov was all smiles, as if he had trouble believing how much fun it was. The dispatcher nonchalantly propped beside the open doorway was taking periodic drags on his hand-cupped cigarette, apparently oblivious to the strong smell of aviation fuel suffusing the cabin. If the inevitable explosion didn't kill him, Russell thought, then the fall was bound to. He checked his harness for the umpteenth time and reminded himself why he had agreed to this madness. 'The things we do for love,' he muttered under his breath.

He and the young physicist had spent the previous twenty-four hours rushing through lessons that usually lasted a fortnight. They had mastered exit technique, flight technique, landing technique. They had jumped off steps, off the end of a ramp, from the dry equivalent of a high-diving platform, and, finally, off a hundred foot tower. And now, against every inclination his mind and body could muster, they were about to leap from a thoroughly airborne plane.

The dispatcher was beckoning. Russell fought his way forward against the wind and looked down. The patchwork of forests and fields seemed both alarmingly close and alarmingly distant. He turned to the dispatcher expecting some final message of comfort, just as a hand in the back pushed him firmly into space.

The shock took his breath away. The transport plane, so solid and loud and all-encompassing, had vanished in an instant, leaving him plummeting through an eerie silence. He frantically tugged at the ripcord, thinking as he did so that he was pulling too hard, and that he'd be left with only a piece of broken rope and a perplexed Buster Keaton expression on his face as he dropped like a stone. But the chute snapped open, the heavens tugged him back, and he was floating down exactly the way he was supposed to. He dropped his head on his chest, held his elbows in, tried to keep his lower limbs behind the line of his trunk – all the things their instructors had been pummelling into them for the last twenty-four hours.

It was extraordinarily peaceful. He could hear the plane again now, a low drone in the distance. He could see the aerodrome below, the huts and training tower on the eastern rim, the wide expanse of grass at which he'd been aimed. Away in the distance sunlight was glinting on a clutch of golden domes.

Looking up, he could see Varennikov dangling beneath his red chute. The Russian's smile would be broader than ever.

After seeming no nearer for most of his fall, the ground rose to meet him at breakneck speed. He told himself to concentrate, not to let his legs out in front of his body. This was the moment his rational self feared most, when his forty-five-year-old bones were put to the ultimate test. A broken ankle now, and that would probably be that, though he wouldn't put it past the Soviets to drop him in a cast.

At least he was falling onto flat grass – the dispatcher's shove had been well-timed. He took a deep breath, mentally rehearsed his technique, and rolled away as he hit the ground, ending up in a relieved heap. He looked up to see Varennikov hit the grass running some twenty metres away. He hardly needed to roll, but did so with all the graceful agility of youth. 'Show-off,' Russell murmured to himself. He lay on his back, staring up at the blue sky and wondering whether kissing the ground was in order, only clambering to his feet when he heard Varennikov anxiously ask if he was all right.

A jeep was on its way to collect them, their plane coming in to land.

'Again,' their chief instructor barked from the front seat of the jeep.

'Why?' Russell wanted to know. 'We know how to do it now. Why risk an injury?'

'Five by day, two by night,' the instructor told him. 'The minimum,' he added for emphasis.

A bomb fell through the roof of the Pathology block extension on the Sunday morning, burying one male prisoner alive in the cells which lay below. It took them most of the morning to dig him out, but the young man managed a smile as they carried him through the basement rooms en route to the hospital. Rosa had been crying on and off since the news of his entombment, and Effi guessed that the incident had triggered some family memory.

When an orderly came for Effi early that afternoon, she was glad that Johanna was on hand to look after the girl. 'I'll be back soon,' she shouted over her shoulder, hoping it was true.

Dobberke's office was at the end of a book-lined corridor on the top floor. He gestured Effi into a chair and stared at her for several seconds before picking up what looked like her papers. The famous whip was in view, hanging from a nail in the wall. The black German shepherd was asleep in a corner.

'You are from Fürstenwalde?' he asked.

'Yes.'

'I know it well,' he said with a smile. 'What was your address?'

The smile told her he was bluffing. 'Nordstrasse 53,' she said. 'It's a few streets north of the town centre.'

He grunted. 'How long have you lived there?'

'Eight years,' Effi said, picking a figure out of the air.

Dobberke laughed. 'You expect me to believe that a Jew could survive detection in a small town like Fürstenwalde for eight years?'

'I am not a Jew.'

'You look like one.'

'I can't help that.'

'And the girl you have in tow – is she not a Jew?'

This was a question that Effi had expected, and she had considered saying no. But the only explanation of the faded star that she could think of – that Rosa had somehow ended up with the blouse of a young Jewish girl of similar size – sounded almost ludicrously unconvincing. 'She is a half-Jew, a *mischling*,' she told Dobberke. She explained about her sister's marriage to a Jew, and how she herself had come to be Rosa's guardian. 'I think there's been a mistake,' Effi concluded. 'We should be in the hospital, not the collection centre.'

Dobberke stared at her for a few more seconds, almost admiringly, she thought. 'I don't believe a word of it,' he said at last. 'You arrive here with papers that are less than a day old, a girl with a star on her dress, and a very practised story. I think there's more to you than meets the eye...' He cocked his head, and she heard the rising whine of the siren. 'If you had arrived a week ago,' he continued, rising to his feet, 'you would be on your way to Französische Strasse for a real interrogation. That may no longer be possible, but the war isn't over yet. In the meantime, you will stay exactly where you are.'

They were ripped from sleep by unearthly thunder – even deep inside the dugout the onset of the Soviet bombardment seemed loud enough to awaken comrades long since dead. This is it, Paul thought, leaping down from his bunk. The beginning of the end.

Haaf stared at him wide-eyed, apparently paralysed. 'Move,' Paul told him. 'We have guns to man.'

Outside it was light enough to check his watch by, and dawn was still three hours away. Vehicles were hurrying west on the road – supply trucks probably, caught too close to the front. They had to be German at any rate – the Soviets would not be moving until the bombardment ended. Paul watched as stretches of earth heaved up around them, wondering which would be hit.

Exploding shells flashed a few hundred metres away to the south, the noise of their detonations engulfed in the wider cacophony. Shaken out of his trance, Paul raced across to the deep trenches that connected their gun emplacements and leapt in, almost landing on Hannes. Haaf was right behind him, barefoot and clutching a boot in either hand.

The shells were drawing closer, ripping a corridor of destruction through the wood with mathematical precision. They waited, grim faces lit by the flaring sky above the trees, for death to descend, but this time the maths were on their side, and the line of fire passed harmlessly in front of their position.

'I can't stand this,' Paul thought. But he could. He had in the past.

The level of noise grew no easier to endure – as he knew from experience it rose until increasing deafness provided its own defence. He looked at his watch. It was three-twenty, which probably meant another ten minutes. He stared up at the long rectangle of sky, trying to lose himself in the swirling patterns of light and smoke.

At exactly three-thirty the sound quality shifted, and the decibel level dropped a merciful fraction. The full-on bombardment of the front areas had shifted to a rolling barrage, as the Soviet artillery concentrated on clearing a route across the Oderbruch for their tanks and infantry, and on obliterating the first line of defence on the lip of the escarpment. The latter, Paul knew, would be more or less devoid of troops, the German commanders having finally learned that it paid to pull them out before the bombardment started, and quickly return them once it was over.

Soon they could hear the Soviet tank guns, and the answering 88s. machine-gun fire began filling the spaces in between. Like a fucking orchestra, Paul thought.

No shells were falling around them now, but all knew the reprieve was temporary. They ate their breakfasts mostly in silence, thinking ahead to the moment when the tanks would appear in their sights. Not for the first time, Paul felt an intense need to be moving. He could understand why people in the rear lines sometimes ran screaming towards the front, eager to settle things once and for all.

Soon after five-thirty, nature's light began seeping into the sky, and by six the sun was rising above the eastern horizon, illuminating a world of drifting black smoke. Low-flying Soviet fighters were soon whizzing in and out of the man-made clouds, but clearly found it hard to pick out targets on the ground. A horse-drawn ambulance cart hurried by on the Seelow-Diedersdorf road, headed for the aid stations farther back. The first of many, Paul thought.

There were too many ways to be killed, and too many hours in the day.

Soon after two o'clock a shell suddenly struck the upper trunk of a tree nearby, setting it ablaze. As they all scrambled for the shelter of the front walls, other shells followed, straddling and surrounding their emplacements without ever hitting them, like some malign god intent on scaring them half to death before finishing them off. The noise and heat were so intense that Neumaier started screaming abuse at the Soviet gunners. Haaf, he noticed, had tears streaming down his adolescent face.

And then, as suddenly as it had begun, the shelling stopped, and the war was once again several kilometres distant.

'Why don't you send Haaf back to the command post for our welfare stores?' Paul suggested to Sergeant Utermann.

'Does he know the way?'

'I'll go with him,' Hannes volunteered.

Darkness had almost fallen when the pair finally returned, loaded up with cigarettes and other necessities.

'They're still handing out *razors*?' Neumaier expostulated. 'Who are we supposed to be impressing – fucking Ivan?' He seemed much better pleased with the chocolate and biscuits in the front line packets.

'Don't forget your buttons' Hannes told him. 'You wouldn't want your dick to fall out in Red Square.'

Paul smiled, and stared at his allotment of writing paper. There was no post anymore. Maybe he should start writing war poetry. The other day someone had shown him a poem by Bertolt Brecht, one of his father's old favourites, a communist writer who'd left Germany when the Nazis came to power. He'd been living in America ever since, but he hadn't forgotten Hitler or the Wehrmacht. 'To the German Soldiers in the East' was the name of the poem Paul had read, and one line had stayed with him: 'there is no longer a road leading home.' Perhaps Brecht had meant that they would never see Germany again, in which case he'd been wrong – here they were, defending German soil. But that didn't matter – there was a bigger truth there, for Paul himself and so many others. They might die in front of Berlin, but even if they survived, the home they had known was gone.

Hannes and Haaf had also brought news. The Russians had lost hundreds of tanks and thousands of men trying to cross the Oderbruch, and the line was still holding. They wouldn't be coming up the road today.

There was also a Führer Order, which Sergeant Utermann insisted on reading aloud. 'Berlin remains German,' it began. 'Vienna will be German again, and Europe never Russian. Form yourselves into brotherhoods. At this hour the whole German people are looking at you, my East Front warriors, and only hope that through your resolve, your fanaticism, your weapons and your leaders, the Bolshevik onslaught will drown in a sea of blood. The turning point of the war depends upon you.'

Utermann carefully folded the sheet and put it in his breast pocket. 'East Front warriors,' he repeated, looking round at the others. 'He has a way with words.'

'We mustn't give up,' Haaf said earnestly. 'There's always hope.'

No there isn't, Paul thought but refrained from saying.

It was still dark when Effi was woken by Rosa shaking her shoulder and urgently asking: 'What's that noise?'

Effi levered herself onto one elbow and listened. There was a dull booming in the distance, a sound neither continuous nor broken, but something between the two. All around the room others were stirring, heads raised in query. 'It's the Russians,' someone said breathlessly.

The news raced around the room, the initial excitement swiftly turning to anxiety. Everyone knew what this meant, that the decision about their own fate had just been brought a whole lot closer. Suddenly the horrors of the present – the hunger, the fear, the living in perpetual limbo – all seemed much more bearable.

About fifteen hours had passed since Effi's interview with Dobberke, and she hadn't been summoned to another. She had met a new friend though, a young Jewish woman in her twenties named Nina. Effi had noticed her on the Saturday, a pale, thin, almost catatonic figure sitting in a corner with knees held tight against her chest. But on Sunday a package from the outside world had worked a miracle, turning her into the vivacious and talkative young woman who, that evening, introduced herself to Effi and Rosa. Nina, they learned, had been in hiding since the big round-up of March 1943. She had lived with a gentile friend – the way she talked about the other woman made Effi think they'd been rather more than 'friends' – and only been caught when a female *greifer* recognised her from their old school days together. That had been four weeks ago.

That morning, the mood engendered by her friend's visit was still in evidence. When she, Effi and Johanna discussed the one question occupying every mind in the camp – what would the SS do when the Russians drew near? – Nina was the most optimistic. They would release their prisoners, she thought – what else could they do? The answer to that was depressingly obvious, but neither Effi nor Johanna put it into words. Were there enough of them to kill a thousand Jews, Effi wondered. Or would they just settle for murdering the hundred or so pure Jews in the collection camp? Making those sorts of distinctions with the world crashing down around them seemed utterly absurd, but when had they ever been anything else?

Later that morning, when the latest raid forced everyone down to the basement, she studied Dobberke's face, hoping for a clue to his intentions. There was none, and when he suddenly glanced in her direction she quickly looked away; she had no desire to provoke another interrogation.

She tried to imagine herself in his situation. He had committed crimes which she hoped the Allies and Russians would consider serious enough to warrant the death penalty. It was often hard to believe that the people bombing Berlin had any sort of moral sense, but surely sending civilians to their death for being members of a particular race would be considered worthy of the ultimate punishment. So Dobberke had to be fearing the worst. Of course, it was possible that he had already decided on suicide – Hitler, she was sure, would take that way out – and, if so, he might well want to take them all with him. But Dobberke hadn't struck Effi as the suicidal type. And if he wanted to survive he needed to provide his future captors with an ameliorating circumstance or two. Like letting his current charges go.

So maybe Nina was right. As the day wore on Effi felt more optimistic, right up to the moment when two of the Jews from the Lübeck train were escorted through the basement rooms, en route to the cells. The third Jew, the young man who had stayed in Bismarck Strasse, was nowhere to be seen, but one of these recognised her from the night in the forest, the eyes widening in his badly bruised face.

It didn't matter, she told herself. It was too late in the day for Dobberke and his goons to start investigating individual stories. Whatever the fate awaiting those in their care, it seemed increasingly certain that everyone would share it.

It was long past dark when the chauffeur-driven Ford dropped Russell and Ilya Varennikov outside the NKVD barracks that served as their temporary home. They had done five drops that day, one in the pre-dawn twilight, three in daylight, and one as dusk shaded into night. The first had been the scariest, a long fall through gloom in which distances had been hard to measure, and only a serendipitous patch of bog had saved Russell's legs from the clumsiness of his landing. The last, darker drop had been easier, the various lights on the ground providing more of a yardstick for judgement, but there was no guarantee of similar assistance in the countryside west of Berlin. A moon might make things easier, but it would also render them more visible. Russell found himself hanging on to the thought that the Soviets really wanted this operation to succeed, and would not be dropping him to a likely death just for the fun of it.

Although he and Varennikov were physically shattered, a day spent falling from the heavens had left them both with an undeniable sense of exhilaration. It had also brought them together, as risk-sharing tended to do. Russell had expected the usual Soviet caution when it came to dealing with foreigners, but Varennikov had been friendly from the start, and now, tucking into a large pile of cabbage and potatoes in the otherwise empty canteen, he was eager to satisfy his curiosity about Russell. How had an American comrade ended up on this mission?

It occurred to Russell that the young scientist might had been primed to ask him questions, but somehow he didn't think so. And if he had, what did it matter? He gave Varennikov an edited version of the true story – his long career as a foreign correspondent in Germany before and during the war, his eventual escape with Soviet help, his time in America and Britain, his determination to rescue his wife and son in Berlin and his consequent arrival in Moscow. If only it had been that straightforward, he thought to himself in passing.

He expected questions about America and Britain, but Varennikov, like many Soviet citizens, seemed oblivious to the outside world. He also had a wife and son, and pulled two photographs from an inside pocket to prove it. 'This is Irina,' he said of the smiling chubby-faced blonde in one snapshot. 'And this is Yakov,' he added, offering another of a young boy gripping a large stuffed bear.

'Where are they?' Russell asked.

'In Gorki. That is where I work. My mother is there also. My father and brother were killed by the Nazis in 1941. In the Donbass, where my family comes from. My father and brother were both miners, and my father was a Party official. When the Germans came in 1941 anti-Party elements handed over the list of local Party members, and they were all shot.'

'I'm sorry.'

Varennikov shrugged. 'Most Soviet families have such stories to tell.'

'I know. Yours must have been proud of you. Doing the work you do.'

'My father was. He used to say that before the Revolution, the sons of miners had no chance of going to university, or of becoming scientists. All such jobs were taken by the sons of the bourgeoisie.' He gave Russell a smile. 'I was born the day after the Party seized power in 1917. So my father decided that my life should be like a chronicle of the better world that the Party was creating.'

It was Russell's turn to smile. 'And has your life gone well?'

Varennikov missed the hint of irony. 'Yes, I think so. There have been troubles, setbacks, but we are still going forward.'

'And were you always interested in atomic physics?'

'It's been the most interesting area of research since the mid-thirties, and I... well, I never really considered any other field. The possibilities are so enormous.'

'And what are you hoping to discover in Berlin?'

'More pieces of the puzzle. I don't know – there were so many brilliant German physicists before the war, and if they received enough government backing they should be ahead of us. But they probably didn't – the Nazis used to describe this whole field as 'Jewish physics'. Or the German scientists might have refused to work on a bomb, or worked on it without really trying. We don't know.'

'How powerful will these bombs be?' Russell asked, curious as to current Soviet thinking.

'There's no obvious limit, but large enough to destroy whole cities.'

'Dropping them sounds a dangerous business.'

Varennikov smiled. 'They'll be dropped from a great height, or attached to rockets. In theory, that is.'

'And in practice?'

'Oh, they won't actually be used. They'll act as a deterrent, a threat to possible invaders. If we had owned such a bomb in 1941 the Germans would never have dared to invade us. If every country has one, then no one will be able to invade anyone else. The atomic bomb is a weapon for peace, not war.'

'But...' Russell began, just as footsteps sounded behind him. The openness of their discussion might, he realised, be somewhat frowned upon in certain quarters.

Varennikov seemed unconcerned by such considerations.. 'And harnessing atomic power for peaceful purposes will transform the world,' he continued. 'Imagine unlimited, virtually free energy. Poverty will become a thing of the past.'

Colonel Nikoladze sat down beside the physicist.

'We're imagining a better world,' Russell told him.

'Don't let me stop you,' Nikoladze replied. He didn't care what they were talking about, Russell realised with a sinking heart. Varennikov could tell him that Stalin was partial to goats, and no one would protest. They hadn't even forbidden him from writing about the mission once the war was over. Why bother when he wouldn't be around?

'I hear it went well today,' Nikoladze said.

'We're still in one piece,' Russell agreed. 'When do we go?'

'We leave for Poland early tomorrow. And if all goes well, you'll be dropped over Germany early on Thursday.'

'Four of us?'

'Yes,' Nikoladze answered. 'The two of you, Major Kazankin who you've already met, and Lieutenant Gusakovsky.'

It seemed small for an invading army, but that was probably the point. If the Germans noticed them, it wouldn't matter if they were a thousand-strong – they still wouldn't get away with a single sheet of paper. But four men had a reasonable chance of passing unobserved. They could all get under one big bed if the situation demanded it. And the smaller the group, the better his own chances were of eventually cutting himself loose.

'The final offensive began this morning,' Nikoladze was saying. 'More than a million men are involved. Assuming all goes well Stavka hopes to announce the capture of Berlin on this coming Sunday – Lenin's birthday. So you'll have three days to complete your mission and remain undetected. An achievable target, I think.'

Later, back in the small two-bunk room they shared, Russell asked Varennikov where Nikoladze was from.

'He's from Georgia. Tiflis, I think.'

Georgians seemed to be running the Soviet Union, Russell thought. Stalin, Beria – Nikoladze would have powerful friends.

'He seems competent enough,' Varennikov said with a shrug.

'I'm sure he is. What made them select you from all the other scientists working on the project?'

'Several reasons, I think. I speak English well enough to talk with you, I speak and read a little German, and I know enough about the matter in hand to recognise anything new. There are other scientists with a much better grasp of German,' he added modestly, 'but their minds were too valuable to risk.'

There was no obvious let-up in the Soviet bombing of the German defences during the night, and the members of Paul's anti-tank unit saw little in the way of sleep. Roused bleary-eyed from the dugout shortly before dawn, and fully expecting a re-run of the previous day's all-out artillery bombardment, they were pleasantly surprised to find nothing more immediately threatening than a cold but beautiful sunrise. A steaming mug of ersatz coffee had rarely seemed so welcome.

The respite lasted several hours, the Soviet guns finally opening up, in deafening unison, on the stroke of 10 a.m. Low-flying aircraft were soon screaming overhead, shells and bombs exploding in the wood around them. For thirty long minutes they huddled in their trenches, knees drawn up against their tightened chests, praying that they didn't receive a direct hit. When a shell landed close enough to shake their ramparts, Paul fought off the temptation to risk climbing out in search of the new crater. Everyone knew that no two shells ever landed in the same spot.

As on the previous day, the gunners shifted their focus after half an hour, and began pummelling the German forward defences some two kilometres to the east. A look through the unit's periscope revealed the familiar curtain of smoke above the invisible Oderbruch. Tank guns boomed in the distance.

An occasional plane still flew over their position, but the rain of shells had stopped, making movement beyond the trenches a relatively safe affair. The gun emplacements had survived several near misses, and the outer door to the dugout had been blown in, but the only real casualty was their football pitch, which now featured a large crater where the centre circle should be. Neumaier looked ready to kill, and Paul's consoling remark that further fixtures were unlikely elicited a bleak stare.

Hours of nervous waiting followed. They could hear the battle, see it reaching for the sky in smoke and flame, but had no way of knowing how it was going. Were the Russians on the point of breaking through, or simply piling up corpses in the meadows? No one, with the possible exception of Haaf, actually expected the 'turning of the tide' their Führer was demanding, but stranger things *had* happened. Maybe Ivan had finally run out of cannon fodder. It had taken him long enough.

More likely, he was just taking his time, grinding down his opponent with the same remorseless disregard for life he'd demonstrated from day one. And any moment now his tanks would rumble into view.

But when? The unit radio just crackled, and no runners arrived with orders. Utermann sent two men off to battalion, in search of news and additional shells. Paul, on observation duty, watched a steady stream of laden ambulance carts lumber west towards Diedersdorf, and found himself remembering a long-ago birthday party, and the seemingly endless string of coloured flags which the hired magician had drawn from his sleeve.

The emissaries returned with neither news nor shells, but bearing two dead rabbits. The smell of cooking soon wafted along the trenches, and by three in the afternoon they were all licking grease from their fingers. As they dined a Soviet plane passed high overhead, and several leaflets drifted down amongst them. 'Your war is lost – surrender while you still can' was the basic message – one that could hardly be argued with. But here they were.

'I bet they're not having meat for lunch,' Hannes muttered.

An hour or so later German troops, most of them Waffen-SS, appeared in the distance, falling back across the fields. The trickle soon turned into a flood, soldiers with smoke-scarred faces and dark-rimmed eyes, half walking, half running, passing them by with barely a glance. There were vehicles too, self-propelled guns and the occasional tank, with lines of soldiers clinging to whatever purchase they could find, bumping up and down like amateur horsemen as their mounts rumbled across the uneven ground and blundered their way through the trees.

A grey-haired Hauptsturmführer told them that Soviet tanks had broken through on either side of Seelow, and were close to surrounding the town. He looked as tired as any man Paul had ever seen. 'They're not far behind us,' the SS officer said, looking back across the fields as if expecting to find the Russians already in view. 'We're moving back to the Diedersdorf line,' he added, then managed the ghost of a smile. 'But I doubt we'll be there for long.'

He raised a weary hand in farewell and walked off towards the west. So this is it, Paul thought.

But it was another couple of hours before the enemy appeared, and by that time the fields ahead were bathed in the golden light of the setting sun. The first Soviet tank, a T-34, appeared as a flash of light, then coalesced into the familiar profile. As Hannes manned the sighter, Paul and Neumaier spun the direction and elevation wheels to his bidding, and Haaf stood waiting with the second shell.

'Wait for it,' Utermann warned. He might be an idiot, Paul thought, but he knew how to run a battery. 'On the left,' the sergeant reminded them. The other 88 would take out the tanks on the right.

A second T-34 slid into view, and a third. Soon there were ten of them, fanning out on either side of the road. They were advancing slowly, with all due caution. A big mistake.

'Fire,' Utermann said, almost too quietly to hear.

Paul's left hand tugged on the trigger, and the gun shook with the force of the discharge. A split second later the other 88 followed suit. As the smoke cleared Paul could see two of the T-34s in flames. He thought he heard a distant scream, but was probably imagining it.

One of the other Soviet tanks opened fire, but it was still out of range. Haaf rammed another shell into the breech as Hannes barked instructions, and the other two adjusted their wheels. 'Now,' Hannes shouted, and Paul pulled the trigger again.

The target slumped to a halt, but no flames erupted. The crew were already tumbling out.

Three further tanks were destroyed, but more were moving into view, and the 88s were running out of shells. Another two burst into flame, and another two. It was like shooting ducks in the fairground on Potsdamer Strasse, Paul thought, only these ducks would outlast the supply of shot. And those that survived would be angry.

They were down to five shells when the first tank turned away, and the others soon followed suit. Their commander had probably just been told there was no chance of air support that evening, and had preferred a ten-hour wait to losing his entire brigade. He had no way of knowing his opponent was down to his last few shells.

It was time to get out. With two shells needed to render the 88s useless, there was no point waiting for morning to fire the other three. They might as well charge the Russians on foot.

'Prepare the guns for demolition,' Utermann told the two crews fifteen minutes later, apparently satisfied that the Russians weren't about to reappear. 'And get all the fuel into one of the half-tracks,' he told Hannes.

They set to work. Ten minutes later Hannes returned with the bad news. 'There's no fuel in either tank,' he said. 'Those SS bastards must have siphoned it off.'

Utermann closed his eyes for a second and breathed out heavily. He was still opening his mouth to speak when they all became aware of the roar in the distance which heralded a *katyusha* attack. 'Stalin's organs!' Utermann shouted unnecessarily, as everyone bolted for the nearest trench. Most were still running as the roar transmuted into a hissing howl, and an area of the wood some hundred metres to the west exploded in flames. By some merciful chance, Ivan had got the range wrong.

Over the next ten minutes he did his best to make amends. As Paul and his comrades hunkered down helplessly in the emplacement trenches, the rocket-launcher crews systematically worked their way across the wood, drawing ever nearer to the German guns. Looking up, Paul saw that the stars were lost in smoke, the branches above bathed in orange light. This is it, he thought, the moment of my death. It felt almost peaceful.

And then the salvo fell, straddling their position with a flash and crash that threatened to obliterate the senses. Paul had his eyes closed at the vital moment, but still had trouble focusing when he opened them again. Haaf, he realised, was screaming his head off, though he couldn't hear him. Something had landed in the boy's lap – a head, Paul realised – and he had leapt to his feet to shake it off. Before anyone could stop him, the boy had clambered out of the trench and disappeared from sight.

Someone shone a torch on the head. It was Bernauer, the other gun's loader. His emplacement must have taken a direct hit.

Another salvo landed, sounding much further away but still turning nearby trees into torches. They had all been deafened, Paul realised. It would pass in a few hours. Or at least it always had.

The rockets kept firing for another ten minutes, the hiss of their incoming flights barely discernible above the hissing in their ears. Once they had stopped, Utermann gestured them out of the trench – the Soviets might be playing games, creating a false sense of security before launching more salvos, but an immediate infantry assault was much more likely.

There were no obvious human forms in the other emplacement, which was itself barely recognisable. Paul had seen such sights in daylight, and felt grateful to the darkness for cloaking this particular jigsaw of blood, flesh and bone.

Hannes cursed as he tripped over something in the dark. It was Haaf's lifeless body – a large chunk of the boy's head had been sliced off.

A red flare suddenly blossomed above what was left of the wood – Ivan was on his way.

Utermann was waving his arms around like a demented windmill, trying to get their attention. 'Let's go,' he shouted, if Paul's lip-reading was any good. The sergeant must have been feeling pretty lucky, Paul thought. Up until this evening, he and Corporal Commen had always taken shelter in the other emplacement.

The five of them moved off through the battered wood, clambering over fallen trees and sheared limbs, working their way through the mosaic of fires still raging. Fifteen minutes went by with no sign of pursuit, and Paul began to wonder whether the Russians had decided to call it a night. The hissing in his ears had almost gone, and he found he could hear his own voice, albeit from some distance away. As he walked on, the sounds of his and his companions' progress grew steadily clearer, as if someone in his skull was cranking up the volume.

'How's your hearing?' he asked the man walking behind him.

'I can hear you,' Neumaier said.

Another fifteen minutes found them staring out across depressingly open fields. The moon had just climbed over the horizon, and the landscape was visibly brightening with each passing minute.

'The next line runs through Görlsdorf,' Utermann said, gesturing to the right, 'and along there,' he added, sweeping a finger from north to south, 'across the Seelow road to Neuentempel. It's about a kilometre away.'

'When does the moon go down?' Hannes asked.

'About two o'clock,' Neumaier told him. He'd been on watch the previous night.

'So we wait?' Hannes suggested.

'Yes,' Utermann decided. 'Unless Ivan turns up in the meantime.'

Russell had a night of anxious dreams, and was relieved when a hand shook him roughly awake. It was still dark and cold outside, but by the time they had downed mugs of tea and chewed their way through hunks of bread and jam, light was seeping over the eastern horizon. A long walk across the tarmac brought them to their transport – a Soviet-built version of the American DC-3 which Varennikov told him was designated a Lisunov LI-2. It had space for thirty men, but the two pilots were their only fellow-travellers. Five minutes after clambering aboard they were airborne.

It was Russell's first meeting with the fourth member of the insertion team. His first impression of Lieutenant Gusakovsky was favourable – the youngish Ukrainian accompanied his handshake with a pleasant smile and seemed less full of himself than Kazankin. He was tall, good-looking and seemed extremely fit. He had, Varennikov revealed, played centre-half for Dynamo Kiev before the war.

The Lisunov had rows of rectangular windows, and one of these offered Russell a panoramic view of Warsaw as they came into land just before noon. He had expected damage – the city had been bombed for a couple of weeks in 1939 – but nothing like this. As far as he knew, there had been no fighting inside the city, but the centre looked like a giant had danced all over it. A farewell gift from the Nazis, Russell could only assume. It didn't bode well for Berlin.

The airfield, which lay several kilometres to the south, was awash with Soviet planes, personnel and flags. The one lone Polish emblem tagged to a long row of hammers and sickles might have been an accident, but looked more like an insult. A glimpse of the future, Russell thought.

Rain began falling as they walked across the grass, and was soon beating a heavy tattoo on the corrugated roof of the canteen. Nikoladze and the two soldiers disappeared in search of something or other, leaving Varennikov and Russell to pick at the dreadful food. Working on the assumption that Berlin's current cuisine would be even less rewarding, Russell consumed as much as he could, sealing his achievement with a stinging glass of vodka. Varennikov had brought a book of mathematical puzzles to amuse himself, but Russell was reduced to reading the army newspaper *Red Star*. There were several stories of tragic heroism, a few slices of that cloying sentimentality which Russians seemed to share with Americans, and a bloodthirsty piece by Konstantin Simonov encouraging Red Army soldiers to take their revenge on the German people. Russell checked the newspaper's date, thinking that it must have been printed before Stalin's recent edict emphasising the need to distinguish between Nazis and Germans, but it was only a few days old. Simple inertia, he wondered, or something more sinister? Whichever it was, Berlin would pay the price.

They took off again in mid-afternoon, this time aboard a smaller two-engined plane which only had room for the four of them. It was a rough ride through clouds, with Poland's mosaic of fields and woods only occasionally visible a few thousand feet below. Kazankin seemed worst-affected by the bumpy flight: he sat rigid in his seat, carefully controlling each breath, a study in mind over stomach.

It was getting dark when they bounced back to land on another make-shift airstrip. 'Where are we?' Russell asked Nikoladze, as they walked towards a single small building surrounded by large canvas tents.

'Leszno,' the Georgian told him. 'You know where that is?'

'Uh-huh.' It had been the German town of Lissa until 1918, when it found itself a few kilometres inside the new Poland. They were about two hundred kilometres – an hour's flight – from Berlin.

Nikoladze disappeared inside the building, leaving the rest of them outside. The clouds further west were breaking up, offering glimpses of a red setting sun, and a series of Soviet bombers were dropping down onto the distant runway. 'Where have they been?' Russell asked a passing airman.

The man's initial reaction was dismissive, but then he noticed the NKVD uniforms. 'Breslau, comrade' he said curtly, and hurried off.

So 'Fortress Breslau' was still standing. It had been surrounded for two months now – a mini-Stalingrad on the Oder. A beautiful city, once upon a time.

Nikoladze emerged with the news that a tent had been reserved for the team. As they walked towards it, the landing lights on the distant runway winked out. The Luftwaffe was still out there, Russell deduced. He wasn't looking forward to the next night's flight.

In the tent they found a sackful of foreign worker uniforms, rough dark trousers and jackets with the blue and white *Ost* patch. 'Find one that fits,' Kazankin told him and Varennikov.

The uniforms obviously hadn't been washed in living memory, but Russell supposed that a band of sweet-smelling foreign workers might be deemed suspicious. He found an outfit that seemed a reasonable fit, and didn't actually stink. There was a torn square of paper in one pocket with a couple of strange-looking words scribbled across it. Finnish perhaps, or possibly Estonian. A fragment of a life.

'Will we be carrying guns?' he asked Kazankin.

'You won't,' was the instant answer.

A few minutes later Nikoladze arrived with two pieces of bad news. The Germans on the Oder was putting up a stiffer resistance than expected, and Berlin by Lenin's birthday was beginning to look a trifle optimistic. More germane to their own operation, there was no sign of the inflatable dinghy which Nikoladze had been promised. The plan, as Russell now discovered, involved a dropping zone a few kilometres west of Berlin, a long walk to the Havelsee, and a short voyage across that body of water. A further hike along the paths of the Grunewald would then bring them to the edge of the city's south-western suburbs.

It seemed an ambitious programme for a single night.

Paul was woken by a tap on the head. He had fallen asleep with his back against a tree.

'Ivan!' Neumaier hissed in his ear.

Paul could hear the Soviet infantry crashing through the wood behind them. They couldn't be more than a few hundred metres away. Scrambling to his feet, he followed Neumaier across the lane, swung himself over the gate and joined in the headlong flight. The moon was almost down now – another few hundred metres and the night might hide them.

The field was mercifully unploughed, its owner probably somewhere west of Berlin by now. Racing across the turf, Paul had a memory of one *Jungvolk* instructor urging him to run faster on a weekend exercise in the country. It must have been around the time of the Berlin Olympics, because the man had screamed: 'this is not some fucking gold medal you're running for – it's your fucking life!'

He caught up with Utermann, who was always moaning that his right knee hadn't been the same since Kursk. By this time they were over three hundred metres from the trees, and no bullets were flying past their ears. Glancing over his shoulder, Paul thought he caught a hint of movement in the wall of trees behind them.

They caught up with the others, who had gone to ground in a ditch between fields. Paul had no sooner sunk gratefully onto his front than two 'Christmas trees' rippled into life above them, the Soviet parachute flares scattering what looked like blazing stars across the night sky. The five men kept their heads down, pressed into the wet earth of the bank. All that talk about German soil, Paul thought. And here it is, stinking in my nostrils.

As the flares dimmed they cautiously raised their heads. A host of shadows was advancing towards them.

Once the lights had flickered out, they made their way across the stream and up into the adjoining field. As they began running an excited shout rose up – one of the Russians had seen them. A single rifle cracked, and Paul thought he heard the bullet pass by. A volley of shots followed, with no more effect. They were firing blind.

But someone would be asking for another flare, Paul thought.

There was an explosion behind him. He was looking back when another went off – mortar rounds were landing amongst the Russians.

And then the machine-guns opened up, and Neumaier, twenty metres ahead of him, suddenly stopped in his tracks and toppled to the ground. Paul came up as Hannes turned his friend over – one eye was staring, the other gone. Utermann and Commen were still running, screaming out that they were Germans, when both went down together, as if tripped by the same wire.

Paul crouched there with Hannes for what seemed an age, waiting his turn, almost revelling in the breathtaking absurdity of it all. But the machine-gun had fallen silent – Utermann had obviously been heard, albeit too late to save himself – and voices were calling them forward.

They did as they were told, almost falling into the foremost German trench, but there was no time to rest. Someone gave them each a rifle, shouted something vaguely encouraging, and moved on. Paul stared at the gun for several seconds as if unsure what it was for, shook his head to clear it, and took a position at the parapet. Many Russians were down, but hundreds of others were still charging towards them, screaming at the top of their lungs, the leading echelons no more than fifty metres away. Paul took aim at one, and saw another go down. He took aim again, and his first target went down bellowing.

A few seconds more, and the first Russians were amongst them, some leaping across the trenches, other straight in, rifles firing then swinging, blades glinting and falling. One swung wildly at Paul, and he swung equally wildly back, catching the man across the neck with a sickening crack.

He scrabbled in desperation at the wall of the trench, and managed to haul himself over the edge. All around him, men were heaving, grunting and rasping, like warriors from some ancient battle between Teutons and Romans. In the dark it was hard to distinguish friend from foe, and Paul saw no reason to try. Weaving his way between personal battles, he ran for the next line of trees.

Since the weekend bombing of the ground-level extension above the cells, the latter's capacity had been severely diminished, and the two Jews from the Lübeck train had been allowed to share in the relative freedom of the fourth basement room. Effi had initially thought it prudent to stay away from them, but she badly wanted to know what had happened to their friend, the young man she had once sheltered in the Bismarck Strasse flat. After two days had passed she decided it was safe to make contact.

From the doorway of the furthest room, she could see them sitting against a wall. Their faces still bore the marks of the last interrogation, but they still seemed more animated than most of their fellow-prisoners. Both got warily to their feet as she approached.

The thought crossed Effi's mind that they might suspect her of betraying them. 'Do you remember me?' she asked unnecessarily.

'Yes,' the younger of the two replied. He was about twenty-five, and looked intelligent.

'What happened in Lübeck?' she asked them quietly.

'We don't know,' the young man said after a moment's hesitation. 'We were already on board the ship. We'd been hiding in the hold for a few hours when the roof slid open and there were the Gestapo, shining their torches down at us and killing themselves laughing.'

'They never let slip how they tracked you down?'

'No.'

'What happened to your friend?'

'Willy? He's dead. He made a break for it as they led us off the ship, jumped off the gangplank. There was some sort of stanchion sticking out of the wall, and he landed right on it. He looked dead, but they shot him a few times just to make sure.'

'I'm sorry.'

'He told us he'd met you before, that you'd helped a lot of Jews.'

'Some,' she admitted.

The obvious question must have showed in her face. 'Don't worry,' he told her. 'He didn't tell us your name or anything else about you.' Or we would have told them, went the unspoken coda.

It didn't seem to matter now. 'It's Dagmar. Dagmar Fahrian,' Effi said. There was a hint of guilt in the older man's eyes, she thought. He had probably given the Gestapo her description. She couldn't blame him.

'I'm Hans Heilborn,' the younger one said. 'And this oaf is Bruno Lewinsky.'

'May we meet again in better times,' Effi said simply. 'Have you heard any news of the fighting?'

'Yes,' Lewinsky said, speaking for the first time, 'I heard two of the guards talking.' He had a surprisingly cultured voice.

He'd probably been a university professor, Effi thought. So many academics, scientists and writers had been Jews. How much knowledge and wisdom had the Nazis destroyed?

'The Russians have broken through on the Oder,' Lewinsky was saying. 'They should be in the outskirts by the weekend. And the army defending the Ruhr is surrounded by the British and Americans. It's bigger than the army we lost at Stalingrad.'

Effi noticed the 'we' – after everything that had happened, these two Jews still thought of themselves as Germans – but mostly she was thinking about Paul, and hoping that he'd been taken prisoner. She wasn't sure John would ever forgive himself if his son was killed.

As dawn broke Paul was sitting on a wall in Worin. He was one of around fifty men who had reached the deserted village through the darkened woods. Most of the others were from the misleadingly named 9th Parachute Division – their airborne status had long been merely honorary –

along with some stray panzergrenadiers. All were remnants of remnants, of those units once entrusted with the defence of the Seelow Heights.

Paul had not seen Hannes since the hand-to-hand battle with the Russians, and rather doubted he would again – if his friend was still alive, he'd probably been taken prisoner. And if he, Paul, was the unit's only survivor, then God had to be smiling down on him for some strange reason.

Or perhaps not. If all of them were going to die, then someone had to be last.

He bit another chunk off the sausage he had found in one of the abandoned houses, and eyed the growing light with some alarm. Soviet planes would soon be overhead, and a further withdrawal seemed advisable. He assumed that his battalion had been pulled back *en masse*, probably in the direction of Müncheberg, but heading that way without orders might prove a risky business. The two military policemen on the far side of the village square had already given him – and just about everyone else – suspicious looks, and Paul suspected that their current passivity was well calculated. They would have loved to order everyone back in the Russians' direction, but feared, with ample justification, that they might be shot if they tried. If Paul tried to strike out on his own, they would have no such worries. For him, for the moment, safety lay in numbers.

A panzergrenadier lieutenant seemed to be working his way round the square, talking to men and probably canvassing opinions. He looked like an officer who knew what he was doing, and Paul hoped he was planning a further withdrawal.

More men were trickling in all the time, but Hannes was not among them. Most of the arrivals looked as if they hadn't slept for days, and when a Soviet plane roared across the rooftops only a few bothered to take evasive action. One man raised a weary fist at the sky, but his heart wasn't it. This plane dropped nothing, but more would be back. It was time to move.

A few minutes later the roar of approaching tanks did get men reaching for their rifles. And then, to general amazement, two Tigers rumbled into view. This was good news and bad news, Paul thought. Good because it made the village slightly more defensible, bad because it would encourage the idiots to defend it.

The latter forecast proved distressingly accurate. While village beds were stripped of mattresses to bolster the tanks – a trick learned from Ivan – trenches were started at either end of the single street. But the earth had barely been broken when the familiar roar sent everyone rushing for cover. Paul made a run for the nearest building and threw himself down behind a large wooden horse trough. With hands over head and knees almost up to his chest, he shook with the earth and tried to think of something beautiful. Madeleine came to mind, but she was dead. Another shower of human flesh.

When it became clear that the barrage was over, he stayed where he was, shaking gently to and fro, feeling the burn of uncried tears.

A few minutes later, walking aimlessly up the street, he came upon a young officer he hadn't seen before. The man was foaming at the mouth, talking gibberish, and several of his subordinates were standing there looking at him, not unkindly, but with a sort of grim impatience.

Both military policemen had been seriously injured. 'That'll teach 'em to get this close to the front,' one grenadier joked in Paul's hearing.

The Tigers were unscathed, their crews sufficiently humbled by their irrelevance to be moving out. The village would be abandoned, which seemed just as well, as there wasn't much left of it to defend.

The panzergrenadier lieutenant had also been slightly wounded, and the shock had apparently removed any inhibitions he had about taking charge. When darkness fell they would withdraw into the woods that lay west of the village, and try to shake off the Russians with a night march into the west.

The Lightning Tower

April 18 – 20

The PS-84 transport rumbled down the sparsely-lit runway for what seemed an eternity, before bouncing itself hopefully into the sky. The four men glanced at each other, feeling, for the first time, the solidarity of danger shared. Even Kazankin gave Russell a rueful smile, and he was probably the designated executioner.

It had been a day of waiting, first for news of their inflatable boat, and then for departure. Their dinghy had eventually shown up somewhat the worse for wear, having collected two bullet holes crossing the Oder crossing. They'd been patched to Kazankin's satisfaction, and survived a trial inflation. There had been better news from the front – the German defences on the Seelow Heights had been penetrated, and Zhukov's tanks were on the last lap of their thousand-mile journey to Berlin. It seemed unlikely that they would reach the city in time for Lenin's birthday, but they were only a couple of days behind schedule.

These had been the day's high points – the four of them had spent most of the morning poring over maps, checking their equipment and endlessly rehearsing contingency plans for when things went wrong. Russell had then spent several hours watching the Soviet bombers run through their routine: taking off and heading south, returning two hours later for another bellyful of bombs, taking off again. There had been 80,000 Germans in Breslau when the Soviets surrounded the city in February, and each receding plane would subtract a few more. Like a fist that couldn't stop hitting a face.

Now, as their transport droned on towards Berlin, he wondered how badly the German capital had suffered. He had seen aerial photographs of the destruction, but somehow they hadn't seemed real, and whenever he imagined the city it was the old Berlin, the one he had lived in, that appeared in his mind's eye. The one that wasn't there anymore.

He would soon have a new picture. His task was to guide the team to the Institute that night, get them back before dawn to the safety of the Grunewald, then move them on to the Hochschule on the following evening. Their last stop, as Nikoladze had told him that afternoon, would be the railway yards outside Potsdam Station, where an underground cell of German comrades was still in contact with their Soviet mentors. They would hide out there until the Red Army arrived.

In case of accidents or misunderstandings, the members of the team had letters signed by Nikoladze sewn into their jackets. These testified that the holders were on an important mission for the NKVD, and demanded that any Red Army soldier who ran into one or all of them should both provide any necessary protection and immediately notify the relevant authorities.

In the meantime, there was the small matter of the Nazi authorities. How tight was their grip in these final days? One could hope that the demands of the front had thinned the police presence in Berlin, though it seemed more likely that all of the bastards would be needed to keep the population in order as the Russians approached. But who would be out on the streets – the *Kripo*, the military police, the SS? All of them? As Nikoladze had reluctantly admitted, their knowledge of the restrictions placed on foreign workers was several weeks old. Would the four of them be challenged as they made their way across the city, or simply taken for granted?

How easy was movement, come to that? Were any trains or trams still running, or had they been bombed to a halt? And if public transport continued to function, were foreign workers still allowed to use it?

Not to worry, Russell decided, as the plane took a sudden lurch – the parachute drop would probably kill him.

They seemed to be veering northwards now, and he thought he could detect the faintest of glows in the eastern sky. They'd been hoping for more, but the recently risen quarter-moon was concealed behind a thick layer of cloud, and the drop looked set to take place in almost total darkness. That might lessen the chances of their descent being spotted, but there didn't seem much point in arriving unnoticed with a broken neck.

The minutes ticked by. The pilot was under orders to draw a wide arc around the southern outskirts, in the sanguine hope that Berlin's air defences would all be narrowly focussed on the approaches used by the British. So far, it seemed to be working – no searchlights had leapt to embrace them, and neither flak nor fighter had sought to blow them away.

'Five minutes,' the navigator shouted from the cockpit doorway. Russell felt his stomach lurch, and this time it wasn't the plane.

Kazankin and Gusakovsky were instantly on their feet, checking their harnesses one last time. According to Varennikov, both men had served with the partisans, and had ample experience of landing behind enemy lines. He was in excellent hands, Russell reminded himself. Up until the moment that they no longer needed him.

Varennikov, he noticed, had lost his usual smile, and was tugging at his own harness with what seemed unnecessary violence. Kazankin took over, testing each strap, jollying the young physicist along. Satisfied that his charge was under control, he gestured Russell to his position at the front of the queue. A position that Russell realised was logical – jumping last, the two experienced men would have a better shot at working out where everyone was – but it still seemed a bit like punishment.

'One minute,' the navigator shouted.

The door was wrenched open and the wind swept in, causing the plane to rock, almost blowing them over. Recovering his balance, Russell looked out and down. There were no lights, no hint of land, only a writhing pit of darkness and cloud. 'Oh shit,' he muttered.

'Go!' the dispatcher yelled in his ear, and out he leapt, childishly intent on pre-empting the helpful shove. Proud of himself, he forgot to pull the ripcord until several seconds had passed, and then tugged at it with a ferocity born of panic. As the chute burst open the quality of darkness suddenly shifted – he had fallen out of the clouds and into the lightless air beneath. There was still no sign of a world below, and no sign of other chutes above.

As he drifted down he noticed that the sky to his right was slightly lighter. The hidden moon, he realised, and felt strangely comforted – there were shades and dimensions, an east and a west, an up and a down.

The world below took form and shape, one second a blur, the next a faceful of wet grass and the smell of loamy earth. He lay there for a second, checking his body for pain, and almost shouted for joy when he realised there was none. He had done it. He had jumped out of a plane in total darkness and lived to tell the fucking tale.

But where were the others? He gathered in the chute, rolled it up, and looked around for somewhere to stuff it. There was nowhere. A flat open field stretched into nothingness in all directions. There were no trees, no moving shadows, no sounds of other humans. His three companions had been swallowed by the night.

First things first, he told himself – work out where you are. The paler sky away to his left had to be the east. He sought confirmation from his Red Army compass, but there wasn't enough light to read it. Still, it had to be the east. And since the plane was flying roughly northward when he jumped, his companions would have hit the ground further to the north. 'Somewhere over there,' he murmured to himself, turning on his heels and peering hopefully into the gloom.

Should he go looking for them? Or wait for them to find him? They knew when he had jumped, and should have a pretty good idea of where he was. And if they didn't show up in, say, twenty minutes, he could head for the rendezvous point they'd arranged for exactly this contingency.

Or perhaps not. Was this the moment to abandon his new Soviet buddies? They'd gotten him into Berlin – well, almost – and there was nothing more he needed from them. Not this week, in any case. And he was fairly sure that they intended to kill him before the week was out. So why hang around?

Because, he told himself, he believed in Nikoladze's promise of retribution. Given that they were planning to kill him anyway, that particular threat was only designed to keep him on board, but they'd still be hell-bent on punishment if he left them in the lurch. The Soviets would own half the world in a month or so's time, and their assassins would be roaming the other half. It wouldn't be wise to antagonise them. Do the job and then get lost – that was the best of several poor options. Once the war was over, everyone would calm down a bit. He could promise to keep their secrets, and mention in passing that he'd arranged for their publication in the event of his sudden demise.

He couldn't read his watch either, but it must have been at least ten minutes since he fell to earth. He would give them another ten.

There was noise above, he realised – a low drone in the distance. For a moment he thought their plane must be circling, but soon realised his mistake. This sound was slowly filling the sky.

As if in reply, a beam of light reached into the sky. Others swiftly followed, like the lights going on in a theatre. The lowness of the clouds was visible now, so the bombers would be up above them. The gunners below had no more chance of seeing their prey than the bombardiers had of picking out targets. Either someone had got the weather forecast wrong or the Allies no longer cared where their bombs fell.

The invisible bombers seemed almost above him, perhaps a little to the north. The first flashes erupted away to the north-east, swiftly followed by a staccato series of distant explosions. Spandau, he guessed. And Siemenstadt. Industrial areas.

Over the next few minutes the line of flashes crept around to the east, heading for the city centre. He heard the booms of the flak guns, saw flashes of exploding shells through newly diaphanous clouds. But no blazing plane fell through the veil.

His twenty minutes were up, and there was still no sign of the others. It was, he decided with some reluctance, time to move on. With the bundled-up chute under one arm, he began working his way across the increasingly boggy field, hoping to find the first of two roads. On several occasions his second-hand boots – stolen by the NKVD from God knows who – sunk deep into patches of mire, and a misjudged leap across a small stream resulted in one waterlogged foot.

A line of trees loomed ahead, and perhaps marked the looked-for road.

He was some thirty metres away when voices rose above the almost constant rumble of distant explosions. German voices. Russell sank to his haunches, thankful that what light there was, was ahead of him.

He could see them now, two male figures walking northward, one wheeling a bicycle. What were they doing out here after midnight?

'Spandau's catching it,' one of them said, with the tone of someone lamenting bad weather.

'Seed potatoes!' the other one exclaimed. 'That's what I forgot.'

'You can pick them up tomorrow,' his friend told him.

They walked on out of earshot, apparently heading for the cluster of roofs to the north, silhouetted by burning Spandau.

Bombers were still droning overhead.

He clambered in and out of a ditch that ran alongside the road, slipped across the narrow ribbon of tarmac, and slid down a small bank on the other side. The new field seemed even boggier, and the smell of shit grew steadily stronger as he worked his way across the waterlogged ground. The Soviet map of the area had placed a sewage farm slightly to the north-east of their intended route, so he was probably in the right area.

Above the horizon yellow-white flares crackled and danced in an almost orange sky. The word 'devilish' came to mind. He was walking towards hell.

If he was remembering the map correctly, another kilometre would bring him to a second, wider highway, which ran south from Seeburg towards Gross Glienicke and Kladow. The point, a kilometre south of Seeburg, where this road entered a sizable wood, had been chosen for the reunion of an accidentally scattered team.

It took him twenty minutes to reach the empty road, and another five to sight the dark wall of trees that lay ahead. A direct approach seemed unwise – there might be other locals about, and who knew what sort of strain the night's events had wrought on Kazankin's nerves – so he took the long way round, walking out across the adjoining field and entering the wood from the west, before working his way back to the rendezvous point.

But the only cracking twigs were the ones he stepped on, the only sounds of breathing the ones provided by his own lungs. There was no one there.

He settled down to wait. His watch told him it was almost one – they were supposed to have reached the Havelsee by one-thirty. There was no chance of that now, but he had always thought the timetable absurdly optimistic. Expecting to reach, search and get away from the Institute before a six o'clock sunrise had never been on.

He closed his eyes. His feet were wet and cold, and he was feeling his age. One war was enough for anyone. What had his generation done to deserve two?

The intensity of the bombing was lessening, and the sky above seemed empty of planes. It occurred to him that once the searchlights went off movement would again become difficult.

Noises away to his left jerked his eyes open. It sounded like footsteps coming his way. There were whispers, a louder rustle, a muttered curse. Three vague shadows moving between the tree trunks.

'Russell,' a voice hissed. It was Kazankin.

'I'm here,' he murmured, mostly to himself. 'This way,' he added, with rather more volume. It was hard to believe that anyone else would be skulking in this particular patch of forest.

Kazankin was the first to reach him, and his surprise at finding Russell was written on his face. He was holding a large canvas holdall in one hand, like a plumber with his tools.

'What happened?' Russell asked.

The Russian exhaled with unnecessary violence. 'Comrade Varennikov decided his chute was faulty,' he said coldly. 'By the time we got him through the door you were long gone. We landed on the other side of Seeburg.'

'I'm sorry,' Varennikov said, for what was probably the hundredth time. 'I panicked,' he explained to Russell. 'It was just...' His voice tailed off.

'We need to get going,' Kazankin said, looking at his watch.

'It's too late,' Russell told him. 'We're already an hour behind schedule, and we didn't have one to spare.'

He expected Kazankin to argue with him, but the Russian just looked at his watch again, as if hoping for a different time. 'So what do you suggest?' he asked when none was forthcoming.

'Get as close to the lake as we can tonight, lie low during the day, and then cross as soon as it looks safe tomorrow evening. That'll give you most of the night to ransack the Institute.'

'We still have time to get across the lake tonight.'

'Yes, but the Grunewald is popular with walkers. They'll be more chance of our being spotted on that side of the water.'

'You think the people of Berlin are still going for walks?'

It was a reasonable question, Russell realised. And he had no idea what the answer might be. 'I don't know,' he admitted.

'We'll go on,' Kazankin decided.

They crossed the road, and plunged into the wood on the other side. Kazankin took the lead, with Russell behind him, then Varennikov. Gusakovsky, carrying the inflatable dinghy, brought up the rear. They had hardly gone a hundred metres when the light suddenly dimmed. The searchlights were being turned off.

Their progress slowed, but Kazankin, as Russell reluctantly acknowledged, was good at picking a path. It only took them an hour to reach the wide and empty Spandau-Potsdam highway, and soon after two-thirty they emerged from the forest close to the road connecting Gatow to Gross Glienicke. They followed this for a while, and almost ran into trouble, hearing the raised voices of some approaching cyclists with barely enough time to find cover. The cyclists, who looked in the dark to be wearing Luftwaffe caps, had obviously been drinking, and were singing a rather ribald song about that organisation's beloved leader. They were presumably heading home to Gatow Airfield, which lay a couple of kilometres to the south.

If the airmen hadn't been singing, Russell thought, they would never have heard them in time.

Kazankin led them off the road and out across empty fields. There was no sign that these were being worked, either for crops or pasture. German agriculture, at least in the vicinity of Berlin, seemed a thing of the past.

Eventually they reached another road, and passed into another stretch of woodland. Russell was beginning to feel tired, and the younger Varennikov seemed only slightly more energetic. Kazankin and Gusakovsky, by contrast, looked capable of walking all the way home to the Soviet Union.

There were big houses in these woods, but neither lights nor barking dogs. The rich owners were long gone, probably up in the Alps, lamenting the fact that they couldn't ski all the year round.

And then, suddenly, they were standing on a small pebble beach, staring out across the dark Havelsee. The lake was at its narrowest here, little more than five hundred metres across. There were no lights visible, and all they could hear were breeze-ruffled leaves and their own breathing.

Kazankin was right, Russell thought. The Grunewald was big – almost fifty square kilometres. If they ran into walkers, so what? – they were foreign labourers, looking after the paths and the trees. They should get across tonight.

Gusakovsky was already inflating the boat, although where he was finding the breath was beyond Russell.

'On the map,' Kazankin said, 'there was an island a few hundred metres south of here.'

'Lindwerder,' Russell said.

'Is it inhabited?'

'It was used for test-firing rockets in 1933,' Russell remembered. 'But only for a few weeks. As far as I know, it was only used as a picnic spot in the years before the war.'

'It might be a good place to spend the day,' Kazankin said, as much to himself as Russell. 'We would have advance warning of any visitors.'

'A good idea,' Russell agreed.

Ten minutes later, Gusakovsky had inflated the boat. He took it out into the water, rolled himself in, and kept it in situ with one of the wooden paddles that Kazankin had extracted from his holdall. The others waded out to join him, and somehow got themselves aboard. The dinghy seemed alarmingly low in the water, but showed no sign of sinking any lower. The two NKVD men started paddling them towards the island.

Russell sat gazing out at the barely visible shores, remembering Sunday afternoons here with Effi, Paul or both. A Berlin institution – a sail on the Havelsee, with a shore-side stop for a picnic. He didn't think he'd ever seen the lake in darkness.

Lindwerder hove slowly into focus, a low forested hump in the water around two hundred metres long. They grounded the dinghy on a gravel beach, then carried it up into the trees. 'Wait here,' Kazankin ordered, and disappeared into the darkness.

He was back ten minutes later. 'There's no one here,' he said. 'Follow me.'

He led them up through the trees, over the crest of the island's slight ridge, and came to an abrupt halt. Looking down, Russell could just about see a natural hollow in the slope.

Kazankin took two small spades from the holdall, and handed one to Gusakovsky. Both men began to dig, their breathing growing steadily heavier as the minutes went by. After about fifteen, Kazankin pronounced himself satisfied.

Russell wondered how many hides like this the two men had built in their time with the partisans.

'It's almost dawn,' the Russian commander said, staring up at the eastern sky. 'We'll wait for light to build the roof. And take another look at the maps.'

Half an hour later the roof was in place, and Kazankin was pulling the briefing material from his trusty canvas bag. There was a street map of Dahlem and Zehlendorf, an aerial photograph of the area surrounding the Kaiser Wilhelm Institute, and, most useful of all, a hand-drawn plan of that part of the Institute supposedly used for atomic research. The map was only a few years old, the photograph reasonably clear, and the diagram, according to Nikoladze, had been drawn by an Institute worker only three years before. Russell had seen them all at the Lissa airfield, and been impressed – the NKVD researchers had exceeded his expectations. Kazankin was no slouch either. As the Russian commander described their intended course of action, Russell felt a reluctant admiration. The man said what needed to be said and nothing more; he seemed determined and utterly fearless.

Outliving him would not be easy.

Despite sleeping with Rosa tucked into her body, Effi awoke in the middle of the night feeling colder than she could ever remember. The hospital's electricity supply had been cut off on the previous day, and what little heating there was had disappeared with it. According to rumour, they were also running out of water. Some sort of end seemed near.

Any day now they might all be led outside and shot. Come to that, they might be shot where they were.

It was, she thought, about three in the morning. Rosa was sleeping soundly, but many of the adults seemed as wakeful as she was – all across the room limbs were shifting, murmurs and whispers being traded.

The idea of dying here, in the last days of the war, was almost too much to take. She had thought about trying to escape – she assumed almost everyone had – but not to any useful effect. Even with the end so near, the camp was efficiently guarded by locks, walls and guns. On her own, she would have preferred any risk to simply waiting, but she wasn't on her own anymore. How many people, she wondered, had gone to their deaths with their children, when they might conceivably have saved themselves on their own? It was wonderful really, if you could say that of something so tragic.

Would she ever have a child? She had been asking herself that question with increasing frequency since her forced separation from John. Which was somewhat ironic – when they'd been together the subject had rarely been raised. They'd had each other, and he'd had Paul, and she'd had her career and her nephew. They'd never ruled out having a child with each other, but there had been a tacit acceptance that they wouldn't, or at least not yet.

Well, if she had another birthday in May, it would be her thirty-ninth. Which might well be too late, although miracles happened. And then there was Rosa, or whatever her real name was. Effi had only known the girl for ten days, but already found life without her hard to imagine. And there was no one to send her back to. She wondered how John would feel about adopting a daughter. She wasn't sure why, but she felt fairly confident that he'd like the idea. And Paul, if he lived, could be the grown-up brother.

The thought brought tears to her eyes. She lay there in the dark, the sleeping girl enfolded in her arms, trying not to sob.

The makeshift defence line on the eastern outskirts of Müncheberg was still in German hands when Paul's adopted combat group reached it just before dawn. This was almost a pleasant surprise, given how over the course of the night the Russians had often seemed ahead of them.

Around fifty of them had slipped out of Worin and across the open fields when darkness fell on the previous day. Once assembled in the next patch of forest, they had struck out for Müncheberg, some ten kilometres to the west. It had been a long and twisting journey, in which the sights or sounds of fighting nearby had often dictated a change of course. Stopping to rest while the moon was up, they had watched in petrified silence as one line of enemy lorries had passed a mere stone's throw away, the soldiers within filling the night with their songs of triumph. Only a kilometre or two from Müncheberg they had found themselves forced between two burning villages, not knowing which side was setting the fires.

And Müncheberg itself, it transpired, was soon to be parted from the Reich. According to the latest reports the Russians had broken through to both north and south, leaving most of Ninth Army in peril of encirclement. All troops were being pulled back to the Berlin defence lines, either with their own units or as members of combat groups newly formed by the military police who controlled the crossroads outside the town. Paul, to his intense annoyance, was told to join up with a new unit built around the remnants of a *Hitlerjugend* battle group. When he protested this decision, arguing that his gunnery skills would be utterly wasted in an infantry unit, he was treated to a lecture on the bravery and commitment of the *Hitlerjugend*, who could 'give the fucking army a lesson in how to stand and fight.'

They probably could, but only because they were too young to know any better. Most of his new comrades seemed to be fifteen or sixteen, and Paul doubted whether their life expectancy warranted shaving kits. Scanning the smoke-blackened child faces lining the road he felt a further lurch towards total despair. Some seemed utterly blank, others close to feral. Some were on the verge of tears, and probably had been for weeks. Understandable reactions, each and every one.

The good news, from Paul's point of view, was that the *Hitlerjugend*'s suicidal devotion to the Führer had earned them transport – their unit, unlike others, had been allotted trucks and fuel enough to reach Erkner. He climbed aboard his vehicle with relief, and tried not to notice the age of the other passengers. Get to Erkner, he told himself, and a chance would occur to seek out his old battalion, most of whose members still considered personal survival a more than worthwhile goal.

The lorry moved off, and he closed his eyes for some much-needed sleep.

'I'm Werner Redlich,' a small voice interrupted him. 'I heard you tell the MP you're a gunner.'

'Yes,' Paul said without opening his eyes.

'I wanted to be a gunner,' the boy persisted.

Paul looked at him. He had noticed him at the crossroads – a sad and far too thoughtful face for one so young. Like most of the others, he was wearing a brown shirt, short trousers and an oversize helmet. 'How old are you?' he asked.

'Fifteen,' Werner replied, as if were the most natural age for a soldier to be. 'Nearly fifteen,' he corrected himself. 'Are your family in Berlin?'

'No,' Paul said, shutting his eyes again, 'they're all dead. And I need some sleep.'

'Okay,' Werner said. 'We can talk later.'

Paul smiled to himself, something he hadn't done for a while. He spent the next couple of hours drifting in and out of sleep, the lorry jerking him half-awake each time it accelerated away from road blockages caused by refugees, retreating soldiers or the earlier depredations of the Red Air Force. When he fully came to, the back of the lorry was empty, and Werner was offering him a can of food and a mug of coffee. 'Where are we?' he asked, looking out over Werner's head. 'And where is everyone?'

'Stretching their legs. We're in Herzfelde.'

The sky above the houses was purest blue, and the war seemed, at that instant, a long way away. He levered the tin open, and began spooning its contents into his mouth. 'Why have we stopped here?' he asked between mouthfuls.

Werner was looking down the road. 'We're wanted,' he told Paul.

'Who by?'

'SS.'

'Then we'd better go.' Paul took one last mouthful of soup, and lowered himself down to the road. Fifty metres away, the unit was coalescing around a couple of black uniforms. A Führer Order, he guessed, as they walked forward to join the throng.

He was right. The SS Sturmbannführer leaning on the windshield of his APC had paper in hand, and after gesturing successfully for everyone's attention, began reading the latest bulletin: 'Hold on another twenty-four hours, and the great change in the war will come! Reinforcements are rolling forward. Wonder weapons are coming. Guns and tanks are being unloaded in their thousands.'

Paul looked around, expecting at least the odd smirk, but every young face seemed enraptured. They wanted so hard to believe.

'The guns are silent on the West Front,' the Sturmbannführer continued. 'The Western Army is marching to the support of you brave East Front warriors. Thousands of British and Americans are volunteering to join our ranks to drive out the Bolsheviks. Hold on another twenty-four hours, comrades. Churchill,' the Sturmbannführer concluded with the air of a magician saving his biggest rabbit for last, 'is in Berlin negotiating with me.'

Now there were smiles on the young faces. They were going to win after all.

Paul reminded himself that it wasn't so long since he had taken official pronouncements seriously. Even now, a small part of his brain was wondering whether the British leader might really be in Berlin.

'Do you believe it?' Werner asked quietly, as they walked back towards their vehicle.

'Of course,' Paul said in a tone that implied the opposite.

'Neither do I,' the boy said, removing his helmet to run a finger along a still-healing gash in his forehead.

'Where are your family?' Paul asked him.

'In Berlin. In Schöneberg. My father was killed in Italy, but my mother and sister are still there. At least I think they are. I've heard nothing since we were sent to the front.' He raised his eyes to meet Paul's. 'I promised my father I'd look after them.'

'Sometimes there's no choice and you have to break a promise. Your father would understand that.'

'I know,' Werner said, sounding more like fifty than fifteen. 'But...' He let the word hang in the air.

'We're loading up,' Paul told him.

Ten minutes later they were on their way, heading off the main road, driving south-west towards Erkner, which until recently had still been functioning as a terminus for Berlin's suburban trains. There were lots of refugees on the road, many with possessions piled in pushcarts or prams, some with a dog strutting happily alongside, or a cat curled up among salvaged bedding. Did these people imagine safety ahead, or were they simply putting as much distance as they could between themselves and the guns? Paul hoped they were planning to bypass the German capital, because heading into Berlin would, as the English saying had it, exchange the fire for the frying pan. Over the next couple of weeks, with the Nazis desperate and the Soviets hungry for revenge, his hometown seemed like a place to avoid.

They were only about fifteen kilometres from the outskirts now, rolling down the sort of road – sun-dappled forests on one side, gently rippling lakes on the other – that had featured on pre-war Reichsbahn posters. 'No longer a road leading home,' he murmured to himself.

Half an hour later they drove into Erkner, eventually stopping in a still-busy street close to the town centre. People emerged from houses and shops to stare at this children's army, anxiety warring with disapproval in many of the faces. Some ducked back in, only to return with food and cigarettes for the soldiers. One woman in her forties, catching Paul's eye, and presumably noticing his less than pristine condition, asked him and Werner if they would like a wash.

They were only too pleased – it was a while since either had seen soap of any description, and even the wartime variety, which tended to remove skin along with the dirt, seemed like a rare luxury. Werner was not yet shaving, but Paul took the opportunity to remove four days' worth of stubble. Some of the wildness in his face came away with the razor, but there was no disguising the sunken cheeks, the dark semi-circles under the eyes, the loss staring back at him. He turned hurriedly away, and went back out to find Werner eating cake in the kitchen.

The woman silently ushered Paul into the front room, and shut the door behind them. 'He's only fourteen,' she said, as if Paul himself might not have noticed. 'I can hide him here. Burn the uniform and say he's my nephew. No one will be able to disprove it, and it will all be over soon.'

Paul looked at the woman. Presumably she realised that her suggestion, if reported, would result in her being shot. He wondered where she and all those like her had been for the last twelve years. 'You can ask him,' he said.

Back in the kitchen, Werner listened to the woman's offer, and politely rejected it. 'I must get back to Berlin,' he told her. 'My family are relying on me.'

'Time to get up,' Kazankin announced, pulling back the branches that covered them. The sky was still clear, the light fading fast.

Despite being bone tired, Russell had managed only three or four hours of sleep. He had spent most of the day lying on his back, examining the blue sky through the lattice of vegetation which Kazankin and Gusakovsky had created, listening to Varennikov's snoring and the war's relentless soundtrack. Hardly ten minutes had passed without a bomb exploding, a flak gun booming or a plane droning overhead. How had Berliners managed to sleep during the last two years?

He struggled out of the dug-out, and reluctantly opened the can of cold mystery rations that Kazankin handed him. He wasn't hungry, but forced himself to eat whatever it was, envying his companions' apparent appetite.

'Time to go,' Kazankin said.

The canvas bag was left in the refilled dugout, and Russell and Varennikov were given spades to carry, bolstering the impression that they were foreign labourers. The two NKVD men, Russell noticed, were now carrying their machine pistols in the smalls of their backs.

They all took to the dinghy, and paddled their way across the short stretch of water that separated Lindwerder from the mainland. Once ashore, Gusakovsky dug a shallow hole while Kazankin deflated their craft, the hiss of escaping air sounding preternaturally loud in the silent forest. Boat buried, they set off through the trees, Kazankin in the lead, Russell wondering who might they run into. In pre-war summers they might have stumbled over any number of trysting couples, and if London's blacked-out streets were any guide, a life of constant danger seemed to heighten the desire for outdoor sex. But surely it was still too cold for assignations in the woods. There were always a few eccentrics who liked a walk at night, but he could see no reason for the police to patrol the Grunewald. With luck, they might manage the whole five kilometres without meeting a single soul.

Kazankin strode on ahead, his body radiating bullish confidence. They crossed a couple of paths and one clearing dotted with picnic tables which Russell thought he recognised from years before. At one point Kazankin halted and gestured for quiet, and a moment or so later Russell saw the reason – a cyclist was crossing their line of travel, the beam from his handlebar lamp jerking up and down on the uneven path. Where on earth could he be going?

After half an hour's walking they reached the Avus Speedway, which had served as the world's narrowest motor racing circuit until 1938, its eight kilometres of two-way track topped and tailed by hairpin bends at either end of the Grunewald. The two lanes had been part of the autobahn since then, but that evening's traffic was decidedly sparse, an official-looking car heading towards Potsdam, two military lorries rumbling north-west towards the city. Once they had vanished, the road lay eerily empty, two ribbons of concrete stretching away between the trees. As they walked across, Russell remembered driving Paul down the Speedway in his new car, early in 1939. His son had been only eleven years old, still young enough to be thrilled by a 1928 Hanomag doing a hundred kilometres an hour.

He wondered if the car was still where he'd left it in 1941, gathering rust in Hunder Zembski's yard. If the authorities had known it was there, they would surely have confiscated it. But who would have told them? The Hanomag had probably fallen victim to Allied bombs – only a brick wall separated Hunder's yard from the locomotive depot serving Lehrter Station, an obvious target.

They crossed the railway tracks on the eastern side of the Speedway and plunged back into forest. Russell knew this part of the Grunewald reasonably well – his son Paul, his ex-brother-in-law Thomas and Effi's sister Zarah had all lived fairly close by – and the paths seemed increasingly familiar. Another twenty minutes and they would reach Clay Allee, the wide road that separated the Grunewald from the suburbs of Dahlem and Schmargendorf.

Which was far from comforting. He felt safe in the forest, he realised. Streets would be dangerous.

As if to confirm that thought, a siren began to wail. Others soon joined in, like a pack of howling dogs.

This could be construed as good news – the streets would be emptied, making it less likely that they would encounter the authorities. The familiar drone of bombers grew louder behind them, and the search-light beams sprang up to greet them. Tonight though, there were no clouds to turn back the light, and the overall effect was to deepen the darkness below.

The first bombs exploded several kilometres to the east, and through the remaining screen of trees Russell saw rooftops silhouetted against the distant flashes. Closer still, a car with thin blue headlights drove towards them, and then turned off down an invisible road.

Kazankin halted. He had brought them out of the forest at exactly the right place, not much more than a kilometre from the Institute. Russell was impressed, but wasn't about to say so. 'That's Clay Allee,' he told the Russian. 'The Oskar Helene Heim U-Bahn station is down to the right, about two hundred metres.'

They had discussed this last lap earlier in the day. They could approach the Institute through Thiel Park, a long, twisting ribbon of greenery which stretched from Clay Allee almost to their destination, but Russell, looking at the Soviet map, had argued for the shorter, simpler route. Two minutes on Clay Allee, ten on Gary Strasse, and they would be there. There would be nothing furtive about their progress, nothing to raise suspicion.

Rather to his surprise, Kazankin had agreed. Now, eyeing the prospect, Russell began to wonder. The street looked far too empty, and not nearly dark enough. And who in their right mind would be promenading down a suburban street in the middle of a bombing raid? So far the bombs seemed to be falling on other parts of the city, but would Berliners be that blasé? Would anyone?

He said as much to Kazankin, and got short shrift in return. 'This is perfect,' the Russian insisted. 'They'll be no one on the street. Let's go.'

They went, abandoning the single file of a partisan detachment for the sort of tired grouping a quartet of foreign labourers might form on their way back from a long day's work. As they reached Clay Allee and turned south towards the U-Bahn station a military lorry without lights roared into view and out again, leaving Russell's heart thumping inside his jacket.

It seemed to be the only vehicle moving in Dahlem. They crossed the bridge over the U-Bahn tracks and turned left onto Gary Strasse. Several houses had been hit in earlier bombing raids, and much of the debris was still lying in the road, which shocked Russell almost as much as the level of damage. The fact that the German authorities could countenance such levels of civic untidiness spoke volumes.

Their boots had not been chosen for softness, and their footfalls on the city pavements sounded distressingly loud. As if to confirm Russell's fears, he saw a curtain twitch in a bedroom window. He imagined someone reaching for a telephone, then told himself it wouldn't be working. No system could function in these conditions.

They turned a bend in the road to find two men walking towards them. In uniform. One hastened his stride, as if eager to deal with them. 'What are you doing out?' he asked, while still ten metres away.

'We're on our way back to our barracks,' Russell told him, in what he hoped was Polish-accented German. 'They kept us working on the new defences until late,' he volunteered, holding up his spade as evidence, 'and there was no transport to bring us back. We've walked about ten kilometres.'

The policeman was in front of them now. 'Papers,' he demanded preemptorily. His companion, walking up behind him, looked a lot less interested.

The first man was at least fifty, Russell thought. Probably sixty. But he seemed confident of his ability to deal with four potential opponents. He was probably used to ordering foreign workers around.

Russell handed over the papers that identified him as Tadeusz Kozminski, a construction worker from Kattowitz in Silesia.

The officer examined them, or at least pretended to – it was hard to believe he could read anything in this much gloom. Behind him a series of flashes lit the night sky, swiftly followed by the sound of explosions. They seemed to be getting nearer.

The others passed over their papers.

'Your name?' the policeman barked at Kazankin.

'He doesn't speak German,' Russell interjected. 'I'm the only one who does.'

'Where is your barracks?' he was asked.

This was the question they had feared. During their discussions at the Polish airfield, Nikoladze had asked Russell whether he knew of any places in Dahlem where foreign workers might be billeted, and the only one he could think of was a stormtrooper barracks once infamous for its book-burning excesses. It was in the right area.

'On Thiel Allee,' Russell said. 'Just up from Berliner Strasse.'

'Where do you mean?' his interrogator asked, suspicion in his voice. His hand was busy unclipping the leather holster on his hip.

Russell saw surprise bloom in the man's eyes, heard the sudden 'pff'. As the policeman sank to his knees, revealing the dark shape of his companion, the noise was repeated. The other man collapsed with little more fuss, leaving life with only the slightest of gasps.

The two NKVD men just stood there for a moment, their silenced pistols pointing down at the ground, ears straining for any indication that the crime had been witnessed. There was only the rumble of distant explosions.

Satisfied, they each grabbed a pair of legs, hauled the fresh corpses across to the low hedge bordering the road, and tipped them over. They would doubtless be visible in daylight, but by then...

Varennikov's mouth was hanging open, his eyes reflecting the shock that Russell felt. He had seen a lot of dead bodies over the last few years, but he couldn't remember ever watching another human being lose his life at such close quarters, and with such astonishing suddenness. And the sangfroid of the Soviet security men was breathtaking. Two Germans, two bullets, two bodies dumped in the shadows. And if there were wives or mothers who loved them, who the hell cared?

Kazankin urged them back into motion with the jerk of an arm. They had to be nearly there, and sure enough, a sign for Ihne Strasse soon emerged out of the gloom. They were only a block away.

Russell had visited the Institute once before, on a journalistic assignment in early 1940. He had made an appointment to see Peter Debye, the Dutch physicist then in charge, but had received a less than fulsome welcome when he reported at reception. Debye, it later transpired, had just been fired for refusing to accept Reich citizenship, but the news had not been cleared for official release, and Russell had spent an hour strolling around the grounds before he received the definitive no. If Nikoladze was right and it hadn't been bombed, he was fairly sure he would recognise the building. The Lightning Tower – the large cylindrical structure at its western end – was too distinctive to miss.

It would probably still be. The Americans would have done their damnedest to destroy the whole complex once they discovered that atomic research was going on there, and they would have redoubled those efforts once they knew that the Soviets would be reaching Berlin before them. But trying and succeeding were two very different things where aerial bombing was concerned. If any country's bomber command had won medals for precision in this war, then Russell hadn't heard about it. The fact that they'd been aiming at the Institute seemed a near-guarantee of its survival.

A few moments later his cynicism was rewarded, as the stark silhouette of the Lightning Tower reared up against the flare of a distant explosion. They had reached their first objective, and much quicker than he had expected. 'That's it,' he told Kazankin in a whisper.

They advanced along their barely discernible road, and crossed another. Beyond the dim shape of the tower, the long three-storeyed building stretched away. As they drew nearer the deepening orange of the sky reflected in the even rows of windows that lined the sides and roof. There were no lights visible, but blackout curtains were bound to be in place. The whole German scientific establishment might be inside, all working flat out on some new monstrosity for the Wehrmacht to use.

But Russell didn't think so. The building felt empty. In fact the whole area – all the large shapes in the darkness that made up Wilhelm II's dream of 'a German Oxford' – felt empty. As if the German scientific establishment had finally summoned the nerve to say 'Fuck you, Adolf', and headed on home.

He remembered the building standing in an open, well-manicured square of parkland, but the war had taken a toll, and patches of unkempt vegetation now offered useful camouflage for a raiding party. Kazankin pushed his way through the surrounding hedge and led them to one such patch, not far from the base of the Lightning Tower. Looking up, Russell could see the vertical ribs, and the small rectangular windows just below the coolie hat roof which gave the tower its resemblance to a fat medieval turret. When the war began it had housed a particle accelerator for atomic experiments, but that was probably long gone.

The eastern sky was growing lighter with each new blaze, and Kazankin found he could read his watch. 'Almost eleven,' he told Gusakovsky – they were slightly ahead of schedule. The moon would rise in twenty minutes, and on a clear night like this would make a considerable difference. But it would only be up for four hours, which they'd spend in the hopefully empty Institute, out of sight and searching for secrets. When it went down at a quarter past three, they would still have three hours of darkness in which to reach the sanctuary of the Grunewald forest.

They crouched there for what seemed an age, until Kazankin was satisfied that no one had seen them. He then led them across to the nearest porticoed entrance, and hopefully depressed the handle on one of the double doors. It swung slowly open. This implied human occupancy, but the complete lack of light suggested the opposite. Which was it? Had the Institute been closed down? Had its scientists decided that the war was over and gone back to their families? Or had the whole shebang been transferred to some safer location? That would explain the absence of security – there would be nothing left to guard.

There should at least be a caretaker, though. Some hapless old man, down in the basement, waiting for the all-clear to sound.

Kazankin disappeared into the darkness, and for what seemed like several minutes the others waited where they were, listening to the muffled sounds of his exploration. Finally the thin beam of the Russian's masked flashlight blinked on, revealing a long corridor in which every door seemed to be closed.

'Is it empty?' Varennikov asked in a whisper.

'No,' Kazankin answered shortly. 'There are no blackout curtains down in the offices, so we must lower them ourselves before we use any light. Now...' He took the folded diagram of the building out from inside his jacket, flattened it against the corridor wall, and shone the flashlight on it. Several rooms at the western end, close to where they stood, were marked with crosses. So was the Lightning Tower.

'I think we're wasting our time,' Russell heard himself say.

'That is possible,' Kazankin said coldly. 'But since we have three hours to waste I suggest you and Comrade Varennikov start here' – he picked out the nearest cross in the diagram, which marked a large room facing onto the inner courtyard – 'and work your way down this side of the building to the tower.'

'Where will you be?' Russell asked, thinking about the possible caretaker.

Kazankin paused for a long moment, as if he was wondering whether to divulge the information. 'Shota will stay here by the entrance,' he said eventually. 'I will check the building next door. According to our information, it has a lead-lined basement area known as the Virus House where certain experiments have been performed. If I can find it, and if anything looks interesting, I will come back for Comrade Varennikov. If not, you must be back here by three-fifteen. Understood?'

Russell nodded. It was the first time he'd heard Gusakovsky's first name, and the extra intimacy was somehow comforting. Once he and Varennikov were inside the first office, Russell closed the door behind them and carefully closed the blackout curtains before trying the light. Unsurprisingly, the electricity was off – they would have to rely on their flashlights. Which was probably no bad thing, he decided. Most curtains bled a little light around the edges, and the brighter the source the sharper the glint.

Varennikov started rummaging through the desks and filing cabinets. They had not been cleared out, which might bode well, but the young physicist gave no sign of finding anything significant. Outside, the level of bombing seemed to have abated, although it might just have moved further away. 'There's nothing here,' the Russian concluded.

They moved on to the next room, a laboratory. Once Russell had blanked off all three windows, Varennikov used his flashlight to explore the room. The various items of scientific equipment meant nothing to Russell, but the physicist seemed encouraged, and swiftly applied himself to sifting through several filing cabinets' worth of experimental results.

To no avail. 'Nothing,' he said, slamming the last cabinet shut with a loud bang, and then wincing at his own stupidity. 'Sorry.'

The next room was almost bare, the laboratory that followed devoid of anything useful. Only two small offices remained on this side of the corridor, and the first was replete with papers. Halfway through the first pile, Varennikov extracted a single sheet and sat staring at it for what seemed a long time.

'Interesting?' Russell asked.

'Maybe,' the Russian said. He put that sheet and several others to one side.

The next office was even more rewarding. Halfway through one folder of papers the Russian's excitement became almost palpable. 'This is very interesting,' he murmured, apparently to himself. 'An ingenious solution,' he added in the same tone, taking out the relevant sheet and placing it with the one he had taken from the previous room. Others followed: the beginnings of a nuclear pile in more ways than one.

At the end of the corridor a door and small passage brought them into the Lightning Tower. The particle accelerator had been removed, leaving a vast echoing space, and only the metal stairway spiralling up the sides and the Manhattan-style island of filing cabinets in the centre of the floor precluded the tower's re-employment as a fairground wall of death. The perfect metaphor for Nazi Germany, Russell thought. Once the petrol ran out, it had dropped like a stone.

'It must have been huge,' Varennikov was saying, a look of awe on his face. Almost reluctantly, Russell thought, the Russian turned his torch beam on the filing cabinets, and began rummaging through their contents.

He was soon lost in the task, throat clicking in apparent appreciation as he added more papers to the Moscow-bound sheaf. It took the better part of an hour to riffle through each cabinet, and by then the file was bulging, the physicist smiling. 'We'll have to be quick with the rest of the offices,' Russell told him.

'Yes, yes,' Varennikov agreed, with the air of a man who already had what he needed.

Which, as they soon discovered, was just as well. The outside offices contained only administrative records. They found no further evidence of Heisenberg's progress in creating a German atomic bomb, but they did discover what the famous physicist's salary was. Russell thought about translating the Reichsmarks into roubles for Varennikov's enlightenment, but decided it would be unkind.

They were in the last room when two things happened. First there was a shout, a few frantic words in German that included *nein*. And then, only a heartbeat later, the window blew in, sucking in the roar of an exploding bomb with a hail of shattered glass. Russell felt a sharp pain in his face, and heard Varennikov gasp. An instant later, a second bomb exploded, then another and another, each one sounding a blissful stretch further away.

Russell picked a small shard of glass from his check, and felt the blood run. He trained each eye in turn on the moonlit gardens – both were still working. Varennikov, his flashlight revealed, had lost his right earlobe, and the stub was bleeding profusely. He seemed more shocked than harmed.

Russell suddenly remembered the shout. He switched off his flashlight, carefully opened the door, and stepped out into the dark corridor. There was nothing moving, and no sign of Gusakovsky or Kazankin, but a thin wash of light filled the lobby area some twenty metres to his left. And there was a dark shape on the floor.

Two, as it turned out. The old man was nearer, a neat black hole drilled through the left side of his forehead, a few locks of silver hair draped across his right eye. Gusakovsky was just beyond him, unnaturally twisted, the back of his head glistening in the dim light. He had been thrown against the wall by the blast, Russell guessed. The bomb must have landed almost on the doorstep, blowing the doors inwards, a split second after Gusakovsky's shooting of the caretaker.

The Russian's gun was lying close to his splayed hand. Russell bent down to pick it up, and placed it in his belt.

'Wh-where's Kazankin?' Varennikov stuttered behind him.

It was a question that needed answering, but far from the only one. Were there any emergency services still operating in Berlin? If so, were they already fully occupied? If any were spare, how long would it take them to arrive? Sooner or later someone was bound to. They had to get away from the Institute.

But where to?

And where was Kazankin?

Russell worked his way between pieces of furniture to the open doorway, and clambered gingerly out across the ruined portico. The moon was almost down, but flames were rising from a building away to his left, flooding the world in yellow light. The bomb had gouged a sizable crater across the pathway leading to the street gates, and the remains of a body lay heaped on the grass ten metres beyond. From a distance, it looked like a shapeless mass of bloodied flesh; closer up, Russell could identify shreds of the foreign worker uniform. One quarter of the face was strangely untouched, and in it a single staring eye. Kazankin's.

He wasn't supposed to feel sorry for his potential executioner, but he almost did.

He looked around. One building on Gary Strasse was merrily burning, but the other three bombs had only inflicted blast damage. No more were falling, and the sky sounded empty of planes. Had Kazankin and Gusakovsky fallen prey to a single stray stick, not so much aimed as discarded?

Varennikov had followed Russell out, and was now standing there, clutching the sheaf of papers, staring down at what was left of Kazankin. He ran a hand through his hair. 'What now?' he asked. It sounded more like a plea than a question.

Russell responded. 'This way,' he ordered, leading the Russian out through the gates and across the empty street. As they approached the intersection with Boltzmann Strasse they both heard vehicles approaching from the Thiel Allee direction. Russell broke into a run, Varennikov following. They turned the corner into Boltzmann Strasse and headed for the pool of deep shadow offered by two large trees.

They had barely reached it when two vehicles drove across the intersection they had just left behind. Fire trucks of some kind, Russell guessed. They would find three bodies, one caretaker and two foreign workers.

One of whom, he realised, was still carrying his Soviet pistol. Fuck!

It was too late to do anything about it. With any luck the Nazis would assume that there'd only been two of them. 'Let's go,' he told Varennikov.

'Where are we going?' the Russian asked as they walked towards the Thielplatz U-Bahn station.

'To my brother-in-law's house,' Russell told him.

'Your brother-in-law? But he's a German!'

'Yes he is. And he's probably the best chance we have of saving our lives.' He certainly couldn't think of any others. But was it fair to land on Thomas's doorstep with a Soviet physicist, and half the Gestapo in probable pursuit? The thought crossed his mind that he could simplify matters no end by taking out Gusakovsky's silenced gun and leaving Varennikov in a Dahlem gutter. But he knew he couldn't do it. The Soviets might find out. And he rather liked the young Russian.

He asked himself how he would feel if Thomas turned up at his door with a ticking bomb. He would take him in, he knew he would. He and his ex-brother-in-law had fought on opposite sides in the First War, but they'd been on the same side ever since.

Thomas even had a cellar – Russell could remember him remarking how they'd probably need it after one of Goering's speeches on the invincibility of the Luftwaffe. They should be able to hide out there until the Red Army reached Berlin. And once they did, then saving Varennikov should earn both him and Thomas some much-needed credit with the Soviets.

All of which assumed Thomas being there. He could imagine him evacuating Hanna and Lotte to Hanna's parents in the country, but he found it hard to imagine Thomas leaving his factory or his Jewish workers. As far back as 1941 he'd been all that stood between them and the trains heading east – he had even taken to cultivating a few Nazi acquaintances as insurance. And things was unlikely to have improved. If the bombing had spared him, Thomas would be there.

'How far is it?' Varennikov asked, interrupting his thoughts.

'About two kilometres,' Russell told him. He couldn't remember hearing an all-clear, but the bombers seemed to have gone. With the searchlights dimmed, the moon down, and the blackout still in force, it could hardly have got any darker. Even the whitened kerbs offered little help – six years of weather and footfalls had worn the paint away.

They took the bridge across the U-Bahn cutting, and headed up the narrow Im Schwarzen Grund. It might be dark, but the main roads carried a heavier risk, and he was fairly confident of finding his way through Dahlem's suburban maze. Varennikov looked less certain, but plodded dutifully along beside him. If the sheaf of papers under his arm amounted to a bomb for Stalin, then the Americans would eventually have questions for Russell. He decided that Thomas didn't need to know what this was all about. For everyone's sake.

The street was quiet. In the poorer parts of Berlin, people would be hurrying home from the large public shelters, but in richer suburbs like Dahlem most houses and blocks had their own. And for obvious reasons the police presence had always been thinner here than in the old socialist and communist strongholds of working-class Wedding and Neukölln. In some areas of Wedding even the Gestapo had needed military back-up.

The streets were quiet, but not entirely empty. Twice on Bitter Strasse the two men were forced to skulk in the shadows while people went by, an air-raid warden on an unlit bicycle, a woman in a long coat. Two of the phosphorescent badges that Russell remembered from the early years of the war were pinned to her chest like pale blue headlights.

There was no sign that Dahlem had been bombed that night – apart, that is, from the four which had fallen around the Institute – but it had clearly suffered during the preceding months. As they crossed the wide and empty Königin Luise Strasse, Russell noticed several gaps in the once imposing line of houses, and the depredations on Vogelsang Strasse seemed, if possible, even heavier. Had the Schade residence survived?

It had. Identifying the familiar silhouette against the starry backdrop gave Russell an intense sense of relief. He had spent many happy hours in this house and the garden that lay behind it. Thomas had bought it in the early 1920s, soon after taking over the family's paper and printing business from his ailing father. Russell and Ilse had stayed there when they returned, as lovers, from the Soviet Union in 1924. Through the 1930s he and Effi had spent many a Sunday lunch and afternoon as part of the extended family, eating, drinking and lamenting the Nazis.

Unsurprisingly for four in the morning, the house lay in darkness. But the small front garden did look unusually unkempt, and the thick spider's web which Russell encountered on the porch implied a distinct lack of human traffic.

'It looks empty,' Varennikov said. He sounded relieved.

'Come,' Russell told him, heading for the archway at the side of the house, where another web was waiting. Many years earlier, Thomas had invited him back to the house, only to realise he'd forgotten his keys. 'There's a spare one round the back,' his friend had said, and there it had been, gathering moss under a water bucket.

The bucket was in the same spot, and so was the key. It felt a little rusty, but still opened the back door. Russell ushered Varennikov into the huge kitchen that Hanna loved so much, and told the Russian to stand still while he attended to the blackout curtains. Once these were closed, Russell used his flashlight to reveal the room's geography.

Two things immediately caught his eye. The documents on the large kitchen table were Thomas's Volkssturm call-up papers. They had been issued the previous autumn.

And on the mantelpiece above the stone fireplace there was one of the black-bordered memorial cards that Russell remembered from 1941. Joachim Schade smiled out of the photograph. Thomas had lost his son.

We killed them all

April 20 – 21

Paul let himself out of the temporary barracks just before seven, and took a deep breath of fresh air – most of the *Hitlerjugend* still sleeping inside had probably forgotten what soap and water were for. The sound of aircraft lifted his eyes – high in the sky above Erkner the sun glinted on the silver bellies of Allied bombers. All through the night he had listened to the dull thud of distant explosions, and day it seemed would bring no mercy. To the west, Erkner's Rathaus was silhouetted against a sky laced with the colour of fire. It was, he realised, Hitler's birthday.

He walked across to the railway station and down the short street to the town centre, intent on finding someone from his own division, or at least news of its whereabouts. How else was he going to get away from a bunch of deluded children with a collective death-wish?

But he was out of luck. The traffic clogging the main road west was mostly civilian; the only uniforms in motion were black, and they belonged to embarrassed-looking Waffen-SS soldiers clinging to a farm tractor. At the crossroads an unusually cheerful MP had no idea where the 20th might be, but more than enough information about the Russians, whose advance was apparently gathering speed.

'How far away are they?' Paul wanted to know.

The man shrugged. 'Two days? Maybe only one. But we'll all be pulled back into the city before they get here.'

He made Berlin sound like a real barrier, but Paul had seen French prisoners-of-war hard at work on the so-called 'obstacle belt' on his last trip to the city. A few trenches and gun emplacements weren't going to hold up the Red Army for long, even when manned by soldiers too young to know fear.

Returning to the canteen, he saw Werner across the road, happily chatting to the woman from the day before. 'Frau Kempka's husband was in Italy with the same division as my father,' the boy announced happily, as if that was some consolation for them both being dead.

'Was he really?' Paul said. 'Good morning, Frau Kempka,' he added. She had a coat on, and a suitcase sat by the front door.

'I'm going to try and reach Potsdam,' she said, noticing his glance. 'My brother lives there, although I expect he's serving in the Volkssturm now. It seems safer than staying here, don't you think?' She looked at Paul, as if confident he would know the answer.

I'm only eighteen, Paul felt like saying. 'You're probably right,' was what he said. Potsdam, about twenty-five kilometres south-west of Berlin, seemed as good a place as any.

'We're moving out,' Werner told him. 'They told us fifteen minutes ago – you might have been left behind.'

'Where are we going?'

'A few kilometres east. There's a gap between two lakes, and we're supposed to plug it. Us and a police battalion. And the local Volkssturm.'

Paul groaned inwardly – police battalions were notoriously prone to disappearing without warning, and the Volkssturm would probably just get in the way.

Over the next couple of hours, as they waited for the fuel they'd been promised for their lorries, he saw nothing to make him more optimistic. The members of the police battalion were all armed with rifles, but their eyes looked inward and their faces were pale with fear. The older men of the Volkssturm looked more depressed than frightened, but they were woefully short of weapons. They would only have a rifle each when half of them were dead.

The fuel finally appeared, two barrels on the back of a horse-drawn cart which needed siphoning. It was almost ten when they finally set off, and by then the sky was clouding over. The *Hitlerjugend* sat clutching their rocket-launchers; apart from a few exceptions like Werner, they seemed eager for battle. Today was the Führer's birthday, they kept reminding each other, the day on which the wonder weapons would be unleashed. This would be the moment the Soviets were stopped and driven back, and they would be able to tell their children that they had been part of it.

Staring out through the back of the lorry at the huge pall of smoke hanging over Berlin, Paul wondered how anyone could still believe in victory.

Their new position was only about three kilometres away, but forcing their way through the oncoming tide of refugees took almost two hours. Paul saw a mix of emotions in the passing faces – faint hope, pity tinged with resentment, even a hint of the old respect – but the commonest look was of incomprehension. It was the one he had seen in Gerhart's mother's eyes, the one that couldn't fathom how anyone might still believe there was anything to fight for.

At the spot where their road passed under the orbital autobahn a large hoarding carried the increasingly ubiquitous 'Berlin Remains German!' slogan, and some joker had added the words 'for one more week' in what looked like large slatherings of gun grease.

No defensive positions had been prepared across the isthmus which divided the lakes, and the next two hours were spent digging themselves in. There were just over a hundred of them, Paul reckoned, enough to hold the position for a few hours, assuming the promised artillery support turned up. If it didn't... well, Ivan would just plough right on through them.

The two *Hitlerjugend* in the neighbouring foxhole were still talking about the wonder weapons. Both were certain of their existence, but one seemed less than certain of their imminent arrival. Werner, by contrast, was digging in silence. He was strong for a fourteen-year-old, Paul thought. Another way in which he had grown up too fast.

Russell was woken by the sirens, and for one all-too-brief moment thought himself back in Effi's flat. It was only nine o'clock, and the bed seemed as damp as it had when he first lay down. Sunshine was pouring in through the window, lighting the Hertha team portrait which Joachim had pinned to his wall. It was the 1938–39 team, Russell realised. The four of them – he, Paul, Thomas and Joachim – had gone to most of the home games that season.

Was Paul dead too? He felt his chest tighten at the thought of it.

He swung himself off the bed and went for a piss. Varennikov was still sleeping, one arm stretched out above his head with palm averted, as if he were warding off an attacker. The sheaf of papers from the Kaiser Wilhelm Institute peeked out from under the pillow.

Russell went downstairs in search of food and drink. There was water in the taps and, rather to his surprise, a weak flow of gas from the oven hob. There was a can of ersatz coffee, some sugar, and several tins of Swedish soup – a gift from someone with influence, no doubt. He stared out of the window at the overgrown garden while he waited for the water to boil, then left a saucepan of soup above the derisory flames.

Taking care to keep clear of the windows, he worked his way through the downstairs rooms. The living- and dining-room furniture was wreathed in sheets, Thomas's office a dustier version of what he remembered. Standing in the front hall, he idly picked up the telephone, and was astonished to hear a working tone.

On impulse, he dialled the Gehrts' number. It rang, but no one answered.

Next he tried Effi's old flat. He knew she couldn't be there, but he loved the idea of hearing the telephone ring in their old living room.

There was no answer.

Who else could he call? Zarah, he decided. If Effi had spent the last forty months in Berlin, he found it hard to believe that she hadn't made contact with her sister. But what was the Biesingers' number. Did it end with a six or an eight?

He tried the six. He counted ten rings, and was about to hang up when someone picked up. 'Yes?' a tired male voice asked.

It was Jens, Russell realised, Zarah's Nazi husband. He broke the connection.

Outside, the sound of bombs exploding seemed to be getting nearer. They should move to the cellar.

It was early evening when the rumour spread through the basement rooms of the collection camp, leaving something close to terror in its wake. Effi could feel the rising sense of panic before she knew its cause, that Dobberke had finally received the order to kill them all. Like everyone else, she instinctively turned her eyes to the door, for fear that their killers were about to burst through it.

It was almost dark outside. Would they do it at night or wait for the dawn? Effi had heard of wounded people lying motionless for hours under corpses, waiting for the moment to crawl away. Had they just been lucky, or was there a trick she needed to know?

'What's happening, Mama?' Rosa said, jolting her out of the dark reverie. Over the last few days, the girl had voiced none of those questions that she must be asking herself, but the look in her eyes was too often fearful. And this was the first time she had ever called Effi 'Mama'.

'I'm not sure,' Effi told her. How could you tell a seven year-old that her execution had just been ordered?

The sirens started wailing, welcome for once. Would their jailers all come down to the basement as if nothing had changed? Would Dobberke stand there smoking his cigarettes, sharing an occasional joke with his prisoners?

He did, although he looked more uncertain than usual, at least to Effi. She decided she couldn't bear to wait. She needed to know if the rumours were true.

The men in the fourth room would know, the ones who'd been locked in the cells until the weekend bombing. 'You stay with Johanna,' she told Rosa. 'I'm going to find out what's happening. I'll be back in a few minutes.'

She came across Heilborn and Lewinsky in the third room – the old mortuary, as Nina had told her. 'What's happening?' she asked them without preamble.

The rumour was apparently true. A fourteen-year-old Jew named Rudi, who worked as a shoeshine boy for their Gestapo jailers, had overheard one end of a telephone conversation between Dobberke and his superior Sturmbannführer Möller, and then listened in as Dobberke passed on the news to his subordinates. Möller had ordered the 'liquidation' of the camp. 'At once.'

That sounded like good news to Effi – by taking his time Dobberke was already disobeying orders.

There was more. The Hauptsturmführer had agreed to a meeting after the air raid with two representatives of the prisoners. Which suggested a willingness to consider counter-proposals.

'What are they planning to say?' Effi asked. She felt more than a little resentful that a few men had taken it upon themselves to speak for everyone, but reluctantly conceded that time might be short for democracy.

'They're going to ask him to release everyone,' Heilborn told her. 'And to tell him that the gratitude of a thousand Jews might well save his life in the weeks to come.'

Effi made her way back to Rosa, and passed on what she had heard to Johanna and Nina. On the other side of the room Dobberke still looked unusually tense. She prayed he would know a good bargain when he saw one.

An hour or so later she still had no answer. The two prisoners had returned from their meeting with the Hauptsturmführer. They had offered him signed testimonials from each and every one of his thousand Jewish prisoners in exchange for freedom, and he had promised to think about it.

Whatever Dobberke decided, it would happen in the morning. Effi doubted whether many of the collection camp's inmates would sleep that night. She knew she wouldn't.

Paul and Werner spent their afternoon waiting in the trench. Given some encouragement, Werner talked about his family – the engineer father that he'd lost, the mother who loved to sing while she cooked, his younger sister

Eta and the doll's house which he and his father had made her. And as he listened, Paul caught mental glimpses of his own childhood. One in particular, of decorating a cake with his mother when he was only four or five, had him fighting back tears.

Twice during the afternoon Soviet fighters flew low over their positions, one offering a desultory burst of machine-gun fire which killed one of the policemen, and soon after four o'clock tank fire was heard in the distance. But as dusk fell it grew no louder, and Paul was daring to believe they would survive the day when a lone T-34 tank emerged from the trees a few hundred metres down the road. Then the world exploded around them, a barrage of incoming shells straddling their positions, sucking earth and limbs skyward. They pressed themselves up against the wall of their foxhole, and tried to remember to breathe.

The shellfire soon abated, which only implied one thing – Ivan was coming through. As if in confirmation, a 'Christmas tree' flare burst out above them, sprinkling the blood-red sky with searing lights. Raising his eyes over their parapet, Paul could see a swarm of advancing T-34s, and the bulkier silhouettes of several Stalin tanks. As he looked, a boom sounded behind him, and one of the smaller Russian tanks exploded in flames. Two German Panthers had put in an appearance, and many of the *Hitlerjugend* were whooping and cheering as if the war had been won.

The Stalins were clearly unimpressed. One moved forward at a frightening pace, tracer rounds ricocheting off its hull in all directions; the other took careful aim. A whoosh and a flash left one of the Panthers ablaze, the other frantically traversing its gun as it scuttled backwards towards the dubious shelter of the trees. Looking to his left, Paul was sure he could see T-34s already level with their position – the police battalion had fled or been overrun. They had to withdraw.

A figure suddenly emerged above them, apparently oblivious to the bullets shredding the air. Orders to fall back, Paul assumed, but he couldn't have been more wrong. 'We're going for them,' the boy said, a 'Christmas tree' lighting his excited face. 'They won't be able to see us until we're right among them,' he added nonsensically, before hurrying on to the next foxhole.

Paul slumped back into his own. Werner was looking at him, waiting for direction, for encouragement, for permission to die. Well, he was damned if he was going to offer any of those. Why die defending a gap between two small lakes that the enemy could easily bypass? The thought crossed his mind that if his body was found in a pile of *Hitlerjugend* his father would think he'd learnt nothing. And he would hate that.

The light of the last 'Christmas tree' was fading. Glancing back out over the rim, he could see the shadowy figures of *Hitlerjugend* leaving their trenches and starting towards the oncoming Soviet tanks, each with a panzerfaust slung over his shoulder. Another 'Christmas tree' and they would all be mown down.

Paul felt the urge to go with them, and dismissed it as ridiculous. 'Do you want to see your mother and sister again?' he asked Werner.

'Yes, of course...'

'Then put that down and follow me.' He levered himself out of the foxhole, and started running, crouched as low as he could manage, towards the nearest trees. Werner, he realised, was close behind him. Reaching the shelter of a large oak, they stopped to look back. The second Panther was also burning, the T-34s roaming this way and that like cowboys rounding up cattle in an American Western. As they watched, one erupted in flames – at least one *panzerfaust* had found its mark. But the *Hitlerjugend* had vanished from sight, swallowed by darkness and battle.

They moved on into the trees, keeping the road some fifty metres to their right and moving as fast as the darkness would allow. Behind them, the 'Christmas trees' were increasing in frequency, like a firework display reaching for its climax.

They had gone about half a kilometre when three Soviet tanks rumbled past on the road – they would, Paul guessed, soon be sitting astride the autobahn intersection. He led Werner towards the south-west, intent on crossing the autobahn further down, and after jogging on for another half an hour they finally came to the lip of a cutting. But there was no autobahn below, only twin railway tracks. As they reached the bottom of the bank they heard something approaching. A train, Paul supposed, but it didn't sound like one.

Werner started forward, but Paul pulled him into the shadows. A tank loomed out of the gloom, half on and half off the tracks. Someone was standing up in the hatch, and several other human shapes were draped across the hull, but it was several seconds before Paul could be sure they were Germans.

He thought about trying to attract their attention, but only for a moment. They probably wouldn't see him, and if they did the chances were good that they'd open fire.

Following them, though, seemed a good idea – if there were any Russians on the line to Erkner, the tank would find them first. He and Werner started walking down the tracks, the sound of the tank fading before them.

After around an hour Paul realised they were coming into Erkner. A few seconds later the tank loomed out of the darkness, still straddling the rails. His first thought was that it had run out of fuel, but it hadn't been abandoned – a man was still standing up in the turret, smoking a cigarette. Paul risked a shout of 'kamerad'. The man quickly doused his cigarette, but invited them forward when Paul supplied the names of their units.

The tank had fuel enough, but the commander, fearing that the Russians were already in Erkner, had sent his grenadiers ahead on reconnaissance. If they came back with a good report, then he'd drive straight through the town. If Ivan was already ensconced, then he'd find another way round. In either case, they were a panzergrenadier short, and Paul was welcome to the vacancy. The boy could come along for the ride.

The grenadiers came back a few minutes later – Erkner was still in German hands. Everyone climbed wearily aboard, and the tank moved off, swapping rails for road. They rumbled down the sleeping streets, talked their way through the MP checkpoint on the canal bridge, and headed out onto the Berlin road. Reaching the city's outer defence line near Friedrichshagen, they discovered that their regiment was ordered to Köpenick, five kilometres further on. They arrived in the hour before dawn to find their supposed assembly area – the western end of the Lange Bridge across the Dahme – occupied by a company of Volkssturm. With no other tanks in sight, and confident that the Russians were at least a day behind them, the case for sleep seemed overwhelming.

Werner, however, was hard to turn off. He had been quiet throughout the journey, and now Paul discovered why. The boy couldn't shake the feeling that he'd let his comrades down.

Paul understood why Werner felt that way – only a week ago he had felt the same himself. But not any longer. Maybe it was only him, but over that week the rules had seemed to change. 'They chose their fate,' he told Werner, hoping the boy wouldn't notice all the questions he seemed to be begging. 'Look, there are only a few days left. There's nothing you and I can do anymore that will help win the war, nothing we can do to prevent it from ending in defeat. Nothing at all. All we can do is to try and survive it. And I want to survive,' he said, surprising himself with the vehemence of the thought. Had losing Gerhard and Neumaier made him more determined to live?

'So do I,' Werner admitted, as if it were a guilty secret.

'Good,' Paul told him. 'So can we get some rest?'

'Okay.'

Paul closed his eyes and let the sound of the river lull him to sleep.

Russell woke to darkness, and it was several seconds before he remembered where he was. On the other side of the basement Varennikov was gently snoring, and somewhere in the outside world bombs were falling to earth with a series of distant thuds. 'Welcome to Berlin,' he murmured to himself.

Waking briefly in the middle of the night, he had found the young scientist reading the papers by torchlight, and was somewhat surprised not to find him still at it. He had let Varennikov sleep until five in the afternoon on the previous day, mostly because he couldn't decide what their next step should be. When the Russian had finally woken up, he had assumed that they would wait there for the Red Army – 'we stay, yes? – but Russell was not so sure. And while Varennikov had spent his evening engrossed in the papers, Russell had spent his sifting through options. Without reaching a decision.

Things seemed no clearer this morning. It might make sense to wait for the Soviets – they should be here in four or five days, a week at the outside. And if he handed Varennikov and the papers over in one piece, then Nikoladze might help him find Effi and Paul. But it didn't seem likely. Even more to the point, he wanted to find Effi before a drunken gang of Russian soldiers did, not several days later.

And if they let the Russian tide wash over them in Dahlem, those areas of central Berlin still in Nazi hands would be forever out of reach. Effi might be hiding in the outlying suburbs, but he doubted it. That wasn't the city she knew, and she had always liked being at the centre of things.

So should he leave Varennikov behind? The Russian would probably be okay, provided he kept to the basement and remembered to eat. But Russell was loath to do so: Nikoladze might well decide he'd abandoned his charge – he was, after all, under orders to seek out a second atomic research laboratory and deliver his charges to the railwaymen comrades. The other laboratory could safely be forgotten – without their NKVD enforcers, and with valuable papers already secured, the risks were not worth taking. And he could always stand up the German comrades at the rail yards, given a good enough reason. But the one thing Nikoladze would expect to find, when he eventually set foot in Berlin, was someone protecting his precious scientist with a new mother's fervour. 'I left him in a basement on the other side of town' would not go down too well.

It had to be the Potsdam goods yard – Varennikov could hardly object if Russell insisted on following their original orders. But not until tomorrow. Today he would go to Zarah's house in Schmargendorf. If Effi had told anyone that she was still in Berlin, it would be her sister, and during the day Zarah's husband Jens would be at work, always assuming that there was anything left for Nazi bureaucrats to do. He could also visit Paul's house in Grunewald, which was only a short distance farther away. It didn't seem likely that Matthias and Ilse were still in Berlin, but it was possible, and they would have some idea where Paul was. In fact, he would go there first.

He went up to the kitchen, poured two cupfuls of water into the kettle, and lit the gas. The flames seemed even smaller than before, but he was in no hurry. Bombs were still falling in the far distance – on the government district, most likely. He wondered whether Hitler was still in residence, and decided he probably was – if the Führer ever let go of his reins, it was hard to imagine any of the disciples having the gumption to pick them up. And someone was keeping the whole futile endeavour going.

Upstairs, he went through Thomas's clothes – the two of them were much the same size – and picked out the oldest suit he could find. In the bathroom he found a strip of bandaging, in Thomas's study a bottle of red ink. The latter looked the wrong colour for blood, but it would have to do. A stick and a limp would complete the illusion of someone unfit for battle.

Or at least it might. Russell had the feeling that death was the only excuse the Gestapo would find acceptable, and only then if you had papers to prove it.

He had no papers of any kind, but without Varennikov in tow he could probably talk himself through a random check. If all else failed he still had Gusakovsky's gun.

It was time to get moving. Back down in the basement he shook Varennikov awake, and told him he was going out for a few hours. He expected dissent, but the Russian just grunted and went back to sleep.

Closing the front door quietly behind him, he walked down the overgrown path to the arched gateway and took a peek at the outside world. There were other people about, but none looking or moving in his direction. He slipped out into the street, and walked slowly north towards the main road. Halfway up, an old man leaning on a gate wished him a cheery good morning, and predicted a nice day. The Allied bombers still dotting the sky were clearly not a factor worth mentioning.

As Russell limped north, cutting through suburban back streets and avoiding the main thoroughfares, the bombing damage seemed ever more serious – Schmargendorf had fared much worse than Dahlem. Houses were missing from every row, streets and gardens cratered. At least half of the trees were burnt or broken, and those that weren't had been pollarded for fuel. Green shoots were now rising from the stumps – Eliot had been right about April being the cruellest month.

An all-clear sounded in the distance, but crowds no longer rushed from the shelters as they had in the early years. The visible population seemed almost exclusively female, and there was little in the way of purposeful activity. Women of all ages stood outside their doors and gates, alone or in groups, smoking or chatting or both. Their lives were in limbo, he realised. They were waiting for the war to end, waiting for news of a husband or son, waiting to discover what would be left for rebuilding their streets and their lives.

He crossing the wide and mostly empty Hohenzollerndamm. There was a tram further up the street, but it showed no signs of being in service. So far, he had seen a couple of official-looking cars and several bicycles, but no trace of public transport. No electricity, no petrol. The city, it seemed, had ground to a virtual halt.

He walked on into Grunewald, and finally reached the peaceful suburban avenue where Paul had lived with his mother, stepfather and stepsisters. A few trees had been cut down, but only one dwelling, several hundred metres from Matthias Gehrts' large detached house, had been completely destroyed by a bomb.

Working on the thesis that boldness was best – skulking seemed much more likely to get him reported – he limped straight up the driveway and reached for the iron knocker. He already feared that the house was empty – it had that indefinable air about it – and the lack of response confirmed as much.

He considered peering through the windows, but decided that would look overly suspicious. He walked back to the gate, played out a pantomime of noting something down, and limped off down the road. As he neared the next corner, he noticed that Paul's old school was standing empty, chains tied across its rusting gates.

A quarter-hour later he reached the road where Effi's sister lived. Skulking was his only option here, because Jens might answer a knock on the door. They had never liked each other, and it seemed safe to assume that he and Effi becoming fugitives had only made matters worse. For all Russell knew, Jens had been expelled from the Party for having traitorous relatives.

He had bought a *Volkischer Beobachter* from a still-functioning kiosk on Hubertusbader Strasse – the Nazi paper had shrunk, he gleefully noted, to a single large sheet – and duly positioned himself behind it some fifty metres from the relevant door. It was, he knew, a less than convincing stratagem, but he couldn't think of a better one. He was, in any case, probably wasting his time. Zarah was probably in the country with Lothar, and he had no intention of approaching Jens.

According to the paper, there was heavy fighting in the vicinity of Müncheberg. Which, in Goebbels-speak, meant that the town had already fallen. The Red Army was almost at Berlin's door.

An extra issue of rations was announced, supposedly in honour of the Führer's birthday. And rations for the next two weeks could be collected in advance – someone at least in the Nazi hierarchy seemed reasonably aware of how much time remained.

No one had emerged from the house, which was disappointing but hardly surprising – it would have been something of a coincidence if anyone had appeared during these particular ten minutes. But he could hardly stand there for hours. The temptation simply to walk up and knock grew stronger, and after completing his perusal of Goebbels' latest bleatings he felt on the verge of succumbing. If Jens answered the door he'd just have to play it by ear.

He was saved by an old man in a milkman's uniform, who beat him to it, climbing the steps and hammering on the front door with all the insistence of someone intent on settling a long outstanding bill.

There was no answer. The milkman placed a piece of paper against t he door, licked his pencil, and scribbled what looked like a furious message.

Russell started back towards Dahlem. There were more people on the streets now, and most seemed to be smiling. He assumed the extra rations were responsible, but soon learned otherwise. A bald old man with a Hindenburg moustache – he had more hair under his nose than Russell had seen on many heads – insisted on shaking his hand. 'We made it through,' he said exultantly.

'Through what?' Russell asked.

'You haven't heard? That was the last air raid this morning. It was on the radio.'

The BBC, Russell assumed. 'That is wonderful,' he agreed, and allowed his hand to be shaken again. Walking on, he could think of only one reason why the Allies would stop their bombing – the Soviets was poised to enter the city.

As if in response to that thought, a rippling wave of explosions erupted away to the east.

There were no planes in the smoke-smeared sky. It could only be Soviet artillery. They were close enough to bombard the city centre.

Things would get worse, he realised. The gaps between air raids allowed time to shop, to collect water, to enjoy a few precious hours of natural light. But the Soviet guns would keep pumping shells around the clock. There would be no respite, no time of safety on the surface. From this point on the residents of Hitler's rapidly shrinking realm would be spending all their time underground.

There were no shells landing in Dahlem – yet. Reaching Thomas's gate, he checked the street was empty before hurrying down the path. If anyone was watching from a window, he could only hope that any sense of social responsibility had worn thin. If seeing their city go up in flames didn't stop people reporting their neighbours, then what would?

Varennikov was awake, standing in the kitchen scratching his bare chest and staring hopelessly at the kettle. There wasn't enough gas to warm a flea.

'Someone knocked on the door,' he told Russell.

'When?'

'Oh, fifteen minutes ago.'

'Where were you?'

'Here.'

'You didn't see who it was?'

'No. I was afraid they might see me if I moved the curtain.'

'You were right. Did they only knock once?'

'No twice. After a half-minute they knocked again.'

'They?'

Varennikov shrugged. 'I don't know. I didn't see.'

It might be nothing, Russell thought. But what innocent reason could anyone have for knocking on Thomas's door? An old friend looking them up? Perhaps. It would be a coincidence, someone appearing so soon after their own arrival. A neighbour would be more likely, and a neighbour would know there was no one supposed to be here. Unless, of course, their arrival – or his own exit that morning – had been noticed.

If a neighbour had seen them, he or she might have come over to check them out, might now be phoning the police to report the presence of burglars. Would the police care? Surely they were too busy saving their own skins to worry about crime?

He walked out into the hall and tried the telephone. It was still working.

If a policeman turned up he supposed he could shoot him. And he supposed that he would, if that seemed the only way to save himself and Varennikov. But he would much rather not, particularly if the policeman was some poor old sod from the *Orpo*.

It was time to move on, he decided. If they could find sanctuary with the comrades in the Potsdam goods yard, then Nikoladze would be happy, and he would be within walking distance of the bolthole Effi had bought in Wedding almost four years ago. They had stayed there for a week while arranging their escape from Berlin, and she might, conceivably, still be living there. He had nowhere else to look. 'We have to leave,' he told Varennikov.

'Why?' the Russian asked, alarm in his eyes.

'I think we may have been seen...'

'You shouldn't have gone out.'

'Maybe, but I did. And if I was seen then someone may report it. The plan was to hide out in the railway yards – remember?'

'But what if we're stopped?' Varennikov wanted to know. 'They'll take the papers. They'll destroy them. The Party needs this information.'

'I understand that,' Russell said reassuringly. Rather more seriously, possession of the damn papers would be grounds for summary execution. 'We can hide them in the house somewhere' he improvised. 'Once the Red Army's in control of the city, we can come back and collect them. Okay?'

'What if the house is shelled or bombed?'

'All right. We'll bury them in the garden. After dark. We'll just have to hope no one turns up this afternoon.'

Varennikov seemed satisfied. 'I do have most of the important stuff in my head. And I can memorise more this afternoon. We will go tonight? How far is it?'

'About ten kilometres, maybe a bit less. And I'll have to think about when. Early tomorrow morning might be the better bet, because lots of foreign workers will be on their way to work. And if we reach the yards around first light, we'll have a better chance of finding our contact.'

All of which sounded like sense, Russell told himself later. As long as you ignored the fact that railway yards would be high on any list of artillery targets. Perhaps the Russians would become bored with targeting their fire, and simply lob their shells into the city, like the Western allies with their bombs. In which case he and Varennikov would have much the same chance of survival as anyone else.

And if he reached the centre in one piece, his chances of finding Effi would be that much better.

In the Pathology building on Schulstrasse the dull grey dawn had seemed an ill omen – the last few days had been full of sunshine. Fear, hunger and sleep deprivation had eroded what little equanimity remained, and the air seemed full of angry mutterings and semi-hysterical whispers. Two women were praying in one corner, rather too loudly for their neighbours, one of whom begged them to shut up.

The arrival of a single uniformed Gestapo officer silenced the entire room. Seemingly oblivious to the reaction he had provoked, the man approached the nearest group of prisoners. Effi watched him ask a question of one man, then search through the papers he was carrying. When he found what he was looking for, he handed the man a pencil, and pointed out where he should write.

As the Gestapo officer worked his way through the first group, word of what he was doing spread through the basement. The papers had two parts: a statement attesting Dobberke's refusal to liquidate the camp and kill his prisoners, and a list of the latter. Each prisoner was expected to endorse the statement by affixing a signature beside his or her own name.

Reaction varied wildly. Some were almost overcome with relief, while others asserted that it must be a trick. Effi wasn't sure what to think. When their turn came, she signed for herself and Rosa, and searched the Gestapo officer's eyes for more than the usual deceit. All she saw was boredom, which seemed like reason for optimism. So did the absence of guards that morning, and the fact that the signatures would be worthless if all the signatories were killed.

As the Gestapo officer moved on into the next room, the sirens sounded outside, and soon they could all hear bombs exploding in the distance. To the south, Effi thought. On what was left of the city centre.

Around half an hour later Dobberke arrived. He had several guards with him, but none were brandishing guns. Commandeering a chair and table, he sat down with a large pile of papers before him, and called forth the nearest prisoner. The guards began forming all the others into a queue.

The piled-up papers were release certificates, and Dobberke was intent on signing each one in the presence of its recipient. It was either the most convoluted and sadistic hoax in history, or they really were being released.

Halfway down the queue Effi felt her body go weak with relief, her legs almost folding beneath her. She put an arm round Rosa's neck and pulled her in. 'We're going to be all right,' she whispered in the girl's ear.

The all-clear had sounded a few minutes earlier, and several prisoners were now hovering near the unguarded open door, clutching their release certificates and clearly wondering whether they could just walk out. The first one did so, hesitantly, as if he couldn't quite believe his luck. Others followed, walking faster, as if afraid of missing their chance. There was no gunfire, no sign that anything bad was waiting outside. On the contrary, Effi caught a glimpse of one man through the high windows. He was almost skipping his way down Schulstrasse.

But many, even most, of the released prisoners seemed happy to stay where they were. And Johanna and Nina were among them. 'We should just wait here for the Russians,' Johanna suggested. 'We won't starve, and we'll be safer down here than out in the street. And when the Russians arrive we'll have enough strength in numbers to make them behave.'

Effi conceded that she might be right, but had no intention of staying. She told them she wanted to find her sister, which was true in itself, but far from her only reason. Strength in numbers or not, she felt vulnerable out here in Wedding, far from those parts of the city in which she had always lived, and which she knew like the back of her hand. And now she knew that 'Willy' had not given away her address, they could go back home to Bismarck Strasse. Admittedly her new papers went with a flat in Weissensee, but that could hardly matter now.

Their turn at the table arrived. Dobberke greeted her with a crooked smile, then signed the two certificates and wished Effi luck. She didn't reciprocate.

They collected their suitcases, and waited for Nina and Johanna to collect their certificates before saying their goodbyes. Effi thought of suggesting a post-war meeting, but the habitual caution of the last few years weighed more heavily. Rosa was less encumbered, and insisted on setting a time and place. The Zoo Cafeteria at 11 a.m. on August 1st was solemnly agreed.

They turned for a final wave, Effi still a little nervous as they walked past the empty guardroom and out through the iron archway. Further down Schulstrasse other former detainees could be seen heading south towards the city centre under the slate grey sky.

A light rain was falling, but had stopped by the time they reached Wedding Station. Effi's suitcase had never been searched, and she still had the small, refugee-like wad of Reichsmarks that she had taken to Fürstenwalde. But she could not spend the money on transportation – only those with red passes were now permitted to travel on the U-Bahn, the old woman in the booking office told her apologetically. And the same was apparently true for trams, not that any seemed to be running. She and Rosa would have to walk.

The shortest way to the Bismarck Strasse flat ran north of the Tiergarten through Moabit, a part of the city that Effi didn't really know. She opted for simplicity; they would head straight for the city centre and then west along the southern rim of the park. It would add a couple of kilometres to the walk, but remove any chance of their getting lost.

They started down Reinickendorfer Strasse, heading for the junction with Chaussee Strasse. There were more people on the street now, and a large queue spilling out of the old market hall. There was a vibrant buzz of conversation and no shortage of smiles on the women's faces, which both surprised and heartened Effi. Had something good happened? Had Hitler finally thrown in the towel? She thought about crossing the street to ask, but decided not to bother – peace, when it came, would hardly need announcing.

There were similar queues on Chaussee Strasse, and signs that the war was close by. Around twenty *Hitlerjugend* rode past them on bicycles, heading north with rocket-launchers strapped to their handlebars. The leading pair of boys were chatting gaily with each other, and might have been on a pre-war exercise, but most of their followers looked sick with fear. A little farther on, outside the barracks which book-ended the fortress-like Wedding police HQ, a company of *Volkssturm* was forming up. They all wore the relevant armbands, but their uniforms were anything but, a mish-mash of colours, styles and suitable sizes. A battalion of scarecrows, Effi thought, in more ways than one. The Russians would roll right over them.

Rosa walked alongside her, showing no sign of tiredness, eyes devouring the sights. This was probably only her fourth or fifth trip outside in years, Effi thought. No wonder she was curious.

Several women walking in the opposite direction gave them a passing glance, and one gave Rosa a big smile, but that was all the attention they received. Effi began to relax and accept the reality of their release. They really did look like ordinary Berliners; no one was going to point a finger at them and scream out 'Jews!' or 'Traitors!'.

But there was no point in pushing their luck. As they approached the junction with Invaliden Strasse, Effi saw that a barricade was being erected on the road ahead, and instinctively altered course to avoid it. She might have Dobberke's release certificates in her pocket, but their validity was another matter. By this time the man might be under arrest for disobeying his murderous orders.

Invaliden Strasse was almost empty, and so was Luisen Strasse. A number of fires were burning in the half demolished Charité Hospital complex, and several buildings on the other side of the street were smouldering. Organ music was coming from somewhere, suitably funereal against a background crackle of flames. They passed several corpses, some apparently untouched, others charred and riven.

The carnage continued beyond Karl Strasse. A headless woman lay twisted in the street a few metres short of the S-Bahn bridge, but Effi could see no sign of the head. There was a bicycle though, which the woman must have been riding. It was a man's machine, with a crossbar which Rosa might perch on, and a frame at the back for carrying their luggage. Effi stood it up and spun the wheels. It seemed fine.

Turning in search of Rosa, she saw the girl staring down at the headless corpse, making drawing motions with her right hand. It was how she distanced herself, Effi realised. Drawing the world kept it at bay.

'Rosa,' she said, breaking the spell. 'Come here.'

The girl did as she was told, her eyes brightening at the sight of the bicycle.

'We're going to see if we can both get on this,' Effi told her. Two suitcases were impossible, so she forced as much as she could into one, and tied it shut with a rope of torn clothing. She lifted herself onto the seat, helped the girl onto the crossbar, and set the wheels rolling. The first few metres seemed a trifle perilous, but soon they were gathering speed and approaching the Marschall Bridge.

In 1941 they had all watched Udet's funeral procession from the side of this bridge, Paul angry at his father for being English, Russell angry with his son for making him give the Nazi salute. Now the bridge itself was half gone, with only one lane open and men at work below, probably wiring the rest for destruction. She expected to be stopped, but the guards on the bridge just waved them through, one throwing Rosa a kiss.

She pedalled on down towards Unter den Linden, turning right past the walled-up Adlon as a queue of men bearing laden stretchers filed in through the makeshift entrance. The Zoo Bunker flak towers loomed in the distance; the whole Tiergarten seemed, from Pariserplatz, like a military camp. She continued on down Hermann Göring Strasse, intent on following the road that formed the southern boundary of the park, and was just approaching the turning when she heard it – a whistling sound that rapidly gathered pitch and volume as it turned into a scream. A split-second later the earth in the adjacent park erupted, showering them both with fragments of soil and grass.

As Effi applied the brakes another screech ended with flames leaping out of a nearby government building. These weren't bombs, she realised. They were artillery shells. The Russians had brought their guns within range.

Another one landed in the road behind her, drawing a squeak of alarm from Rosa. Yet another exploded in the Tiergarten, spinning an already bomb-damaged tree up into the air. The shells were arriving every few seconds, and in a seemingly random pattern. They had to find shelter, and quickly.

The large bunker under Potsdam Station seemed the nearest. Effi resumed pedalling, pushing her weary legs faster and faster, weaving her way through rubble as the world exploded around her. Potsdamer Platz hardly seemed to draw any nearer, and she found herself wondering if she would even feel a blast that blew her off the bicycle. Would someone find her headless body by the side of the road?

As she reached the top of the square two shells smashed into buildings on the western side, sending out gouts of flame. A car was on fire in the middle, people screaming on the pavements away to her left, but she rode straight on, swerving between still-moving victims and heading straight for the steps that led down to the shelter. Reaching it, they both leapt off, and Effi frantically untied their suitcase. She was reluctant to leave the bicycle, but knew how crowded the shelter would be. Letting it drop, she grabbed the suitcase and hustled Rosa down the steps.

She'd been in this bunker once before, when an early air raid had caught her between trams in the square above. There had been a lot of rooms, some the size of school assembly halls, with electric lighting, pine chairs and tables, and a reasonable number of clean, working toilets. People had sat around having picnics, and made jokes about the feebleness of the British bombing.

That was then. Now furniture and lights were gone, the population had risen ten-fold, and no one was making jokes. Effi led Rosa deeper into the labyrinth, hoping for a space to sit down in. They passed a couple of blocked toilets, and several corners used for the same purpose. The smell was appalling.

All the rooms were full of people. Most were women, but there were some old men and a fair number of small children. They sat or lay in mostly silent misery, their suitcases beside them, often attached to their wrists with string.

The corridors and stairways were also heavily populated, except for those that connected the underground hospital to the outside world. These had to be kept clear for the stretcher-bearers. Two *Hitlerjugend* patrolled them, moving on anyone who tried to settle.

Eventually they found a place, a niche off the cleared corridor where residence was apparently permitted. The previous tenants, their nearest neighbours told them, had just been taken away. The baby had died of hunger, and the mother had tried to stab herself with a shard of broken glass. She'd been taken to the hospital.

Effi leant back against the wall, and enfolded Rosa in her arms. 'At least we're safe,' she whispered.

'I'm all right,' Rosa said, then repeated the phrase, just to be sure.

'Good,' Effi murmured, and gave the girl a squeeze. They'd be here for a while, she told herself. She wouldn't take Rosa back outside until the shelling had stopped, and why would it stop before the fighting was over? The Russians seemed unlikely to run out of ammunition, and she couldn't see the Wehrmacht pushing them back out of range.

When Paul awoke the daylight was almost gone, and a tall figure was leaning over him, gently shaking his shoulder.

'Hello, Paul,' the man said.

He recognised the voice before the face. 'Uncle Thomas!' he exclaimed, throwing off the greatcoat and scrambling to his feet. They looked at each other, burst out laughing, and embraced.

'Come, let's sit down,' Thomas said, indicating one of the cast-iron seats that lined the river promenade. 'I'm much too tired to stand up.' He took off his helmet, unbuttoned his coat, and lowered himself wearily onto the seat.

He looked a lot older than Paul remembered. They had last met three years ago, when his uncle had tried to defend his father, and he had refused to listen. How old was Thomas now – fifty, fifty-one? His hair, cut back almost to nothing, had gone completely grey, and the lines on his face had multiplied and deepened. But the deep brown eyes still harboured mischief – Uncle Thomas had always found something to laugh at, even in times like these.

'What are you doing here?' he asked Paul.

'God knows,' Paul replied. My unit was overrun on the Seelow Heights.

The usual story – too little ammo and too much Ivan. I've been back-pedalling ever since. Looking for my unit.'

'Still in the 20th?'

'What's left of it.'

'And who's that?' Thomas asked, twisting in his seat to look at the sleeping Werner.

'His name's Werner Redlich. I picked him up... no, he picked me up – a couple of days ago. The other boys in his unit all wanted to die for the Führer, but Werner wasn't so sure.'

'How old is he?'

'Fourteen.'

'He looks younger.'

In sleep he did, Paul thought. 'What are you doing here?' he asked his uncle.

'Defending Berlin,' Thomas said wryly. 'I was called up last autumn. They spent several months training us to fight a street battle, then sent us out here to defend a river.' He shrugged. 'The earthworks are good enough, but there's nothing to put in them. No artillery, no tanks, just a bunch of old men with rifles they might have used in the First War. And a few disposable rocket launchers. It would be a farce if it wasn't a tragedy.' He smiled. 'But at least I'm getting some exercise.'

'How are the family?'

'Hanna and Lotte are with Hanna's parents in the country. They should be behind American lines by now.'

'And Joachim?'

'He was killed last summer, in Romania.'

'I'm sorry, I didn't know.'

'Yes. I should have found a way to let you know at the time. But, well, I wasn't thinking too clearly for a while, and then there was the factory to deal with, and then the call-up...'

They sat in silence for a few moments, both staring out across the darkening river.

'What's happening at the factory?' Paul asked eventually. The last he'd heard, the Schade Printing Works was one of the few businesses in Berlin still employing Jews. Thomas had fought a long rearguard action against their deportation, insisting that their expertise was irreplaceable if he was to fulfil his government contracts.

'It's still running,' Thomas said, 'but most of the workers are Russian POWs. The Jews are gone.' He grimaced. 'People always told me it would end badly, and it did.'

'How?'

'Oh, the Gestapo just kept coming back. I don't know whether you knew it at the time, but I was cultivating some pretty disgusting people before your father left. I hoped they would provide me – and the Jews – with some protection. It might even have worked, but the two with the most clout both died in the bombing – and on the same day! A third man was arrested for plotting against the Führer – I couldn't believe it, the man seemed such a shit! And the rest... well, they just refused to stick their miserable necks out. One did give me a day's warning, which helped a great deal. There were about forty Jews still working for me then, and I was able to warn them. Half took the chance to go underground, and didn't turn up for work the next morning. The rest were carted off to God knows where. I assume they were killed.'

Paul said nothing for a moment, remembering a lecture his father had once given him in London about Jews being people too. 'I saw the remains of a camp,' he said slowly. 'In Poland, a place called Majdanek. The SS had flattened all the buildings, and a local woman told us they'd dug up thousands of bodies and burned them. If they did, they did a good job. There was nothing left.'

Thomas sighed.

'We killed them all, didn't we?' Paul said quietly. 'All those we could get our hands on.'

Thomas turned to face him. 'Did you kill any?'

'No, of course not...'

'Then why the "we"?'

'Because.... because I'm wearing a German uniform? I don't really know.'

'The victors will want to. Did the Germans do this, or just the Nazis? – that's what they'll be asking. And I don't think they'll find a simple answer.'

'We voted for him. We knew he hated the Jews.'

'Berlin never voted for him. But yes, a lot of Germans did, and we all knew he hated the Jews. But we didn't know he meant to murder them all. I doubt even he knew it then.'

Paul managed a wry smile. 'It's good to see you, Uncle Thomas.'

'And you.'

'I thought I saw Effi a couple of weeks ago. There was a woman standing on the opposite platform at Fürstenwalde Station – she had a young girl with her. And there was something about the woman. I only caught a glimpse of her before a train came between us, but I could have sworn it was Effi. Of course it wasn't. I expect she's living the high life in Hollywood.'

'Perhaps,' Thomas said. 'There was always a lot more to Effi than most people realised. Your father has been lucky with women,' he mused, 'first my sister, and then her. I expect you miss them both,' he added.

'I do,' Paul said, and felt suddenly ashamed. Uncle Thomas had lost his son and his sister, and his nephew had refused to talk to him for three years. 'The last time I saw you, I behaved like a child' he admitted.

'You were a child,' Thomas said drily.

Paul laughed. 'I know, but...'

'Have you forgiven your father yet? In your own mind, I mean?'

'That's a good question. I don't know.'

Thomas nodded, as if that was the answer he'd expected. 'We may never see each other again – who knows? – so will you listen to what I wanted to tell you that day?'

'All right.'

'Your father abandoned you – there's no denying it. But he had to. If he'd stayed, you'd have had a dead father instead of a missing one.'

'That might have been easier,' Paul said without thinking.

Thomas took it in his stride. 'Yes, for you it might have been. No one would deny that it was hard on you.'

'On all of us,' Paul said.

'Yes, but particularly on you. And then you lost your mother. But Paul, it's time you stopped feeling sorry for yourself. You had a father and a mother who loved you – a father, I'll warrant, who still does – and that's more than a lot of people get in this world. Your father didn't abandon you because he didn't care about you; he didn't leave you because of who he was or who you were. It was the war that divided you; it was politics, circumstance, all that stuff that makes us do the things we do. It had nothing to do with the heart or the soul.'

In the back of Paul's mind a child's voice was still intoning 'but he left me'. 'I do still love him,' he said out loud, suddenly aware that he was fighting back tears.

'Of course you do,' Thomas said simply. 'Shit, I think I'm wanted,' he added, looking over Paul's shoulder. His Volkssturm company seemed to be gathering at the end of the bridge. 'There's always another hole to dig,' he remarked in the old familiar tone as he got rather slowly to his feet. 'It's been wonderful seeing you,' he told Paul.

'And you,' Paul said, throwing his arms around his uncle. 'And you take care of yourself.'

'I'll do my best,' Thomas said, disentangling himself. There was a hint of moisture in his eyes too. 'Don't worry, I have no intention of throwing my life away in a lost cause, particularly this one. I've got Hanna and Lotte to think about. I shall surrender the first chance I get.'

'Choose your moment. And your Russian, if you can.'

Thomas gave him an approving look. 'I shall remember that,' he said. He smiled once more, then turned, one hand briefly raised in farewell, and walked away down the promenade.

After almost twelve hours in the shelter Effi was beginning to wonder whether she'd exaggerated the dangers of the outside world. Perhaps the shelling stopped at night, or at least grew less intense. Perhaps they could try to get home in the hour before dawn.

Or perhaps she was being foolish: hunger and lack of sleep were unlikely to be improving her judgement. But how could they survive here, without even water?

'Effi?' a voice asked, sounding both surprised and pleased.

Startled, she raised her eyes to a familiar face. 'Call me Dagmar,' she whispered. The woman might denounce her, but there seemed no reason she should do so by accident. Effi had met Annaliese Huiskes almost four years ago. She had been a staff nurse at the Elisabeth Hospital, and Effi had been one of the film stars who had volunteered to visit the hospital's swelling population of wounded soldiers. Over the weeks of their acquaintance the two women had discovered a shared taste for hospital-flavoured pure alcohol and a shared disgust for the war.

'Dagmar?' Annaliese said, amusement in her voice. 'Is it really you, Dagmar?'

Effi smiled back. 'It is.' It was, she realised, an enormous relief to be who she really was.

'How did you end up here?' Annaliese asked, squeezing herself into the niche as a stretcher party went past. There was just enough space for her to sit down.

'A long story,' Effi told her. 'But we were just outside when the shelling started. This is Rosa, by the way,' she added, as the sleeping girl shifted her body.

'Your daughter?'

'No. Just someone I'm looking after. She's an orphan.' Annaliese looked much the same as she had four years earlier – small, blonde and worn-out. But there was something heartening about her, something that hadn't been there in 1941. She was wearing a wedding ring, Effi noticed.

'I hope you're going to stay here,' Annaliese said.

'I don't know. We were on our way home, and this place... If we leave before dawn...'

'Don't. The shelling hasn't stopped since it got dark. And it's not like the bombing, where you get some warning. You'd just be gambling with your lives. And even if you get home... Effi – sorry, Dagmar – you have to think about the Russians now. Have you heard the stories? Well, they're all true. We've had hundreds of women who've been raped, and not just raped – they've been attacked by so many men, and so violently, that many are beyond help. They're just bleeding to death. So stay, see the war out here. It can't be many days now. The Russians are in Weissensee already.'

'I understand what you're telling me...'

'Have you ever done any nursing?' Annaliese interjected.

'Only in movies.'

'Well, how you would like to learn? We're ridiculously short-handed, and what you see makes you want to weep, but there's food and water and we do some good.'

'What about Rosa?'

'She can come too. I forgot to say – you'll also get somewhere to sleep. You'll have to share, but it'll be better than this.'

'Sounds wonderful,' Effi said.

'Okay,' Annaliese said, levering herself back to her feet, 'I'll tell them you're an old friend, and willing to help. I'll be back soon.'

She disappeared up the corridor, leaving Effi wondering about Zarah. If her sister was still out in Schmargendorf, then the Russians would probably get to her before she could. And if Zarah was in a government bunker with Jens, there was no way that Effi could find her. There was nothing more she could do.

Annaliese was true to her word, returning a few minutes later. Effi woke Rosa and introduced her friend, who led them through rooms full of wounded men, and down some stairs to a small room with bare brick walls and two pairs of bunk beds. A single candle was burning in the middle of the floor.

'That bottom one's yours,' Annaliese told here. 'You start in the morning with me. Now I'll get you a little water.'

Rosa sat down on the bed and smiled up at Effi. The smell of shit was weaker here, the smell of blood much stronger. An appropriate spot to see out a war.

Corpse brides

April 22 – 23

Russell could only find one spade in the pitch-black shed, so he sent the Russian back inside, fought his way through the brambles to where he thought Hanna's vegetable patch had been, and began digging. There was little chance of his being heard – the rain and wind would see to that. Not to mention the occasional slam of an exploding shell. It was a night for burying oneself, not atomic secrets.

Varennikov had insisted on a depth of two metres, in case a shell landed on top of his precious papers. Russell decided on a third of that – if the choice was between him getting pneumonia and the Soviets an atomic bomb, he knew damn well which he preferred.

At least it wasn't cold. He dug on, careful to pile the excavated earth alongside the hole. Once he'd gone down a couple of feet – he supposed he still measured digging in English units because of his experience in the trenches – he pulled the papers out from inside Thomas' raincoat and placed them at the bottom of the hole. Varennikov had wrapped them in a piece of oilskin that he'd found in the larder, which should protect them from damp for a couple of weeks.

After a moment's hesitation, he added Gusakovsky's machine pistol to the hoard – a weapon for emergencies was all well and good, but being caught with it would see them both shot as spies.

He shovelled back the earth and tamped it down, first with the spade and then with his feet. The rain seemed to be easing.

After returning the front door key to its hiding place he went back inside.

'You dug two metres already?' Varennikov asked with a lamentable lack of trust.

'At least,' Russell lied. 'The soil is soft here,' he added for good measure. 'Let's go.'

Dawn would be around six, which gave them three hours to cover the ten kilometres. This had seemed like plenty of time, but, as soon became clear, it was not. For one thing, Russell was uncertain of the route – he had driven in from Dahlem on enough occasions in the past, but only along those main thoroughfares which he now wished to avoid. For another, visibility was atrocious. The rain had stopped, but clouds still covered the heavens, leaving reflected fires and explosions as the only real sources of light. It took them more than ninety minutes to reach the inner circle of the Ringbahn, which was less than halfway to their destination.

They saw few signs of life – the occasional glimmer of light seeping out of a basement, a cigarette glowing in the window of a gouged-out house, the sound of a couple making vigorous love in a darkened doorway. Once, two figures crept furtively past on the other side of the street, like a mirror image of themselves. They were in uniform, but didn't appear to be carrying guns. Deserters most likely, and who could blame them?

As Russell and Varennikov entered Wilmersdorf, the sky began to break up, and patches of starlight emerged between fast-moving clouds. This offered easier movement, but only at the price of enhanced visibility. They narrowly avoided two uniformed patrols by the fortunate expedient of seeing them first – in each case a flaring match betrayed the approaching authorities, giving them time to slip into the shadows. As dawn approached an increasing numbers of military lorries, troop carriers and mounted guns could be seen and heard on the main roads. Everyone, it seemed, was hurrying to get under cover.

Once in Schöneberg, Russell felt surer of directions. He followed a street running parallel to the wide Grunewald Strasse, on which he and Ilse had lived almost twenty years earlier, and passed what was left of the huge Schöneberg tram depot, before turning up towards Heinrich von Kleist Park, where Paul had taken his faltering first steps. The park was in use as some sort of military assembly area, but a short detour brought them to Potsdamer Strasse a few hundred metres south of where Russell had intended. At the end of a facing side street the elevated tracks leading north towards Potsdam Station were silhouetted against the rapidly lightening sky.

The sprawling goods complex was a few hundred metres up the line. Russell had visited the street-level offices once before, accompanying Thomas in search of some printing machinery supposedly en route from the Ruhr. On that day the areas beside and under the tracks had been choked with lorries, but the only vehicles in sight on this particular morning were bomb victims. One lorry had lost the front part of its chassis, and seemed to be kneeling in prayer.

Russell found it hard to believe that anyone would still be working in the goods station – what, after all, could still be coming in or out of Berlin? And it was only six-fifteen in the morning. But he followed the signs to the dispatch office, Varennikov meekly in tow. And lo and behold, there was a Reichsbahn official in neat uniform, two candles illuminating the ledger over which his pencil was poised. After their long night walk across the broken city, the normality seemed almost surreal.

The official looked up as they entered, surprise on his face. Customers of any kind had doubtless become rare, let alone men in foreign worker uniforms. 'Yes?' he asked, with a mixture of nervousness and truculence.

'We've been sent by the Air Ministry,' Russell began. 'Our boss was told last week that a shipment of paintings had arrived from Königsberg, but he hasn't received them. If you could check that they're here, a vehicle can be sent to collect them. I was told to say that our boss has already spoken to Diehls.'

Comprehension dawned on the official's face, causing Russell to breathe a sigh of relief. 'We were told to expect you,' the man continued, in a tone that suggested they hadn't believed it. He came out from behind his desk and shook their hands. 'Please, come with me.'

He took a flashlight from his desk, led them out through the back of the building and up a steep iron stairway to rail level. The rising sun had barely cleared the distant rooftops, but the smoke from explosions and fires had already turned it into a dull red ball. As they walked by a line of gutted carriages a shell landed a few hundred metres further down the viaduct, but their guide showed no reaction, ducking under a coupling and crossing a series of tracks to enter a huge and now roofless depot. Inside, the loading platforms were lined with what had once been wagons, and now looked more like firewood. Another shell exploded, closer this time, and Russell was glad to take another staircase down, their guide using his flashlight to illuminate the abandoned office complex beneath the tracks. More stairs and they were actually underground, which had to be an improvement. A corridor led past a row of offices still in apparent use, though none had human occupants. Two more turnings and they reached a half open door, which their guide put his head around. 'The men for the Königsberg paintings,' Russell heard him say.

There was the sound of a chair scraping back, and the door opened wide. 'Come in, come in,' their new host said, suppressed excitement in his voice. He was also wearing a Reichsbahn uniform, but was much younger than their guide. No more than thirty-five, Russell guessed.

'I am Stefan Leissner,' he said, offering his hand.

'This is Ilya Varennikov,' Russell said. 'He doesn't speak much German.' He introduced himself. 'We had two companions, but they were both killed.'

'How?' Leissner asked. He looked shocked, as if the notion that Soviet officials were mortal had not occurred to him.

'In an air raid. They were unlucky.'

'I am very sorry to hear that. But it is good to see you, comrades. I hope your mission has proved successful.'

'I think so,' Russell told him. He had no idea whether Leissner knew what their mission had been, and decided that he probably didn't – the NKVD were not known for their chattiness. 'And you are able to hide us until the Red Army arrives?'

'Yes, of course.' Leissner looked at his watch. 'And I should take you to... your quarters, I suppose. I doubt whether many will come to work today, and those that do will mostly be comrades, but there is no point in taking risks. Come.'

Their original guide had been outside, presumably keeping watch. Dismissed, he walked back down the corridor, his flashlight beam dancing in front of him, while Leissner turned the other way, and quickly brought them to the top of a spiral staircase. 'You go down first,' he said, shining his torch to show them the way. When they all reached the bottom, the flashlight revealed two pairs of still-shining tracks – they were in a small lobby adjoining a railway tunnel.

'This is the S-Bahn line that runs under Potsdam Station and north towards Friedrichstrasse,' Leissner explained, stepping down onto the sleepers. 'There are no services on this line anymore, just a few hospital trains stabled beneath Budapester Strasse.' He set off alongside the tracks, assuring them over his shoulder that the electricity was off. The tunnel soon widened, platforms appearing on either side. They climbed up, and turned in through a corridor opening. Tiny feet scurried away from the questing flashlight beam, awakening memories of the trenches which Russell would rather forget. Much to his relief, they went up another spiral staircase, emerging into a wide hall with a high ceiling. The old skylights had been covered over, but light still glinted round the edges.

A door led through to a large room, in which several camp beds had been set up. There was water, cans of food and a bucket toilet. For illumination there were candles, matches, and a railway headlamp. 'It's only for a few days,' Leissner said apologetically. 'And it should be safe. The only way in is the one we used – the old station entrance was bricked up before the First War. A comrade will stand guard in the tunnel – if you need anything, just go down and tell him. The army might decide to flood the tunnels by blowing up the roof where it passes under the Landwehrkanal, but that wouldn't be a problem for you. Not for long, in any case. You wouldn't be able to get out until the waters went down again, but you'd still be fine up here.' He lit one of the candles, and dribbled wax onto to the tiled floor to hold it upright. 'There,' he said, 'just like home.'

It was almost light when Paul awoke. He had spent most of the last twelve hours under their tank, catching up on the sleep he was owed. Ivan's planes had provided several unwanted alarms, but his own thoughts hadn't kept him awake, as had happened all too often of late. And he knew he had Uncle Thomas to thank for that. It was incredible how calming simple decency could be.

He slid himself out from under the Panzer IV's exhaust, and found that a light rain was falling. He clambered up the low embankment behind which the tank was positioned, and walked across to the promenade parapet. The dark waters of the Dahme slid north towards their meeting with the Spree, and a host of shadows were streaming across the Lange Bridge. All German, all civilian, as far as he could tell.

Looking round for Werner, he saw the boy walking towards him with a mug of something hot, and had a sudden memory of 'Orace, the breakfast-serving batman in many of the Saint books. He had loved those stories.

'There's a canteen in Köllnischerplatz,' Werner said, offering him the mug, 'but they've run out of food.'

Church bells were ringing away to the west, faint and somehow sad. As they listened to the distant tolling, Paul realised that the sounds of war had died away. Could peace have been declared?

Seconds later, a machine-gun opened up in the distance, leaving him absurdly disappointed.

'Do you believe in God?' Werner asked.

'No,' Paul said. His parents had both been convinced atheists, and even his conservative stepfather had never willingly set foot in a church. In fact, though it pained him to admit it, one of the things his younger self had most admired about the Nazis was their contempt for Christianity.

'Me neither,' Werner said, with far too much assurance for a fourteen-year-old. 'But my mother does,' he added. 'My granddad was a chaplain in the First War. He used to say that people always behave better when they believe in something more powerful than themselves, so long as that something isn't other people.'

'Words of wisdom,' Paul murmured.

'He was a clever man,' Werner agreed. 'He used to tell me bedtime stories when I was really young. He just made them up as he went along.'

The eastern sky was lightening, the drizzle easing off. There were men at work under the bridge, Paul noticed. Planting charges, no doubt. He was still watching them when a Soviet biplane flew low up the river, and opened fire with its machine-gun. Several men dropped into the sluggish current, but Paul couldn't tell whether they'd been hit or simply taken evasive action. At almost the same moment the first shells of an artillery barrage also hit the water, sending up huge plumes of spray. They had no doubt been aimed at the western bank, and he and Werner made the most of their luck, hurrying for cover while the Soviet gunners fine-tuned their range. They were still scrabbling their way under the tank when a shell landed on the stretch of promenade which they had just abandoned.

The barrage, which only lasted a few minutes, set a pattern for the rest of the day. Every half-hour or so the invisible Soviet guns would launch a few salvoes, then fall silent again. In between time, Soviet bombers and fighters would appear overhead, bombing and strafing whatever took their fancy. The only sign of the Luftwaffe was a sorry-looking convoy of ground personnel, who had been sent forward to the fighting front from their plane-less airfields.

The German tanks, guns and supporting infantry were well dug in, and there were, for once, few casualties. As far as Paul could tell, the German forces in and around Köpenick were strong enough to give Ivan at least a pause for thought. There were more than a dozen tanks, several of them Tigers, and upwards of twenty artillery pieces of varying modernity. If Paul's tank was anything to go by, they were all likely to be low on fuel and shells, but Ivan couldn't know that. And if he wanted to find out, he first had to cross a sizable river.

The bridge was finally blown in mid-afternoon, the centre section dropping into the river with a huge 'whumpf'. It was neatly done, Paul thought – the Wehrmacht had certainly honed a few skills in its thousand-mile retreat.

Russell's watch told him it was almost seven o'clock – he had slept for nine hours. He didn't regret it – he had needed the rest, and the middle of the day seemed far too dangerous a time to be wandering the streets. After dark seemed a much better bet, although Leissner might have other advice. Now he came to think about it, the Reichsbahn man might be reluctant to let him go. He would have to persuade Leissner that Varennikov was the one that mattered, the prize the Red Army would be hoping to collect.

He fumbled around for the matches and lit a candle. The Russian kept on snoring, which wasn't surprising – he'd had even less sleep than Russell over the last few days. After Leissner had left them that morning, Varennikov had asked Russell over and over whether he thought they could trust the Reichsbahn official. Was there any reason they shouldn't? Russell had asked him. There was, it turned out, only one. The man was a German.

Internationalism had not, it seemed, taken root in Soviet soil.

Feeling hungry, Russell drank some cold soup from one of the billycans. Its tastelessness was probably its primary virtue, but he certainly needed some sort of sustenance.

Taking the candle with him, he descended the spiral staircase. The flickering went ahead of him, and the lookout was already on his feet when Russell reached the platform. Leissner was either very efficient or very determined not to lose his prize. Or both. He probably had hopes of an important post in a new communist Germany.

'I need to talk to Comrade Leissner,' Russell said.

The man thought about that for several moments. 'Wait here,' he said eventually, and disappeared up the tunnel.

He returned five minutes later. 'You can go up to his office. You remember the way?'

Russell did.

Leissner was waiting at the top of the stairs. He ushered Russell into the office, and carefully closed the door behind them. 'Just habit,' he explained, seeing Russell's face. 'Only a handful of people came in today, and they've all gone home. For the duration, I expect. It can't be long now,' he added with a broad smile. 'It really is over.'

Not quite, Russell thought, but he didn't say so. He had only known this particular comrade for a few hours, but his expectations of the Soviets were likely to be somewhat overblown. Leissner had probably joined the KPD in the late 1920s when he was still a teenager, and spent the Nazi years concealing his true allegiance. His looks would have helped – blonde hair, blue eyes and a chiselled face were never a handicap in Nazi Germany – but living a double life for that length of time could hardly have been easy, and he would certainly have become adept at deception.

But, by the same token, a life spent down the enemy's throat provided one with few opportunities to learn about one's friends. For men like Leissner, the Soviet Union would have been like a long-lost father, a vessel to fill with uncritical love.

'How can I help you?' the German asked.

'I have to find someone, and I'm hoping you can help me,' Russell began.

'Who?' Leissner asked.

'My wife,' Russell said simply, ignoring the detail of their never marrying. 'When I left three years ago, she stayed. I'm hoping she might still be living in the same place, and I need to know the safest way to get there.'

Leissner had lost his smile. 'I don't think that would be wise. The Red Army will be here in a few days...'

'I want to reach her before... before the war does,' Russell said diplomatically.

Leissner took a deep breath. 'I'm sorry, but I'm afraid I can't allow you to leave. What if you were caught by the Gestapo, and they tortured you? You would tell them where Varennikov was. I don't say this to impugn your bravery of course.'

'But this is my wife,' Russell pleaded.

'I understand. But you must understand – I must put the interests of the Party above those of a single individual. In the historical scheme of things, one person can never assume that sort of importance.'

'I agree completely,' Russell lied. 'But this is not just a personal matter. My wife has been working undercover in Berlin since 1941, and the leadership in Moscow wishes her to survive these last days of the war. My orders,' he went on, with slightly greater honesty, 'were to bring Varennikov to you, and then do what I could to find her.'

'Can you prove that?' Leissner asked.

'Of course,' Russell said, pulling from his pocket Nikoladze's letter of introduction to the Red Army. If Leissner could read Russian he was sunk, but he couldn't think of anything better.

Leissner stared at the paper. He couldn't read it, Russell realised, but he wasn't going to admit it. 'All right,' he said at last. 'Where do you hope to find your wife?'

'The last place she lived was in Wedding. On Prinz Eugen Strasse. How would I get there? Is the U-Bahn still running?'

'It was yesterday, at least as far as Stettin Station. Your best bet would be to walk through the tunnels below here as far as Friedrichstrasse, then catch a U-Bahn if there is one, walk if there isn't. But I don't know how far south the front line has moved. The Red Army was still north of the Ringbahn this morning, but...' He shrugged.

'It'll be obvious enough on the ground,' Russell reassured him. Rather too obvious, if he was unlucky.

'But you can't go through the tunnels dressed like that,' Leissner insisted. 'The SS are all over the place, and they won't take kindly to a foreign worker wandering around on his own. I'll get you a Reichsbahn uniform from somewhere. I'll send it down to you before morning.'

'Would dawn be the best time to go? Are there any times of day when the shelling is less intense?'

'No, it is more or less constant,' Leissner told him. He seemed proud of the fact.

The pieces of the broken bridge had barely settled on the bed of the Dahme when the first Soviet tanks appeared on the river's eastern bank, drawing yells of derision and an almost nostalgic display of firepower from the German side. It seemed too good to last, and it was. As darkness fell, signs of battle lit the northern and southern horizons, and less than an hour had passed when news of a Soviet crossing a few kilometres to the south filtered through the few barely coordinated units defending Köpenick. No order was issued by higher authority for the abandonment of the position, but only a few diehards doubted that such a move was necessary, and soon a full withdrawal was underway.

A gibbous moon was already high in the sky, and their driver had few problems manoeuvring the Panzer IV across the wide stretch of heath that lay to the west of the river. At first their intention was to follow the line of the Spree, but numerous battles were clearly raging on the eastern bank, and it seemed more prudent to drive west, through Johannisthal, before turning north. Another stretch of moonlit heathland brought them to the Teltowkanal, and they headed north alongside it, looking for a bridge across. The first two had already been destroyed, but sappers were still fixing charges to the third as they drove up. Once across, they found themselves among the houses of Berlin's southern outskirts.

Soon after midnight they emerged from a side street onto the wide Rudower Strasse, which stretched north toward Neukölln and the city centre. It was full of people and vehicles, military and civilian, almost all heading north. The edges of the road were littered with those who would go no further – a dead man still seated at the wheel of his roofless car, a whimpering horse with only two legs. And every now and then a Soviet plane would dive out of the moon, and release a few souls more.

And there were other killers on the road. A gang of SS walked by in the opposite direction, their leader scanning each passing male. A few hundred metres up the road, Paul saw evidence of their work – two corpses swaying from makeshift gallows with pale anguished faces and snapped necks, each bearing the same roughly-scrawled message – 'We still have the power.' Looking ahead down the long wide road, Paul could see the taller buildings of the distant city centre silhouetted by the flash of explosions. The Soviet gunners had got there before them.

Their tank was crossing the Teltowkanal for the second time when its engine began coughing for lack of fuel, and the driver barely had time to get it off the bridge before it jerked to a halt. Not that it mattered anymore – the Teltowkanal, which arced its way across southern Berlin, was the latest defence line that had to be held at all costs, and strengthening the area around the bridge was now the priority. While the tank commander went off in search of a tow, his grenadiers were put to work digging emplacements in the cemetery across the road. It was gone two when they were finally allowed to stretch out on the wet ground and try to snatch some sleep.

It was a three-kilometre hike through the S-Bahn tunnels to Friedrichstrasse. As Russell walked northward many slivers of light – even beams in places – shone down through the cut-and-cover ceiling. This evidence of bomb and shell damage didn't inspire much confidence in the integrity of the tunnel, but the thin grey light allowed him to walk at his usual pace, and it only took about twenty minutes to reach the S-Bahn platforms underneath Potsdam Station. These were lined with people, most still sleeping, others staring listlessly into space. No one seemed surprised by his appearance in the borrowed Reichsbahn uniform, but he stopped to take a close look at the track in several places, as he had once seen a real official do. Up above, the Soviet artillery seemed unusually fierce, and one near-miss caused a shower of dust to descend from the ceiling. A few heads were anxiously raised, but most people hardly stirred.

The next section was the worst. As he moved north, the smell of human waste grew stronger in his nostrils; a little further on, and he was picking up the metallic odour of blood. The stationary hospital trains had only just become visible in the distance when he heard the first scream, and not long after that the lower, more persistent groaning of the wounded soldiers on board became increasingly audible. It sounded like Babelsberg's idea of a slave's chorus, only the pain was real.

The trains seemed barely lit, and there was no way of knowing what sort of care their passengers were getting. The only person Russell saw was a young and rather pretty nurse, who was seated on some vestibule steps, puffing on a cigarette. She looked up when she heard him coming, and gave him a desolate smile.

The tunnel soon curved to the right. He guessed it passed under the Adlon Hotel, where he'd spent so many hours of his pre-war working life. He wondered if the building was still standing.

Unter den Linden Station suggested otherwise. Large chunks of sky were visible in several places, and no one was using the rubble-strewn platforms for shelter. By contrast, the long curve round towards Friedrichstrasse was the darkest section so far, and when he heard music drifting down the tunnel he thought he must be imagining it. But not for long. For one thing, it grew steadily louder; for another, it was jazz.

As he reached the Friedrichstrasse platforms he could hear the music quite clearly: the players were somewhere close by in the subterranean complex beneath the main-line station. Many of those camping out on the platforms were obviously enjoying it, feet tapping to the rhythm, smiles on their faces. He had seen nothing stranger in six years of war. Or more heartening.

He followed several corridors to reach the U-Bahn booking hall. The trains were still running all the way to See Strasse, which seemed another small miracle – the terminus couldn't be that far from the front line. Russell waited while a woman pleaded in vain for permission to travel – her eighty-five-year-old mother was alone in her Wedding apartment, and needed help to get out before the Russians arrived. The man on the barrier was sympathetic but adamant – only people with official red passes were allowed on the trains. As she walked despairingly away Russell flashed the one that Leissner had loaned him, and hurried down to the U-Bahn platforms.

He needn't have bothered. The trains might be running, but not with any regularity, and if the rats playing between the tracks were any judge, an arrival wasn't imminent. When a train did arrive an hour or so later, the front four carriages were already packed with old-looking soldiers, presumably en route to the front. Russell squeezed into one of the others, almost losing his Reichsbahn cap in the mêlée.

The train must have stopped a dozen times in the tunnels between stations, and on each occasion Russell feared an announcement that it would go no further. He and his fellow-passengers were finally told as much after the train had sat at the Wedding platform for almost half an hour. This was not the nearest station to Prinz Eugen Strasse, but it was not that far away. As he walked up the platform towards the exit he noticed that the Volkssturm were not getting off, and that the front half of the train was being uncoupled for further progress up the line.

As he climbed the stairs towards street level the sounds of the war grew louder, and by the time he emerged onto Müller Strasse it was clear that the fighting front could only be a few kilometres away. The sudden detonation of several artillery shells a few hundred metres up the street was encouraging, implying, as it did, that no Soviet units had yet penetrated the area. The last thing Russell wanted to meet was a T-34.

Haste, he decided, was probably more important than caution. He walked swiftly up the eastern side of Müller Strasse, conscious of how empty this part of the city seemed. Most people would be in their basements, he supposed, just waiting for the Russians. Those still working in the city centre would be sleeping in their offices, not commuting through shellfire.

As he crossed Gericht Strasse he caught a glimpse of the Humboldthain flak towers, which had still been under construction when he left Berlin. The main tower was giving and receiving fire, its guns pumping shells towards the distant suburbs, while incoming Soviet rounds exploded on impact with the thick concrete walls to little apparent effect. The whole edifice was wreathed in smoke, like a wizard's castle.

He took the next turning, and soon reached the intersection with Prinz Eugen Strasse. The block containing the apartment that Effi had rented as a possible bolthole was down to the right. Or had been. There was only a field of rubble there now. The neighbouring block had lost an entire wall, leaving several storeys of rooms open to the air, but Effi's had been razed to the ground. And not recently, Russell realised with some dismay. He was sure she'd come back here, but how long had she stayed?

Each pair of blocks had its own shelter, he remembered. As he strode along the street to the next entrance, a shell exploded behind a block on the other side, throwing what looked like half a tree into the air. He broke into a run, reaching the shelter of a courtyard just as another shell landed somewhere behind him. Taking the steps to the shelter two at a time, he suddenly found himself the object of numerous stares.

The Reichsbahn uniform was obviously reassuring, and most of the shelter's occupants wasted no time in returning to what they'd been doing. One old woman continued smiling at him for no apparent reason, so he walked across to her.

'My husband used to wear that uniform,' she told him.

'Ah.'

'And before you ask – no, he wasn't killed in this war. He didn't live to see it, the lucky old sod.'

Russell laughed, then remembered why he was there. 'Can you tell me when the block across the street was bombed?' he asked.

'Autumn of '43,' she said. 'I can't remember the month. Did you know someone who lived there?'

'Yes.'

'No one survived, I'm afraid. The whole building came down, and went right through the basement ceiling. They were digging for days, but they didn't find anyone alive.'

Russell felt cold spreading across his chest, as if his heart was a heat-pump and someone had just switched it off. He told himself that she'd probably moved out long before, that the Effi he knew would never have settled for simply waiting out the war. She had to be alive. Had to be.

He went back up to the street, and began retracing his steps towards Wedding Station. Shells were now landing several blocks to the north, which was just as well, because he was in the mood for tempting fate. If she was gone, then Berlin could have him splashed across its walls.

But he couldn't really believe that she was. And if she wasn't, then how the hell was he going to find her? Where else could he go, who else could he ask?

As he approached the station he suddenly remembered Uwe Kuzorra, the police detective who had helped him escape in 1941, and who lived only half an hour's walk away. He would have access to state records, to lists of bomb victims, and of those arrested.

No, Russell told himself. If Kuzorra was still working for the police, he wouldn't be at home. And if he wasn't, then he wouldn't be able to help. There was no point.

Heading underground once more, he wondered who else he could go to. The only person he could think of was Jens. At least he knew that Jens was still in Berlin. He might know something, and if Russell had to beat it out of him, he was more than willing to do so.

The train at the platform eventually pulled out, but had only reached Oranienburger Strasse when its journey was abruptly cut short. Russell had sometimes used this stop when visiting the Blumenthals in 1941, and felt a pang at the memory. Martin and Leonore were almost certainly dead, but their daughter Ali had always said she would rather go underground than accept a Gestapo invitation to the east. If she had, she might still be alive. There had been a lot of decent 'aryans' in Berlin before the war, and Russell was willing to bet that some would have offered their Jewish friends a helping hand.

Two other memories caught up with him as he walked down the stretch of Friedrichstrasse that lay between the Spree and the railway bridge. First he came to Siggi's Bar, half in ruins and boarded over; it was there that he'd waited for Effi on that terrible evening, believing that he'd never see her or Paul again. And there, on the other side of the street, was the model shop that he and Paul had often visited, with the proprietor who never tired of talking about his customer, the Reichsmarschal. That too was boarded up, and so, Russell guessed, was Goering's hunting lodge out at Karinhall, where the Reich's largest model railway was reputedly laid out. Perhaps the Russians were out there now, playing with the trains. Or perhaps they'd shipped them home to Stalin.

There was no music playing beneath Friedrichstrasse Station, which was something of a disappointment. Down in the tunnel there was nothing to distract him from thoughts of Effi, and the possibility that she had died in Prinz Eugen Strasse. There was not even consolation in the certainty of a quick death – she might have been under the rubble for days.

The hospital trains gave him something else to think about. He remembered that Leissner had talked about a possible flooding of the tunnels, and wondered if any provision had been made for an emergency evacuation of the wounded. Knowing the SS, he doubted it.

Back at their hideaway in the abandoned station, Varennikov looked up from the book he was reading by candlelight. 'No luck,' he deduced from Russell's expression.

'No.'

'I'm sorry,' the Russian said in a heartfelt tone. 'I don't know how I'd survive without my Irina.'

Dawn brought a quickening of the long range artillery attacks, but Paul's area around the Schulenburg Bridge only received a couple of hits. Most of the shells were falling far behind them, on the Old Town, the government quarter and the West End. Either Ivan was having a particularly inaccurate morning, or he was saving the more obvious military targets for when his infantry was poised and waiting on the other side of the canal.

Sent in search of something to eat by his fellow-excavators, Paul ran into soldiers from his own division. There were about forty of them in the immediate vicinity, a lieutenant told him. Their situation had been reported, he said, but they hadn't yet received any new instructions. Until they did, it seemed wisest – he nodded his head in the direction of the SS officer who seemed in overall charge of the Schulenburg Bridge position – to follow the orders of those on the spot.

A mess had been set up in the underground booking hall of the Grenzallee station. It was staffed by local volunteers, women in their forties and fifties with gaunt faces and dead eyes. A huge tureen of soup was all they had to offer, but it smelled and tasted good – the ingredients, one women told him in a whisper – had come from the Karstadt department store on Hermann Strasse, two kilometres up the road. The SS in charge of the adjoining warehouse had been cajoled into releasing some supplies for the fighting men at the front.

Back in the cemetery, Paul shared out the contents of his billycan. There had been a handbill delivery in his absence, and he read through one as he ate. Hitler, it seemed, was actually in Berlin, and still directing the military traffic. And General Wenck was on his way to relieve the capital. According to the Führer Order reprinted as part of the leaflet, 'Wenck's Army' had been summoned to Berlin's aid, and was now approaching the city. 'Berlin is waiting for you! Berlin longs for you with all its heart!' the order concluded. It sounded like some idiot hero in a Babelsberg weepie.

Paul didn't believe a word of it, and could hardly bear the look of hope on Werner's face.

A couple of hours later, a passing corporal filled them in on the latest news. The Soviet shelling, unlike the Allied air raids which preceded it, was more or less continuous, and those Berliners that could had taken up more-or-less permanent residence in underground shelters of one sort or another. After two whole days of this many had begun to wonder where their food would come from when present supplies ran out. It was no great secret where the authorities had stored the ration supplies, and that morning crowds had gathered outside many of the relevant premises, invading and looting those that were insufficiently guarded.

At the Karstadt department store on Hermann Strasse, the SS were in charge, and seemed intent on blowing up the building rather than leave the Russians such a treasure trove of supplies. The people of Neukölln had turned up en masse, and been grudgingly permitted a few hours to cart away all of the food. Some had taken the opportunity to seize less edible ware, like silk dresses and fur coats, but Karstadt staff had guarded the doors and taken such items back. Having their stock reduced to rubble was obviously preferable to giving it away.

'And there's a big drive on to round up deserters,' the talkative corporal added. 'It started this morning. There are roadblocks everywhere, and gangs of the black bastards are going round the basements. Those they find, they hang, so I advise you all to wait here for Ivan.'

He laughed at his own joke, re-lit the stump of his cigarette, and wandered off down the cemetery path.

It wouldn't be long, Paul thought. Looking around, he could see smoke rising in every direction. Soon this cemetery would erupt all around them, throwing up old corpses, sucking in new. Berlin was waiting for an army all right, but it wasn't Wenck's.

It was mid-afternoon when a private came to fetch him. The largest remnant of his division was deployed four kilometres to the east, where the road to Mariendorf and Lichtenrade crossed over the same canal, and he and his fellow stragglers were to join it at once. The assembly point was outside the Grenzallee U-Bahn station.

'I'm on my way,' Paul said, stabbing his spade into the earth.

'Can I come too?' Werner asked. 'Where you're going is only a few kilometres from my house.'

The SS on the bridge might argue, but only if someone was foolish enough to ask them. 'Okay', he told the boy. After wishing the tank team luck they left the cemetery by the back gate, and worked their through the side streets to the station, where thirty-odd men were scattered across the staircase leading down to the booking hall. The lieutenant looked twice at Werner, but said nothing.

There was no transport, but it was only an hour's march, and still light enough outside for vehicles to be something of a mixed blessing.

The lieutenant fell them in and sent them off in pairs, keeping a decent distance between them to minimise the damage a single shell might do. The first street they walked down was almost intact, but the hospital district on the other side of the Britzer Damm had been almost obliterated, and the area of small streets which lay between the canal and the Tempelhof aerodrome was in equally terrible shape. There were ruins and rubble everywhere, and no sign that anyone was interested in clearing anything up. The few adults they passed looked either angry and resentful or listless and indifferent; the only child they encountered ran alongside them firing an imaginary gun and making the appropriate noises, until Paul felt like shooting him.

It was getting dark by the time they reached the Berliner Chaussee, and another long hour was spent waiting in the deepening cold while the lieutenant sought out the divisional HQ. He found it in the basement of a factory which overlooked the canal basin just east of the Stubenrauch Bridge. The remnants of the division – all 130 of them – were deployed in and around the basin, mostly in other industrial buildings. The division's last four artillery pieces were well dug in and camouflaged, ready for the Soviet onslaught. Paul had been hoping to find a place with one of them, but there was already a waiting list. At least ten men had to die before he got his old job back, and only then if the gun survived its minders.

Still, there was food enough, and old acquaintances to pass the time with. Not everyone had died. Not yet.

The *Hitlerjugend* held his watch up to the kerosene lamp. 'It's after nine,' he told Effi.

She'd lost track of the time, something easy to do in what smelt and felt like the bowels of the earth. She could no longer hear or see the war, but the constant turnover of casualties was proof enough of its continuance. The smell of fresh blood had been with her all day.

The shift had lasted twelve hours. She was working as a nursing assistant, her uniform a bloodstained apron, her tasks mostly menial – fetching and carrying, boiling instruments, cleaning what had to be cleaned with water collected from the pumps outside. Her only close contact with patients lay in bandaging the wounded and trying to comfort the dying.

Rosa had been with her throughout, sometimes helping but mostly just drawing. Effi had no idea what mental and emotional havoc was being wreaked on the already traumatised seven-year-old, but she didn't dare let her out of her sight. She told herself that watching people so intent on saving life must surely have a positive effect, but she didn't really believe it.

The girl seemed okay. They'd just shared a can of sardines and some bread in the room which passed for a hospital staff room, and were sitting at their table, listening to the moans of the wounded next door. The hospital was running out of morphine, and only those in excruciating pain were getting any. Some of the unlucky ones were stoical beyond belief, but most found it easier to groan or scream. Effi had hardly noticed while she was working, but now it made her want to join in.

Annaliese Huiskes sat down beside them. She had somehow got hold of a hot cup of tea, which she offered to share. 'I'm sorry about earlier,' she told Effi in a low voice.

'Don't worry about it,' Effi told her. 'You made a brilliant recovery.' Annaliese had let Effi's real name slip, but answered the questioning looks with an explanation of staggering simplicity. Dagmar had been given that nickname, Annaliese explained, because she looked so much like the film star Effi Koenen.

'The traitor,' one doctor had murmured. Another had denied the resemblance.

'I've been meaning to ask you,' Effi said, gesturing at the ringed finger. 'Did you get married?'

A shadow passed over the other woman's face. 'A corpse marriage,' she said. 'I shouldn't call it that – I hate it when other people use that phrase. But it's more than three years ago. Maybe you'd disappeared by then, but there was a Führer decree allowing women who'd just lost their fiancées to marry them post-mortem. There was a pension included, and that's why I went for it, but I did love Gerd, and I'm sure he'd have seen the funny side of it – marrying me when he was already dead.' She smiled to herself. 'After the war I'll find a real husband. Or try to. I suppose there'll be a shortage of men, and I'm not exactly young any more. What about you? What happened to John?'

'Who's John?' Rosa asked.

'He was my boyfriend. He went away to Sweden, and I hope he'll be back when all this is over.'

'Why shouldn't he be?' Annaliese asked.

'Three and a half years is a long time.'

Annaliese made a face. 'He was crazy about you. I only met him once, but that much was obvious.'

'He was then. But if you're not young any more, what does that make me?' Effi lowered a voice to a whisper. 'Do you know you're the first person who's recognised me in three years?'

'You look different, but your eyes are the same. And you don't look old. I think we'll both look pretty good once we've had some decent food and slept through the night a few times. How about your career? Are you going back to it?'

Effi shrugged. 'Who knows? There aren't many parts for women in their forties.'

Rosa had been paying attention. 'Were you an actress?' she asked in a whisper.

'I was,' Effi admitted. 'Quite a good one.'

After his trip out to Wedding, Russell had felt physically and emotionally exhausted. Lying down for a few hours had given his body some rest, but his brain was too busy contemplating Effi's possible fate for sleep to take over. He had to do something, had to keep on the move. He decided he would go back to Schmargendorf and confront Jens. That evening, after dark.

Once the last hint of light had disappeared from the cracks in the booking hall ceiling, he made his way down to the tunnel. A different comrade was on guard, and saw no problem in Russell seeing his boss. He found Leissner in his office, head bent over a ledger. When the men from Moscow arrived they would all be up-to-date.

The Reichsbahn man greeted Russell with a glimmer of a smile, and raised no objections to another foray. He had realised – or been told – that Varennikov was the one who mattered. Or – perish the thought – Moscow had let it slip that Russell himself was far from indispensable.

Maybe he was being paranoid. Leissner was friendly enough, and seemed more than happy to give him a run-down of the current military situation. The Red Army had breached the Teltowkanal defence line in the south-western suburbs that morning, and were expected in Zehlen-dorf and Dahlem sometime tomorrow. Schmargendorf should still be safe, but only for forty-eight hours.

The U-Bahn, Leissner added, was no longer working – the tunnels were being booby-trapped to prevent the Soviets from using them. And the SS had spent the afternoon setting up lots of checkpoints, particularly in the western half of the city. Russell was unlikely to face summary execution in his Reichsbahn uniform, but now that the trains had stopped running he might be pressed into military service. It would, Leissner suggested, be advisable not to argue.

Russell thanked him, and made his way up and over the elevated tracks to the goods yard entrance. Night had now fallen, and Berlin was bathed in the grim orange glow of cloud-reflected fires. It felt like rain, which might at least put some of them out.

He walked west, keeping clear of the main thoroughfares and inch-ing his head around corners to check what lay ahead. Twice he avoided checkpoints in this manner, carefully working his way around them. And on three other occasions he came upon those who'd not been so careful, who were now swinging from makeshift gibbets with the signatures of psychopaths pinned to their chests.

Incoming shells exploded at irregular intervals as the evening wore on, some as close as a neighbouring street, but there was no point in wor-rying about them. If staying alive was his goal he should have stayed in London.

By the time he reached the Biesinger house in Schmargendorf it was gone ten, and he felt like falling over. It occurred to him that he'd hardly eaten all day, which hadn't been very sensible. If he ever did find Effi, she'd be looking after him.

There were no lights visible through the uncurtained windows, but Jens had his own basement shelter, as befitted a high-ranking Party of-ficial. If he was home, he'd be ensconced down there, probably drown-ing the Reich's many sorrows. Russell hoped he'd be conscious enough to hear the door-knock.

He gave it a mighty series of bangs, which the Russians probably heard in Teltow, and was about to repeat the effort when he heard footsteps. As the door began to open he pushed his way through, forcing a gasp from the person inside. A woman's gasp. It was Zarah.

'What do you... who...'

'It's John,' he told her, shutting the door behind him.

'John?' she exclaimed in astonishment. What are you...'

'It's a long story.'

'I can't believe it. Come downstairs, where we can see each other.'

He followed her down to the cellar. There were camp beds against three of the walls, tables, chairs and armchairs crammed into the centre of the room.

She turned to look at him, and saw the uniform. 'What...?'

'Don't ask. I take it Jens isn't here?'

It wasn't really a question, but she answered with an almost defiant 'no'. She looked different, much thinner than the last time he'd seen her, and her copper hair was cut much shorter. She should have looked less attractive, but there was something in her eyes that hadn't been there before.

'Will he be back tonight?'

'I don't think so. What are *you* doing here?'

'Looking for Effi. I...'

'I don't know where she is,' Zarah said despairingly, as if she should know.

'You've seen her,' Russell said, hope rising inside him.

'Not for almost a month.'

'But you've *seen* her. She's alive.' He felt joy sweep through his head and heart.

'I hope so. She must have been arrested.'

That was an eventuality that Russell hadn't even considered. 'What for?' he asked stupidly.

Zarah smiled ruefully. 'I don't know that either. She has never told me anything about the life she's been living. I know she must be involved in some sort of resistance movement. With the communists, perhaps. I really don't know.'

'But what makes you think she's been arrested?'

'She didn't turn up at our usual time. And she hasn't been in contact since.'

'Yes, but what makes you think she's been arrested?' Russell repeated. 'She might have been hurt in an air raid. Or even killed,' he added, almost against his own will.

'No, I would know,' Zarah insisted. 'John, I know you always thought we were like chalk and cheese – and we are – but there's a bond... I can't explain it, but it's there. Sometimes I've wished it wasn't, and I know Effi has too, but it is. I would *know* if she'd been killed.'

Russell believed her, or wanted to. 'Okay. So you met regularly. Since when?'

'It was the end of April, I think. In 1943. She waylaid me in the cinema, sat down beside me at a matinee on Hardenberg Strasse. I nearly had a heart attack. She sounded just the same, but when the lights came on I found that I'd been talking to an old woman. I don't think I would recognised her if we'd met in the street. Anyway, we went for a walk in the Tiergarten, and she told me everything that had happened, and that you had escaped to Sweden.'

'How did she find that out?'

'I don't know, but she did. She asked me to pass it on to your ex-wife, so that she could tell your son. Which of course I did. And after that we met every two weeks, usually at the same time, but in different places. She soon had another identity, younger than the one before, but still older than her real age. She had her hair cut much shorter, and she just looked different somehow. It was extraordinary. I don't how she does it.'

'Where is she living?'

'She wouldn't tell me. She wouldn't even tell me what name she was using.' Zarah smiled, and for the first time in their long acquaintanceship Russell saw something of Effi in her sister. 'But I found out. I almost ran into her on the street one day, but she didn't see me, and I was afraid I might mess something up if I just went up to her. And then it occurred to me – I could follow her. And I did, all the way to her home. It was an apartment at Bismarck Strasse 185. Number 4.

'I never told her that I'd found out, because I knew it would worry her, my knowing. I used to give her ration stamps and money. She took them, but I never got the feeling she needed them.'

This was wonderful, Russell thought, so much better than he'd feared. Or it had been until three weeks ago. 'So when was this meeting she didn't turn up for?'

'Ten days ago. Friday the 13th.' She wrung her hands. 'I wasn't that worried at the time – it had happened before. But she'd always contacted me within a couple of days and set my mind at rest. So I waited a few days, and then I really did start to worry. I went round to Bismarck Strasse on the Wednesday, and the *portierfrau* told me that she hadn't seen any of them since the previous Thursday. When she said 'them' I thought I'd got the wrong flat, but I managed to get her talking, and it all came out. Frau von Freiwald and her grown-up niece Mathilde had been living there for almost two years, and only the previous week another niece – a small girl – had arrived from Dresden. Frau von Freiwald and the young girl had been there on the Thursday, but no one had seen them since. They must have been arrested, John – Effi wouldn't leave Berlin without telling me. And who are these fictional nieces – have you any idea?'

'None at all. Have you been back there since?'

'Yesterday. There was no one there, and the *portierfrau* still hadn't seen any of them.'

Russell ran a hand through his hair. 'Have you asked anyone... no, silly question – who could you ask? Jens, maybe – did he know you were seeing Effi?'

'No, I couldn't risk telling him. It wasn't that I thought he would turn her in, not really. It was just easier not to, and... well, he's had a lot to deal with lately. Look,' she went on, responding to the look which Russell failed to suppress, 'I know you never liked him...'

'I never liked his politics.'

'No, John, be honest, you didn't like him.'

'Not much, no.'

'I was never interested in politics, and I used to think he was a decent man. He was a good father to Lothar until the war took up all his time.'

'Where is Lothar?'

'With my parents. Effi wouldn't even let me tell them that she was still alive.'

'Why aren't you there too?'

'Why do you think? Lothar's as safe as any German could be, and I had to be here in case Effi needed me.'

'Of course,' Russell said, though until that evening he'd never quite appreciated just how close the sisters were.

'But now that she really needs me, I haven't been able to do anything,' Zarah bitterly admitted. 'I did ask Jens to look into it – I said Erna von Freiwald was an old friend from school who'd recently got in touch, and had then been arrested. I made up a story about her involvement with a group printing leaflets of Pastor Niemöller's speeches – the Christians are the only dissidents Jens has any sympathy for. He promised he would look into it, but I don't think he looked very hard. He discovered there was no one of that name in Lehrter Prison, or in the women's prison on Barnim Strasse. That was yesterday, and when I asked him again today he told me to forget the whole business, that we had our own fates to worry about. And then he showed me these suicide pills he'd gotten hold of, and seemed to think I would shower him with gratitude. 'What about Lothar?' I asked him. 'And do you know what he said? He said Lothar would know that his parents had been "true to the very end". I couldn't stand being with him for a moment longer. I just walked out of his office and came home. I tell you, John, I feel like a corpse bride.'

'So what will you do now?'

'Wait for the Russians, I suppose.'

'That could be dangerous,' Russell replied without any thought. What other choices did she have?

'You mean I might be raped?'

'Yes.'

'Then that's what'll happen, John. I intend to see my son again.'

'That sounds like a very sane way of looking at it.'

'I hope so. But what are you going to do?'

'I came to find Effi. And my son. I'll keep on looking until I do.' He smiled to himself. 'You know Effi rented a flat in Wedding in case we needed to hide from the police?'

'Yes, she told me that.'

'I went up there yesterday, hoping against hope that she might still be there. And the whole building was gone, absolutely flattened, and I thought, well, you can imagine, and my heart seemed to shrivel inside me...'

'She's alive, John, I'm sure she is. We'll get her back'

'I love you for believing that,' he said, and took her in his arms. 'I must get back,' he said after a while. At the outside door they wished each other luck, and Russell had a fleeting memory of standing on the same stoop more than three years earlier, after a drunken Jens had more or less confessed to the deliberate starvation of occupied Russia.

'And here we have the come-uppance,' he murmured to himself, as he began the long walk back. Two more hours of screeching shells and sudden flares, of wending his way through ruins and evading the occasional patrol, and he was back in the abandoned station. Varennikov was already asleep, so Russell pinched out the still-burning candle and laid himself out on his bed. He had probably walked further in the last five days than in all the five years that preceded them, and he felt completely exhausted.

Eyes closed, he suddenly remembered Kuzorra again. If the detective still worked at the 'Alex' police headquarters he would have access to arrest records. But how could he could be contacted?

Yorck Strasse

April 24 – 26

Soon after dawn Ivan announced himself with an artillery barrage, shattering every window that overlooked the Teltowkanal and blinding several of the divisional lookouts. A *katyusha* barrage followed, blasting holes in brickwork, cratering towpaths and sending up huge spouts of water. Fires broke out in several buildings, but were all put out with buckets of canal water collected the previous day. A steady stream of wounded disappeared in the direction of the field hospital three streets to the north.

The two nearest bridges had both been destroyed in the night, but there was still no sign of Soviet tanks on the far bank. They'd lose a lot of men getting across, Paul reckoned, but that had never worried their commanders in the past. He wondered if ordinary Russian soldiers were, like their German counterparts, becoming more survival-conscious as the war entered its final days.

Not that it would matter to him. The Russians would fight their way across this canal sooner or later, just as they had every watercourse between the Volga and Berlin. Just as their comrades moving in from the north would fight their way across the Hohenzollernkanal and Spree. And when they all came together the shouts of 'hurrah' would ring through the wastes of the ravaged Tiergarten. Nothing could stop them now, so why try?

Paul wasn't sure he knew. It wasn't the fear of being hanged as a deserter that stopped him from slinking away, though he realised it was a distinct possibility. Nor was it any great sense of responsibility to his current comrades, most of whom were complete strangers. It was more a case of having nowhere to go. When the war began he'd had two sets of parents, a home, a city and a country. All were broken or gone.

His relief on watch arrived, a boy named Ternath with floppy blonde hair and glasses with one cracked lens. Paul made his way to the back of the building, where the rest of his platoon were gathered in relative safety. Werner was sitting on the wooden floor, his back against the far wall, a ferocious scowl on his face as he tried to make sense of the morning newssheet. Paul found himself hoping that the boy's mother and sister were still alive. Some people had to be, even in Berlin.

He was halfway across the room when a wind half lifted him up and almost threw him at the opposite wall. As he slowly picked himself up the sound of the explosion was still rippling in his ears.

Another shell exploded, this time further away. 'Ternath,' someone shouted, and they all rushed lemming-like across the corridor and into the empty machine room which overlooked the canal. The shell had taken out a large chunk of wall, some ten metres down from the window they'd been using. Ternath had been hit by the blast, and by any number of flying bricks, but his head and limbs were still apparently attached to his body. Blood was pouring from several cuts, but no severed artery was fountaining life away. Even his decent lens was still in one piece. He'd been lucky, and Paul told him so.

'I'm alive?' the boy whispered, in a tone that suggested this might be a mixed blessing.

A stretcher appeared, and Paul, having just completed his watch, was one of the obvious bearers. Werner grabbed the other handles, and they carried the wounded man across the building and down a wrought-iron fire-escape to the roadside yard. The nearest dressing station was two streets away. It had been set up in an infant school basement, but was already overflowing onto the ground floor. Heading for the stairs, they passed two classrooms carpeted with occupied stretchers.

Down in the basement, candles provided most of the lighting. A triage nurse in bloodstained overalls gave Ternath a quick examination, and told them where to leave him. 'He'll live,' she said curtly, and moved on to the next. As he gave the boy a last encouraging look, Paul didn't feel so sure. The last time he'd seen eyes like that, the man had died an hour later.

Walking back towards the stairs, he saw an amputation underway through an open doorway. Across the table from the saw-wielding surgeon a man was crouched beside a bicycle, pedalling with both hands to power the handlebar light. A moment later the ceiling shook as the first rocket of a *katyusha* barrage landed somewhere close by. The surgeon glanced upwards, then quickly leant forward to shield the open wound from falling masonry dust.

The barrage continued for about five minutes, but no other rocket fell so close. On the ground floor the two classrooms full of stretchers had miraculously escaped, but several of the immobilised men were now whimpering with fear. Outside, the street was cloaked in swirling dust and smoke. Hurrying back towards the canal, they heard a woman shouting over crackling flames, but couldn't see a fire.

One or more rockets had hit their building, taking a room-size chunk out of the western end. The team had moved down a few rooms, and was setting up the sandbags by another south-facing window. There was a major looking out over their shoulders, a man that Paul hadn't seen since the January retreat. His name was Jesek, and he had a good reputation, at least among his subordinates. He was one of the old school, a bit of a stickler for the rules, but someone who cared what happened to the men in his charge.

His eyes now fixed on Werner, first taking in the baby face, then the bloodstained *Hitlerjugend* uniform. 'Name?' he asked without preamble

'Werner Redlich, sir.'

'And how old are you?'

Werner hesitated. 'He's fourteen,' Paul volunteered.

'I'll be fifteen next week,' Werner added.

Major Jesek sighed, and stroked two fingers down his left cheek. 'Are you from Berlin?'

'Yes, sir. From Schoenberg, sir.'

'Werner, I don't want you to take this the wrong way – I'm sure you've been a brave soldier – but I don't believe children belong in battle. I want you to take off that uniform and go home. Do you understand me?'

'Yes, sir,' Werner said, his face torn between hope and anxiety.

Once Jesek was gone, he turned to Paul. 'You won't think I'm a coward?'

'Of course not. The major's right. You go home and look after your family.'

Werner looked down at his uniform. 'But I have no other clothes.'

'Go back to the dressing station. They'll have something you can wear.'

Werner nodded. 'Can we meet again when this is over?' he asked.

Paul smiled. 'What's your address?'

The boy gave it to him, and they shared a farewell embrace. Werner hoisted up his panzerfaust rocket-launcher out of habit, then gently put it back down. He gave the rest of the men a shy wave and was gone.

Paul sat down with his back against the wall, feeling pleased for the boy but sad for himself. He had enjoyed the company.

Russell's day went badly from the start. He woke from a nightmare, Varennikov shaking him by the shoulder and shouting his name. He'd been in France, in the trenches, his head swinging left and right like a tennis spectator, watching shells explode on either side, throwing up sprays of blood like waves coming over a promenade wall. And all in perfect silence, except that church bells were tolling in the distance, and he was screaming for them to stop.

'You were screaming,' Varennikov told him.

'I know,' Russell said. The sense of being yanked back into the present was almost physical. 'I was back in France, in the First War,' he explained reluctantly.

'The trenches,' Varennikov said carefully in English. 'I have read about them. It must have been terrible.'

'It was,' Russell agreed tersely, eager to change the subject and allow the dream to fade. He asked Varennikov what his parents had done in the First War, and got himself dressed as the Russian told the story of his father's capture in the Brusilov offensive, and his three years of imprisonment in Hungary. The man had come home a communist, and discovered, much to his astonishment, that his country's government had undergone a similar transformation.

Before getting to sleep the previous night Russell had decided that there was no choice but simply to turn up at the Alex. He would walk in, wearing his Reichsbahn uniform, and say he had an appointment with Kriminalinspektor Kuzorra. Or that he was an old friend. Or something. There was hardly likely to be anyone around who'd recognise him from three-year-old wanted posters. The only real risk was strolling down firing ranges that used to be streets.

Leissner had no objections, and didn't even ask where Russell was going. He supplied the usual military bulletin – the Red Army had entered Weissensee and Treptow Park to the north-east and south-east, and had reached the northern S-Bahn defence line and Hohenzollernkanal. They were across the Teltowkanal in the south-west, and advancing into Dahlem. The ring around the city was almost complete.

'Where do you get your information from?' Russell asked, purely out of curiosity.

'The military authorities still use trains to move weapons and ammunition to the front,' Leissner explained. 'So they have to tell us where it is.'

Which made some sort of sense, Russell thought, always assuming the overriding insanity of continued resistance. Halfway down a street on the other side of Anhalter Station he came across a message that expressed his own feelings with great simplicity. On the last remaining wall of a gutted house someone had painted the word '*Nein*' in letters two metres high.

Most of the streets in the city centre were like obstacle courses, and it took him over an hour to reach the river. Travel on the surface resembled a long drawn-out game of Russian roulette, but these were odds that he had to accept – if he waited underground for a break in the shelling he might be there until doomsday. The streets were literally plastered with the flesh of those whose luck had run out, but his continued to hold, at least until he reached the Spree.

He had chosen the Waisenbrücke as the least likely bridge to be guarded, but there was a checkpoint at the western end. It was manned by regular military police, and there seemed a good chance that the Reichsbahn uniform would limit any expression of official disapproval to simple refusal. He decided to risk it, and was amply rewarded – once he told them he was on his way to police headquarters they simply waved him across.

It took him only ten minutes to discover the reason for their benevolence. There were SS-manned checkpoints on all the exits from Alexanderplatz, and these were in the business of gathering volunteers. Spotted before he had the chance to gracefully withdraw, Russell reluctantly presented himself for inspection. His claim of urgent business with the police was answered with the gift of a spade and a finger pointing him down Neue König Strasse. An incipient protest died in his throat as he caught sight of the corpse a few metres away. There was a bullet hole in the forehead, and the Russians weren't that close.

He got a glimpse of a battered but still-standing 'Alex' as he crossed the square, but that was all. He spent the morning digging gun emplacements in gardens off Neue König Strasse, the afternoon helping to build a barricade with two trams and several cart-loads of rubble. Apart from a few careless strays like himself, the workforce was made up of *Hitlerjugend* and *Volkssturm*, the former painfully enthusiastic, the latter replete with sullen misery. They were reinforced in the afternoon by a posse of Russian women prisoners, all wearing pretty headscarves, all barefoot. It rained most of the time, drenching everyone but the SS supervisors, who strode around holding umbrellas. Their uniforms were astonishingly immaculate, their boots the only shiny footwear left in Berlin, but there was a brittleness in their voices, the hysterical stillness of a trapped animal in their eyes. They were living on borrowed time, and they knew it.

Late in the afternoon a sad-looking horse slowly clip-clopped into view with a mobile canteen in tow. Even the Russian women were given tin cups of soup and a chunk of bread, and Russell noticed one of them surreptitiously feeding the horse. He had no idea what the soup was made of, but it tasted wonderful.

The canteen moved on, and everyone went back to work. An hour or so later, their task completed, Russell's team stood around awaiting instructions. But the senior SS officers had vanished, and their subordinates seemed uncertain of what came next. Without the noise of their own labours to mask them, the sounds of battle seemed appreciably closer. The machine-gun fire was no more than a kilometre away, the boom of tank cannons maybe even closer.

'They'll be giving us rifles soon,' one of Russell's fellow-strays remarked. He looked about sixty-five, and far from pleased at the prospect of battle.

'That would be good news,' an even older man told him. 'Most likely they'll put us with the *Volkssturm* and tell us to use their guns once they've been killed.'

As it began to grow dark, Russell gave serious consideration to walking away. But how far would he get? There were still SS in sight, and no doubt others around the next corner. The corpse by the checkpoint was still vivid in his memory. But waiting for the Red Army with a bunch of rocket-bearing children and a handful of geriatrics armed with First War rifles seemed no less life-threatening. When the light was gone, he told himself. Then he would make a run for it.

It was almost gone when an argument broke out further down the street between SS and army officers. 'I'm off,' one of Russell's fellow-workers muttered. He stepped out of the emplacement they had dug that morning, and strode calmly off in the direction of the nearest street corner.

No one seemed to notice him, and within seconds the darkness had swallowed him up.

Russell followed his example. No shouts pursued him either, and soon he was jogging down an empty side street towards Prenzlauer Strasse. This was barricaded in the direction of the river, so he continued north-westward, searching for an unguarded route back into the Old Town. Several adjacent houses were burning in one such street, a crowd of people apparently watching. He joined it surreptitiously, and realised that an effort was underway to rescue people trapped in an upper storey. Curiosity kept him watching for a few moments, until he realised he was being stupid. He slipped on down the street, and eventually recognised the silhouette of the elevated S-Bahn. He was just heading under the bridge when he had the idea of climbing up – he still had to get over the river and there wouldn't be a checkpoint on a railway crossing.

He followed the viaduct until he found a maintenance stairway, managed to scramble over the gate, and laboriously hauled himself up to the tracks. He was two or three hundred metres east of Börse Station. Feeling every one of his forty-five years, he began walking westwards between the two tracks.

It was an eerie experience. Berlin was spread out all around him, a dark field in which a thousand fires seemed to be burning. As Leissner had said, the Soviet encirclement was almost complete – only a small arc to the west seemed free of intermittent explosions and tracer ribbons.

He walked on, through the dark and silent Börse Station, past the stock exchange building after which it was named, and out over the first arm of the Spree. As he stopped in mid-bridge, drawn by the terrible beauty of the fire-lit river, something let loose an unearthly screech in the distance. It sounded like one of the Zoo's big cats, which it probably was. It would be more of a miracle if their cages were still intact.

A little further on, the railway viaduct had taken a recent hit, and the whole structure seemed to sway alarmingly as he inched his way along one edge. The adjacent museum was also badly damaged, but the barracks on the other side of the river's second channel seemed simply empty. A few kilometres to the north a fierce night battle seemed to be taking place. The distance and direction suggested the area around Wedding Station, where he'd stepped from the train less than thirty-six hours ago.

Another ten minutes and he was walking across the bridge into Friedrichstrasse Station, his feet crunching through broken glass from the now skeletal roof. Standing alone in the dark and cavernous ruin, he felt, almost for the first time, the enormity of what had been done to his city. Of what was still being done.

He took the glass-strewn steps to street level, then descended further to the noisier realm below ground. Once again he heard music somewhere in the underworld, this time a lone trumpeter blowing the melody of a Billie Holiday song. He wended his way down the crowded platforms and disappeared into the familiar tunnel, the words of the song playing on his lips:

The world was bright when you loved me,
sweet was the touch of your lips;
the world went dark when you left me,
and then there came a total eclipse.

He had escaped a pointless death defending Alexanderplatz from the Russians, but that was all. He had come to find Effi, and in that he had failed. There was no one else to ask for help, nowhere else he could go. It would only take the Red Army a couple more days to roll over the last pockets of resistance, and then he would have to trust to Nikoladze's gratitude. Some hope.

The hospital trains were still parked in the darkness – where could they go? – but the sounds of lamentation seemed more restrained. There was no nurse sat on a step, but as he walked past he saw one cadaverous face up above him, pressed tight against a window, staring out at the tunnel wall.

Back in the abandoned station, he found Varennikov reading his novel by candlelight. The Russian looked up. 'Someone came to see you,' he said. 'A German comrade named Ströhm. He said he'd come back tomorrow.'

It was five in the morning, and the men in Paul's unit were readying themselves and their weapons for the expected dawn attack. Some were writing their wills, some last notes to their loved ones, some a combination of the two. Most had done so many times before, littering Russia and Poland with their urgent scribbles.

They all looked depressed, especially those who'd been drinking the night before. Paul had never really taken to alcohol, and imbibing large quantities of the stuff on the eve of battle seemed less than clever – why dull the reflexes that your life might depend on? And he could also hear his father telling him not to 'turn off', to live with it, learn from it. If he did survive this, and he ever got to speak to his father again, he would take great pleasure in asking him what more there was to learn from this, once you'd realised that human stupidity was a bottomless pit.

On the previous evening a couple of idiots from the Propaganda Ministry had turned up out of the blue. One had a roll of posters under his arm, the other a hammer and a pocket full of tacks, and between them they had solemnly pinned their boss's latest message – 'The darkest hour is just before the dawn' – to a wall. They had offered the unit a 'hope-that-helps' look before moving on in search of another grateful audience.

It was hard to believe, but there was the poster, waiting for a shell to contradict it.

It was all over – any fool could see it. Here they were, waiting to die in defence of the Teltowkanal, when the enemy was already across it in the south-western suburbs. The Russians were in Dahlem, someone had said. Any day now they'd be camping out in his own bedroom.

Would they ever go home again? He supposed they would. Armies always had.

He felt frightened, which was no surprise. At the beginning, first as a *flakhelfer* and then on the Eastern Front, he had half expected that the fear would diminish, that he would gradually become immune. But it had never happened. Your body just learned to ignore your mind. His first *katyusha* attack, he had crapped himself almost instantly, and felt terribly ashamed. But no one had laughed at him. They'd all done it, sometime or another. These days he still felt a loosening, but that was all. Progress. You went with the fear rather than under it. He liked that. Maybe he would become a psychiatrist after the war. There'd be quite a demand.

When Stefan Leissner came to see them on the following morning, he brought Gerhard Ströhm with him. Both were wearing Reichsbahn uniforms, but Ströhm's had none of the braids and fancy epaulettes, only the sewn-on badge below each shoulder, the eagle and swastika motif above 'RBD Berlin'. His hair was shorter, the moustache gone, and he no longer resembled the young Stalin. He looked ten years older than the man Russell had known four years earlier.

There was no obvious friction between the two German communists, but he sensed that they didn't have much time for each other. Ströhm deferred to Leissner, who was presumably his Reichsbahn superior, but their relative positions in the Party hierarchy might well be different. From what Russell had seen of them – which admittedly wasn't much – their different temperaments reflected very different ways of looking at the world. Leissner, he suspected, would have no trouble working with the Soviets, whereas Ströhm probably would.

'I understand you are an old friend of Comrade Ströhm,' Leissner said to Russell, sounding less than thrilled. 'You can catch up on old times in a moment, but first I must give you an update on our advance.'

It was much as Russell expected. The city's encirclement had been completed on the previous evening, and Soviet forces were pushing steadily in toward the centre from all directions. That morning a battle was raging along the Teltowkanal, only four kilometres away.

'Tomorrow they should be here,' Leissner said with barely suppressed excitement. 'The following day at the latest.'

He departed, leaving Ströhm with them.

'It's really good to see you,' Russell said. 'I must admit, I assumed you were dead.'

'Not yet,' Ströhm said wryly, walking over to embrace him. 'It's good to see you too. A welcome surprise. I won't ask how you got here – or why – I gather it's not a subject for discussion...'

'According to Comrade Leissner?'

'Yes.'

'Well, I wouldn't want to upset him. But I would like to know how you escaped the Gestapo in 1941. We were told in Stettin that the whole Berlin network had been arrested.'

'Most, but not all. A few were saved. Like myself.'

'How?'

'In the usual way. The Gestapo got careless – in one case they applied too much pressure and the comrade died, in another they gave the comrade a chance to take his own life. And those two deaths cut the only links to several cells, mine included.'

Ströhm's recitation of tragedy was as matter-of-fact as ever. He had initiated their relationship in 1941, in the hope that Russell, as an American journalist, could somehow get news of the accelerating Holocaust to the outside world. Together they had witnessed the first steps of the process, the trains loading up under cover of darkness, at several different Berlin yards. Ströhm's passionate concern for the Jews was personal – his Jewish girlfriend had been murdered by stormtroopers – but Russell had always known that the man was a communist, and when he and Effi needed to flee Berlin, Ströhm was the man he had turned to. Ströhm had taken the matter to his comrades, and they had arranged the first leg of his eventually successful escape.

Russell sighed. 'And now it's almost over,' he said, as much to himself as to Ströhm. 'How are the Russians behaving in the suburbs?'

Now it was Ströhm's turn to sigh. 'Not well. There have been many rapes in Weissensee and Lichtenberg. Even comrades have been raped.'

'I can't say I'm surprised,' Russell said. 'The Soviet papers have been almost inviting the troops to take their revenge,' he went on. 'They've changed their tune over the last few weeks, but I think the damage has already been done. '

'You're probably right, but I hope not. And not just because the women of Berlin deserve better. If the Red Army behaves badly, it'll make things so much more difficult for the Party. The people already lean towards the English and Americans, and we need the Red Army to behave better than their allies, not worse.'

Fat chance, Russell thought. 'Indiscriminate shelling is not going to win the Soviets many post-war friends in Berlin.'

'No, probably not. But at least there's *some* military point to that – the

Nazis *are* still resisting. But raping hundreds of women... there's no excuse for that.'

'None,' Russell agreed, thinking about Effi. 'Look, I owe you a great deal...'

'You owe me nothing.'

'Well, I think I owe you something, but it's not going to stop me asking another favour.' He told Ströhm about Effi, how she'd come back to Berlin, and probably become involved with a resistance group. 'She suddenly disappeared a few weeks ago, and her sister is convinced that she's been arrested. Is there any way you could check if that's true, and if it is, find out where she was taken? She's using the name Erna von Freiwald.'

Ströhm looked up. 'I've heard that name in connection with one of the Jewish escape committees. But I never dreamt it was Effi Koenen. I thought she escaped to Sweden with you.'

Russell explained why Effi had chosen to stay behind.

'We have men in the police, but I have no idea if any of them are still at work. The area around the Alex is being turned into a strongpoint.'

'I know,' Russell said wryly. He told Ströhm about his attempted visit, and the day of hard labour that had resulted.

'Ah. Well, I will see what I can find out, but don't get your hopes up – it may well be nothing. But before I go, tell me, the work we were doing in 1941 – did you get the story out?'

'I did,' Russell told him. 'But not in the way we wanted. The big story I had – the gas that Degesch produced for the SS without the usual warning odour – that must have gone into a dozen papers. But no editor was willing to headline it, to put it all together, and tell the whole story for what it was – the attempted murder of an entire people.'

'Why?' Ströhm asked, just as Kenyon had in Moscow.

Russell offered him the same guesses, and shrugged. 'I tried. I made such a pest of myself that one editor actually hid in his cupboard rather than see me. I think that was when I realised I was onto a loser.'

'That's a terrible shame,' Ströhm said quietly. 'But perhaps we were foolish to expect more.' His face was lined with sadness, and Russell found himself wondering how Ströhm would make out in a Soviet-dominated Germany. Here was a man who wanted to believe in a better world – who had no hesitation about putting his own life on the line in pursuit of it – but who found it harder and harder to muster the required suspension of disbelief. He had seen through the lie that was Western capitalism, seen through the lie that was fascism. And soon he would see through the lie that was communism. He was too honest for his own good.

They embraced again, and Ströhm disappeared down the staircase, calling out over his shoulder that he'd return with any news.

Varennikov, it seemed, had understood enough of the conversation to form his own judgement. 'Your friend seems more of a German than a communist,' he said casually.

'Maybe,' Russell said non-committally. Ströhm had actually been born in America, but he doubted whether Varennikov would find that reassuring.

'It will take many years to rebuild our country,' Varennikov said, with an air of someone addressing a hostile meeting.

It seemed like a non-sequitur, until Russell realised that his companion was using the German despoliation of western Russia to justify the Red Army's behaviour in Germany. 'I'm sure it will,' he agreed diplomatically.

'But America has not even been touched,' the Russian went on, as if Russell had disagreed with him. 'I know a few English cities have been bombed, but my country has been laid to waste. You must remember – until the Revolution we had no industry, no dams, everything was backward. People worked so hard to build a modern country, and now they must do it all again. And they will. In fifty years the Soviet Union will be the richest country on earth.'

'Perhaps.'

'Of course, we must avoid another war. That is why the papers we found are so important – if we have an atomic bomb no one will dare to invade us, and all our socialist achievements will be safe from destruction.' His earnest face suddenly broke into a grin, making him look about twenty. 'Who knows? Perhaps we will both be made Heroes of the Soviet Union.'

The battle began badly. The machine-gun was destroyed by only the second shell of the opening barrage, killing two of them. The rest ran for the nearest exit, shells exploding around them like the lashes of a giant whip. Had they emerged at the back, they might have kept running till evening, but a wrongly chosen door led them out into enemy fire, and a choice between death and going to ground. Paul had a ten-metre crawl to reach the nearest communication trench, and it seemed a lot farther.

Once inside, he was little more than a spectator. A hail of shells whooshed over him, provoking a sporadic response from the surviving German machine-guns and artillery. The latter, he assumed, were conserving their ammunition.

Clouds of smoke and brick dust coalesced and spread, until the whole area seemed choked in a brown haze. Around nine o'clock, lines of Soviet infantry came charging out of the fug, singing and shouting like there was no tomorrow. For most of them, there wasn't – the first wave succumbed almost to a man. Some had been carrying small boats, but only a single soldier reached the edge of the canal, toppling into the oily water with blood pumping from his neck.

The Soviet artillery redoubled their efforts, slowly reducing the buildings around the harbour to their constituent bricks. Planes came swooping out of the smoke on low-level bombing runs, and stretches of the trench system on either side of Paul were plastered with human gore.

More infantry appeared, and this time some succeeded in launching their boats. None got safely across, but the bodies now floating in the water were like marks left by a rising tide. It was all so fucking predictable, Paul, thought. So many pushes, so many corpses, and sooner or later...

Soviet tanks were now firing across the canal, and drawing no response. The next wave would wash over them, Paul realised. And so, apparently, did Major Jesek. As more Soviet infantry loomed on the southern bank, the order was given to pull back.

Paul joined the rush along the trench, clambering over the dead and still groaning, out into a rubble-strewn gap between ruins. Jesek was there, looking in his element, giving each soldier an encouraging smack on the shoulder until his head blossomed blood and his body pitched into the bricks.

Paul stumbled on, out of the industrial area and into residential streets. There were houses missing in all of them, and houses burning in most. Ahead of him, a soldier was frantically shaking his hands, as if he was trying to dry them – catching him up, Paul saw that the man's mouth was hanging open in a silent scream.

The soldier suddenly sank to his knees.

Paul put a comforting hand on his shoulder, and the man violently shook it off. 'Go fuck yourself,' he hissed.

Paul left him where he was. Looking back once, he saw the man still kneeling in the middle of the road, his former comrades passing by on either side, like a stream divided by a fallen rock.

A kilometre to the north, under the S-Bahn bridge by Tempelhof Station, the MPs were waiting for them. They joined the fifty or so men who had already been rounded up, and listened to the sound of the battles still raging while they waited for stragglers. When the road to the south was empty they were marched through the Tempelhof aerodrome gates and delivered to those in charge. There were lots of tanks dug in around the airport buildings, tanks they could have used that morning.

'Guess why they're here?' the Volkssturm man beside him asked, as if he was reading Paul's mind.

'Tell me.'

'Someone special might need a last-minute flight,' the man replied. The thought seemed to amuse him.

It didn't amuse Paul, and neither did the prospect of yet more digging. If he'd stayed in one place he'd be in China by now.

The emplacements, as it turned out, had already been dug, and all that remained was the wait for Ivan. It was actually a beautiful day, the sun shining out of a perfect blue sky until just before noon, when a horde of Soviet IL-4 bombers appeared out of nowhere and started blowing holes in the hangars and terminal buildings. They were careful not to damage the runway – mindful, presumably, of their own future needs.

Paul was assigned to one of the PaK41 emplacements in the aerodrome's north-eastern corner, and had only a distant view of the afternoon's battle, which raged between the S-Bahn defence line and the aerodrome's southern perimeter. Every now and then a jeep full of *Hitlerjugend* armed with *panzerfaust* would careen away across the tarmac to take on the Soviet armour, and several familiar-sounding explosions would eventually follow. The gun commander claimed he could see several burning hulks through his binoculars, and Paul had no reason to doubt him. But none of the jeeps came back.

Darkness fell with the Soviets still held at arm's length, but scattered engagements rumbled on by the light of the full moon, and as midnight approached the Russian infantry were still pushing forward. Paul's own gun was down to eleven shells, which didn't bode well for the dawn.

It had been a long and so far fruitless day, in which Varennikov had almost driven him mad with his non-stop ramblings. Sometimes Russell could hear the idealism of his own younger years, but mostly it was just the stupidity. There was nothing he really disliked about the young Russian, but Russell wished he would shut up. After a while he simply tuned him out, and focussed his ears on listening for sounds on the stairs.

It was well into evening before he heard them, and Ströhm's head emerged from the stairwell. 'You didn't tell me she was Jewish,' he said without preamble.

'Effi? She isn't.'

'Well, she was arrested as one. On the 13th of April. She was taken to the detention centre for Jews on Schulstrasse – the old Jewish hospital – do you know it?'

Russell felt something grip his heart. 'Yes, I went there once... but that's out beyond the Ringbahn. It'll be in the Soviet hands by now.'

'It is. But Erna von Freiwald was released on the 21st. Last Saturday. It's in the records – all the remaining prisoners were released that day. I assume the people in charge were trying to earn themselves some credit for the future.'

'Where did she go?' Russell asked automatically.

'I'm sorry, there's no way of knowing.'

'No, of course not.'

'Perhaps she went home,' Ströhm suggested.

'No, her sister went to the apartment only two days ago.'

'Then she's probably in one of the mass shelters – you know where they are: underneath the flak towers in the Tiergarten, under Pariserplatz. There's one right next to Anhalter Station. They're all incredibly over-crowded at the moment. Lots of women are hoping that there's strength in numbers, that the Red Army will behave better in front of a thousand witnesses.'

After finishing her shift and eating, Effi could stand it no longer. She had to get some fresh air, had to convince herself that the moon and stars still shone. 'Would you like to go outside, just for a minute?' she asked Rosa.

The girl thought about it for a moment, then nodded.

'Then let's go,' Effi said, taking her hand.

The rooms beyond the hospital seemed more crowded than ever, the smells of sweat, urine and excrement almost impossibly pungent. There were guards on the bunker entrance, but they had no objection to people taking the air – it was, as one of them said, 'their funeral'. Perhaps it would be, Effi thought, but she was beyond caring. She stood for a few moments at the bottom of the steps, inhaling the smoke-laden breeze and listening for sounds of explosions close by. In the sky above, a few faint stars glimmered in the murk.

They went up into the Berlin night. The square was not silent, as Effi had expected, nor empty of movement. Several walkers were visible, all keeping close to those walls that remained. Far up Hermann Goering Strasse a lorry was driving away. Berlin still had a heartbeat, albeit a faint one.

They could see no fires, but the sky was a deep shade of orange, and several of the surrounding buildings were silhouetted against areas of bright yellow. Streamers of dark smoke hung in the air, like photographic negatives of the Milky Way. Far in the distance, she could hear the faint rattle of machine-gun fire. .

The familiar keening turned into the familiar scream, and for one dreadful second Effi thought she'd managed to kill them both. But the shell hit a building on the far side of the square, starting an avalanche of masonry and igniting a furnace within.

What people had built, people destroyed, and would no doubt build again. She felt weighed down by the utter pointlessness of it all.

She knew they should go back down, but stubbornly put off the moment. One semi-delirious soldier had recognised her that afternoon, but the doctor had cheerfully put him right. Her acceptance as an Effi Koenen look-alike felt rather strange, but everyone knew that fugitive film stars avoided working in underground hospitals.

Rosa snuggled up to her. 'Is everyone going to die?' she asked, matter-of-factly.

'Not in this war,' Effi told her. 'Everyone does eventually, but I think you and I are going to have really long lives.'

'How long is a long life?'

'Well, according to the Bible, God thinks we should get at least three score years and ten – which is seventy. So let's add another thirty for good luck, and live to be a hundred.'

Rosa digested that in silence for a few moments. 'Is God hiding in a shelter until it's over?' she asked. 'Like us?'

It was a long night. A storm raged in the early hours, adding thunder, lightning and pelting rain to the sporadic Soviet artillery fire, but it all passed over, and by five o'clock there was only smoke to blur the heavens, and a huge red moon seeking shelter behind the western horizon. Dawn brought the usual bombardment, but once again the Soviet artillery and air force seemed fixated on the city centre.

Paul was hunkered down in his unit's emplacement on the north-eastern corner of the Tempelhof field, reading a copy of the *Panzerbär* newsletter that Goebbels had introduced in place of newspapers, and trying to ignore the bombers droning overhead. 'We are holding on!' the headline claimed, but, as an announcement further down the page made obvious, some believed otherwise. Those who hoisted white flags of surrender from their window would be dealt with as traitors, the propaganda minister promised, and so would all the other occupants of their building.

After exactly sixty minutes – the Soviets, sloppy in so many ways, were remarkably precise when it came to timing their bombardments – the artillery barrage abruptly died away. Another ten minutes and they could expect to see the armour creeping forward across the smoke-laden field, supported by the usual hordes of infantry. With only eleven shells remaining, it felt like the Seelow Heights all over again, only this time there seemed no point in destroying the gun – by the time the Soviets lifted it out of its emplacement the war would be over.

There was little point in firing it at all, in Paul's estimation, but little point in saying so either. He scrambled to his feet just as an SS Hauptsturmführer with one arm in a bloodstained sling loomed over their trench asking for a volunteer. There was a job needed doing on the roof of the terminal building.

'You go,' the sergeant ordered Paul.

Cursing inwardly, Paul followed the Hauptsturmführer across the tarmac and around behind the huge concrete edifice. A fire escape zigzagged up the side of the buildings, and Paul spent most of the long climb wondering what the officer needed him for.

He soon found out. Once they reached the huge flat roof, the officer unfolded the map he was carrying, carefully laid it out on the ground, and asked Paul to stand, legs spread, with a foot on each of two corners. He stood on the other two, and began scanning the surrounding city through his binoculars.

Paul resisted the temptation to point out that a couple of chunks of masonry could have done the same job – SS Hauptsturmführers were notoriously unwilling to take criticism. Every now and then his companion would lower the binoculars, fall to one knee, and scrawl lines across the map with a piece of pink chalk. Watching him work, Paul decided he must be plotting the latest Russian advances.

It wasn't so easy to do. The flash and peal of cannonades and explosions were coming from every direction, but only a few of these could be attributed to actual fire-fights on the ground. Away to the east, on the far side of the aerodrome, one such battle was underway in Neukölln – Paul could hear the distinctive sound of tank fire, and the faint rattle of machine-gun fire. The same was true to the south-west, where a battle was raging on their side of the S-Bahn. On the airfield itself German forces were still dug in to the north of the main runway, but their resistance would serve no purpose if the Soviets bypassed Tempelhof to both east and west.

A loud explosion turned both their heads round. Two kilometres to the east a vast cloud of smoke and dust was rising into the sky. As it cleared, it became apparent that the huge Karstadt department store was no longer there. The SS had done what they promised, and Paul's companion duly grunted his pleasure.

The view to the north was presumably less to his taste – following the morning air raid most of the centre seemed to be on fire. The blessed Führer was somewhere under that lot, no doubt safe and sound in a concrete bunker. Paul wondered how Hitler's morning was going. Surely he must realise it was all over – for all his increasingly apparent faults, the man was not stupid. But if he did, then why were they fighting on? Did his own troops' lives mean nothing to him? That was hard to believe after all they'd been told of his First War experiences, but what other explanation could there be?

'You can take your feet off now,' the Hauptsturmführer said, breaking into his reverie. The SS officer folded his map back up, took one last look round, and headed for the fire escape. Paul followed with some reluctance. On the way up he had expected to feel appallingly vulnerable on the flat roof, but no plane had swooped down on them with machine-guns blazing, and a wonderfully deluded sense of being above the fray had slowly come over him. Now, each step down felt a little closer to hell.

It proved an accurate assessment. They were just rounding the corner of the building when incoming *katyushas* started ploughing a wide path towards them. The Hauptsturmführer ran for the nearest door, and, for want of anything better, Paul followed in his wake. There was nothing to open – the door had already been torn off its hinges – and a down staircase offered sanctuary on the far side of the lobby. By the time the rockets crashed into the front of the terminal Paul was halfway down the stairs, but the Hauptsturmführer, hindered by his wounded arm, had only just reached the top. Thrown over Paul's head, he hit the wall above the staircase with massive force, and dropped like a stone onto the bottom steps. His map, opened by the blast, fluttered down beside him.

Though he tumbled down the last few steps, Paul sustained nothing worse than bruises. The barrage had rolled over, but he had been through enough *katyusha* attacks to know that another might plough the same furrow, and after a cursory glance at the dead Hauptsturmführer, he clambered over the body and continued on down the steps, only stopping two floors down when another SS officer told him he could go no further – his men were booby-trapping the building.

He had no objection to Paul waiting out the barrage, and even offered him a cigarette. When Paul declined, he lit his own before delivering a rueful monologue on the evils of smoking. 'You should hear the Führer on the subject,' he said. 'As I was once privileged to do. His hatred of smoking will one day seem prophetic – mark my words!' He drew deeply on his cigarette and smiled through the smoke he exhaled.

Paul said nothing – the only question seemed to be whether Berlin would be renamed Wonderland before the Russians razed it. After fifteen minutes the *katyusha* barrages abated for a while, half convincing him that they had stopped. Big guns were now firing somewhere close by. German ones, he hoped.

He went back up. Someone had moved the Hauptsturmführer's body to the side of the stairs, but had not bothered to close his eyes. Paul did so, and, on impulse, took the binoculars that were still hanging from the man's neck. The machine pistol might come in useful, so he took that too. Some of Himmler's officers liked to mark their guns with SS insignia, but this one had not, which was just as well.

The doorway was a lot wider than it had been, and there was now a large crater on the threshold. Smoke and dust obscured most of the field ahead, but there seemed to be a lull in the bombardment. He worked his way round the rim of the crater, and hurried out past the still-standing 'Welcome to Tempelhof' sign in the direction of his gun emplacement. A few seconds later the curtain of smoke drew apart, and he could see the long barrel pointing straight up at the sky. He feared the worst, but the emplacement was empty – his comrades had fired their shells and gone. And so, he realised, had everyone else in this sector. While he'd been discussing Hitler's tobacco-phobia there'd been a general pull-out.

Abandonment was becoming something of a habit. But he wouldn't be alone for long – the moving shapes in the distance looked like T-34s and their accompanying infantry. Was this the moment to surrender? He thought not. As he'd told Uncle Thomas, surrender was a risky business, best attempted away from the heat of an ongoing battle, when emotions were raw and trigger-fingers itchy.

No, it was time for another retreat. There couldn't be that many more. If the Soviet forces to the north of the city had breached the Ringbahn defence line, then all that remained in German hands was a corridor about five kilometres wide.

He clambered out of the gun emplacement and started running, only stopping when he reached the sheltered rear of the terminal building. The Soviet artillery had thoughtfully pounded holes in the high wire fence that surrounded the aerodrome, and he had a clear run to the U-Bahn station on Belle Alliance Strasse. He took it at top speed, almost tumbling down the steps as shells exploded further down the road. The booking hall was packed with civilians, most of them women, and none seemed pleased to see him. 'Either go or get rid of the uniform and gun,' one old man told him imperiously. Paul could see his point, but still felt like hitting him.

He went back up the stairs. The Landwehrkanal, just over a kilometre to the north, was the next obvious line of defence, and he supposed that should be his destination. He could think of none better.

Out on Belle Alliance Strasse he could see men in the distance, heading in the same direction. Behind him, the battle for Tempelhof seemed to be winding down. The centre of the wide, traffic-free road offered the clearest path, but he kept to the edge for fear of shell-blast, wending and climbing his way along the rubble-choked pavement. The bodies he came across were mostly women's, though sometimes it was hard to tell.

A single shell exploded a couple of hundred metres up the road, taking the corner off a three-storey block and conjuring flames from within.

As he passed another bombed-out house the Kreuzberg loomed into view, crowning the wooded slopes of Viktoria Park. Why choose blood and stone, he asked himself, when grass and trees were there for the taking? He took the first available turning and worked his way through to the park's eastern gate, then followed a path up through blossoming trees to the summit. He and his Dad had come there often, catching a tram to the depot at the bottom of the hill, walking up, and sitting on a wooden bench, ice cream in hand, with Berlin spread out before them. On a clear day they could usually see the Hertha grandstand away across the city.

There was no such clarity today, but he could still see enough to be shocked. Myriad fires were burning across the city's heart, from the Ku'damm away to the west, through the district south of the Tiergarten, to the Old Town and Alexanderplatz in the east. Every few seconds the flash of another explosion would spark in the smoke-leaden gloom, reminding Paul of the matches flaring to life in the Plumpe grandstand as spectators lit their half-time cigarettes.

Turning his head, he caught sight of Soviet tanks. They were crossing Immelmann Strasse and entering the street that ran along the bottom of the park's western slope. And away to the west, marching up Monumenten Strasse towards him was an absurdly neat formation of infantry. There had to be a couple of hundred men, but there was something odd about them...

Remembering the binoculars, he brought the formation into focus.

The 'something odd' about them was their size – they were children. Two hundred neatly-turned out *Hitlerjugend* were marching out to meet the Red Army, panzerfausts at the ready. And they were walking into a trap.

A machine-gun rattled but no one fell down – either the Russians were too drunk to shoot straight, or they were firing warning shots. The column visibly hesitated, but kept on coming, and more warning shots seemed only to encourage whichever heroic nincompoop was in command. The machine-guns opened up in earnest and the front lines went down, exposing those behind them. As bullets scythed through them, the rear echelons broke and fled, dropping their panzerfausts and sprinting back across the railway bridge. Ivan, to his credit, ceased fire.

Other Russians were visible at the southern foot of the hill. It was time to go. Paul strode back down through the empty park, the clashing smells of death and spring mingling in his nostrils. The depot at the bottom had taken several hits, and through the wide-open entrance he could see one tram half raised on the rear of another, like a dog mounting a bitch. He walked round the corner of the building and started up Grossbeer-en Strasse, which had lost most of its houses. At the first intersection he found six bloodied female corpses around a standpipe. Two were still clutching the water buckets they'd come to fill.

A little further on a three-legged dog gave him a hopeful look, and started whining piteously once he'd gone past. Paul wanted to cry, but no tears came. Something inside him was irreparably broken, but he had no idea what it was.

A Soviet plane flew low overhead, and opened fire on something be-hind the houses to his left. He walked on towards Yorck Strasse, where several women were gathered round a prone casualty. There was an air of hopelessness in their postures, and in the way they glanced up the street, as if they were pretending for everyone's sake that help was on the way. Beyond them, outside the Yorck Strasse police station, another two corpses hung slack-necked from lampposts. Paul walked towards them. The first, a moustachioed man in his forties or fifties, was in army uni-form. The second was Werner.

The boy's mouth was open, his fists clenched, his dead eyes full of terror. A piece of card bearing the message 'All traitors will die like this one' had been looped over the second button of his *Hitlerjugend* shirt.

Paul stood there staring at the boy's body until his legs suddenly folded beneath him, and a sound he didn't recognise, a cross between a wail and a high-pitched hum, welled up from his soul and erupted through his lips.

A few moments later he felt a hand on his shoulder. 'Did you know him?' a woman's voice asked.

'Yes,' Paul managed to say. 'He was only fourteen.'

'He never said. He was a brave little bugger.'

'You saw this happen?' Paul asked. He climbed slowly back to his feet. Why hadn't the boy ditched his uniform?

'From my window. It was the redhead – we've seen him before. He's an Obersturmführer, I think – I can never remember their uniforms. My husband was in the real army.'

'By what authority...'

She shrugged. 'Who knows? He's a law unto himself. He has a few helpers, but he's the judge and the executioner.'

Paul looked up at the body. 'I'm going to cut him down.'

'It's your funeral.'

He took out his knife, clambered up onto the police station wall and managed, with a couple of hacks, to slice through the rope. Werner's corpse dropped to the pavement.

Paul sank to one knee and closed the dead boy's eyes. He went through his pockets, hoping to find something he could take to Werner's mother and sister. Inside the *Hitlerjugend* documentation there was the family photograph that he'd showed Paul when they first met. It seemed like years ago, but was less than a week.

'Where can I bury him?' he asked the woman. Two of her neighbours had appeared, and all three of them looked at him as if he was mad.

If there was a reply, he didn't hear it. There was a sudden whoosh and the briefest sensation of flight. The earth seemed to explode, a hundred hammers seemed to hit him at once, and then all noise was sucked away, leaving only a shimmering silence. He felt a moment of enormous relief, and then nothing at all.

Under the gun

April 26 – 27

Russell was woken by the thump of distant explosions. It had to be an air raid, but sounded louder than anything that had gone before. On and on it went without respite, like a berserk drummer with no sense of rhythm.

Some of the bombs seemed to be falling not too far away, but as Leissner had said, it would take extraordinary bad luck for a shell or bomb to land on their roof, protected as it was by surrounding buildings and a secondary ceiling of elevated tracks. Sound reasoning, which didn't quite still his nerves, or black out the images of trench life under shell-fire which rose unbidden from his memory.

'What are you going to do now?' he murmured to himself, partly in search of distraction, partly because he needed some sort of plan. Was his best bet to stay where he was, wait for the Russians, and hope for their help in finding his family? Mounting a tour of the giant shelters in search of Effi would be pointless. His chances of finding her would be minute, his chances of death by shellfire depressingly high. If Effi was in one of those shelters she should be safe; when the war ended and the shelling stopped, she would doubtless go home, and he would find her there.

It was the sensible option, but still hard to take. Since 1941 a sense of failure, of letting her down, had churned away in the shallower recesses of his subconscious, and inaction always brought it bubbling to the surface. The urge to keep looking was almost irresistible, and he had to keep reminding himself that behaving like a headless chicken might very well lose him his head.

Several hours went by. Varennikov woke up, and the two of them breakfasted on cans of cabbage and cold water. They talked for a while about Russia, and Russell's first visit in 1924, when the hopes were still high. Listening to himself talk, and seeing the pride in Varennikov's face, Russell felt sadness rather than anger. He was getting old, he told himself.

Stefan Leissner had come to see them each morning so far, but noon passed without a visit. And, as a quick trip downstairs revealed, the sentry in the tunnel was gone. What was happening? Russell went back up to Varennikov, and asked the Russian if he fancied a trip to Leissner's office – 'you haven't been out since we got here.'

Varennikov demurred. He knew he was being over-anxious, he said, but there was always a chance that the papers they'd buried would be destroyed by a shell or a bomb. 'Or even eaten by an animal,' he added. 'So I must keep myself safe until what I've learned has been passed on.'

Fair enough, Russell thought. Crazy, but hardly grounds for committal. He descended once more on his own, walked down the short stretch of tunnel, and climbed the other spiral staircase. It seemed deathly quiet in the underground office complex, and neither Leissner nor anyone else was in residence,

He took the two flights of stairs to the elevated goods warehouse, which was equally deserted. The short walk along the elevated tracks offered a panoramic view of hell, the sort of thing Hieronymus Bosch might have painted if he'd been born a half-millennium later, but, for the moment at least, no shells were landing nearby. He hurried across the tracks, noting only the curtain of fire that hung above the northern horizon, and what looked like a rail-mounted flak gun further down the viaduct.

He found Leissner in the goods station forecourt. A bomb had fallen on this side of the elevated tracks, killing two men he didn't recognise and almost severing their host's right leg. He – or someone else – had tied a tourniquet above the knee, but that had been some time ago, and if Russell was any judge the unconscious man was in serious danger of losing the limb. He loosened the tourniquet and wondered what else he could do. Nothing much, was the answer. He could haul Leissner back down to his underground office, but the leg might break off in the process. Or he could leave him here, on the old principle that two bombs never fall on the same spot. Out in the open he might attract a passing medic's attention.

Or not. If he fetched Varennikov, Russell realised, the two of them could carry the man down to his office. They could all stay there until the Russians came. It would be just as safe as their current abode.

He made his way back through the offices and up towards the tracks, still juggling options in his mind. Perhaps he should head for Effi's new flat now, and leave Varennikov with Leissner. They could welcome the Red Army just as well without him.

As he emerged onto the viaduct he heard a rumbling sound. The rail-mounted flak gun was grinding its way along the viaduct some two hundred metres to the north. Spasms of black smoke rose behind it, as an invisible steam engine propelled it forward. The barrel of the gun was questing to and fro, as if it was smelling the air.

Where the hell did they think they were going? Russell wondered. Poland?

He didn't wait to find out, hustling down two sets of stairs to the tunnel below. Here he received an unpleasant surprise – there was gunfire in the tunnel leading south. It still sounded some way away, but over the last few days Russell had learned how being underground could warp one's sense of distance.

He scurried down the tunnel to the abandoned station and headed for the spiral staircase. He had climbed about five steps when the blast of air and sound hit him, blowing him backwards against the handrail and spilling him onto the platform. The debris cascading down the stairwell sounded like a coalman emptying his sack.

Russell scrambled unsteadily to his feet. He felt like he'd been hit by a wall, but no bones seemed broken.

He started up the iron staircase, holding his collar against the swirling dust. He was used to darkness above, but the old booking office was now awash with beams of light, flooding down and around a mountain of metal. The flak gun and its mount had fallen through the roof, crushed the interior walls of the old station building, and come to rest on solid earth, half in the old booking office, half in the room where Russell and Varennikov had spent most of their time. The long barrel of the 88mm gun lay across the remains of the inner wall, as if it was resting from its long labours.

Varennikov was somewhere underneath it. Russell squeezed himself between a wall and several huge wheels, then through a gap between buffers. There was more space left in the other room, and he allowed himself a moment of hope that the young Russian had survived. But no – there were his legs, both severed by an edge of armoured plate. The rest of his body was underneath the fallen carriage, crushed to a pulp.

It would have been quick. Varennikov might have heard the viaduct give way, but he would barely have had time to look up before nemesis fell through the ceiling.

Russell worked his way back into the old booking office. There were two more corpses behind the gun, both of boys in *Hitlerjugend* uniforms. There were probably more outside. The viaduct above looked as if someone had taken a huge bite out of it, but there were no signs of charring or smoke. The structure had probably been compromised already, the gun just a little too heavy.

So what now? Russell asked himself. With the viaduct half-destroyed he might find it hard to reach Leissner, and what, in any case, would be the point? – there was nothing he could do for the man, other than keep him company. There were people with more claim to his attention, people he loved.

Not that he knew where they were. He decided he would try to reach Effi's flat. If she stayed in one of the big shelters she should be all right, but if she ended up at home his protection – and Nikoladze's letter – might be worth something.

The Reichsbahn uniform was somewhere under the wreckage, but the foreign worker outfit he was wearing should be almost as safe. Surely the Nazis had better things to do with their final hours than check credentials.

He hesitated for a moment at the top of the staircase, wondering what he could say to mark Varennikov's passing, but nothing came to mind. He remembered what the young Russian's father had said, that his son's life would unfold like the chronicle of a better world. So much for a father's dreams.

He gingerly worked his way down the wreckage-strewn staircase. At the bottom he hesitated, uncertain which way to go. North would take him away from the West End and Effi's apartment, but south was where he heard the gunfire. He opted for the latter. One thing about Russian soldiers – you could usually hear them coming.

He passed the bottom of the other spiral staircase and entered uncharted territory. It was hard to be certain underground, but the tracks seemed to be rising, which suggested they would soon emerge into the open. He knew there was an east-west running U-Bahn line somewhere in the near vicinity, but had no idea if there was any way of accessing it from the tunnel he was in. Iron ladders rose up to the roof at regular intervals, but the U-Bahn line would surely pass beneath him.

He was making his way around a long curve in the tracks when the walls ahead briefly shone with a faint yellow light. A split-second later he heard the scream, also faint, but no less bloodcurdling in its intensity. A flamethrower, he guessed. A few moments of agony before you died.

He could hear voices now, and the echoes of running feet. German voices, not that it mattered. No one coming down that tunnel would hesitate to shoot him.

He turned on his heels and hurried back towards the first iron ladder. It seemed much further than he remembered, and the voices behind him were growing louder. Had he missed one in the dark?

If so, he almost missed another, catching the gleam of metal as he hurried past. He grabbed hold of the ladder and started up, just as a burst of machine-gun fire erupted in the tunnel behind him. He was climbing into utter darkness, but assumed that the ladder had to lead somewhere.

And then his head made painful contact with something hard – an iron railing. He hung there for several seconds, gripping the ladder until the dizziness abated, then risked using the flashlight to examine his surroundings. He was at the top of a cylindrical shaft, where the ladder ended in a small platform, just beneath a circular plate.

The running feet sounded almost beneath him. He hauled himself onto the platform and pushed in desperation at the heavy-looking plate. Much to his surprise, it almost shot upwards, losing him his balance and tipping him back into the tunnel. He clambered swiftly out onto into the open air, rolled the cover plate back into place and looked around for something to weigh it down. He seemed to be in another goods yard, and the only movable objects with any weight were a couple of porters' trolleys lying on the ground nearby. He dragged them over and piled them on top of the plate, realising as he did so that they weren't heavy enough. But there was nothing else.

Time to go, he told himself. But which way? It was late in the afternoon, so the smoke-wreathed sun was in the south-west. There was a narrow roadway heading westward, and it soon passed under several elevated tracks, which had to be those heading south out of Potsdam Station. Rounding a corner, he received confirmation in the familiar silhouette of the Lutherkirche. He knew where he was.

He hurried up past the church, conscious once again of the city's ominous soundtrack. A short distance down Bülow Strasse some women were dissecting a fallen horse, its innards a vivid splash of red in the sea of greys and browns. For the moment no shells were exploding nearby, but that of course could change in an instant, and the women were working at a feverish pace. Walking past on the other side, Russell noticed several of their faces were streaked with white plaster, giving them the appearance of theatrical ghosts. Intent on securing their family's next few meals, they didn't seem to notice him, and when a shell landed a hundred metres down the street, none ran for the nearest shelter. When Russell glanced back from the Bülow Strasse station entrance they were all still carving at the bloody carcass.

This U-Bahn line ran underground all the way to Bismarck Strasse, and as far as Russell knew the Russians were still some kilometres away. There was no one to stop him descending to the platforms, and the tunnels, as he soon found out, were already in service as civilian highways. The current was obviously off.

He joined the steady stream of people heading west. Ventilation shafts provided occasional patches of light, but rendered the darkness between them even more intense, and progress was extremely slow. Despite the absence of any direct threat an almost hysterical atmosphere seemed to pervade the tunnels. There was always a child crying somewhere, and every now and then a sudden shriek would echo down the tunnel. It wasn't much more than three kilometres to Effi's building on Bismarck Strasse, but it took him the best part of two miserable hours to reach Zoo Station. The sight of several SS officers in conclave at the far end of the westbound platform offered all the incentive he needed to head back above ground.

Reaching the surface, he almost regretted the decision – night had fallen, most of Berlin was ablaze, and the Russians seemed much closer than he'd expected. A surprising number of people were hurrying across the wide expanse beside the Stadtbahn station, and he joined the rush, heading north up Hardenberg Strasse under the blood-coloured sky. Just beyond the railway bridge several figures were swaying on gibbets, reminding him to look out for SS patrols. The bastards might ignore him in his foreign worker uniform, but they could just as easily be looking for scapegoats.

And the uniform, he suddenly realised, was unlikely to win him a welcome at Effi's apartment building. In the last resort he could tear off the badge, but something smarter would be an improvement. From a corpse, he thought. There were enough of them lying around.

Some sort of fracas was underway at the Knie intersection, so he turned up the smaller Schiller Street, meaning to join Bismarck Strasse a little further down. There was a female corpse outside a bomb-damaged shop, and another close to the junction with Grolman Strasse, but no sign of the dead male he needed. A car with all its windows broken was parked in front of the ruined Schiller Theatre, and Russell had almost gone past it when he noticed the man slumped back in the driving seat, a gun still stuck in his mouth. After quickly scanning the street for witnesses, he pulled the body onto the pavement and into a niche in the rubble. The man looked about the right height, and he'd been kind enough not to get blood on his suit. Russell changed into the jacket and trousers, and congratulated himself on his luck – they fitted almost perfectly. The papers in the jacket pocket included a Nazi Party card with a suspiciously low number, and the bookmark in the man's diary was inserted beside a map of the Reich in 1942. No wonder he'd shot himself.

Russell hesitated a moment, then tossed the papers and diary away. If they weren't out of date, they soon would be.

As he reached Bismarck Strasse a welcoming shell landed half the way down to Adolf Hitler Platz. Effi's latest home was only a few buildings down, one of those an old and elegant Berlin mansions that they'd sometimes thought of buying, should they ever want to raise a family. The blackout regulations were presumably in abeyance, but none of the windows were lit – the residents would all be in the shelter. The front door opened to his push, and he walked upstairs in search of Number 4. That door was locked, and one half-hearted bang with a shoulder showed no sign of forcing it open.

A shell exploded nearby, causing the floor to slightly shift – perhaps the shelter was good idea.

He polished his story on the way down, and sought out the communal basement. Conversations faltered as he stepped inside, but only briefly. He scanned the hundred-odd faces; he was not expecting to see Effi's, but he wanted to give the impression that he did. Those still staring at him seemed relieved, probably at his lack of a uniform.

When he asked for 185's block-warden, a stout-looking woman in her forties was pointed out to him. 'That's Frau Esser.'

Russell introduced himself as Rainer von Puttkamer, Frau von Freiwald's older brother.

Frau Esser looked upset. 'I'm afraid she left over two weeks ago. And she didn't tell anyone where she was going.'

'Oh,' Russell said, 'that's a pity. She was expecting me. At least, she knew that if the Russians reached Beeskow – that's where our family home has always been – then I would be coming to her. Perhaps she left me a message in the apartment. But of course I don't have a key. Does the *portierfrau* have one, do you know?'

'I expect so. She's over there. Come with me.'

Russell obediently followed. He'd been ready with dramatic tales of a miraculous escape to explain his lack of papers, but it seemed that they wouldn't be needed – the imminent end of the war had finally made it all seem irrelevant. The *portierfrau* proved more than willing to let him use her key, and remarked on how much he looked like his sister. Perhaps it was true that couples grew to resemble other, Russell thought. He felt rather pleased by the notion, until he remembered that Effi was disguising herself as an older woman.

He was tempted to go up immediately, but an explosion nearby persuaded him otherwise. The camp beds that belonged to Frau von Freiwald and her niece were still waiting for them, a fact which Russell found surprising, but which Frau Esser took obvious pride in – the idea of personal property still meant something in *her* shelter. He introduced himself to his new neighbours, and received fulsome expressions of sympathy for the loss of the family estates. Declining the offer of a game of skat, he lay down and closed his eyes.

When he woke a few hours later, the only people still awake were an old couple reading a book by the glow of a Hindenburg light. The outside world seemed quiet, and after testing the silence for several moments he wended his way through the gently snoring bodies to the stairs. The sky above the courtyard was a fiery red, but the absence of shellfire persisted.

There was no electricity in the apartment, but once he'd pulled up the blackout blinds there was enough fire-reflected light to see by. Nothing reminded him of Effi though, until he came upon the blouse she'd been wearing that night in the Stettin Station buffet, when she'd calmly announced that she wasn't going with him. He lay down on the bed, and succumbed to the urge to sniff the pillow. He was hoping for the familiar scent of her hair, but all he could smell was damp.

Elsewhere in the flat he found clothes belonging to a child and another, bigger woman. But there was nothing to tell him anything more – no writing, no letters, only a collection of pencil drawings. He doubted they were Effi's – he couldn't remember her ever drawing anything. The other woman's probably – they seemed too good for a child. He leafed through them – they were like a visual diary of the city's fall.

In the Potsdam Station shelter it was almost midnight, and Effi had only just finished another long stint in the hospital. Now that the fighting was only a few kilometres away the medical staff were even busier, and the proportion of wounded soldiers to civilians was growing ever-higher. The presence of so many field grey uniforms had unfortunately attracted the attention of those in black, many of whom were now patrolling the corridors in search of possible deserters.

She had sent Rosa to bed an hour ago, and was on the way to join her when a young man on a corridor trolley caught her eye. He was wearing only undershorts, and his pale legs and trunk contrasted markedly with the dark stains of dried blood that covered his arms, neck and face.

It was Paul.

His eyes were closed but he was breathing well enough. The grim expression on his face gave her pause, but only for the briefest of moments. She had known him since he was eight years old. He would never betray her.

She touched him lightly on the shoulder, and his eyes jerked open. 'Paul,' she said softly. 'Remember me? Dagmar?'

He took in the familiar face, the nurse's uniform, and realised he was smiling. 'I saw you at Fürstenwalde Station,' he said.

'I saw you too. Aren't you cold? Where are your clothes?'

'A bit. My uniform's underneath the trolley. I had to take it off – it's covered in blood and brains.'

'Why, what happened to you?'

'A shell. I was on Grossbeeren Strasse. I've no idea how I got here.' He could see the expression on Werner's face. 'A friend had just been killed...' he began, but let the sentence die.

She saw the pain pass across his eyes. 'I'll get you a blanket,' she told him. 'I'll only be a moment.'

While she was gone he levered himself into a sitting position. He felt strange, but that was hardly surprising. Everything else seemed in working order. He vaguely remembered a doctor. He'd also been covered in blood.

Effi came back with a blanket and wrapped it around his shoulders.

'How did you end up here?' he asked her.

'A long story.'

'It must be,' he said with a wryness that reminded her of his father.

'One for later,' she warned him, as one of the doctors went past.

'You know that Dad escaped?' he whispered.

'Yes.'

'Do you know where he is now?'

'No,' Effi admitted. 'But I expect he'll arrive with the first Americans, whenever that is.'

'Why didn't you go with him?' Paul asked, without really meaning to. It felt like the question had asked itself.

'That's another long story.'

'Okay,' he agreed. He could hardly believe she was standing there in front of him. 'I saw Uncle Thomas a few days ago,' he told her.

Her face lit up, only to darken as Paul outlined the circumstances.

'He was planning to survive,' he concluded, as if that alone might save his uncle. He suddenly realised that a young girl had joined them, the one he'd seen with Effi on the Fürstenwalde platform.

'You're supposed to be asleep,' Effi scolded her, without any noticeable effect. It was hard to imagine Effi as an effective chastiser of children.

'You must be Paul,' the girl said in a very grown-up voice.

'I am. And who are you?'

'I'm Rosa at the moment. Rosa Borinski. My aunt has told me all about you. She's been taking care of me since my mother died.'

'That's right,' Effi agreed. 'Look, I'll leave you two together while I do what I can with Paul's uniform. Okay?'

'Okay,' Rosa said, looking suddenly shy.

'So what did Effi – Dagmar – tell you about me?' Paul asked her.

'Oh, that you like football. And models of ships. And that it was difficult for you having an English father.'

It had been, Paul thought. For a while it had coloured everything. And now it seemed utterly irrelevant.

'And that you lost your mother like I did.'

'It's all true,' Paul admitted. His mother's death seemed a long time ago.

A shadow loomed over them, two men in black uniforms with belts so stiff that they squeaked. Their insignia said they were Untersturmführers, the SS equivalent of lieutenants.

'Name?' one of them asked. He had a thick blubbery face with the sort of pop-out eyes that gave the master race a bad name. His companion, by contrast, was a trifle on the weaselish side. Both had one hand on their holsters, as if mimicking each other.

'Gehrts, Paul.'

'Papers.'

'They're in my uniform. It's just been taken to be cleaned.'

'Are you actually injured?' the second man asked.

'I was knocked out by shell-blast. The doctor said I have mild concussion,' he added, suddenly remembering as much.

'Do you have a chit?'

'I don't think so,' Paul admitted.

'The doctor's been too busy,' Effi said, coming up behind the two SS. 'But I can vouch for this patient.' She handed Paul his uniform. It still wore the stains of a messy death, but at least the fragments had been brushed away.

'What is your unit?' the first man asked.

'20th Artillery Regiment, 20th Panzergrenadier Division.'

'Their command base is now in the Zoo Bunker. You will report there immediately.'

'As soon as I'm dressed, Unterrsturmführer,' Paul agreed.

The man looked vaguely dissatisfied, but nodded his head and turned away. He and his partner walked off down the dimly lit corridor in search of other victims.

'I think I can persuade one of the doctors to write out a chit excusing you further service,' Effi told Paul. 'And then you can come back to the flat with us.'

Paul smiled and reached for his trousers. 'No, I couldn't do that.'

'Why ever not? There's no point in getting yourself killed at this stage.'

'I know. But I couldn't duck out on a lie. I owe my comrades better than that. If I decide to take my chances as a deserter I will – there's an honesty in desertion. But I won't cheat the system. Not while honest men are still dying.' He looked her straight in the eye. 'Does that sound childish to you?'

'No, just stubborn.' And she knew there'd be no budging him. There never had been once he'd decided on something. 'But if you change your mind...' She told him their address, and was about to add that his presence might offer them some protection when she realised that the opposite would probably be true. If he came between them and the Russians then the latter would probably shoot him. 'Just come when you can,' was all she said.

'Yes,' Rosa added, offering him a small hand to shake. Taking it, he found himself fighting back tears.

It was around two in the morning when Paul reached the Zoo Bunker flak towers. He had hitched a lift across town in a Ministry of Propaganda lorry – the Reich's few remaining tanks might be crying out for fuel, but delivering the latest edition of *Panzerbär* obviously had a higher priority. Skimming a copy by the light of the burning buildings on Tiergarten Strasse, he had discovered that treachery was rife and help on its way.

Despite the sporadic shellfire, tanks and infantry were scattered among the trees outside the Gun Tower, offering an illusion of control which shattered the moment he stepped inside the vast concrete edifice. Here the only deterrent to utter chaos was the degree of overcrowding, which rendered physical movement almost impossible. Every stairway, landing and room of the multi-storey block was occupied by a bewildering mixture of civilians and soldiers, all jostling for enough space in which to lie down.

It took Paul more than half an hour to seek out any semblance of military authority, and when he did the news was bad. The Untersturmführers at the Potsdam Station shelter had got their facts wrong – the remains of the 20th Panzergrenadier Division had been sent to Wannsee Island in the south-western outskirts, and the Russian occupiers of Dahlem and Grunewald now stood between Paul and his former comrades. A weary major suggested he attach himself to the 18th Panzergrenadiers, who were actually on the premises, but Paul's request for a precise location went unanswered. There were, the major added in explanation, over twenty thousand people crammed into the tower.

Paul went off in search of somewhere to sleep, and eventually found a large enough space to sit down in, provided his chin touched his knees.

As Saturday morning wore on it became increasingly clear to the inhabitants of the Potsdam Station shelter that some sort of crisis was brewing. More and more soldiers were arriving, many of them foreigners serving in the Waffen-SS. They had the air of men expecting to die, and no interest at all in those hoping for reprieve. If death was catching, they seemed like carriers.

'The doctors are all moving to the Zoo Bunker,' Annaliese told Effi.

'And the nurses?'

'Unofficially, we've been told to choose our own fate. We can go along, or stay here, or whatever we want. There's a group of us going west through the tunnels – one of the soldiers used to work for the S-Bahn and he says he can get us most of the way to Spandau.'

'What's so great about Spandau?'

'Nothing much. Gerd's parents live out there, so if all else fails I'll have somewhere to stay. But people say you can still get out of the city from there, and I'd like to leave the Russians behind. The Americans may not be any better, but they can hardly be worse. You should come with me. Both of you.'

'I have a sister to find' Effi said automatically. It occurred to her that the U-Bahn tunnel towards Spandau passed under Bismarck Strasse. 'But can we come with you as far as Knie?' she asked.

'Of course. The more the merrier. We're leaving now, by the way – I only came up to see if you wanted to come. And to say goodbye if you didn't.'

Effi picked up their suitcase. 'Let's go.'

Their route to the platforms took them through the hospital, which was still crowded with wounded.

'What will happen to them?' Effi heard herself ask. She already knew the answer.

'There's no way of moving them,' Annaliese confirmed. 'The Russians will have to look after them.'

They emerged into a wide corridor still plastered with Promi slogans, and descended a staircase lined with identical posters bearing the single word 'Persevere!' As they emerged onto the dimly lit platform, Annaliese spotted their group of around a dozen people. There was only one other woman, dressed somewhat incongruously in a long fur coat and hat. Most were middle-aged men in civilian clothes, without weapons or insignia. Minor government officials most likely, the holes still showing in their suit lapels where they'd pinned their badges of loyalty. A couple of *Hitlerjugend* bearing rifles made up the party; they were busy telling all who would listen that they were just heading back to their Ruhleben barracks.

After checking that everyone was present – the whole business had the air of a school outing, Effi thought – the ex-railway worker led them off the platform and down another staircase. They were still descending when a dull boom reverberated in the distance, then faded into silence. They all stood there listening for several moments, but there were no aftershocks, no sounds of roofs collapsing or soldiers approaching.

The lower of the two S-Bahn platforms was even more crowded, mostly with hungry-looking women and children. The ex-U-Bahn employee had just leapt down to the track bed when a low swishing noise became audible down the south-leading tunnel. It rapidly swelled in volume, rising above the cries of alarm, and exploded from the tunnel mouth in a surging wave of water. The ex-railway worker was knocked off his feet and carried along for at least twenty metres, before managing to fight his way out of the torrent.

All along the platform people were leaping to their feet, frantically gathering children and possessions, and looking round for the nearest exit. Most of the adults seemed to be shouting, most of the children crying. At the mouths of corridors scrums were already underway, as people fought for precedence in their desperation to get away.

Effi resisted the pull, fixing her eyes on the flooded track bed. The tide was slowing, the water rising, but the platform was a metre high and there seemed no immediate danger. Another few moments and they might have been inside the tunnel, with God only knew what results, but for now the platform seemed a much safer bet than the struggle on the stairs.

Rosa was standing beside her, staring open-mouthed at the dark, swirling water. As the tumult around the stairs grew less, they could both hear the screams of those trapped in the tunnels.

It was hot in the Zoo tower, and Paul awoke streaming with sweat from a few hours of miserable sleep. His body was stiff as a board, and there was a sharp pain in his back where the SS officer's machine pistol had pressed against it. He forced himself painfully to his feet, and watched the bodies around him expand into the few square centimetres he had relinquished.

The smells of sweat, shit and blood – the latter emanating from the continuous activities of the operating theatre on the ground floor –

permeated the entire structure, and the loudly whirring air extractors seemed incapable of shifting them. What they did do, was force everyone to shout above them, which only exacerbated the overriding sense of barely suppressed hysteria.

It was, Paul thought, as if they'd all been placed in a huge coffin. The lid was on, with only the burial to look forward to.

He had to get out.

His stomach rumbled, reminding him that he'd hardly eaten since the previous morning. There had to be food somewhere in the tower, or people would be even more agitated. He would seek it out, and maybe stumble across the 18th Panzergrenadiers in the process.

He eventually found the canteen he had frequented as a *flakhelfer*, and joined the long queue. There was only *wassersuppe* on offer, but it would improve the taste in his mouth. There was even a table to sit at, and after emptying the tin mug he laid his forehead on his folded arms and closed his eyes.

But sleep wouldn't come. On first joining the army he'd slept through anything quieter than a *katyusha* barrage, but that knack, like so much else, had eventually deserted him.

Two seats down a young soldier with a Rhenish accent was insisting that Wenck's Army could only be hours away. No one in his group disputed this, although some comrades were more inclined to put their faith in the imminent appearance of the long-anticipated wonder weapons. One corporal had heard rumours of bombs that could destroy whole cities, and of their intended use against London this coming weekend. When another man argued that Moscow should be the target, the corporal could only agree with him. But, sad to say, the Soviet capital was temporarily out of range.

Across the table a young army captain almost choked on his *wassersuppe*. 'Bunch of fools,' he spluttered in explanation when Paul caught his eye. The young soldiers seemed about to answer back, but were probably inhibited by the Knight's Cross at their critic's throat. Instead they rose in unison and made their way out, muttering indignantly amongst themselves.

Another group arrived to take their place, and were soon broadcasting their own rumours. Someone had heard that the Führer was getting married that day, to an actress that nobody had heard of. And that the actress was to going to feature on a new twenty mark note, dressed as a milkmaid.

The captain just shook his head at this one, and got up to leave. Paul thought about following suit, but where was there to go? Here he could stretch out his legs, and there was something comforting in listening to his fellow soldiers' conversations, no matter how moronic they were.

The ones to his right were discussing the benefits of life in the flak towers. For one thing they were safe from shellfire; for another they were safe from the SS squads now combing the city for deserters. Many civilians were putting out white flags to mollify the approaching Russians, but some were acting too soon, and drawing down the wrath of the SS. Buildings had been emptied, and all their inhabitants shot.

Paul's thoughts turned to Werner, and the red-headed Obersturmführer who had hanged him. If they both survived the war he would seek some kind of reckoning. The boy deserved a better epitaph.

He felt depression settling over him. Meeting Effi had lifted his heart, but the effect was wearing off. He found himself thinking about Madeleine, and their few weeks together. They'd shared their innermost secrets, even talked of marriage after the war, but their sexual relationship had never gone beyond passionate fumblings in the darkened Tiergarten. She had died in this building, and the chances seemed good that he would too.

He looked round the packed room and told himself to get a grip. With this many people and this much confusion there had to be some way out.

It was after five in the afternoon when Effi and Rosa climbed the staircases up to the shelter. After the initial rush the water had risen steadily for more than an hour, peaking at a point only a few centimetres beneath the rim of the platform. And then it had slowly begun to recede.

She had spent several hours pulling shocked and frightened people from the water. Most had needed no more help than that, and were soon on their way, heading up the stairs in search of sustenance and dry clothes. She reeled in the first few corpses that drifted by, but they appeared at such distressingly frequent intervals that she started letting them go. Most were children, and she ached at the thought that Rosa could well have been one of them.

Back in the shelter the SS presence seemed even more foreboding. The glint of guns was everywhere, and the children were all in *Hitlerjugend* uniforms. They found Annaliese in their old room, writing out a note. 'Thank God you're safe,' she said when she saw them. 'Where on earth have you been?'

As Effi told their story, she noticed the bruises on her friend's face and arms.

'I fell on the stairs,' Annaliese explained. 'Others were not so lucky,' she added. 'At least one child was trampled. It was insane.' She grimaced. 'I say that, and I was as bad as all the others.' She managed a rueful smile. 'I assumed you were right behind me. Anyway, I've given up on Spandau. There's a last transport leaving for the Zoo Bunker when it gets dark, so I thought I might as well join it. Why don't you come?'

'Okay,' Effi said without hesitation. The bunker at the Zoo towers might be terrible, but it could hardly be worse than this.

They spent the next couple of hours in a room close to the entrance. The shelter was less crowded than it had been – many long-term residents had concluded that the outside world, with all its Russian shells and soldiers, offered a better chance of survival than a last-ditch SS fortress. And if Effi was not mistaken, some of the SS felt the same. As she and Rosa waited to leave, several young supermen stopped to stroke the girl's hair and wish them good luck, tears in their pure blue eyes.

The transport was late arriving, and it was almost nine when the call came to climb the stairs. Effi hadn't breathed any outside air for several days, and the stars sprinkled above the shelter entrance gave her reason to smile. Potsdamerplatz, by contrast, was a wilderness of rubble. Since their vigil earlier in the week, the last facades had been torn away, and what remained bore an eerie resemblance to an ancient ring of stones.

Their lorry was pumping dark exhaust, its tailgate lowered to allow them aboard. There were fifteen of them, mostly medical staff that Effi recognised, with only a couple of hangers-on. Most seemed in high spirits, as if they were heading off on an adventure, rather than driving through shell-fire to another bastion of useless resistance.

In fact, there seemed to be a lull in the shelling. As they drove south on Potsdamer Strasse a full moon rose through the ruins behind them, and the city seemed more at peace than it had for weeks. They rattled over the hump-backed Potsdamer Bridge and turned right along the southern bank of the Landwehrkanal. Through the open back of the lorry Effi saw moonlight dancing on the gently rippling water, and the sudden eruption of flames from a building on the north bank. Another explosion followed, this one further back.

The lorry's engine started to cough. It limped on a few more metres and then suddenly jerked to a halt.

The driver was still fending off complaints when shells began landing all around them. Everyone scrambled out of the lorry, most seeking cover between the wheels. Others crammed themselves into the nearest convenient doorway, leaving Effi, Annaliese and Rosa running for the shelter of an alley. They had only just reached it when a shell exploded behind them with an enormous 'whumpf', and hurried them on like a strong gust of wind. Effi turned to see another building ablaze on the far side of the canal, and a shell explode in the shallow water, sending up a huge spout for the moon to burnish. A shower of drops landed all around them.

'Let's find somewhere better,' Annaliese insisted, already on her way. Effi went after her, Rosa's hand held tight in her own.

Another shell landed behind them, and this time there were human screams as well. The entrance to the alley was a wall of flames.

They emerged into a small and apparently deserted mews. A garage with open doors looked inviting, but offered no real protection. They hurried on down the narrow street, Effi conscious that they were heading south, and probably towards the Russians. The shell-fire seemed to have stopped, and she was wondering whether they should walk back towards the canal, or at least look for a road leading west, when she saw the car peeking out of its garage.

It was a black Hanomag, like the one that John had owned, the one in which he'd taught her to drive. She told Annaliese to wait, put down the suitcase, and went to inspect it. It had diplomatic plates, which was hardly surprising in an area known for its embassies.

'You don't suppose it has any petrol?' Annaliese asked at her shoulder.

'We have no key,' Effi reminded her. Squeezing in alongside the driver's door, she lowered the handle. It opened, but there the miracles ceased. There was nothing in the ignition.

Effi's face fell, but Annaliese was smiling. 'Gerd was a mechanic,' she said impatiently. 'I can start a car without a key if there's any fuel in its tank. Here are some matches. Have a look at the gauge.'

Effi struck one, and tried to make sense of the instruments. 'There might be some,' she said hesitantly.

'Well, get out of there and let me have a go.'

Effi did as she was told, and waited with Rosa outside the garage. 'Can we just take a car?' Rosa asked doubtfully.

'As long as we bring it back,' Effi reassured her. She had almost given up on Annaliese's promise when the car's engine sprang noisily to life. There was a grinding of gears, and it inched forward out of the garage, a beaming Annaliese at the wheel. 'Your taxi, Madam!'

Effi climbed in beside her, Rosa in the back.

'Where shall we go?' Annaliese asked.

'I'd like to go home,' Effi said.

'Me too,' Rosa agreed from the rear.

'And you can stay with us until it's over,' Effi suggested to Annaliese.

'I'll think about it. I might just drive on to Spandau once I've delivered you two. If that's all right with you. You found the car.'

'You're welcome to it.'

They drove slowly down the mews, turned right at the end, and soon found themselves on Lützow Strasse. Two military lorries went by in the opposite direction, but the once-busy avenue was otherwise empty of traffic. The moonlight was strong enough to steer by, and Annaliese turned off the lights. Driving round Lützowplatz she struck two pieces of rubble in quick succession, which shook everyone up but failed to slow the Hanomag.

It was ten in the evening but felt like four in the morning. Distant explosions flared in the wing mirrors but the world ahead seemed fast asleep. They arced round the ruined Memorial Church and under the railway bridge on Hardenberg Strasse. There was a barricade up ahead, so at Effi's suggestion Annaliese took a tight left turn and drove back down to Kant Strasse. A right fork at Savignyplatz brought them onto Grolman Strasse, which was just about passable.

'Our place is just round the corner,' Effi said hopefully, as they passed the ruins of the Schiller Theatre. If Grolman Strasse was anything to go by, the area had taken a pasting in her absence.

Annaliese stopped the car a prudent few metres short of the intersection, and examined the petrol gauge by the light of a struck match. It had risen slightly. 'I'll keep going,' she decided. 'It can't be much more than five kilometres from here, and Gerd's family could probably do with some help – they're quite old. And if they don't I can try and reach the Americans.'

The two women embraced, and Effi got out. Rosa primly reminded Annaliese that she had to take the car back once the war was over, and looked somewhat put out when the nurse just laughed.

She inched the car round the corner and, once reassured, accelerated out of sight.

Effi and Rosa followed. Bismarck Strasse had suffered fewer recent depredations than Grolman, and their building was still standing. This was reassuring, even though life was now lived in the shelter. Descending the steps, the first person they met was Frau Pflipsen, happily puffing on a Turkish cigarette. 'Where have you been?' she asked. 'Your brother's been here since yesterday.'

'My brother?' Effi echoed. 'Which one?' she improvised. 'I have so many.'

'I don't know. He's upstairs in your flat, I think. I've told him several times what a risk he's taking, but he doesn't seem to appreciate the danger. I don't suppose they've had much bombing in Beeskow.'

'No, probably not. I'll go up and get him. But you stay here with Frau Pflipsen,' she told Rosa. 'I won't be long.'

Effi hurried back up the steps, across the yard and into her building. It had to be Aslund, she thought. But what was he doing here? Was he on the run, after all this time? It didn't seem likely.

She trudged wearily up the stairs, and opened the unlocked door.

It was John, sitting in the chair by the window, apparently asleep. She let out a small gasp of delight. She couldn't believe it. Where had he come from? And how? She rushed towards him.

As she placed her hands on his shoulders his eyes opened.

'Effi,' he said, as if everything was right with the world. She looked thinner, exhausted, about ten years older. He had never seen anything half so beautiful.

He stood up, and they dissolved into each other's arms.

'How did you find me?' she asked after a few moments.

'Zarah told me where you lived.'

'But she doesn't...'

'She saw you in the street once and followed you. She needed to know where you lived.'

Effi shook her head in amazement. 'But how did you find Zarah? How did you get to Berlin?'

The Russians brought me. Would you believe I jumped from a plane out beyond Gatow?

She couldn't help laughing. 'Oh John, this is so wonderful.'

'I had to get to you,' he said simply. They stood there, hands on each other's shoulders, staring into each other's eyes.

'I saw Paul yesterday,' Effi said.

He gripped her shoulders a little tighter. 'Where? Is he okay?'

'It was in the big shelter at Potsdam Station. He was in the hospital, but he wasn't badly hurt – just a concussion. He's in uniform, of course, but he'd lost touch with his unit. Some SS bastards told him to report in at the Zoo Bunker, and I suppose he's still there.'

Russell's elation was edged with panic – his son was alive, but still at risk. And only a couple of kilometres away. 'How did he seem?'

Effi grimaced. 'It's hard to say. He was the same old Paul, and he wasn't. He's so much bigger than I remember, but that's... he seemed overwhelmed, but what young man wouldn't be after what they've all been through? You know that Ilse and Matthias were killed?'

'No, no I didn't. When? How?'

'Last year in a car accident. Out in the country. They reached the crest of a hill at the same moment as an army lorry. They were both killed outright.'

'Christ.' Russell had a sudden picture of Ilse in the foreign comrades' canteen, all those years ago. Paul would have been devastated. An utterly selfish thought crossed his mind: his son would need him now. 'Has Paul forgiven me?' he asked Effi.

'I don't know. He asked after you. He didn't sound angry.'

A shell exploded some way up the street, momentarily lighting up the room.

'Where did you see Zarah?' Effi asked. 'Is she all right?'

'"All right" might be an exaggeration. Jens tried to interest her in some suicide pills, so she walked out on him.'

'Ten years too late – no, I suppose Lothar was worth it. But... So she's back in Schmargendorf. Aren't the Russians there already?'

'Yes. She was expecting them. She... well, I don't think she's under any illusions. She told me she plans to stay alive for Lothar.'

'Oh God,' Effi murmured, as another explosion echoed down the street. But there was nothing she could do for her sister – the Russians would be between them by now. 'We really should go down to the shelter,' she told Russell.

'Okay.'

'Why were you up here?' she asked, taking his hand.

He smiled. 'Would you believe I wanted to be close to you?'

'I think I might,' she said, and gave him a kiss. 'But we must go down,' she insisted, as another shell exploded, closer this time. 'There's someone I want you to meet,' she added, as they descended the stairs.

'Not a new boyfriend, I hope.'

'No, just a new member of the family.'

'What?'

Effi paused at the top of the basement steps. 'She's seven years old and Jewish, and all her family are dead. I've more or less adopted her.'

'Right,' Russell said lightly. He could see a small fair-haired girl hovering at the bottom of the steps, staring up at them.

They went down. 'This is John,' Effi told the girl, after checking that no one else was in earshot. 'But we'll pretend he's my brother until the war ends.' She turned to Russell. 'And this is Rosa. We've had a lot of adventures together.'

The girl gave Russell a hopeful look, and offered a hand to shake.

Russell took it. 'I hear you're part of the family now,' he said with a smile. 'And I'd love to hear about all your adventures.'

'Of course,' Rosa told him, 'but we have to wait until after the war is over. We sleep through here,' she added, leading the way into the large basement room. Most of the inhabitants had already turned in, and one of two burning candles was snuffed out as they wended their way to the far corner. 'Our beds are still here, but someone has slept in mine,' Rosa whispered.

'That would be me,' Russell whispered back. 'I didn't know it was yours.'

'That's all right.'

Rosa and Effi took one camp bed, Russell the other, which suited the child rather better than him.

Despite trying hard to stay awake – she didn't want to feel left out, Effi realised – Rosa was soon asleep. The two grown-ups conversed in whispers, and she told him about Paul's meeting with his uncle. 'Thomas is also planning to survive,' Effi remembered. 'Like Zarah.'

The shelling outside was much more sporadic, and Russell realised he wouldn't need much encouragement to let desire get the better of sense.

He got none. 'I can't leave her down here on her own,' Effi said, in answer to his suggestion of a trip upstairs. If she woke up and found we were both gone... well...'

'You're right,' Russell told her. 'It was a stupid idea.'

'Not that stupid,' she said, carefully disentangling herself from the sleeping child. 'And I can at least join you over there.'

But entwined and kissing on the narrow camp bed, the issue became rather more pressing. 'Have the customs changed since 1941?' Russell eventually whispered. 'Is lovemaking in air-raid shelters permitted these days?'

'Not between brother and sister.'

'Oh.'

'So we'll have to be very quiet.'

No longer a road leading home

April 28 – May 2

It had been light for about an hour, and already the city centre was taking a frightful hammering. As Russell and two other men from the shelter worked their way down Grolman Strasse in search of a working standpipe, the sky to their left seemed choked with Soviet planes, the rise and fall of whining shells overlapping each other like a gramophone needle stuck in mid-symphony. In the centre of it all, the Zoo Bunker Gun Tower loomed above the ruined city, giving and taking fire, half cloaked in drifting smoke.

Paul was inside it.

Russell remembered what Effi had said about the boy seeming overwhelmed. He couldn't think of a better word to describe his own feelings. Seeing Effi again had filled him with joy, yet left untouched the dread of losing his son.

And Thomas too. If anyone deserved to survive this war then Thomas did.

A crowd up ahead suggested water, which proved to be the case. Joining the queue, they stood there scanning the sky like everyone else, knowing that a bomb could perhaps be outrun, that a shell would give no warning.

Neither fell, and soon they were hurrying back up the street with their containers, trying not to slosh any water overboard.

Effi was waiting at the bottom of the steps, looking almost angry. 'What happened?' she asked. 'You've been so long.'

Russell put the containers down, and explained that the usual standpipe had taken a direct hit. 'We had to go further afield. One of the men I was with remembered a tap on Grolman.'

'I...' she started to say, and just pulled him to her.

'There were soldiers here while you were gone,' Rosa announced from behind her.

'Two of them,' Effi confirmed. 'They said the Russians are in West-kreuz, so it shouldn't be long.'

'Where did they go?'

Effi shrugged. 'Who knows? They seemed lost, but they wouldn't abandon their uniforms, so Frau Essen had to ask them to leave.'

The three of them made their way back to their corner. There was a drawing on Rosa's bed, one of Effi that almost brought tears to his eyes. Russell realised that the girl had drawn the pictures he had seen upstairs. 'This is wonderful,' he told Rosa. 'We must get it framed, and hang it in our new house.'

Effi smiled at that, and Rosa's face lit up. 'I can do one of you too,' the girl said. 'If you'd like. But I promised Frau Pflipsen I'd draw her next. '

'Whenever you have time,' Russell assured her. It was noisy in the shelter, and while Rosa was across the room immortalising her latest subject, he and Effi had the chance to talk. During the night she had told him where Rosa had come from, and now he asked her if Erik Aslund was still in Berlin.

'As far I know,' she replied.

'We may need him,' Russell said quietly. He made sure that they were not being overheard. 'Look, I've been doing some thinking. The Nazis are history, or soon will be. We can forget the bastards, thank God. Germany will be divided up between the Russians, the Americans and the British. And maybe the French. They've already drawn the boundaries. The same goes for Berlin. It'll be right in the middle of the Russian zone, but the city itself will be shared out.

'But not for a while,' he went on. 'The Russians will want to grab everything they can, so they'll take their time. They'll say the city isn't properly secure – something like that.'

'Whose bit are we in now?' Effi asked out of curiosity.

'Probably the British, but what I'm saying is that they won't be here for weeks, maybe even months. It's the Russians we'll have to deal with, and they'll be eager to talk to me.'

'Why?' Effi asked. 'You still haven't told me why they brought you here.'

He went through the story – the American decision to let the Russians take Berlin, his own trip to Moscow, the offer of inclusion in the Soviet team seeking out atomic secrets. He told her what had happened to Kazankin and Gusakovsky at the Kaiser Institute, and how he and Varennikov had hidden out in Thomas's house.

'There are plans for an atomic bomb buried in Thomas's garden?' she asked incredulously.

'In Hanna's vegetable patch, to be precise.'

'Okay.'

'And I'm the only one who knows where they are,' he added. 'Varennikov was killed a few days later.'

'How?'

Russell sighed. 'A train fell on him.'

'A train fell on him,' she repeated.

'I know. But that's what happened.'

'All right. But what's the problem? You just hand the plans over to the Russians – no one else need know.'

'That might be the sensible thing to do. Or it might not. I can think of two good reasons why it wouldn't be. First off, the Russians might want to make absolutely sure that I don't tell anyone else. Like the British or the Americans.'

'But that's silly,' Effi protested. 'You could never tell them that you'd just helped the Russians to an atomic bomb. They'd put you in prison.'

'Or hang me for treason. I know that and you know that, but the NKVD doesn't like loose ends.'

'I suppose not.' She felt crestfallen. Overnight it had seemed like the worst might be over.

'I've been thinking I need to bargain with them,' he went on.

'The papers for your life,' she guessed.

'Yes, but more than that. If Paul and Thomas survive, they'll end up in Soviet camps. Zarah might be arrested too – she is the wife of a prominent Nazi, and the Russians are certainly feeling vindictive. So I thought I'd offer them the papers in exchange for the whole family.'

Effi smiled, but looked dubious. 'You know the Russians better than I do, but won't they think that a bit of a cheek? And what's to stop them beating the location out of you? Or just agreeing and then reneging on the bargain once they have the papers?'

'Nothing, at the moment. But that's where your Swedish friend might be useful.' Russell outlined what he had in mind, and she began to see a glimmer of hope. 'But first we wait,' he said. 'The Soviets gave me a letter to use when making contact, and I hope it'll offer us – you – some sort of protection when the ordinary troops arrive. Once the battle's over, I'll find someone senior to approach.'

'That sounds good,' Effi agreed. When they woke up that morning, she had half expected him to set off in search of Paul.

'I thought about heading over to the Zoo Bunker,' he said, as if reading her mind. 'But even if I got there safely, and no one arrested me on the spot, what could I do? I can't order Paul to come home. He's not fourteen anymore, and he'll have a much better idea of the situation down there than I have. If he wants to desert, and he thinks he can get away with it, then he will.'

'He has this address,' Effi reminded him.

It was soon after eleven in the morning that an overheard conversation in the soldiers' canteen pointed Paul in the direction of escape. There were, it seemed, over five hundred corpses in the two towers, not to mention a vast and growing collection of amputated limps. All needed burying, but finding men willing to leave the safety of the walls and dig the necessary graves, while Soviet gunners cratered and re-cratered the area concerned, was far from easy. Why risk the living for the dead?, was most people's response to any such request.

A few thought differently. Some were claustrophobic, others beaten by the smell or undone by the stress of waiting. Some, like Paul, saw no point in dying to defend a last fortress when everything else was lost. If they were going to die, then better to die outside, where at least you could move and breathe. And where there was always the chance you might slip through a crack and keep on living.

There were around twenty of them all told, lined up outside the packed mortuary with rags across their nostrils to keep out the appalling smell. Each pair carried a bloody stretcher, but Paul, finding himself odd man out, was given two large sacks of arms, legs and heads to carry. He tried to keep the sacks off the ground, but they were simply too heavy, and once outside the walls he settled for dragging them across the grass.

The plot chosen for the burials was just to the north of the Zoo, around two hundred metres from the Gun Tower, but no one had thought to bring digging implements. A few men went back for them, and while Paul and the others awaited their return a shell struck the Control Tower, gouging a hole a metre deep in a wall three times as thick. He supposed the towers might eventually be battered into submission, but the food would run out long before that.

All the men were privates or corporals, and the only deterrents to walking off were peer pressure and a calculation that life on the streets would prove even more hazardous than life in the tower. Paul had intended burying his two sacks, but as more and more minutes went by with no sign of spades, he felt his sense of obligation fade. When others started back towards the tower, leaving their stretchered corpses on the grass, he abandoned his own bag of body-parts and hurried off towards the nearest bridge across the Landwehrkanal.

It was broken, and so, he could see, was the next one up. He retraced his steps and headed for the Zoo, whose geography he knew by heart from many childhood visits. Using one of several new gaps in the boundary wall, he worked his way between wrecked cages and cratered enclosures in the general direction of the nearby railway station. Several eviscerated antelopes were spread across one area, and a dead hippopotamus was floating in the pool. A few yards further on, he almost tripped over a human corpse, a man with a Slavic face in a tattered suit. They were about the same size, and Paul hesitated for a moment, considering a switch of clothes. He was, he realised, reluctant to shed his uniform. He told himself he'd be safer with than without it – if the SS caught him in civilian clothes they wouldn't waste time with questions.

Walking on, he found another convenient gap in the boundary wall and emerged onto the road that ran alongside the railway embankment. Zoo Station's glass roof was gone, or rather it was dispersed in a million shards. On the far pavement a group of civilians were walking eastward in close formation, like an advancing rugby scrum. Paul crunched his way across the square where he'd often met his father, and turned up Hardenberg Strasse. The railway bridge was still standing, but a gaping hole showed through the tracks.

The occasional plane flew low overhead, and only seconds went by without a shell exploding somewhere nearby, but today he felt strangely immune. It was ridiculous, he knew – maybe the concussion had left him with delusions of invincibility. Maybe the Führer had received a bang on the head in the First War. It would explain a lot.

He heard himself laugh on the empty street, and felt the sting of tears. 'No one survives a war,' Gerhart had told him once.

There was a barricade up ahead, so Paul headed back down to Kant Strasse. At the farthermost end of the long straight street a tattoo of sparks split the gloom. Muzzle flashes, he thought. The Russians were closer than he'd expected.

He worked his way around Savignyplatz, turned the corner into Grolman Strasse, and came to an abrupt halt. On the far side of the street, around thirty metres in front of him, a tall SS Obersturmführer was facing away from him, holding a rifle. His uniform seemed stunningly black amidst the ash and the dust, his boots insultingly shiny. Red hair peeked out from the rear of his cap.

Werner's killer.

He was about to kill again. Two men were kneeling in front of him, one protesting violently, the other looking down at the ground. The muzzle of the rifle was resting on the former's forehead.

Behind them, a line of women with petrified faces were clutching all sorts of kitchen pots. The standpipe beside them was noisily splashing water into the dust.

The rifle cracked and the head almost seemed to explode, showering the victim's companion with blood and brain. Several women screamed, and some began to sob. Paul started forward, pulling the machine pistol from his belt.

Some of the women noticed him, but none of them shouted out. The rifle cracked again, and the second man collapsed in a heap.

Paul was about ten metres away. Hearing footsteps behind him the Obersturmführer turned. Seeing a soldier in uniform he offered Paul a curt smile, as if to reassure him that everything was in hand.

He was still smiling when Paul put a bullet in his stomach. He tried to lift the rifle, but a second shot to the chest put him down on his knees. He looked up with lost puppy eyes, and Paul smashed the pistol across the side of his head with all the force he could muster.

The man slumped to the ground, blue eyes dead and open.

Paul dropped the pistol. He felt suddenly dizzy, and stood there, swaying slightly, only dimly aware of the world around him. A woman was saying something, but he couldn't hear what. He could see something coming towards him, but had no idea what it was.

Someone was calling his name. 'It's me. Your Dad. Are you okay?'

'Dad?' He couldn't believe it.

Russell put an arm around the boy's shoulders. On his way to the standpipe for the second time that day, he'd been lucky enough to see the SS officer before the SS officer saw him, and had witnessed the whole scene from a corner fifty metres up the road. Unarmed, he had watched aghast as the executions took place, and only realised at the last moment that the lone soldier was his son. 'It's me. Are you okay?'

Paul had no idea what the answer to that was. 'He killed my friend, Dad,' was all that came to mind.

'You knew one of those men?'

'No, no. Not today. He killed my friend Werner. Two days ago, or three. Werner was only fourteen, and he hanged him as a deserter.' Paul started to cry and Russell cradled him in his arms, or at least tried to. His son was now taller than he was.

'We'll go to Effi's building,' he told Paul. 'It's only a ten-minute walk, but I have to get some water first.' He had left his containers further up the street, but those that belonged to the dead men were still sitting on the pavement, so he simply collected those and waited for his turn at the tap. Paul stood off to one side, staring blankly into the distance.

Water collected, they each took two containers and started up the street. But they'd hardly gone a hundred metres when two Panthers rumbled across the intersection with Bismarck Strasse, a surprisingly neat formation of troops following in their wake. *Hitlerjugend*, to judge by their size.

Another followed. They stopped and waited for the danger to pass, but eventually another tank slewed round the corner and headed towards them. Russell led Paul off into a side street, looking for somewhere to hide for a while. There was a small enclosed courtyard a little way down, with a full complement of surrounding walls, and they took up refuge inside, straining their ears for approaching men or armour.

Russell knew he should talk to his silent son, but couldn't think where to begin. With what had just happened? With his mother's death? What could he say that wouldn't rub salt in wound after wound? Just what he felt, perhaps. 'It's so good to see you,' he said simply. 'I've missed you so much.'

Paul stared back at him, a solitary tear running down one cheek. 'Yes,' he said, the ghost of a smile forming on his lips.

'It heals,' Russell heard himself say, just as footsteps sounded in the street outside. A moment later a man put his head round the corner of the courtyard entrance. He was wearing a leather jacket and baggy trousers tucked into high felt boots. A star adorned the front of his hat.

Seeing the two of them sitting against the wall, he called out to his comrades and ran quickly forward, rifle at the ready. Russell and Paul raised their hands high, and got to their feet. By this time two others had arrived. Both were wearing around a dozen wrist watches on the outside of their sleeves.

'Comrade, I need to talk to your commanding officer,' Russell told the soldier in his own language. How long had his father spoken Russian, Paul wondered.

The soldier looked surprised, but only for a second. 'Come,' he ordered, swinging his rifle in the requested direction.

They were hustled down the street. In a courtyard further down a Red Army sergeant with pale blue eyes was studying a street map in the front seat of an American jeep. He looked up with a bored expression.

'Comrade, I have been working for the Soviet Union,' Russell told him. 'I have credentials from the NKVD inside my jacket. Will you look at them please?'

The eyes were more interested now, but also suspicious. 'Give them to me.'

Russell handed over Nikoladze's letter and watched the man read it. At that rate *War and Peace* would take the rest of his life.

'Get in the jeep,' the sergeant told him.

Russell stood his ground. 'This is my son,' he told the Russian.

'This says nothing about a son,' the sergeant said, waving the letter. 'And he is a German soldier.'

'Yes, but he is my son.'

'Then you will meet again. Your son is prisoner. Don't worry – he will not be shot. We are not like Germans.'

'Please, don't separate us,' Russell pleaded.

'Get in the jeep,' the sergeant reiterated, a hand on his holstered pistol.

'I'll be all right, Dad,' Paul managed to say.

Russell climbed in beside the driver, and another man climbed in behind them. 'I'll find you,' Russell shouted above the revving engine, and was almost thrown from his seat as the jeep swung out of the courtyard.

Looking back, he had a final glimpse of Paul standing among his captors, his face bereft of expression.

The jeep roared down Kant Strasse, where only a few wary-looking Soviet infantry were in evidence. As far as Russell could see the Russians were advancing eastward up this street while German troops headed west along the parallel Bismarck Strasse, like dogs chasing each other's tails. The Soviets would eventually win through of course, but they might, for the moment, have over-extended themselves in this particular sector. It was hard to tell. It might take them days to reach Effi's building. Or only hours.

He prayed she would be all right.

He prayed that Paul would be all right. He had believed the Russian's promise not to shoot his son, but front-line troops were one thing – they tended to respect their opposite numbers – the men behind them something else. And there was always the chance that Paul would run into someone who was aching for revenge. At best he would end up in a poorly provisioned prison camp, with no prospect of an early release. The Soviets were slow at the best of times, and looking after German POWS would be nowhere on their list of priorities.

Russell found it hard to blame them. If he was Stalin, he'd probably keep his German prisoners until they'd rebuilt every last home and factory.

But the thought of another long separation was almost unbearable. On the last occasion he'd seen his son, Russell had left a fourteen-year-old boy to complete a U-Bahn journey on his own, and worried that something might go wrong. Today he had watched him stride up to an SS officer and shoot the man dead. How many shocks and blows had it taken to get from one to the other? Shocks and blows that a father might have managed to soften or deflect.

But first he had to get him back. The jeep passed over the Ringbahn at Witzleben, and turned onto Messedamm. The loop at the northern end of the Avus Speedway had been turned into a military camp, two T-34s rumbling out as they headed in; others were refuelling from a horse-drawn petrol tanker. The driver parked the jeep in front of an obvious command vehicle and disappeared inside. Russell tried unsuccessfully to make small-talk with the man behind him. This soldier had several watches on one arm, and seemed intent on listening to each one in turn, as if anxious that one might have stopped.

Russell looked around. The mingled smells of manure and petrol made the makeshift camp seem like a cross between a farm and a garage, and he smiled at the thought that such an army had beaten Hitler's.

The driver reappeared, along with a sour-looking major who now had charge of Nikoladze's letter. He gave Russell a long cold stare, and the letter back to the driver. 'Take him to the new HQ,' Russell thought he said.

They set off again, heading south through Schmargendorf. The driver seemed happy with life, whistling as he drove, but disinclined to conversation. It was probably the letter, Russell thought. Any sort of association with the NKVD – as ally or victim – was inclined to inhibit normal interaction.

Now they were driving through conquered Berlin, through districts where the war was effectively over. Soviet troops were much in evidence, gathered round canteen carts or impromptu fires, feeding their animals or repairing vehicles. One soldier wobbled by on a captured bicycle, then delighted his comrades by falling off.

There were more Germans out in the open, and some at least were mingling with their conquerors. They saw several burial parties, but an enormous number of corpses still lay uncollected on the streets. As they drove through Steglitz a woman screamed in a house nearby, and the soldier in the back said something that Russell didn't catch. The driver laughed.

It was a long ride, and one that impressed on Russell just how much of Berlin was in ruins. The building near Tempelhof which proved his final destination stood alone in a field of rubble, with all the pride of a lone survivor. Signs proclaimed it the headquarters of the new Soviet administration.

This time Russell was taken inside, and left in an office still decorated with 'Strength Through Joy' cruise posters. After about ten minutes a tall, handsome Russian with prematurely grey hair appeared. He was wearing a regular lieutenant-colonel's uniform, but the insignia told Russell he was a political commissar.

'Explain,' the Russian ordered, placing Nikoladze's letter on the table between them.

'I can only tell you so much,' Russell told him with feigned regret. 'I arrived in Berlin ten days ago, as part of an NKVD team. I can't tell you the purpose of our mission without compromising state security. I suggest you contact Colonel Nikoladze, because I am forbidden to discuss this matter with anyone else.'

'Where are the other members of your team?'

'They are dead.'

'What happened to them?'

'I can only discuss this with Colonel Nikoladze,' Russell said apologetically.

The commissar gave him a long angry look, sighed, and got back to his feet.

'I have a request,' Russell said.

'Yes?'

'My wife is in Berlin, in the Charlottenburg area. She has been involved in resistance work, here in the city. Once her area has been secured, would it be possible to arrange some sort of protection?'

'It might be,' the Russian said, as he opened the door to leave. 'Why don't you take the matter up with Colonel Nikoladze?'

It was only when Effi caught sight of the two elderly men who'd accompanied Russell on his water-gathering expedition that she realised he hadn't come back. The two returnees were already fending off criticism for returning with empty saucepans, and it took her a while to make sense of their story. An SS officer had apparently executed two deserters whom he found in the standpipe queue, and had then been shot by another soldier.

Russell had rushed from their hiding place to intervene, but they had beaten a hasty retreat. They had no idea what had happened after that, although one man seemed pretty sure that no more shots had been fired.

Effi asked herself what could have happened. Had the soldier taken Russell away? That didn't seem very likely. But what other explanation could there be? – he wouldn't just take off without telling her.

As afternoon turned to evening with no sign of him, her anxiety grew more acute, and when time came for sleep, it proved mostly elusive. She lay beside Rosa, warmed and somewhat comforted by the sleeping child, but plagued by the thought that she had lost him again. When dawn came she volunteered herself for water collection, determined to gather what clues she could at the site of his disappearance.

Approaching the standpipe with two other women, she braced herself for the worst. But there were only three bodies neatly laid out by the side of the street – a red-headed SS Obersturmführer and two men in civilian clothes, all shot. There was no sign of Russell, and no one in that morning's queue who had witnessed the previous day's excitement. Effi thought about waiting for others to arrive, but the sounds of battle seemed closer than ever, and she had to get back to Rosa before the Russians arrived. With heavy heart, she filled the pans with water and slowly made her way up Grolman Strasse.

On Bismarck Strasse, German soldiers were falling back in the direction of the Tiergarten, their hold apparently broken. A succession of muffled booms only confused her for a moment – a battle was raging in the U-Bahn tunnels that ran under the street.

The Russians would be there soon, and perhaps it was better that Russell would not be there to greet them. His letter might have provided protection, but then again it might not. And if the Russians really were intent on rape, she was glad he wouldn't be there. He wouldn't be able to stop them, but he could certainly get himself killed.

On that Sunday morning Paul woke with the scent of lilac in his nostrils. One of several thousand prisoners corralled in a wired-off section of south-east Berlin's Treptower Park, he had staked out a space to sleep beside the blossoming bushes on the previous evening. They smelt of spring, of new beginnings.

The night had been cold, the ground hard, but he'd slept long and well. The sense of relief he'd felt on arrival seemed just as strong that morning – his war was over. There were no more choices to make, everything was out of his hands. If the Russians decided to kill him there was nothing he could do to stop them. In the meantime he would lie there and smell the lilac.

He had arrived at the makeshift camp just before dark. Ivan had been good to him overall. A few unnecessary shoves, but that was nothing. One guard had even offered him a cigarette, and he'd put it behind his ear, the way Gerhart used to. After queuing for ages, his name, rank and number had been taken down by a Russian with an extravagant beard, and then he'd been placed in the teeming pen. The food was terrible, but not much worse than he was used to. He had no injuries, so the lack of medical facilities didn't affect him personally. Captured German medics were doing the best they could with what little the Russians had given them.

Now that the sun was up, he supposed he should take a look round. Maybe Hannes was here, or even Uncle Thomas. But he stayed where he was, pondering the day before. He couldn't have spent much more than half an hour with his father, and there was something dreamlike about the whole encounter. But he knew it had happened – he could remember his father saying how much he had missed him.

He could also remember shooting the red-headed Obersturmführer. He had no regrets about that. If he ever found Werner's mother and sister, he could tell them the killer had paid for his crime.

Russell was pacing the office room that served as his prison. Having spent most of the night agonising about Effi and his son, he was trying to calm himself down. He had to focus on what he could do, and not let his fears and anxieties distract him.

Which was easier thought than achieved. He went over his plan again, talking out loud to keep his concentration. He rehearsed what he intended saying to Nikoladze, in both content and tone. If he'd ever needed to convince another man of something, then this was the occasion.

He would do it, he told himself. The plan would work. Maybe not for him, but at least for the others. And he'd had his three years of freedom, while they'd all been trapped in the nightmare. It was his turn now.

As the morning wore on, he found himself thinking about the future of Germany, and the city that had been his home for most of the last twenty years. Berlin would of course be divided. They would call it a temporary measure, but it couldn't be, not really. The country as well. Anyone expecting anything else was a fool – there was no middle ground between the Soviet system of state planning and the free market. In each zone of Berlin, each zone of the Reich, one or the other would be imposed by the occupying power. And that would be that for the foreseeable future.

Given his current circumstances, Russell doubted he'd be given the choice where to live. But if he had one, which would he choose? Did he want to live in a corner of Stalin's empire? Because that's what it would be. He would probably have given it a try twenty years ago, when the whole Soviet experiment was still a flailing child of hope. But now, looking back over millions of dead, it was clear that the flaws had been there from the start. It was impossible to regret a revolution that championed equality, brotherhood and internationalism, but there had never been any chance of institutionalising those values in a country as backward and traumatised as Russia. Once the German revolution had failed it was all over. Trotsky had been right in that, if in little else – like Varennikov's atomic bomb, socialism only worked as a chain reaction. Cage it in one country or empire, and the result would be brutal. Moscow was no place for journalists interested in truth or criticism, and a Soviet-dominated Germany would be no different.

Did he want to live in the dollar's empire? Not a lot, but on balance it had more to offer than Stalin's. The idea stuck in his throat, though. It had been Europe's communists who had fought Nazism and fascism, who had given their lives while Americans had sat back and profited. He was already sick of hearing them boasting how they'd come again to

Europe's rescue, forgetting the far bigger sacrifices of the Red Army, not to mention the fact that most Americans had been only too happy sitting on the fence until the Japanese pushed them off it.

There was a lot he disliked about America and its priorities. But he could imagine that country producing a Brecht, and he couldn't say the same of the Soviet Union. The dollar was indifferent – it didn't care if you lived or died, and for people with education and means, people like himself, freedom and privilege were there for the taking. The NKVD, by contrast, was caring to a fault. Whatever you did was their business, with all the constraints that that implied. Neither knowledge nor money offered much in the way of protection, and often invited the opposite.

A key turned in the door, interrupting his reverie.

It was the same lieutenant-colonel, wearing a slightly less hostile expression. 'Colonel Nikoladze should arrive here early tomorrow morning,' he told Russell. 'And I've been instructed to provide your wife with protection. If you could give me the exact address?'

Russell did so, and explained that Effi was using an alias. 'And please ask your men to tell her that I'm all right.'

The Russian wrote it all down with the stub of a pencil. 'You are not a prisoner,' he told Russell, 'but you will of course remain here until the Colonel arrives. Consider this room your quarters.'

By noon the Russians were in control of Bismarck Strasse. Street battles could still be heard raging in every direction, but no German forces had been seen since mid morning, whereas Ivan was much in evidence. Soldiers had come to their basement, scared its residents half to death, and left with every available wristwatch, Effi's included. Other men and vehicles passed by at regular intervals, and a horse-drawn canteen had opened for business some fifty metres down the street.

The shelling, of course, had stopped, and while many lingered in the basements, hoping for the safety of numbers, some ventured outdoors, drawn by curiosity and the promise of sunshine. Others, like Effi and Rosa, returned to their apartments, and Rosa spent most of the afternoon by the window, drawing the conquering army. Or, as Effi realised when she saw the drawings, the army of Rosa's liberation. The Russians looked so good, smiling and waving from the turrets of their shiny tanks; even their horses looked glad to be there.

There had been no trouble so far, but Effi feared the coming of darkness. In the event, she didn't have that long to wait – the light was only beginning to fade when the first female screams were heard in the distance. She hesitated a moment, but realised she couldn't just sit there and wait. She took Rosa to the basement and went out in search of someone to plead with.

She found one Soviet officer, but he didn't speak a word of German, and her attempts at mime drew only smiles and shrugs of non-comprehension. Walking back towards her building, she felt eyes following her, and realised how big a mistake she had made. Footsteps behind her confirmed as much, and sent a chill down her spine.

She hurried in through the door, shutting it behind her. Upstairs or downstairs? Rosa was in the basement, but the piece of paper on which Russell had written his Soviet commander's name was up in the flat.

She was still running up the stairs when she heard the front door splinter. She threw herself into the flat and began frantically searching for the paper. It had vanished.

She turned to see them in the doorway. One was short and wiry, with a shock of blond hair and gold front teeth. The other was darker-skinned and burly, with longish black hair and moustache. Boots and caps excepted, both looked as though they'd been outfitted at a rummage sale. And she could smell them from across the room.

They were both grinning at her, the small one with relish, the other with something more like hatred. 'Hello,' the blond one said, as if he was surprised to see her. He muttered something in Russian to his partner and started across the room towards her. The other man was looking round the room, presumably for portable loot.

'No,' Effi said, backing away. 'I'm too old,' she insisted, running a hand through her hair to show the grey. 'Like your mother, your grandmother.'

The big Russian said something, stopping the other in his tracks. He had one of Rosa's new drawings in his hand, and was beaming at it.

'We're friends,' Effi insisted, but the blond soldier refused to be distracted. Lunging forward he caught her by the arm and pulled her towards him. Placing a hand on top of her head, he pushed her down to her knees, then swung her onto her back. With a knee planted either side of her waist, and one hand holding her down at the throat, he started to tear at her clothing.

With a scream of fury Rosa hurtled into the room and flung herself at Effi's attacker. 'That's my mother,' she yelled, wrapping a small arm round his head. 'That's my mother!'

He grunted and swept her away, then ripped open Effi's blouse. She was finding it hard to breathe.

Rosa was still screaming, but the other man had lifted her up and was holding her at arm's length. I have to submit, Effi thought, or God knows what they'll do to her. She let herself go limp, and felt the pressure ease on her throat.

He smiled in triumph, and started undoing his trousers.

The other Russian shouted something. There was a curse from the one on top of her, and what sounded like a command from his partner. Her assailant had been halted for the moment, but was still arguing, and Effi could see the frustration bulging in his trousers. One word was being repeated over and over, and she realised what it was – *Yevr'ey* – the Russian for Jews. The burly soldier was pointing at Rosa's blouse, and the faded star it bore. 'Yevr'ey!' he said again.

Her assailant was reluctant to abandon his conquest, but his partner wore him down. 'Many', 'women' and 'Berlin' were words that Effi thought she recognised, and which made some sort of sense. Eventually her assailant sighed loudly, grinned at her, and pulled the blouse back across her breasts. 'Okay,' he said, as he clambered back to his feet. '*Nyet Yevr'ey.*'

'We tell others. You safe,' the darker man told her in passable German. 'I also Jew,' he added in explanation.

They left, taking one of Rosa's pictures as a souvenir. Effi lay there on the floor, remembering how to breathe. Rosa lay down beside her and put her head on Effi's shoulder. 'I can tell you now,' she said. 'Rosa is my real name. Rosa Pappenheim.'

Ten minutes later two smartly uniformed Russians arrived at their door. They had been sent by the new city administration to protect Frau von Freiwald. 'Mr John Russell,' they assured her, was 'alive and well.'

Soon after eight in the morning Russell was escorted up several flights of stairs to a huge office on the top floor. Four large desks and many more cabinets lined the inner walls, yet still left space for two long leather settees, which faced each other across a low table and a dark crimson carpet. Yevgeny Shchepkin and Colonel Nikoladze were seated at either end of one settee; behind them, through two of the city's last unbroken windows, Russell could see smoke rising from the distant Reichstag.

Neither man got up. Nikoladze offered Russell a curt smile as he waved him onto the other settee, Shchepkin something warmer, and perhaps a little mischievous. His old acquaintance looked awful, Russell thought, but better than he had in Moscow. And he was pleased to see him. Shchepkin was not essential to Russell's plan, but he couldn't shake the feeling that their fates were in some way connected. That was not why Nikoladze had brought him, of course – the NKVD would still be thinking that Shchepkin was someone whom Russell might trust, and who therefore might come in handy.

Russell realised that he might be kidding himself, but he felt his hand strengthened by Shchepkin's presence. And weak as the hand was, that could only be good.

Nikoladze was not a man to waste time on pleasantries. 'So the others are dead?' was his opening line.

'They are,' Russell admitted.

'Yet you are alive,' the Russian noted, as if that should be counted against him.

'As you see.' Russell sneaked a glance at Shchepkin, who was staring into space.

'Give us your report.'

Russell began with the botched landing west of Berlin, avoiding any reference to Varennikov's momentary panic – there was no point in putting Irina's pension at risk. He explained how it had upset their timetable, and resulted in their arriving at the Institute twenty-four hours later than scheduled. He described the successful break-in, and Varennikov's excited reaction to some of the papers.

'He did find something!' Nikoladze exclaimed, leaning forward in his seat. 'Where are these papers?'

'We'll get to that. Let me tell the story.'

Nikoladze gave him a look, but waved him on.

'That was when it all fell apart,' Russell continued. He explained how Kazankin and Gusakovsky had died, then began to blend fact and fiction. 'We spent the whole day hiding in a bombed-out house, and the following night we walked all the way to the Potsdam goods yard. The comrades hid us in an abandoned underground station – we were there for almost a week. And then, four days ago, a rail-mounted gun fell through the ceiling. I wasn't there, but Comrade Varennikov was killed. Since then...'

Neither Russell's subsequent adventures nor his physicist's fate were of any interest to Nikoladze. 'And the papers?' he asked. 'Where are they now?'

'They're safe. Varennikov and I buried them, in case we were stopped and searched.'

'*Where* did you bury them?' Nikoladze insisted, his voice rising slightly.

Russell took a deep breath. 'Colonel, I don't want to be difficult, but there's a problem here.'

'What sort of problem?

'One of survival. My own, that is. Because I've been wondering what my life will be worth once I tell you where they are.'

Nikoladze was speechless for a long moment. Shchepkin, Russell noticed, was suppressing a smile.

'You will tell me where the papers are,' Nikoladze told him coldly. If the threat was palpable, there was also more than a hint of fear in the Georgian's eyes. He could not afford to fail.

Russell refused to be deflected. 'I would lay bets that Kazankin had orders to liquidate me the moment we reached the goods yard.'

Nikoladze's face confirmed as much. 'He told you that?'

'He didn't need to – you people don't like loose ends. So I have nothing to gain from simply handing you the papers. On the contrary, I would simply be signing my own death warrant.'

Nikoladze snorted, and pulled himself forward. 'You are at our mercy. You're in no position to bargain.'

'Maybe not,' Russell admitted. 'But please, Colonel, I did what you asked me to do. So give me a few minutes. Hear my proposal, and we will all get what we want.'

'We might as well hear what he has to say,' Shchepkin said, speaking for the first time. 'What do we have to lose?'

For a moment Russell thought the Georgian would refuse, but he finally nodded his acquiescence.

'You want the papers,' Russell began, carefully marshalling his argument, 'and you don't want anyone else to know that you've got them. I want safe passage to the American zone for all of my family. My son Paul Gehrts is a prisoner-of-war – he was captured with me in Charlottenburg, but I don't know where he was taken. His uncle Thomas Schade was in the Volkssturm, and he was last seen at Köpenick just outside Berlin, about ten days ago. He was planning to surrender, so you probably have him too. My wife you know about. She has a seven-year-old orphan with her, and a sister named Zarah Biesinger in Schmargendorf. I want them all rounded up and brought here, and then driven to the Elbe.' He took a folded piece of paper from his pocket, and offered it to Nikoladze. 'A list of the names and addresses.'

Nikoladze ignored the outstretched hand. 'Why the American zone?' he asked suspiciously.

'Because Zarah's son and Thomas's wife and daughter are already there, and I want my wife and son to be beyond your reach. If I hold the Soviet

Union to ransom, I expect the NKVD to be angry with me. But I don't see why the rest of my family should suffer for my crimes.'

'And the rest of your proposal? I take it there's more.'

'My wife knows a Swedish diplomat here in Berlin. His name is Erik Aslund. He'll travel to the Elbe with the party, see them across, and then report back to me. Once I know they're safe, I'll take you to the papers.'

'And what's to stop us killing you after that?' Nikoladze asked. He was engaged by the logic, Russell realised, which had to be good news.

'Self-interest, I hope. As long as I'm alive, my family will say nothing that could jeopardise my survival, but if I'm dead...' Russell smiled. 'But let's not consider that possibility. Let's be optimistic. Taking my family to the Elbe will cost you a few litres of petrol. You'll get the papers, and no one else will know you have them. None of my family will be able to broadcast the story without incriminating me. And you'll have a lasting hold over me. If you let me go, you can always threaten to expose my involvement in this, and have the Americans hang me for treason. Or you can make use of me. I'm a well-known journalist with a lot of contacts, and I've served you well in the past, as Shchepkin here can testify.'

Nikoladze considered. 'That is all very clever,' he said slowly, 'but direct persuasion still looks the simpler option. And quicker. Or am I missing something?' He glanced at Shchepkin as he said it, and seemed to be challenging them both.

Shchepkin responded. 'It would be simpler, but also more risky. The story would probably get out,' he cautioned. 'If the man died his family would talk, and even if he only disappeared from view, well... And we have no idea who else he might have told, or whether he's left a written account with anyone. He's had several days to set this up. If we do things his way, we still get the papers, and a valuable asset in the Western zone.'

Russell listened gratefully, wondering why he hadn't thought to take such precautionary measures, and marvelling at Shchepkin's quick-wittedness. Here was an asset, the Russian had to be thinking, that only he could control. They would save each other's lives.

Nikoladze was ready to swallow his anger, at least for now. 'Give me the list,' he demanded.

Russell handed it over. The Georgian, for reasons best known to himself, had decided to go along with him. Maybe the NKVD torturers were all fully booked, or he was just a sweetheart in disguise. He might have bought the argument, or at least some of it. Whatever the reasons, he could always change his mind. When he got his hands on the papers, he would still have his hands on Russell.

But the others would be free.

To Russell, the rest of the day seemed endless. He spent several hours in the basement canteen, where all his attempts at idle conversation were either rebuffed or ignored. Back in his room he paced and fretted, or lay on the camp bed and stared at the ceiling. He could sometimes hear guns in the distance, but the building's buzz of activity usually drowned them out.

He eventually fell asleep, and only awoke when sunlight glinted through the boarded-up window. The canteen provided bread and black tea, and a visit to the nearby toilets turned up a bucket of lukewarm water and a paper-thin sliver of soap. The subsequent wash raised his spirits a little, but climbing back into filthy clothes dropped them right back down. He was on his way upstairs when a young NKVD officer intercepted him. 'The people on your list are being brought here,' the young man said. 'They will wait in your room.'

'All of them?' Russell asked, as much in hope as expectation.

'Of course,' the young man answered, as if partial success was an unfamiliar concept. A riotous succession of hurrahs erupted somewhere upstairs, followed by the clinking of glasses. They both looked upwards, and Russell asked if the war was over.

'No, but Hitler is dead. He shot himself yesterday. Like the coward he was.'

The NKVD man carried on down the stairs, leaving Russell to carry on up. Hitler's death seemed almost irrelevant, like a debt already paid.

He let himself into his room and looked around it. An anteroom, he thought. A place between war and peace.

An hour or so later the door swung open, and a soldier delivered Thomas. After exchanging rueful smiles, they embraced like long-lost brothers. 'So what's this all about?' Thomas asked eventually. 'What have I done to deserve Stalin's mercy?'

Russell told him who else was coming, and where they were all going.

Thomas's face lit up. 'Paul's all right? And Effi as well?'

'So the Russians tell me.'

Thomas leaned back against the wall, a smile of wonderment on his face. 'And how have you managed this miracle?'

'I did a deal with the Russians,' Russell said simply. 'A favour for a favour.'

'And what sort of favour are they getting from you? Or shouldn't I ask?'

'A big one, I think,' Russell told him, 'but I don't really know.' The papers had excited Varennikov but, as the young man himself had pointed out, the scientists who mattered were all back home in their nice warm labs. 'And better you didn't,' he added, in answer to Thomas's second question. 'But there is one thing. It's part of the deal that I follow on later – in a few days, I hope, but you never know. In case I don't, well, I saw Paul two days ago, and he seems in bad shape. Not physically...'

'You don't have to ask,' Thomas interrupted. There were footsteps on the stairs.

It was the boy in question. He looked tired, but the haunted look had gone. Russell remembered Armistice Day in 1918, and wondered if Paul was feeling something similar. The reaction came later, of course, but the sense of release was wonderful while it lasted.

Paul was less than happy when he heard the arrangements. He wasn't sure why, but just driving away didn't feel right. And when he heard that his father was staying, he insisted on doing the same.

'I need you to look after Effi and Rosa,' Russell pleaded hopefully.

'Effi's more than capable of looking after herself,' his son retorted, something that Russell knew only too well, but which he hadn't expected from Paul. Three years ago his son would have been flattered by the offer of adult responsibilities, but he was an adult now, and only the truth would do.

'Then do it for me,' he begged. 'If I end up sacrificing myself for the family, then at least let it be the *whole* damn family.'

'What's left of it,' Paul said bitterly. 'But all right. I'll go.'

'I'm sorry about your mother,' Russell said, realising with a shock that her death had never been mentioned. 'I only found out a couple of days ago. It hasn't had time to sink in.'

'It seems years ago,' was all Paul would say.

'And your sisters?'

'With Grandpa and Grandma. I haven't seen them for a couple of years.'

'That won't matter,' his uncle told him, 'they're still your sisters.' There was a sad inflection to Thomas's tone, and Russell realised he was thinking of his own lost son.

The others arrived an hour or so later. Effi threw herself into Russell's arms, and Rosa's offer of a hand made Thomas smile again. Zarah looked like she'd been through hell, but was trying not to spoil the party. 'Later,' Effi told Russell, when he silently asked what was wrong with her sister.

He told Effi he wouldn't be coming with them, which was no surprise but still felt like a blow. 'But you will,' she insisted.

'Tomorrow,' he said. 'Or maybe the next day. What's a few days after more than three years.'

'Several lifetimes,' she told him. 'You should know that by now.'

And then the NKVD troops were at the door, with orders to escort them downstairs. Outside, a line of four jeeps bearing Soviet stars were filling the street with fumes. Nikoladze was there, along with a tall blond Swede whom Effi introduced as Erik Aslund. She had already told Russell about their Jew-smuggling activities, and seeing them together he felt an absurd twinge of jealousy.

He embraced his family one by one, and watched them climb aboard two of the jeeps. A few brave smiles and away they went, roaring down Immelmann Strasse past the blackened hull of a burnt-out German tank.

He turned to go back in. Nikoladze was still on the steps, talking to a Red Army general, and the glance he directed in Russell's direction seemed anything but friendly.

The convoy of jeeps headed west, through Friedenau and Steglitz on the old Potsdam road, the sounds of the battle still consuming Berlin slowly fading to silence. They drove through a landscape of ruins, peopled by shuffling ghosts, smelling of death. In a couple of places Red Army soldiers stood sentry while gangs of German civilians cleared away rubble and gathered in corpses. In a bombed-out space beside one house two piles awaited incineration, one composed of humans, the other of furry pets.

White flags flew from many surviving buildings, red from more than a few. All of the swastikas had vanished, but exhortatory posters still clung to walls, some flapping wildly in the breeze of their passage, as if keen to detach themselves. A dawn had followed the darkest hour, but not the one intended.

And then they were leaving Berlin, and the smell of death wafted away, and the spring seemed suddenly real. A hot sun was beating down, turning dew into mist across the emerald fields.

In the third jeep, Paul found himself thinking about the previous spring, when he and Gerhart had joined the regular army. He could see his friend now, jumping down from the train, and staring entranced at the vast Russian plain that stretched away before them. He could see the surprise on Neumaier's face as the bullets took him, see the love in Werner's face when he spoke of his mother and sister.

But it wasn't painful any more, not for him. It was only painful for the other Paul, the one he had left behind. There was no longer a road leading home for him.

In the jeep ahead, Zarah was crying on Effi's shoulder. For three days and nights she had conquered the impulse to resist, and allowed the same quartet of Russian soldiers to rape her again and again. Proud of their amenable German girlfriend, the foursome had kept their other comrades at bay, and probably saved her from serious physical harm. She knew in her heart she had done the right thing, but still she couldn't stop weeping.

They had all suffered, Effi thought. Herself least of all, or so it now seemed. She'd been in terrible danger on several occasions, but no one had ever laid a hand on her. Those first weeks back in Berlin, alone in the flat in Wedding, had been by far the worst of her life, but often, in the years that followed, she had felt more useful, more complete, more alive, than she ever had as a movie star. Saving lives certainly put acting in perspective.

And then there were Rosa, Paul and Thomas. She could only guess at the damage done to the young girl's heart, and at the damage done to Paul's. Thomas had been through the horrors of the First War, but even his eyes held something new, a weight of sadness that was not there before.

Yet they were the lucky ones, alive, with all their limbs and loved ones to care for.

There was an undamaged farmhouse across the field to her left, smoke drifting lazily up from its chimney. It had probably looked much the same when she and John had driven this road en route to their pre-war picnics. Not all the world was ruins.

There was much to mend, but it could be done. One heart at a time. Just as long as he came back to her.

Russell settled down to wait. It was around 120 kilometres to the Elbe – in ordinary conditions a two-hour drive each way. Add an hour for haggling, then double the lot, and perhaps the Swede would be back by nightfall.

He wasn't. Russell had another night of broken sleep, woken by each step on the stairs, each revving engine on the street outside. Had they run into something on the road, been ambushed by Goebbels' ludicrous Werewolves? Had the Americans refused to take them?

When he finally awoke something seemed strange, and it took him a while to work out what it was. He couldn't hear a war. The guns had fallen silent.

He was still digesting this when a young officer came to collect him.

Erik Aslund was downstairs in the lobby, Nikoladze waiting by the door. The Swede looked exhausted. 'They're across the river,' he told Russell.

'You've only just got back?'

'There were arguments, radio messages to and fro. But we won through in the end. Frau von Freiwald – Fraulein Koenen, I should say, now that I know who she really is – she wouldn't take no for an answer. And when the Americans found out she was a movie star, they didn't dare refuse her. There were a lot of journalists at the American army headquarters, all looking for a story.'

Russell smiled. He wondered what the journalists would say if they knew that the price of the movie star's freedom was a Russian atomic bomb. He thanked the Swede for all his help.

'You're welcome,' Aslund said. 'I hope we meet again, when things are more settled.'

'I hope so too,' Russell agreed, shaking the offered hand. He could feel Nikoladze's impatience.

'So where are the papers?' the Georgian asked, with the Swede barely out of the door.

'In Dahlem. They're buried in my brother-in-law's garden.'

'They had better be,' Nikoladze replied.

They had, Russell thought, as the two of them walked down the steps. He was beginning to wish he'd indulged Varennikov, and buried them deeper. If they got to Dahlem and found a crater in the vegetable patch, he could see Nikoladze shooting him on the spot.

Out in the street, two jeeps sandwiched a gleaming Horch 930V. Russell wondered where Nikoladze had found such a car, and then remembered that the Red Army had passed through the Babelsberg a few days earlier. The model had been a favourite with Goebbels' movie moguls.

A Russian map of Berlin was spread across the leading jeep's bonnet. He, Nikoladze and a Red Army lieutenant gathered round it, pinpointed their destination, and worked out the route.

'In the front,' Nikoladze told Russell, as they walked back towards the Horch.

Yevgeny Shchepkin was sitting in the back, wearing the usual crumpled suit and an expression to match.

Russell got in beside the young Red Army driver, who gave him a crooked grin. The lead jeep started off, small Soviet flags fluttering on the two leading corners. It was a beautiful morning, warm and sunny, with a few fluffy clouds gliding like Zeppelins across a blue sky. Two thin columns of smoke were rising to the north, but the city's silence seemed almost uncanny, the noise of the vehicles unusually loud in the devastated streets.

They made good progress for twenty minutes, but halfway down Haupt Strasse were halted by a Red Army roadblock. The lieutenant walked back to tell Nikoladze that a sniper was being rounded up, and that they'd only be there for a few minutes. They waited in silence, Nikoladze tapping rhythms on his armrest. After almost half an hour had passed without further news, he got out of the car and strode forward in search of someone to bully.

The driver climbed out too, and lit a surreptitious cigarette. It was the first time Russell and Shchepkin had been alone together.

'My daughter told me about your conversation,' the Russian said.

'Natasha? She reminded me of you.'

Shchepkin grunted. 'Then God help her.'

'How long were you in prison?' Russell asked.

'I was arrested in November.'

'For what?'

Shchepkin shrugged. 'I'm still not sure. My boss fell out with Comrade Beria, and I think I got caught in the crossfire. An occupational hazard, I'm afraid.'

'Time for a change of occupation' Russell suggested dryly.

Shchepkin smiled at that. 'What do you think I should do? Retire to the country and raise bees like your Sherlock Holmes?'

'Perhaps.'

'That's not the sort of world we live in any more.'

'No.' Russell agreed. He could see his own potential nemesis in the distance, walking back towards them. 'This is Nikoladze's world,' he murmured, as much to himself as to the Russian.

'Don't be too hard on him,' Shchepkin said reprovingly. 'He staked his life on delivering something, and you made him wait for it.'

Russell turned in his seat. 'Is it really that bad?'

'Oh yes.'

Not for the first time, Russell felt sorry for the Russian. And for his country.

The driver slipped back behind the wheel, smelling of cheap tobacco.

'Do you know what's fetching the highest prices in Berlin these days?' Shchepkin asked in English.

Russell gave it some thought. 'KPD membership cards,' he suggested at last.

'Close,' Shchepkin admitted. 'Jewish stars.'

Of course, Russell thought.

Nikoladze let himself into the back, and soon they were on their way. A couple of hundred metres down the road, Red Army soldiers were standing over the body of a *Hitlerjugend*, like hunters around a kill. The boy's dead face was turned towards them. He looked about twelve.

It took them half an hour to reach Vogelsang Strasse. The Schade house was still standing, and if Russell kept his focus narrow he could see what he'd seen six years earlier, arriving for Sunday lunch with Effi. But let his eyes wander a few degrees, and the past lay around him in ruins.

Heart pounding, he led the way round to the back.

Birds were singing in the blossoming trees, and Hanna's vegetable patch was still a mass of tangled weeds. He realised that he should have used some foliage to camouflage his excavation, which looked like a standing invitation to any passing treasure hunter. Then again, the patch of fresh earth was just the right size for a pet's grave, and who would go digging for dead cats and dogs?

'There?' Nikoladze asked, his finger pointed at the obvious.

Russell nodded.

As two of the soldiers started to dig, Russell looked around the woebegone garden, remembering happier days. Hitler and the Nazis had been evil beyond imagining, but for him and his family the pre-war years had often been a wonderful time. The children growing up, Effi's incredible success; even the Nazis had played their part, giving him and Thomas something to struggle against, a moral and political lodestone to guide their work and lives.

What would there be now? There was something irretrievably wrong with the Soviet Union, but it was so much stronger. And the Americans were reaching for a parallel empire, whether they wanted to or not. It was hard to feel good about a country that still had a segregated army.

It would be a world of lesser evils and uncertain victories, in infinite shades of grey. And after the Nazis he supposed that wasn't so bad.

They all heard the spade strike something hard, and Nikoladze gave him a questioning look.

'It might be Gusakovsky's gun,' Russell suggested. 'I buried it with the papers.'

The soldier put his spade aside, and started sifting through the earth with his hands. He handed up the gun, and then the oilskin parcel. Nikoladze took the papers from their wrapping and quickly riffled through them. They looked stained at the edges, but otherwise undamaged, and his face seemed to sag with relief.

He strode off towards the car without a word.

Russell turned to Shchepkin, and asked him the obvious question: 'So will the bastard let me leave?'

'Oh yes,' the Russian assured him. 'We never waste an asset.'

Russell smiled. As far as he knew, the gulags were full of them. But it didn't seem the moment to say so.

THE EXTRACT THAT FOLLOWS IS FROM THE OPENING CHAPTER OF *ZOO STATION*, THE FIRST 'JOHN RUSSELL AND EFFI KOENEN' NOVEL, SET IN BERLIN IN 1939.

Into the blue

There were two hours left of 1938. In Danzig it had been snowing on and off all day, and a gang of children were enjoying a snowball fight in front of the grain warehouses which lined the old waterfront. John Russell paused to watch them for a few moments, then walked on up the cobbled street towards the blue and yellow lights.

The Sweden Bar was far from crowded, and those few faces that turned his way weren't exactly brimming over with festive spirit. In fact, most of them looked like they'd rather be somewhere else.

It was an easy thing to want. The Christmas decorations hadn't been removed, just allowed to drop, and now formed part of the flooring, along with patches of melting slush, floating cigarette ends and the odd broken bottle. The Bar was famous for the savagery of its international brawls, but on this particular night the various groups of Swedes, Finns and Letts seemed devoid of the energy needed to get one started. Usually a table or two of German naval ratings could be relied upon to provide the necessary spark, but the only Germans present were a couple of age-ing prostitutes, and they were getting ready to leave.

Russell took a stool at the bar, bought himself a *Goldwasser* and glanced through the month-old copy of the *New York Herald Tribune* which, for some inexplicable reason, was lying there. One of his own articles was in it, a piece on German attitudes to their pets. It was ac-companied by a cute-looking photograph of a Schnauser.

Seeing him reading, a solitary Swede two stools down asked him, in perfect English, if he spoke that language. Russell admitted that he did.

'You are English!' the Swede exclaimed, and shifted his consider-able bulk to the stool adjoining Russell's.

Their conversation went from friendly to sentimental, and sentimental to maudlin, at what seemed like breakneck pace. Three *Goldwassers* later, the Swede was telling him that he, Lars, was not the true father of his children. Vibeke had never admitted it, but he knew it to be true.

Russell gave him an encouraging pat on the shoulder, and Lars sunk forward, his head making a dull clunk as it made contact with the polished surface of the bar. 'Happy New Year,' Russell murmured. He shifted the Swede's head slightly to ease his breathing, and got up to leave.

Outside, the sky was beginning to clear, the air almost cold enough to sober him up. An organ was playing in the Protestant Seaman's church, nothing hymnal, just a slow lament, as if the organist was saying a personal farewell to the year gone by. It was a quarter to midnight.

Russell walked back across the city, conscious of the moisture seeping in through the holes in his shoes. The Langermarkt was full of couples, laughing and squealing as they clutched each other for balance on the slippery sidewalks.

He cut over the Breite Gasse and reached the Holzmarkt just as the bells began pealing in the New Year. The square was full of celebrating people, and an insistent hand pulled him into a circle of revellers dancing and singing in the snow. When the song ended and the circle broke up, the Polish girl on his left reached up and brushed her lips against his, eyes shining with happiness. It was, he thought, a better than expected opening to 1939.

His hotel's reception area was deserted, and the sounds of celebration emanating from the kitchen at the back suggested the night staff were enjoying their own private party. Russell thought about making himself a hot chocolate and drying his shoes in one of the ovens, but decided against. He took his key, clambered up the stairs to the third floor, and trundled down the corridor to his room. Closing the door behind him, he became painfully aware that the occupants of the neighbouring rooms were still welcoming in the new year, a singsong on one side, floor-shaking sex on the other. He took off his sodden shoes and socks, dried his wet feet with a towel and sank back onto the vibrating bed.

There was a discreet, barely audible tap on his door.

Cursing, he levered himself off the bed and prised the door open. A man in a crumpled suit and open shirt stared back at him.

'Mr John Russell,' the man said in English, as if he was introducing Russell to himself. The Russian accent was slight, but unmistakable. 'Could I talk with you for a few minutes?'

'It's a bit late…' Russell began. The man's face was vaguely familiar. 'But why not?' he continued, as the singers next door reached for a new and louder chorus. 'A journalist should never turn down a conversation,' he murmured, mostly to himself, as he let the man in. 'Take the chair,' he suggested.

His visitor sat back and crossed one leg over the other, hitching up his trouser leg as he did so. 'We have met before,' he said. 'A long time ago. My name is Shchepkin. Yevgeny Grigorovich Shchepkin. We…'

'Yes,' Russell interrupted, as the memory clicked into place. 'The discussion group on journalism at the fifth Congress. The summer of '24.'

Shchepkin nodded his acknowledgement. 'I remember your contributions,' he said. 'Full of passion,' he added, his eyes circling the room and resting, for a few seconds, on his host's dilapidated shoes.

Russell perched himself on the edge of the bed. 'As you said – a long time ago.' He and Ilse had met at that conference, and set in motion their ten-year cycle of marriage, parenthood, separation and divorce. Shchepkin's hair had been black and wavy in 1924; now it was a close-cropped grey. They were both a little older than the century, Russell guessed, and Shchepkin was wearing pretty well, considering what he'd probably been through the last fifteen years. He had a handsome face of indeterminate nationality, with deep brown eyes above prominent slanting cheekbones, an aquiline nose and lips just the full side of perfect. He could have passed for a citizen of most European countries, and probably had.

The Russian completed his survey of the room. 'This is a dreadful hotel,' he said.

Russell laughed. 'Is that what you wanted to talk about?'

'No. Of course not.'

'So what are you here for?'

'Ah.' Shchepkin hitched his trouser leg again. 'I am here to offer you work.'

Russell raised an eyebrow. 'You? Who exactly do you represent?'

The Russian shrugged. 'My country. The Writers' Union. It doesn't matter. You will be working for us. You know who we are.'

'No,' Russell said. 'I mean, no I'm not interested. I…'

'Don't be so hasty,' Shchepkin said. 'Hear me out. We aren't asking you to do anything which your German hosts could object to.' The Russian allowed himself a smile. 'Let me tell you exactly what we have in mind. We want a series of articles about positive aspects of the Nazi regime.' He paused for a few seconds, waiting in vain for Russell to demand an explanation. 'You are not German but you live in Berlin,' he went on. 'You once had a reputation as a journalist of the left, and though that reputation has, shall we say, faded, no one could accuse you of being an apologist for the Nazis…'

'But you want me to be just that.'

'No, no. We want positive aspects, not a positive picture overall. That would not be believable.'

Russell was curious in spite of himself. Or because of the *Goldwassers*. 'Do you just need my name on these articles?' he asked. 'Or do you want me to write them as well?'

'Oh, we want you to write them. We like your style – all that irony.'

Russell shook his head – Stalin and irony didn't seem like much of a match.

Shchepkin misread the gesture. 'Look,' he said, 'let me put all my cards on the table.'

Russell grinned.

Shchepkin offered a wry smile in return. 'Well, most of them anyway. Look, we are aware of your situation. You have a German son and a German lady-friend, and you want to stay in Germany if you possibly can. Of course if a war breaks out you will have to leave, or else they will intern you. But until that moment comes – and maybe it won't – miracles do happen – until it does you want to earn your living as a journalist without upsetting your hosts. What better way than this? You write nice things about the Nazis –

not too nice, of course, the articles have to be credible… but you stress their good side.'

'Does shit have a good side?' Russell wondered out loud.

'Come, come,' Shchepkin insisted, 'you know better than that. Unemployment eliminated, a renewed sense of community, healthy children, cruises for workers, cars for the people…'

'You should work for Joe Goebbels.'

Shchepkin gave him a mock-reproachful look.

'Okay,' Russell said, 'I take your point. Let me ask you a question. There's only one reason you'd want that sort of article – you're softening up your own people for some sort of deal with the devil. Right?'

Shchepkin flexed his shoulders in an eloquent shrug.

'Why?'

The Russian grunted. 'Why deal with the devil? I don't know what the leadership is thinking. But I could make an educated guess, and so could you.'

Russell could. 'The western powers are trying to push Hitler east, so Stalin has to push him west? Are we talking about a non-aggression pact, or something more?'

Shchepkin looked almost affronted. 'What more could there be? Any deal with that man can only be temporary. We know what he is.'

Russell nodded. It made sense. He closed his eyes, as if it were possible to blank out the approaching calamity. On the other side of the opposite wall, his musical neighbours were intoning one of those Polish river songs which could reduce a statue to tears. Through the wall behind him silence had fallen, but his bed was still quivering like a tuning fork.

'We'd also like some information,' Shchepkin was saying, almost apologetically. 'Nothing military,' he added quickly, seeing the look on Russell's face. 'No armament statistics or those naval plans that Sherlock Holmes is always being asked to recover. Nothing of that sort. We just want a better idea of what ordinary Germans are thinking. How they are taking the changes in working conditions, how they are likely to react if war comes – that sort of thing. We don't want any secrets, just your opinions. And nothing on paper. You can deliver them in person, on a monthly basis.'

Russell looked sceptical.

Shchepkin ploughed on. 'You will be well paid – very well. In any currency, any bank, any country, that you choose. You can move into a better rooming house…'

'I like my rooming house.'

'You can buy things for your son, your girlfriend. You can have your shoes mended.'

'I don't…'

'The money is only an extra. You were with us once…'

'A long long time ago.'

'Yes, I know. But you cared about your fellow human beings.

I heard you talk. That doesn't change. And if we go under there will be nothing left.'

'A cynic might say there's not much to choose between you.'

'The cynic would be wrong,' Shchepkin replied, exasperated and perhaps a little angry. 'We have spilt blood, yes. But reluctantly, and in faith of a better future. *They* enjoy it. Their idea of progress is a European slave-state.'

'I know.'

'One more thing. If money and politics don't persuade you, think of this. We will be grateful, and we have influence almost everywhere. And a man like you, in a situation like yours, is going to need influential friends.'

'No doubt about that.'

Shchepkin was on his feet. 'Think about it, Mr Russell,' he said, drawing an envelope from the inside pocket of his jacket and placing it on the night-stand. 'All the details are in here – how many words, delivery dates, fees, and so on. If you decide to do the articles, write to our press attaché in Berlin, telling him who you are, and that you've had the idea for them yourself. He will ask you to send him one in the post. The Gestapo will read it, and pass it on. You will then receive your first fee and suggestions for future stories. The last-but-one letters of the opening sentence will spell out the name of a city outside Germany which you can reach fairly easily. Prague, perhaps, or Cracow. You will spend the last weekend of the month in that city. And be sure to make your hotel reservation at least a week in advance. Once you are there, someone will contact you.'

'I'll think about it,' Russell said, mostly to avoid further argument. He wanted to spend his weekends with his son Paul and his girlfriend Effi, not the Shchepkins of this world.

The Russian nodded and let himself out. As if on cue, the Polish choir lapsed into silence.